PRAISE FOR THE TUCKER MYSTERIES

Child Not Found

"Daniel is more than generous with the violence, guilt, tweets, craft brews, and compassion."—*Kirkus Reviews*

"By any measure, [*Child Not Found*] is a terrific book. It's got a gripping plot, characters so real you can feel them, and a narrative voice that grips you by the heart and won't let go. A terrific read!"—John Gilstrap, author of *Friendly Fire* and the Jonathan Grave thriller series

Corrupted Memory

*"Compulsively readable … Against a meticulously detailed Boston background, the likable but undisciplined Tucker lurches from one crisis to the next."—*Publishers Weekly* (starred review)

*"Crisp writing, an engaging plot, and well-drawn characters make this … a corker of a mystery. Fans of Boston crime writers Dennis Lehane, Jeremiah Healy, and Hank Philippi Ryan will delight in picking up this new series."—*Library Journal* (starred review)

"A fast-paced crime thriller with an engaging narrator, quirky characters, and explosive secrets … 4 stars."—*Suspense Magazine*

"Excellent and suspenseful."—*Crimespree Magazine*

"A taut novel of high tech and high drama played out against a backdrop of family dysfunction and government intrigue."—Reed Farrel Coleman, *New York Times* bestselling author of *Robert B. Parker's Blind Spot*

"[A] soulful hero."—*Kirkus Reviews*

Terminated

"A lively debut."—*Kirkus Reviews*

"A smart novel with plenty of witty asides, slam-bam action, and it doesn't flinch from depicting sexual violence."—*The Boston Globe*

"Ray Daniel has nailed it. Nailed the story, nailed the writing, nailed the whole clever, original, and quirky deal. An authentically riveting thriller, with wit and skill and a voice you can't forget. Terrific."—Hank Phillippi Ryan, Anthony, Agatha, Macavity, and Mary Higgins Clark Award-winning author

"[A] smart, snappy, suspense-filled entertainment that knows just when to ratchet up the action, just when to turn the plot, just when to twist the knife. And more than that, it's filled with fascinating characters, snarky humor, and some sharp social observations, too. You'll read far into the night and come away with two things: a deep sense of satisfaction and sweaty palms from turning the pages so fast."—William Martin, *New York Times* bestselling author of *Back Bay* and *The Lincoln Letter*

"Ray Daniel delivers a fast moving and engaging story with fully-blown characters, biting wit, and sparkling dialog. *Terminated* is a terrific debut novel. There is a new kid in town who deserves a wide audience."—Gary Braver, bestselling and award-winning author of *Tunnel Vision*

"Ray Daniel not only delivers a suspenseful, twisty, action-packed yarn, he's created an everyman hero named Tucker who will linger in the reader's conscious long after the final page is read. A terrific debut for a promising new series."—Steve Ulfelder, Edgar-nominated author of *Wolverine Bros. Freight & Storage*

"Ray Daniel knows what he writes and has written a winner."—Mike Cooper, award-winning author of *Clawback*

CHILD NOT FOUND

A TUCKER MYSTERY

RAY DANIEL

FIRST EDITION
First Printing, 2016

Book format by Bob Gaul
Cover design by Ellen Lawson
Cover images by Getty Images/139625127/©John Burke
Editing by Nicole Nugent

Midnight Ink, an imprint of Llewellyn Worldwide Ltd.

This is a work of fiction. Names, characters, places, and incidents are either the product of the author's imagination or are used fictitiously, and any resemblance to actual persons living or dead, business establishments, events, or locales is entirely coincidental.

Library of Congress Cataloging-in-Publication Data
Names: Daniel, Ray, 1962– author.
Title: Child not found : a Tucker mystery / Ray Daniel.
Description: First edition. | Woodbury, Minnesota : Midnight Ink, [2016] |
Series: A Tucker mystery ; #3
Identifiers: LCCN 2016003095 (print) | LCCN 2016006726 (ebook) | ISBN 9780738742311 | ISBN 9780738748092 ()
Subjects: | GSAFD: Mystery fiction.
Classification: LCC PS3604.A5255 C48 2016 (print) | LCC PS3604.A5255 (ebook) | DDC 813/.6—dc23
LC record available at http://lccn.loc.gov/2016003095

Midnight Ink
Llewellyn Worldwide Ltd.
2143 Wooddale Drive
Woodbury, MN 55125-2989
www.midnightinkbooks.com

Printed in the United States of America

For Karen
who makes me a better man.

ACKNOWLEDGMENTS

The longer my writing career progresses, the more obvious it is that I wouldn't be here without the help of so many friends and colleagues. Thank you to my wife, Karen, who has shown unwavering confidence in me and so has helped me to have confidence in myself. Thank you to my agent, Eric Ruben, and editor Terri Bischoff for their support of me and my work both professionally and as friends.

Thank you also to my friends and colleagues in Mystery Writers of America, Sisters in Crime, Grub Street, and all the conferences where we writers gather to give each other support and make each other laugh.

Regarding *Child Not Found*, thank you to Karen Salemi, Kay Helberg, Tom Fitzpatrick, and Tim McIntire for reading the manuscript and helping me to improve it. Thank you to Nicole Nugent for her outstanding copyediting. Finally, thank you to Clair Lamb, the extraordinary editor who helps me pull my unruly stories together.

ONE

TAKING A CHILD SLEDDING can almost, but not quite, make you forget how much you hate the winter. You take the kid to the top of a snowy slope and remember yourself, red-nosed and cherry-cheeked, flying down a hill. You recall your friends, your youth, and a simpler time. You convince yourself that you love the winter.

But it's a lie.

I stood at the top of Flagstaff Hill in the Boston Common, keeping watch as my nine-year-old cousin, Maria, launched herself onto the packed powder. The orange fluorescent pom-pom topping her hat helped me track her as she skittered into the crowd at the bottom of the hill. The parents around me had implemented a divide-and-protect strategy, one launching their kids from the top of the hill, the other collecting them at the bottom. I was alone, so I remained at the top to be able to see Maria's entire run. This was my first mistake—my second if you counted buying her a sled.

It started when my cousin Sal heard that I was planning to spend Christmas Day watching football.

"Are you fucking kidding me?" he had said.

"What? I like football," I had said.

"Screw that. You're coming to my house. You're gonna have a real Christmas."

I had arrived like the Nutcracker uncle, batting cold snow off my coat and distributing gifts: a bottle of homemade limoncello for Sal, an amber pendant for Sal's wife, Sophia, and a sled for Maria.

Maria tore at the paper and screeched a happy screech. "A sled. Finally, a sled!"

Sophia gave a strained, "A sled. How wonderful!"

Sal gave me the stink eye.

Christmas at Sal Rizzo's house was a noisy exercise in genealogy. Rizzos stuffed the house, filling every available spot in the apartment and the family tree. There was Sal, the founder of the feast; his sisters, Bianca and Adriana; and the in-laws, Ben Goldman and Catherine Smith.

Bianca was, technically, no longer a Rizzo, having taken her husband's name to become a Goldman. Catherine Smith was a quasi-Rizzo, having married Adriana, though the two had not decided whether they both should become Rizzos, Smiths, or Rizzo-Smiths. Then there was me, a Tucker, who could still claim some Rizzoness through my mother, Sal's aunt.

Maria, as she had proudly calculated, was my first cousin once removed.

The ten of us sat down to a feast of lasagna, meatballs, sausages, beef braciole, broccoli, and sweet potatoes. I learned over dinner that Bianca's converting to Judaism had created a Great Schism in the family and that Sal had been forced to make a choice between inviting his mother (my Auntie Rosa) or Bianca when it came to Christmas dinner. ("A pretty fucking easy choice," Sal confided to me over limoncello.)

The vast assortment of entrees was followed by a vast assortment of desserts: ricotta pies, cannoli, pink and green Italian cookies, a chocolate Yule log, black Bialetti-brewed coffee, brandy, and my bottle of limoncello. Afterwards, Sophia talked with her sisters, the kids played with their toys, and the men argued for no reason other than it was a Christmas tradition.

"A fucking sled?" asked Sal, loosening his tie. The tie, a gift from Maria, featured a portrait of the Virgin Mary holding baby Jesus.

"Yeah," I said, "with a Patriots logo."

"We live in the North End. There's no place to sled."

"There's the Common. I always see kids sledding on the Common."

"All the way out there? Who's gonna take her?"

"I will."

Sal had pointed at me with his drink and said, "Yes you will."

Maria had overheard and had asked, "Will you take me tomorrow?"

And I had said, "Absolutely."

Maria stood in front of me now, having made the climb back up the hill, as I tried to stamp my feet back to warmth. The sun shone uselessly bright and clear over the cold day.

I said, "Maria, how about we go get a cup of coffee to warm up?"

Maria said, "My mother says I'm too young for coffee."

"Okay. Coffee for me. Hot chocolate for you."

"You know," said Maria, "what my mother doesn't know won't hurt her."

"Oh, you want a coffee?"

"Can I have one?"

"Sure," I said, thinking decaf. "It'll be our secret. A Christmas miracle."

"LOL," said Maria.

I said "LOL?"

"Yeah. It means laugh out loud on Facebook."

"I know what it means, it's just that nobody actually says LOL."

"I do," said Maria. "You're just too old."

"And you're too young for Facebook."

"Facebook doesn't know that."

With that, Maria ran down the hill and belly-flopped onto her disk.

I called after her, "And who are you calling old?"

She was out of range. As I watched her pick up speed, I heard my name.

"Tucker!"

I turned and saw Sal, in dress shoes and a greatcoat, running and sliding his way toward me.

He called out again, "Tucker!"

I waved. "Right here!"

"Where's Maria?"

Sal's shoes betrayed him. He fell into a heap in the snow. I ran down the back side of the hill to help him up. As I pulled him to his feet, he shook me off.

"Maria. Where is she?"

"She's sledding. She was just going to do one more run and then we were heading over to The Thinking Cup."

"Jesus. Go get her."

"What's up?"

"Just get her!"

I clomped back to the top of the hill and scanned for Maria. Kids were everywhere, falling, rising, walking, whining, crying, and getting their noses wiped. I couldn't find Maria in the Where's Waldo crowd.

Sal reached the top of the hill, stood beside me.

"Where is she?" he asked.

"I'm looking," I said, shielding my eyes.

"Fucking sun. I can't see anything."

I followed the track where I had seen her launch herself. It traced a straight line down the hill. At the bottom of the track a blue disk rested on its face, its Patriots logo visible as a red, white, and blue smudge.

I pointed. "There's her sled."

Sal said, "Fuck. Where is she?"

I looked beyond the sled and saw Maria's Day-Glo pom-pom. She was leaving the Common with a guy in a Bruins jacket.

I pointed and said, "There she is."

Sal followed my point and yelled, "Maria!"

She was too far away to hear.

Sal started slipping and skiing his way down the hill in those shoes. I ran beside him in my boots. Maria and the guy approached an idling Lincoln Town Car on Charles Street. Sal had been making good time moving down the hill, but he caught an edge and tumbled into a heap.

I stopped to help him up.

"Leave me, just fucking leave me," Sal said. "Go get Maria."

I ran on toward the car. "Maria!" I yelled.

Maria turned, looked at me, climbed into the car. The guy in the Bruins jacket slammed the door shut, jumped into the front seat, and pulled the car into traffic. It took a left onto Beacon Street and was gone.

Sal huffed up next to me.

"What happened?" I asked.

"They fucking took Maria," said Sal.

"Who?"

Police sirens blared. Three police cars slid to a stop in front of us, crunching through the slush. Their doors flew open and cops jumped out, drawing their guns and pointing them at Sal and me. My buddy Bobby Miller, the FBI agent, was with them.

"Tucker!" Bobby Miller yelled. "Get away from Sal."

"What?"

A cop with freckles and red eyebrows yelled, "Hands! Let me see your hands!"

I was still trying to process Bobby's instructions. *Get away? Get away where?*

Sal put up his hands. Mine were still in my pockets, shielded from the cold.

"Hands, you son of a bitch!" the cop yelled, pointing his gun.

Sal hit me in the back of the head with his elbow. "Get your hands out of your pockets, you dumb shit," he said.

I did as I was told. The cops rushed forward. One of them stiff-armed me in the shoulder, grabbing it and pushing me to the ground. He kicked my legs out and said, "Don't fucking move."

I lay on the ground looking up as another cop cuffed Sal's hands behind his back and dragged him to his feet.

Bobby said, "Sal Rizzo, you are under arrest."

TWO

I LAY ON THE salt-encrusted sidewalk watching a fat cop push Sal into a cruiser. The cop placed his meaty hand on Sal's head as Sal ducked into the car. Sal, who was approximately the size and shape of a silverback gorilla, straightened abruptly and caught the cop's hand in the door frame.

"Ow! You son of a bitch!" said the cop. Sal gave a grim little smile as the cop slammed the door shut and waddled around to the driver side. The cruiser took off down Charles, following the path the Lincoln Town Car had taken.

I lay in the gray slush watching a particle of salt destroy a snowflake and processing the last three minutes. Three minutes ago I was standing at the top of the hill, watching Maria and contemplating a cup of coffee. Now I was lying on the ground with ice water soaking into my clothes. Sal was gone and Maria was gone.

Maria was gone.

I stood up.

The red-browed cop said, "You. Back on the ground."

I said, "No."

The cop drew his gun. "I said down."

"What are you gonna do? Shoot me?"

The cop took a step. Bobby Miller intervened.

"For Christ's sake, Mike," said Bobby. "It's over."

"This sonovabitch has to smarten up," Mike said.

Bobby said, "Yeah. Not likely."

I turned away, looked toward the Common. The sledding had stopped. Kids and parents stood at the top of the hill, watching the police cars. Maria's disk lay alone in the snow. I headed for it.

Mike the cop shouted, "Where are you going?"

I ignored him.

"Jesus, Miller, you gonna let him just walk off like that?"

"I'll handle it," Bobby said. He fell into step beside me.

"They took Maria," I said.

The blue disk's Flying Elvis Patriots logo stared into the sun.

"Who is 'they'?"

"I don't know. I just know that Sal came running here in a panic looking for Maria and that she got into a car with some guy in a Bruins jackets."

"They all have Bruins jackets."

"Who?"

"Sal's crew."

I picked up the disk. A kid on an old-fashioned Flexible Flyer shot past. The show was over and parents were letting their charges resume sledding. We were about to become somebody's funniest home video. We headed back for the car.

"You're saying Sal's crew kidnapped Maria?" I asked.

Bobby said, "Kidnapped?"

"Isn't that what it's called when you take someone's kid?"

Bobby blew out a plume of steam, a winter sigh.

"You knew they were going to kidnap her?" I asked.

"You're seeing this thing wrong."

"What am I seeing wrong?"

We reached Bobby's Chevy. He walked around to the driver's side.

"What aren't you telling me?" I asked.

Bobby leaned on the car's roof. "You know you nearly got killed today."

"That guy, Mike? He wasn't going to shoot me."

"He had his finger on the trigger. He could have sneezed and killed you by accident."

"You're stalling," I said. "What's going on?"

Bobby said, "These arrests. They're dangerous situations. No place for a kid."

"Are you saying they took Maria to keep her safe? I could have kept her safe."

"By getting yourself shot in front of her?"

"Oh, screw you."

"I'll bet you that Maria is home right now. C'mon, hop in. Let's bring the sled back."

I stared out across the Common, couldn't shed the feeling that I was forgetting something. The sun shone down on the cold day. Kids skidded down the hill as if nothing had happened. I guess for them, nothing had. They'd have a cool story to tell their friends. I scanned the park for Maria's orange pom-pom. Felt I was leaving her behind. Pulled out my cell to call Sophia to ask if Maria had showed up. I put the cell away. If Maria wasn't there, I didn't want Sophia to learn that way. *You lost my daughter?*

"You coming, Tucker?"

I threw the sled into Bobby's backseat and dropped into the car. Bobby put it in gear, heading for Maria's house in the North End.

THREE

Boston's North End is shaped like the letter D, with the ocean forming the curvy part and the Rose Kennedy Greenway forming the straight part. The Greenway reminds us that an ugly elevated highway once bisected our city. It had taken only ten years and 14 billion dollars to convert the highway into a tunnel and to turn the blighted area beneath the highway into the Greenway. Today the Greenway was white and gray, covered with a layer of city snow.

Bobby had wound his way over Beacon Hill, past Government Center, and was now crossing into the North End. Silence ruled as he and I conducted the aural equivalent of a staring contest. He blinked first.

"Are you okay?" he asked.

I checked out a dirty snow pile by the side of the road and replayed the morning in my head. It was just a final sled run; Maria goes down the slope, comes back up, we go get coffee. Instead, Sal is stumbling through the snow, one of his minions is grabbing Maria, and then I'm lying in a pile of slush.

Bobby said, "Because, you know, I see how this could have been a rough morning for you."

A little warning would have been nice. A little heads-up from my friend Bobby. Maybe I don't take Maria sledding on the day her dad was going to be arrested. Maybe I let her stay home and say her good-byes or something. I rolled this around, considered my responses to Bobby. They all sounded petulant and whiny, so I stuck with silence.

"You knew this day had to come," Bobby said.

I pointed out the window. "Oh look, a beagle. You don't see many of them in the city."

"Sal is a crook."

"Loyal dogs, beagles."

"He murdered his best friend."

I turned to Bobby. "Yeah? Who?"

"Marco Esposito."

The murder of Marco Esposito had floated over and through Christmas dinner like a ghost. Sal was off kilter. Smiling and glad-handing the other Rizzos when directly engaged, but drifting into a dark place as soon as he was left alone.

"It's a tragedy," Sophia had said. "Sal loved Marco."

"Any idea who killed him?" I'd asked.

The *omerta* kicked in and Sophia had said, "I'm going to bring Sal some Yule log."

Then she sat in Sal's lap, kissed him on the forehead, and fed him bits of chocolate cake. He hugged her close, resting his head on her bosom. I had turned away to give them privacy, and had engaged Ben on the relative strengths of the Red Sox and Yankees.

Bobby inched his way around a double-parked car. The rule of law was a faint memory when it came to parking in the North End. He said to the air, "You fuckers double-park even after a snowstorm?"

"Sal didn't kill Marco," I said.

"Oh, really?" Bobby asked. "How do you know?"

"Why would he kill his best friend?"

"Because that best friend was boffing his wife."

"That's a terrible thing to say about Sophia."

"That's what we heard."

"Well, you shouldn't repeat it. Where are you getting this shit?"

"We have our sources."

"Your sources are wrong."

"We'll see." Bobby had wormed his car past the blockage. Now a tourist stood in the middle of the street with his face in a map. Bobby blasted him with the horn. The guy jumped against a parked car.

As Bobby slid past, I rolled down the window and said, "Welcome to Boston, sir." Cold blasted me as I rolled the window back up.

"Almost there," Bobby said.

"Maria better be home."

Bobby said, "She'll be home."

"And if she isn't? How do I tell Sophia that I lost her?"

"She'll be there."

"How do you know?"

Bobby said nothing.

"Oh, I get it," I said. "Your sources. Is this the same guy who told you Sal killed Marco?"

Bobby said nothing. I ran over the morning again. Sledding, Sal, Maria, police. Wished to hell that I hadn't been on the Common this morning.

"You couldn't have given me a little warning?" I said.

"No," said Bobby. "I couldn't give you a warning."

"Afraid I'd tell Sal?"

"It's just not done."

"That's bullshit."

The car hit a pothole on Hanover Street, bouncing and splashing slush against a fire hydrant.

"What do you mean, bullshit?" asked Bobby.

"If it was such a secret, how did Sal know something was up? How did a guy in Sal's crew know to come and grab Maria?"

"I didn't know you were going to take Maria sledding."

"If you knew, you would have told me?"

Silence.

I said, "That's what I thought."

Bobby pulled to a stop behind another double-parked car. I opened my door.

"Where are you going?" Bobby asked.

"It's faster to walk." I opened the back door, pulled out the sled. "She had better be there."

"She'll be there."

I closed the door, climbed through slush to the Hanover Street sidewalk. Hanover cut through the North End's D, running from the Greenway to the harbor. It was a street designed for horses but forced to accommodate cars. Brick buildings loomed above me on either side, hearkening back to a century ago, when Italian immigrants had raised goats in stairwells.

The looming worsened as I turned down Salutation Street. Calling it a street was a kindness; it was more of an alley. One skinny car could travel its length as long as nobody was standing on the curbstones that pretended to be sidewalks. Sal lived here in an unfathomably small condo. He and Sophia loved it, called it cozy. Getting anywhere during Christmas dinner had involved solving a Rubik's Cube puzzle of chairs, legs, walls, and bodies. Crawling over someone's lap to get to the bathroom created a sense of community you didn't get in the dining room of a suburban Colonial. Maybe that's what cozy meant.

The street telescoped away, drawing the door to Sal's apartment with it. The conversation was going to go two ways, neither great. If

Maria was there, then I'd be mad as hell at having her run off and leave me behind. If Maria wasn't there, then—well, then I didn't know what, exactly. How did you tell a mother that you lost her child?

I stopped in front of Sal's door, rang the bell to his top-floor apartment, and realized that I'd probably be the first one to tell Sophia about Sal's arrest. *Aw, crap!* How would I break that news? "The police took Sal. Were you boffing Marco?" Probably not the best tactic.

I rested my hand on the doorknob, waiting for the lock to buzz so I could push through.

No buzz.

Pressed the doorbell again. Perhaps Sophia was busy yelling at Maria for leaving me standing in the Common like an idiot. That would make me feel better.

No buzz.

I looked down Salutation Street. Despite the bright sun sinking in the west, the street was dark. How did people live in perpetual shadow? Rang the bell again, but didn't expect a buzz.

Didn't get one.

Of course there was no buzz. It was ridiculous for me to expect that I'd be the first to tell Sophia. The woman was connected. She probably got phone calls five minutes after the arrest. She was probably at the police station right now. I was standing here like a dope holding a sled. Might as well drop it off.

I buzzed the first floor and peered into the doorway. The first-floor apartment's door opened. Mrs. Iacavelo peeked out. I waved and pointed at Maria's sled. I knew Mrs. Iacavelo from last night's Christmas dinner; she had climbed to the top floor to pay her respects to her landlord. Mrs. Iacavelo and I drank an espresso together and it had turned out that she knew my mother.

"Mrs. Iacavelo, could you open the door?" I called through the glass.

She looked at me and knitted her brow. Forgotten already.

"It's me! Tucker. Angelina's boy. We met at Christmas."

Mrs. Iacavelo called back, "I can't let you in. I'll tell Sophia that you're here."

"She's not answering her bell."

"Then she's not home."

"Please, Mrs. Iacavelo. Just let me drop Maria's sled by their door."

"Leave it." Mrs. Iacavelo turned to go.

I called through the door, trying to draw her back. "I don't want it to get stolen. Sal would be pissed."

At the mention of Sal's name, the old woman stopped. She shook her head, turned back, and opened the door. "Well, if you're just going to drop the sled, then that's fine. But you come right back down."

"Thank you. I'll be right back," I said.

The staircase spiraled up, steep and narrow, its wooden banisters polished smooth by a century of hands. Cooking smells wafted down the stairs. Someone in the North End was always cooking something. I wound around the staircase, bonking the sled behind me. Sal lived in the North End in a penthouse apartment, just as I lived in the South End in a penthouse apartment. "Penthouse" meant that we both climbed lots of stairs to reach our front door, but we had access to sunlight.

The cooking smell got stronger as I spiraled past the second floor, and stronger still as I climbed. I turned the last corner. Light spilled into the hallway through Sophia's open front door. The cooking smell condensed into something recognizable. Coffee. Burnt coffee.

The open door revealed Sal's living room, still a mess from yesterday's dinner. The Christmas tree held pride of place in the corner that was normally reserved for the television. The tree was off, its lights dully reflecting the sunlight in the windows. Coffee was definitely burning.

I called out, "Sophia?"

I inched my way around the extended dining room table, dropped the sled with the other gifts at the base of the tree. Was Sophia hiding?

"Sophia? It's Tucker!"

Nothing.

The coffee smell emanated from the kitchen. An aluminum Bialetti coffeemaker stood on the gas stove over an open flame. Its lower reservoir had boiled dry long ago and would have glowed cherry red if it weren't for the coffee roiling and sputtering in the top reservoir. I turned off the gas and put the Bialetti in the sink to cool.

The house had to be empty. Sophia would not have made a mistake like this. She must have gotten the phone call and gone to the police station. Perhaps the guy who dropped off Maria told her, and they left the door open and the coffee forgotten. Unlikely.

The two bedrooms were down the hall from the kitchen. Condos like this had crazy floor plans, the result of merging Honeymooners-like two-room apartments into one big living space. Maria's room faced the kitchen. I peeked inside. The room exhibited the post-dervish mess of a little girl rushing to go sledding while Sophia had called out, "Maria, get moving. Tucker is waiting."

I turned from Maria's doorway and peeked into the master bedroom, embarrassed at the thought of glimpsing something intimate. Sunlight poured through big windows at the foot of the bed. I stepped into the immaculate room. Immaculate but for a water glass on the floor, and a woman's shoe tossed against the wall.

Took another step. Saw the bed. Sophia lay on the bed, staring at the ceiling, her hands clutching at something that had gouged her throat as it strangled her.

A clock ticked on Sal's dresser. I stepped into the room, stood at the bed. Sophia's eyes bulged. Red dots speckled her face, and her tongue rested against her lower lip. My breath shortened. Sophia's fingers rested on Sal's Virgin Mary tie. The murder weapon.

I looked around the room. Little was disturbed. A crocheted afghan had been kicked to the floor. Sophia's other shoe rested on top of a dresser. Kicking? I reached down, drew Sophia's eyes closed. They slid open again. Bile rose in my gut. I ran to the bathroom, hunched over the toilet, vomited, and dialed 911.

FOUR

TECHNICIANS AND UNIFORMED COPS bustled about as they converted Sal's home into a crime scene. Tape was strung, pictures were taken, and questions were asked—lots of questions, over and over again. The first cop, a uniformed guy, asked me what had happened. I told him that Sophia was dead and Maria was missing. The second cop, another uniformed guy, asked me what had happened. I told him Sophia was dead and Maria was missing.

The third cop didn't wear a uniform. He wore a food-stained green parka with a fur-lined hood, a sweater that looked as if it had been knitted by a vengeful grandmother, and a fleece-lined plaid baseball cap with ear flaps. His name was Lieutenant Lee and we had history—annoying history.

Lee flipped back the parka hood and pulled off the baseball cap, letting his limp black hair splay itself across his forehead. He sat across the dining room table from me and asked, "What happened, Mr. Tucker?"

I said, "Sophia is dead and Maria is missing."

Lee wrote in his book. "Do you have more details?"

"Sophia is dead, Maria is missing, and it's getting dark."

"Did you touch anything in here?"

"I moved the coffeemaker into the sink, tried to close Sophia's eyes, and threw up in the toilet."

"So those are the only places we'll find your fingerprints?"

"I had Christmas dinner here last night."

"Oh."

"And I was here this morning to take Maria sledding."

"So you knew the victim."

"Of course I knew the victim, Lee. What do you think I do, wander the North End breaking into apartments and looking for bodies?"

"I'm just establishing facts."

"The fact is that Maria is missing and her mother is dead. I can't do anything about her mother being dead, but I sure as hell intend to do something about her being missing."

"We'll get to that."

"You'll get to that? When will you get to that?"

"Well, I won't get to that. I will be solving this murder. But someone will get to that."

"Well, who's going to get to it?"

"The Boston Police Department. Now, did you have any arguments with Sophia Rizzo?"

"Arguments?"

"Disagreements."

"What are you talking about? No. She was my cousin's wife, she had me over to Christmas dinner. What would we fight about?"

"And you were alone with her here in the apartment?"

"No, Lee—Jesus Christ. I just—"

"There's no need to swear."

"I'm not swearing."

"You just swore."

"Oh, for God's sake."

"That's a little better. Why don't you start at the beginning?"

I told Lee about my morning, and about how Bobby Miller had said Maria would be here.

Lee listened to my story and said, "So you have an alibi for the murder."

"Ahh—yeah. Yeah, I have an alibi, because a Boston cop stuck a gun in my nose. Can we get back to Maria?"

"Do you know anyone who would want to harm Sophia?"

"Who would want to harm Sophia?"

"I wasn't here for Christmas dinner, you were."

"Well, nobody at Christmas dinner wanted to harm Sophia. Look. Who gets my statement on the fact that Maria is missing?"

Lee sighed. Flipped a page in his book. "How long has she been missing?"

"Almost two hours."

"Did she wander off?"

"No, she got in a car with one of Sal's crew."

"How did you know this man was one of Sal's crew?"

"He wore a Bruins jacket."

"A Bruins jacket in Boston? That doesn't really narrow things down. But, assuming you're right, Maria is with a friend of the family, of sorts. If this were my case, and it is not, I would start by talking to Pistol Salvucci."

"Who's he?"

"One of Sal's captains. He is violent, unpredictable, and something of a sociopath. I'm sure he'd be helpful. Now can we get back to my questions?"

"Fine, what questions?"

"You are an IT person, correct?"

"I'm a computer scientist, a programmer."

"A hacker?"

"A white-hat hacker, sometimes."

"Did you ever do hacking work for Sal?"

"What? Why would—"

The door to Sal's apartment opened and a guy walked in. Tall with a day's growth on a thick, blue five o'clock shadow that reached nearly over his cheekbones. He saw Lee and flashed credentials.

"Lieutenant Lee, I'm Special Agent Frank Cantrell," said the guy.

Lee said, "We are in the middle of an interview, Agent Cantrell."

"I need Tucker."

"I'm not done with him."

"Yes, you are. Say good-bye." Cantrell pointed at me and snapped his fingers in a "get up" motion.

I had had enough of Lee, so I stood.

Lee said, "Agent Cantrell, with respect, I just need a few minutes."

"Get them another time." Cantrell took me by the elbow and started to guide me to the door.

I shook him off and walked. We circled down the stairs and out into the cold street.

FIVE

IT WAS ONLY A quarter past five o'clock, but Boston's winter sun keeps bankers' hours and had set an hour ago. Salutation Street presented a long, dark valley of icy slop. I snapped my coat shut against the cold.

Cantrell asked, "Where'd you park?"

"I'll take the T."

"Good. We're going in the same direction." Cantrell headed up Salutation back to Hanover.

I watched him.

He turned. "Well, c'mon," he said.

"We're not going to your office?"

"Informal conversation. Just you and me."

I fell in next to Cantrell, walking down the middle of the narrow street. "We don't have time for this," I said. "We need to find Maria."

Cantrell said, "We'll get to Maria."

"Maria wasn't at home. Bobby said she'd be home."

"Bobby who?"

"Bobby Miller."

"Why would Agent Miller talk to you about Maria?"

“Because I was responsible for her. I took her to the Common.”

“Yeah,” said Cantrell. “I find that part interesting.”

We hit Hanover, turned, and headed toward Haymarket, walking the reverse of Bobby’s drive.

“Do I need a lawyer?” I asked.

“A lawyer? Why? We’re just two guys talking, figuring out what happened.”

“What do you think happened?”

“I don’t think anything. I know that you took Maria out of her house just in time for her mother to be murdered.”

“That’s just a coincidence,” I said.

“Why did you take her today?”

“Because I bought her a sled for Christmas—”

“Yesterday.”

“Yeah. And she wanted to use it.”

“She didn’t have a sled?”

“No.”

“So you provided one.”

“Yeah. I bought her a Christmas present.”

“So instead of a doll or something you got her a sled, something that would get her out of the house.”

I smelled a rat. “So I do need a lawyer.”

“I’m just listing the facts.”

“Really.”

“If it makes you feel any better, I already knew all that.”

“How?”

“Your friend Bobby Miller.”

“Oh.”

“He’s still an FBI agent, you know. Still interested in justice even when his tech buddy is involved.”

I stopped walking.

Cantrell turned, stepped close, and spoke into my ear. "You got nothing to say? I see a nifty plan where you take Maria to the park and hand her off while Sal murders his wife."

"Why would I hand her off?"

Cantrell filled the silence. "You and Sal are good friends, right?"

"We're cousins."

"What do you know about Sal's line of work?"

"Nothing."

"Oh, the *omerta*, eh?"

"I'm only half Italian. I don't do the *omerta*."

"So why won't you talk about Sal?"

"Because you're a dick."

"A detective?"

"Sure. That kind of dick." I hunched my shoulders. My earlobes ached. "It's freezing out here."

"So let's move it." Cantrell started walking, hands in his pockets.

I followed. My hands were cold in or out of my pockets.

He asked, "Sal ever tell you about his dealings with the FBI?"

"No."

"How long have you known David Anderson?"

"Who's David Anderson?"

"Hah! Good answer."

"Thanks."

"You're telling me you don't know David Anderson?"

"That's what I'm telling you."

"He's a high-tech private equity guy, so I figured a nerd like you would know him."

I stopped walking again. "Quit fishing."

Cantrell stopped. "Do I have to fucking arrest you to get you to walk with me?"

I started walking. Getting arrested wouldn't help me find Maria.

Cantrell said, "Thank you."

"We only have a day or so," I said.

"Forty-eight hours," said Cantrell.

"What?"

"The odds of finding a kid go down like a rock after forty-eight hours."

"So why am I wasting time talking to you?"

"Because you don't want to spend that forty-eight hours in lockup."

"Oh, fuck you!"

"Fuck me? From where I sit, you're Sal's perfect accomplice."

"Sal didn't kill Sophia."

"How do you know?"

"He loved her."

"There are only two people who know what's going on in a marriage. You're not one of them."

"There is no way."

"You do know that your cousin's a killer."

I did know that Sal was a killer. I'd seen him kill. "I don't know what you're talking about," I said.

"Well, let's just say that a guy like that had to earn his stripes."

I had had enough of this. You can't swing a dead cat in the North End without hitting a coffee shop. We were passing one now.

"I'm freezing," I said. "I'm stopping for a coffee."

"Wimp," said Cantrell.

"Whatever, you go on without me—save yourself."

Cantrell stood on the sidewalk, looking down the street and back at me, trying to decide whether he wanted to bully me anymore. Apparently the cold got to him. He beckoned me closer.

I obliged.

Cantrell leaned toward my ear. "That guy, David Anderson?"

I said, "The private equity guy?"

"Yeah. There's something you should know about him."

"What?"

"Sal put a hit out on him. Ten thousand bucks."

I said nothing. What could I say?

Cantrell pointed. "Your cousin is a killer."

"Is there a point to this?"

"His friends are killers."

"Again, is there a point to this?"

"You get involved with these guys and you're likely to get killed."

"Thanks for the advice. Can I go look for Maria now?"

"It's your funeral. I thought you should know."

Cantrell turned, strode down the street, never looking back.

I ignored the coffee shop, stepped into the doorway next to it, and rang the buzzer.

Adriana Rizzo's voice crackled through the speaker. "Speak!"

"It's me, your cousin Tucker."

"What the hell is going on?"

"Buzz me in."

SIX

THE STATUE OF LIBERTY tells the world to send us its huddled masses yearning to breathe free. When those huddled masses arrived in Boston, they did their huddling in the tiny apartments of the North End. First the Irish, then the Italians lived in tiny one-room affairs as they dug Boston's tunnels, filled in its swamps, and earned a place for themselves in the new world.

As prosperity percolated through the North End, landlords combined tiny apartments to create larger ones, except for the studios which stayed tiny and provided a financial toehold into the neighborhood.

My cousin Adriana and her wife, Catherine, lived in just such a studio, the combined income from Adriana's job as a restaurant server and Catherine's as a social worker barely covering the rent.

Catherine opened the door. My cousin-in-law was nearly my height, thin, with short black hair. She made way, closing the door behind me and walking over to a standing desk that held a Facebooking laptop. Adriana sat at the other end of the room at a tiny table, nursing a coffee and poking at a tablet. She had been crying.

I approached and she spun the tablet so I could see it. Facebook statuses filled the screen:

`I'm so sorry Adriana.`

`Sophia is in our prayers.`

`What can I do to help?`

"I had to find out like this?" Adriana asked, then slipped into a new round of crying.

"I came here first thing," I said. "The police were questioning me."

"Why you?"

"I found the body," I said.

"Oh my God. Was Maria with you?"

"No."

"No? You guys were going sledding. It was on her status."

"We did go sledding. Then it all went to shit."

Catherine joined us at the tiny table as I started to tell them how it had all gone to shit. Adriana interrupted me.

"So you lost Maria," she said.

"Well, I mean, she got into—"

"You lost her! It's one of those nightmare stories where your kid disappears."

"But we just have to find—"

"Get out of my house."

"Yeah but—"

"Get out! Get out and don't come back until you find her!"

SEVEN

SELF-MEDICATION HAS A BAD rap. Who's to say that dealing with your feelings by pouring a few fingers of Bulleit rye whiskey into a rocks glass is a worse way to deal with your emotions than watching a *Battlestar Galactica* marathon, mutilating zombies in a video game, or getting into an online screaming match over the political outrage de jour? Certainly not I.

My South End condo runs from the front of the building to the back in shotgun fashion. The living room's bay windows overlook Follen Street, then comes the kitchenette and office. My bedroom at the back of the condo looks out on trees and the next street's houses.

I sat at the kitchenette's breakfast bar, drank my rye, and attacked the problem of finding Maria the way I attacked all problems—by Googling. I started with basic searches about finding lost children, learned that many of them were just cases of miscommunication. Could that be the case here? Sal had been terrified for Maria, running across a field of frozen snow to try to get to her in time. Yet Maria had been calm, getting into the car with just a single glance back toward me. She knew her abductor. The two reactions made no sense. How could Sal be beside himself and Maria just walk away?

My Google searches strayed from the true path of child-finding and slid into questions about Sal and this guy David Anderson. Click and Clack, my hermit crabs, seemed to have been energized by the smell of a good rye whiskey. They climbed onto their feed sponge, and four eyestalks followed me as I drank rye and Googled David Anderson.

The whiskey kicked in, tickling the pleasure centers and loosening my tight gut. I said, "Holy cow, boys. There are hundreds of David Andersons." I refined my search to just include Boston. "Oh, good. There are only ten in Boston."

Still, David Andersons filled my screen. Boston-based David Andersons included two college professors, a lawyer, a state senator, a dead guy, and—there it was—a private equity guy.

"Well. There he is. Why do you suppose Sal would be messed up with a private equity guy?"

Clack scuttled across the tank and plopped into his water dish. I think that's hermit crab for, "You've had a little too much to drink."

"Nonsense," I told him. "What do you know? You're a teetotaler."

David Anderson was a principal in a firm called Battery Street Capital. Battery Street is next door to Salutation Street. The Battery Street website featured a picture of the man himself: dark hair, dark suit, and a toothy, predatory smile. The site went on to list companies in Battery Street's portfolio.

I copied the list of companies into evernote.com and dug in. Found press releases for each company proudly announcing that they had obtained funding in the form of seed-round investments led by Battery Street. Seed-round investments are usually small investments that get a good idea off the ground. They are long-shot bets with a one-in-ten chance of success, perhaps one in twenty.

I dredged around the Internet, determining which of the Battery Street startups had lived and which had died. It was easy to find signs of life, but it was hard to find signs of death. Entrepreneurs love to tell you when they've finally secured funding, but they rarely talk about burning through their cash and slinking away to plumb LinkedIn for a job.

"Happiness is positive cash flow" is the mantra of all successful startups. It means that you can keep running your business forever without having to sell it off or borrow in order to survive. Bill Gates was so enamored of cash that Microsoft always kept a year's worth in the bank—fifty billion dollars—just in case everybody stopped buying Windows and Office.

Startups that get an initial round of funding do it because they can't generate enough cash to survive. In some cases they need inventory: "We've built the Rolex of mousetraps, but we need five pounds of gold." In other cases, the founders can't get employees to work without salaries: "We'll be rich! Rich, I tells ya! We'll all have salaries next year." "Yeah, no thanks."

In the worst cases, the founders blow the cash creating an engineer's Habitrail, complete with Ping Pong, foosball tables, yoga instructors, and weekly massage therapy.

Cash-negative entrepreneurs eventually have to come crawling back to the VCs, hat in hand, begging for more money. This was where David Anderson and his predatory teeth really got cranking. By the time he was done, he owned the company and the entrepreneur was working for him.

I picked up my Bulleit, saw the bottom of the glass, refilled it a finger or two, and got back to Googling. On a rye-induced whim I typed "Sal Rizzo." Sal had his own Wikipedia entry:

"Sal 'Schizo' Rizzo (born September 29, 1962)..."

Schizo?

"... is the reputed boss of the Boston La Cosa Nostra (LCN)."

The entry wasn't telling me anything I didn't already know about Sal being a crook, but reading it made it harder to shunt the knowledge into my peripheral vision. It was front and center on my screen.

I read through Sal's background. It turned out that while I was getting soaked with the fire hose of knowledge at MIT, Sal was blasting his way up the Mafia hierarchy. The entry culminated with the following nugget:

"Sal Rizzo earned his reputation as 'Schizo' from his temper. He can be calm and measured one moment and in a murderous rage the next."

Seriously? I mean, Sal had a temper, but that was a bit much.

I was done deadhorsing the fact that Sal was in the Mafia. Decided to go back to Anderson. Googled him and Sal together. Only one page popped up.

PASSHACK GARNERS SEED FINANCING

PassHack? That was Jarrod Cooper's company. I'd done some consulting for Jarrod on PassHack. I had just clicked on the link to read more when something thwacked against my front door.

The newspaper?

I don't get the newspaper. In fact, I don't order any products that get thrown at my front door. The door's peephole showed an empty hallway. I opened the door a crack, glanced up the stairs to the roof. No ambush. The street door slammed shut three flights down. A manila envelope lay on my welcome mat, the word TUCKER scrawled across it in black marker.

EIGHT

I REACHED FOR THE envelope, then stopped inches away and imagined Bobby Miller yelling at me, *You messed up the fingerprints, you idiot!* He'd be right. I took a picture of the envelope with my phone and texted it to Bobby. He called right back.

"Don't touch it!" he said.

"I didn't," I said. "But I'm going to. They might be waiting for me to call."

"I'll be right over."

"You've got fifteen minutes," I said.

"I've got as much time as it takes, Tucker. Don't mess this up."

I hung up, left my front door open. I didn't want someone taking the envelope back. Considered pouring a little more whiskey, decided against it. Considered it again. Decided against it again. I put the bottle away, washed my glass, and tweeted:

`Was it a mistake to call the FBI? #askingforafriend`

Bobby buzzed my doorbell. Two sets of feet clomped up the steps. Bobby turned the corner, stopped short of the envelope. Frank Cantrell was right behind him.

Cantrell asked, "Did you touch it?"

I asked Bobby, "Why did you bring him?"

"Frank and I are working together on Sal's case," Bobby said.

Frank said, "We've come to collect the evidence and take it back to the office."

"You will surely not 'collect the evidence,'" I said. "We're going to open it together."

Bobby said, "Frank's just—"

"I should never have called you, Bobby," I said. "I wouldn't have if I thought you were bringing him."

"Just calm down," said Bobby. He reached into his pocket, pulled out a pair of blue plastic gloves, and slipped them on. "Frank, we're going to open it here."

Cantrell said, "For what? It's just going to throw more variables into this."

"Time is a variable," I said.

Cantrell said, "Thanks, nerd."

Bobby said, "Frank, do you want to wait in the car?"

"Screw you, just 'cause this guy is your buddy doesn't mean—"

"Tucker didn't need to call us. It was a courtesy."

"So now we're corrupting evidence as a courtesy?"

"Are you guys going to help me find a little girl or not?" I asked.

Bobby picked up the envelope, stepped into my apartment, put the envelope on the kitchen counter, and produced a pocket knife.

Cantrell said, "Wait before you muck it up." He took a picture of the envelope with his phone.

Bobby slid the knife into the top fold, ran it along the manila, sliced it cleanly, jiggled the envelope open, and reached inside with two blue-sheathed fingers. Pulled out a single sheet of paper. It was a printed PowerPoint slide titled DEMANDS. Maria's picture took up one side, three bullet points took up the other.

Maria was duct-taped to a chair, her little wrists trapped against the armrests. She was crying, looking into the camera, probably at someone's instruction.

"Motherfuckers," Bobby and I said in unison.

Cantrell said nothing.

The bullet points listed their demands:

TELL SAL TO PLEAD GUILTY TO THE MURDERS TOMORROW.

IF SAL DOES NOT PLEAD GUILTY WE WILL KILL MARIA.

DON'T CALL THE POLICE. WE WILL KNOW.

Cantrell pointed at the last demand. "Too late for that, I guess."

Bobby said, "Shut up, Frank."

"I mean, they might have seen us coming in."

"Will you shut up?"

What had I done?

"She's dead," I said.

"No, she's not," said Bobby. "They always write that in demands, but if they killed Maria tonight they'd lose their leverage." Bobby slid the picture around, considering it from different angles. "I'm no psych profiler, but this guy's an idiot."

"I can't believe they're not asking for money," Cantrell said. "'Plead guilty'? What kind of shit is that?"

Bobby said, "They know we're charging Sal with murder."

"It wasn't a secret."

"Still, this took planning. They knew we were going to arrest him and knew to grab Maria to force a confession."

"Vigilantes?" asked Cantrell.

"Or competitors."

"That guy who runs MetroWest?"

I said, "Hugh Graxton?"

Cantrell swung around to face me. "How do you know Hugh Graxton?" he asked.

"He's Sal's friend."

Cantrell said, "Friend? What makes you think these guys have any friends? They're animals."

"Hugh's a good guy."

"Yeah, so's Sal, and they'd both kill you as soon as look at you."

"What's your problem, Cantrell?"

"My problem is that you're cozy with these crooks and nobody's even looking at you."

"If I were part of it, why would they send me the ransom note?"

"Who knows if they sent it to you. Maybe this whole charade was the delivery mechanism."

I pointed at the front door. "Get out of my house."

Whatever Cantrell was, he wasn't a vampire. No magical power swooshed him out the front door. Instead, he remained standing in my kitchen.

"You heard me," I said.

Bobby said, "C'mon Frank, we've gotta go."

I asked Bobby, "What are we going to do about this?"

"I think there's only one right thing to do," Bobby said. "We're going to show this to Sal, see if he wants to plead guilty."

"Let me grab my coat."

Cantrell said, "You're not coming. Why would you come?"

"He's my cousin," I said. "And I lost his daughter."

"What's that got to do with it?"

"Frank, let's bring Tucker," Bobby said. "He may settle the situation."

"You're taking his side?" asked Cantrell.

"This isn't about sides."

"Then you two go talk to Sal. Three's a crowd." Cantrell turned and left, running down the staircase and banging the front door closed.

"Tantrum much, Frank?" I asked.

"His heart's in the right place," said Bobby.

"You mean under a rock somewhere?"

Bobby slid the paper back into the envelope. "Let's see if Sal will confess."

NINE

SAL HAD THE SLACK jaw and faraway gaze of a bombing victim sitting in the gutter. Five o'clock shadow bristled from his chin in salt and pepper patches, accentuating his slack jaw and pallid complexion. His eyes darted, jumping from his hands to the wall to Bobby to me and then to the woman sitting at the head of the table.

The woman had red hair, pulled back into a bun, and she wore a sweaty green yoga top. She stood and circled the table to shake our hands.

"Caroline Quinn."

I hadn't seen a woman wearing anything less than a parka in weeks, and my eyes, acting on their own, shot down Caroline's body for an inventory. Tight yoga top, check. Shapely hips in yoga capris, check. Thighs, super-check. My eyes stalled when they hit Caroline's left shin, where a shiny, ornate prosthesis poked out from the capris.

Fluorescent conference-room lighting glinted off the elegant curlicues that adorned Caroline's prosthetic shin. It was as if she'd taken a beautiful tattoo and rendered it in chrome.

Caroline grabbed my hand, shaking it and yanking my eyes back to hers. "I know what you're thinking."

I held her hand. "You do?"

"Nice legs."

Bobby said, "Can we get started here?"

Caroline released my hand, motioned me to a seat, and took hers at the head of the table. "Miller, telling one of my legal secretaries to pull me out of hot yoga was quite a stunt. I hope you're not just messing with me."

"No counselor, I'm not messing with you," Bobby said. "We needed to show you this now."

Caroline nodded at me. "Who's this?"

Sal said, "That's my cousin, Tucker."

Caroline asked, "First name or last name, Tucker?"

"Last name," I said.

"What's your first name?"

"I just go by Tucker." I don't spring *Aloysius* on them until the second date.

"So, Tucker, why are we here?"

Bobby produced a copy of the note, dealt it across the table to Sal. "Because of this. It's a ransom note."

Sal trapped the note with the palm of his hand, slid it toward himself, looked at the picture of Maria taped to the chair.

"Cocksucker!" Sal said. "Fucking Pupo."

Bobby said, "Joey Pupo? What about him?"

Caroline said, "Don't answer that, Sal."

"I should have taken care of him," Sal said.

Caroline said, "Shut UP!"

"What do you mean 'taken care of him'?" asked Bobby.

Caroline said, "No more talking, Sal. Agent Miller, I need you to leave now."

"Why?" I asked. "If Sal knows who has her, that's a good thing, right?"

Caroline blew out a sigh. "What Sal says can and will be used against him in a court of law. Isn't that right, Agent Miller?"

"This is off the record, isn't it?"

"There is no 'off the record,' Tucker," said Caroline. "Miller is fishing."

Bobby said, "I thought Sal should know about the demands."

"And you thought Sal might be more willing to talk to you," said Caroline. "It's time to go."

"They say he needs to plead guilty," said Bobby.

Sal crinkled the note into a ball. "Miller, when did you turn Joey?"

Caroline said, "Not now, Sal."

"You turned my best friend against me," said Sal. "I just want to know when."

Bobby said, "Don't get dramatic, Sal. Joey wasn't your best friend. Marco was your best friend, until you shot him."

"Fuck you!"

"Sal didn't kill anyone," I said.

Bobby said, "You stay out of this, Tucker."

"How long, Miller?" Sal asked. "How long since you turned Joey?"

Bobby didn't respond.

"So he *is* a fucking informant?" said Sal.

"You gonna do him too?" Bobby asked. "Want to just fill out the confess—"

A bleacher whistle, loud enough to be heard from the top of the bleachers, blasted through the room, piercing my ears and driving spikes into my brain. I spun to the noise and saw Caroline Quinn standing, thumb and finger poised. She inhaled and I covered my ears before she blasted us again.

Caroline sat. "You boys ready to settle down?"

Sal rattled a pinky around in his ear. "For Christ's sake, Caroline."

Caroline said, "Agent Miller, I asked you to leave. You can bring Tucker with you."

"I'm not going anywhere," I said.

Caroline said, "I'm sorry. Do you think I'm going to let you fill in Miller after we're done?"

"I just want to find Maria."

Caroline made a flicking motion at Bobby. "Would you leave? C'mon. Shoo."

"Let's go, Tucker," Bobby said.

I said, "I'm not leaving."

Sal said, "Tucker can stay."

"You trust him?" Caroline asked.

"Yeah," Sal said.

Caroline sat. "Fine." She pointed at Bobby, then at the door.

Bobby moved to the door, turned. "Listen Sal. About Sophia. I'm sorry for your loss."

Sal closed his eyes. Crushed the note in his fists. Bobby closed the door behind him.

Caroline patted Sal's hand, worked the note free, and spread it on the table. "That's the stupidest kidnapping demand I've ever heard," she said.

Sal said, "Joey's always been a fucking moron."

"How do you know Joey has her?" I asked.

Sal pointed at the picture. "Those are the dining room chairs his grandmother left him. They're fucking ancient. Nobody else has chairs like that."

I asked, "So why did he take her?"

"Because the douche bag doesn't want to face me in court and spend the rest of his life in witness protection."

"Why would he face you?"

Sal didn't answer, spread out the note some more trying to get it flat. "Thank God Sophia didn't live to see this." Sal's composure slipped. His lip curled, his eyes spilled tears that forged wet trails through his beard. A sob erupted. "Fuckin' church." He dropped his face into his arms. "I'm sorry, Maria."

"What about the church?" I asked.

"I let Joey live—"

"Sal, I shouldn't be hearing this," Caroline said. "Let's focus on—"

Sal grabbed my shoulder, slid his big hand behind my neck, and pulled me close. "You listen to me, Tucker. You never tell a guy you're gonna kill him."

Caroline said, "Sal—"

"You just fucking do it. No warning, no nothing."

"Sal, stop it."

"You fucking warn him and this is what happens." Sal gestured to the room.

"You were going to kill Joey Pupo?" I asked.

"I warned him first," Sal said. "Told him to turn himself in or I'd kill him."

Caroline asked, "Turn himself in for what?"

"He killed Marco."

"Are you sure?"

"I saw him."

"Why didn't you tell the police?"

"Because I'm not a fucking informant," said Sal. "What did I tell you?"

Caroline sighed. "That you'd never turn."

"Don't even bring me a deal."

"I'm still going to bring you a good deal if they offer it."

"I'm telling you, don't do it. I'll never turn on my guys."

"Well, Pupo turned on you, Sal. He told them you killed Marco."

I stood, shrugged on my winter coat, stuck out my hand, and shook Caroline's. "It was nice to meet you."

"Where are you going?" Sal asked.

I said, "I'm getting Maria back."

"You can't just go get her back," Caroline said. "You'll get killed."

"I'll bring Bobby." I opened the door. Stepped into the hall.

Sal called out, "Joey will kill her if he sees you coming."

"Then he won't see me coming."

TEN

Joey's address, Holden Court, turned out to be a long courtyard formed by three brick apartment buildings. Joey's apartment commanded the high ground at the end of the courtyard on the top floor. Bobby Miller peeked around the corner, his bald head steaming in the cold.

"He's got to be up there watching the street," said Bobby. "He'll see us coming. We should wait until early morning. He'd be asleep."

"I'm not waiting," I said. "Maria's terrified."

"Well, walking up that courtyard will get her killed, and that's worse than terrified."

I scanned the buildings around us. I'm certain that the guys who built the North End had never read a computer science book, had never heard of tessellations, and had never even played a game of Tetris. Yet their handiwork on the triangle formed by Battery, Hanover, and Commercial Streets said otherwise; they had managed to cover the entire triangle with buildings by eschewing right angles long before modern construction techniques had made it cool.

The backsides of the triangle-facing buildings formed a little trapezoid, which would have been wasted space, or maybe a park, if the builders hadn't dropped Joey Pupo's house into it. This explained the long courtyard of Holden Court; it was the only way to reach the entombed stack of condos.

"We don't need to go in the front door," I said.

Bobby said, "These places don't have back doors. They're fire traps."

"They're not fire traps. If there's a fire you don't go down, you go up."

Bobby smiled as he got my idea. "You're a genius. Why didn't I think of that?"

"Because you're trapped in mundane two-dimensional thinking."

"Yeah. That must be it."

Bobby popped the trunk on his illegally parked Buick and pulled out a crowbar. We opened the ornate front door next to the courtyard and climbed the steps to the inner door. Three buttons were fitted into the doorjamb. Bobby pressed the bottom one, ringing a buzzer inside someone's apartment. He pressed it again and leaned on it a beat longer than necessary.

"For emphasis," he said.

"Making friends," I said.

An apartment door opened, a head appeared, disappeared, and then a guy came out. He had a short brown beard, neatly trimmed off his cheeks, and a t-shirt that read *Follica: Breakthrough products for hair follicle disorders.* He said, "Can I help you?"

Bobby flashed his ID. "I'm Agent Miller with the FBI, and this is Mr. Tucker. We need to get onto your roof."

The guy stiffened. "You got a warrant?"

Bobby said, "A warrant for what?"

"To search the roof."

"We're not going to search the roof. We're going to walk on the roof."

"I'm sorry, officer—"

"Special Agent," said Bobby.

"What?"

"I'm not with the police, I'm with the FBI. I'm not an officer, I'm an special agent."

"Okay. I'm sorry, Special Agent Miller, but I don't consent to searches."

"I'm not asking you to consent to a search. I'm asking you to let us in so we can get on your roof."

"You need a warrant."

"I don't need—"

"And I'm not with the FBI," I said. "So I don't need a warrant anyway."

The guy said, "What?"

"Listen," said Bobby, "if you're gonna spout the law you gotta know it. You can't ask Tucker for a warrant because he's not an agent or an officer."

"Yeah," I agreed.

"He's an IT guy," said Bobby.

"I'm not an IT guy," I said. "I'm a computer scientist."

"Okay, a fancy IT guy."

"There's a big difference," I said.

The guy in the door said, "Look, I'm a bioengineer, but I still know my rights and I don't have to let you guys onto my roof."

Bobby lunged, bursting through the door and knocking the guy on his ass.

The guy looked up. "Jesus! You can't do that."

Bobby said, "I can do that, because I just did that." Bobby started up the stairs. "I'll let the IT guy explain it to you."

I followed Bobby. "I'm a computer scientist."

The guy yelled up the staircase. "I'm calling the police."

Bobby yelled back, "The police love guys who obstruct investigations. Miller is spelled M-I-L-L-E-R."

"I know how to spell 'Miller'!" The guy stormed into his apartment and slammed the door behind him.

"Do you think he'll call the cops?" I asked.

Bobby said, "It would be good to have some backup."

We climbed an artifact of old city buildings, a spiral staircase mounted in a tall box. The steps, narrow at the inner edge, wide at the outer edge, constantly threatened to send people tumbling to the bottom.

"Have you considered trying Follica?" I asked.

"I don't have hair follicle disorder," said Bobby.

"I'm sorry. I was confused by the lack of hair."

We reached the top. Bobby pulled the door open. Snow tumbled down the staircase. "Oh shit," he said.

Yesterday's storm had dropped two feet of snow onto the city. Most of the snow had already been shoveled, plowed, or brushed away, but nobody had done any of these things on the flat roofs of the North End. Drifting snow reflected the full moon, creating a monochromatic blue snowscape.

I looked down at Bobby's wing tips, encased in rubber. "You'll never make it."

"I'll be fine," said Bobby. "I have galoshes."

"That snow's two feet deep. You think shoe condoms will help?"

"So I get a little cold."

"I'm not worrying about you getting cold. I'm worrying about you falling off the roof."

"What about you?"

I pointed at my boots. "I've got UGGs."

"Jesus, tell me you didn't say that. Did your crush ask you to the prom yet?"

"What? They're great boots."

"And oh so stylish."

"The point is, I can climb through that snow field and you can't. So let's do this. I'll get in the roof door in Joey's house, call you on my cell, then knock on the front door. While he's distracted talking to me, you run up the courtyard."

Bobby looked at the pile of snow. Tested it with a step. His shoe disappeared. "Goddamn, motherfucker, shit. Right down my fucking ankle."

"Well, at least you tried." I took Bobby's crowbar. "See you inside."

I plunged through the drift. Bobby closed the door behind me. I was alone standing on a rooftop courtyard. The city fell away into muffled silence, its traffic noises and energy absorbed by the drifting powder. A tall building loomed next to me like a glacier, while the gap between buildings formed a chasm. This was going to be more like hiking to Everest than walking across the rooftops.

I waded through snow. I had laced my UGGs all the way up, and they performed like champs. Tom Brady champs. My feet stayed dry, and I was able to get traction. *Screw Bobby, I like UGGs.*

I fought my way to the edge of the courtyard. The snow had drifted almost to the top of the fence. I tried to climb the drift, but the light snow compressed into nothing. I hoisted myself up the fence, fell over the top. The crowbar slipped and disappeared into the snow.

Crap!

I pawed through the snow pile, my gloves making it difficult to get a feel for the metal. I could see the spot where it went in, but it had fallen at an angle into two feet of snow. I got down on my hands and knees, pushing snow out of my face and feeling around for the metal. Couldn't find it. I took off my gloves and plunged my bare hands into the snow, all the way to the roof. Felt along the tarpaper with numbing fingers. Hit metal. Pulled the crowbar from the snow with red frozen hands. Jack London would have loved this—"To Build a Fire: Boston."

My burning, frozen hands refused to warm the insides of my gloves. Praying for blood flow, I trudged toward the edge of the building to check out the next one. Peered out at a ten-foot drop to the next roof. I was victim of one of the oldest engineering mistakes in the world: the unchecked assumption. I'd assumed all these buildings would be the same height. I was wrong.

A ten-foot jump into snow. How bad could that be? I looked for a good landing drift but spotted a shed instead. Only a four-foot drop to the shed's roof. Much better plan. I sat on the edge of the current roof. Dropped to the shed.

The snow had hidden the fact that the shed's roof slanted away from a peak. I hit the slant, fell. Rather than break my fall, I gripped the crowbar, determined not to lose it again. Glass shattered. *What the hell?* A chunk of snow fell through a sudden hole. I wasn't on a roof. I was on a skylight, over a stairwell. Cracking sounds tore through the snow as the glass gave way. I threw myself off the skylight and fell through the night onto a drift of snow below. Not sure how I kept from impaling myself on the crowbar.

I rose and headed for Joey's building. The wading became easier, as the snow had drifted to the edges of the roof.

"I might just survive this," I said to the crowbar.

That was when a gunshot blasted the night, followed by a little girl's scream.

ELEVEN

Screw stealth! Time to call Bobby. I ran through a foot of snow, pulled off my gloves, and grabbed my Droid, trying to run and call at the same time. The touchscreen ignored my dead cold fingers as I ran through the powder, and I tripped on a drift-hidden firewall, a thick concrete speed bump that extended a foot above the roof. The firewall caught my boot, sending me sprawling and the Droid flying off the roof. I listened for the sound of it hitting a snow bank. Heard it shatter on freshly salted concrete instead.

On the bright side, I had made it to Joey's roof. The crowbar lay next to me. I grabbed it, climbed through more drifts, and hoisted myself over the fence that surrounded another roof deck. I listened for more shots and, hearing nothing, heel-kicked the rooftop door and flew backward as the door repulsed me. It hadn't budged. Another kick, another rebuff. The UGGs were great for snow, but the big soft heel was dampening my kicks.

Great lock artists study locks the way I study software. They know every weakness, every loose pin, every poorly made tradeoff. For a lock artist, this door was nothing. Too bad I wasn't a lock artist.

Heel-kicked the door again. Nothing.

I jammed my crowbar into the door frame. Hard, frozen wood shattered, giving my crowbar access to the spot right next to the lock. I stuck the straight edge of the crowbar into the door, left it hanging there, and kicked the other end. Wood shattered, splintering into the hallway. The door swung open, the deadbolt still in place.

More silence. I slipped through the door into the dark stairwell. I didn't have a flashlight, didn't have a gun, didn't know who was down there, and had no help. I figured the one thing I could do was be quiet.

I failed.

Someone had been using the staircase as a storage closet for home repair goods. I took a step and kicked over a paint can that clattered down the stairwell. Lost my balance, dropped to the next step. My heel hit a narrow part of the stair, slipped off, and landed in a paint-pan that flipped under my foot and acted as a ski. The paint-pan leg shot out from under me, and I sailed down the stairwell, trying to grab the railing while protecting my face from hammers, two by fours, nail-filled coffee cans, and my own crowbar. I landed flat on my back, hit my head on Joey Pupo's front door, fell through it, and came to a stop looking up at a sink, stove, and refrigerator. I had landed in the kitchen.

I remained still, listening. Nothing happened. Either the apartment was empty or its occupants were hiding. I took a moment to assess the damage. My head throbbed, my elbow was growing a knot where it had hit a wall. I tried to wiggle my fingers and discovered that the pinky finger on my left hand wouldn't move. Brought the hand to my face and saw the poor guy was bent the wrong way. *They're only supposed to bend forward and backward.*

Bobby Miller was tapping my face with a cold hand. "Tucker. Tucker, wake up."

He hadn't been here a second ago. A second ago I was looking at my bent finger. I raised my hand to my face. The finger was straight.

"Must have been a dream," I mumbled.

"What?" asked Bobby.

"I had a dream that I'd dislocated my finger."

"You did. I straightened it out for you."

I flexed my hand. "Where did you learn to do that, Dr. Bobby?"

"On the football field. Can you stand?" Bobby pulled me to my feet. We stood in Joey Pupo's tiny kitchen, looking at the two doors. Bobby picked a door and led the way. We stepped through one bedroom into another. The second room commanded the view of the courtyard that had worried Bobby.

I looked around the empty room with its drawn blinds. "He was never up here."

Bobby shrugged. "Better safe than sorry."

"Maybe not," I said. "Didn't you hear the shot?"

"Shot?" Bobby drew his gun. "What shot?"

"What were you doing down there?"

"Arguing with the Boston cops."

We slipped back through the kitchen.

Bobby peered into the living room. "Shit," he said. He holstered his gun.

A dead guy lay on the living room floor. Blood pooled in a lake on the hardwood.

"Got him in the aorta," Bobby said.

"Oh my God. Maria was here. She saw this."

"How do you know?"

I pointed at the floor. A trail of tiny bloody footprints splashed into the kitchen.

Bobby said, "Those are snow boots."

Small snow boots. Maria's snow boots.

"She ran right through the blood," I said.

"Somebody must have called her over. She was in the back room. The killer shot this guy, watched him bleed out, then called her over."

"So where is she now?"

"Lost," said Bobby.

TWELVE

A SPLASH OF PALE winter sun snuck past my window shade and hit me in the face. I covered up with a pillow, tried to go back to sleep, failed. It was winter; if the sun was high enough to hit me, it had to be nine o'clock. Closed my eyes, saw Maria getting in that car, Sal handcuffed, bloody little bootprints. Last night flooded back.

We had called the Boston police and they had shown up within minutes. We waited in the kitchen, staying out of the crime scene while they strung yellow tape and took pictures.

Lieutenant Lee showed up, crumpled and cold, his hat hair plastered across his forehead. He peeked into the room. Said, "Good Lord."

Bobby said, "Yup."

Lee turned to Bobby, pointing back at the room. "That's Joey Pupo."

"Indeed."

Lee's eyes traced the bloody boot tracks. "Whose footprints are these?"

I said, "Maria Rizzo's."

"Did you find her?"

Bobby said, "No."

"The killer took her?"

I said, "Yes," as Bobby shrugged. "You don't think the killer took her?" I asked Bobby.

"For all I know, Maria killed the guy. Got a gun somehow, shot him, ran out."

"That makes no sense. You were at the end of the court. You would have seen her."

"Probably. Like I said, I was arguing with the Boston cops."

"What was the argument?" Lee asked.

"Long story."

"Just tell me what happened."

We told him, and finished at two in the morning.

I climbed out of bed wearing only my boxers. Thought better of it when my feet hit the cold floor, threw on sweatpants, a sweatshirt, and wool socks. I missed the warm mornings of summer.

A new Bialetti coffeemaker waited on the stovetop. It was my Christmas present from Sal, a single-cup brother to Sophia's family-sized coffeemaker. Its little box had sat under the Christmas tree waiting for me to arrive. When I had walked into the door, Maria ran to the tree and grabbed the box.

"Open it, Tucker, open it!" she'd squealed.

"She's excited because she thought of the present," said Sophia.

"They weren't going to get you a present," said Maria. "But I remembered."

"You got a big mouth for a little girl," said Sal.

"Thank you for reminding us, honey," said Sophia.

"You guys didn't need to get me something," I said.

"Of course they did," said Maria. "You're family. We always buy presents for family."

I had started to disassemble the wrapping paper, being careful not to tear it. Sal lost patience with the process. "Just open the fucking thing."

I opened the fucking thing and discovered the coffeemaker.

"This is so cool!" I said, and hugged Maria. "Thank you, guys."

Sal said, "Make sure you don't put too much coffee into it. Everyone thinks it's an espresso maker, and they pack the coffee into it."

"It's not an espresso maker?" I asked.

"No."

"The box says it makes espresso," I said.

"Don't believe everything you read. Listen to me," Sal had said.

I filled the Bialetti with water and coffee, did not pack it, and set it on the stove. Considered my breakfast options. I needed something hot. The cold had slipped into my chest and my back. I don't know what it is about winter, but the thermostat can read 70 and still you freeze. Click and Clack slept inside their shells.

"Tough day to be cold-blooded, eh, guys?"

I boiled some water, broke out a single pack of oatmeal and stirred it as the little Bialetti began to gurgle, let it finish gurgling just as Sal had shown me, and poured a cup of dark black coffee. The coffee and oatmeal steamed on the breakfast nook. I sat, propped my tablet in front of me, tapped the *Boston Globe* icon, and let its headline drag me right back into yesterday.

GANGLAND MASSACRE

I grimaced at the coffee's bitterness. Read about Sophia's murder, Joey's murder, Sal's arrest. The article implied that Sal had killed them both, along with Marco Esposito, in a wild triangle of terror—this despite the fact that Sal was in jail when Joey was murdered.

The end of the article, in a typical case of the newspaper almost getting it right, mentioned that Maria Rizzo was missing after sledding with "her uncle, Al Tucker."

Al? Seriously? Also, I wasn't Maria's uncle, I was her cousin.

I tweeted:

`If a newspaper gets the news wrong is it still a newspaper? #questions`

The article went on to say that Maria was thought to be with family. Who thought that? I didn't think that, and I was family. I swiped back to the article's byline: Jerry Rittenhauser. Why didn't he call me? He could at least have gotten my name right.

I closed the article, opened Gmail. I had long ago given up the notion of personal privacy and had willfully joined the Google info-verse. Google knew where I was, what I got for email, and, because I used Google's phone service, all my voicemail went to my Gmail account. Voice messages from Jerry Rittenhauser filled the inbox. He had tried to call me, but my phone had been destroyed.

The heating system ticked as I ate my oatmeal, drank my bitter coffee, and reread the article, reread the notion of me being "Uncle Al." This was ridiculous. I moved to my office, fired up the Gmail application that turned my computer into a speakerphone and called Jerry.

"Rittenhauser," he answered.

"This is Tucker. You called me—let's see—five times last night."

"Thanks for get—"

"And still you got the story wrong."

"Well, you know, we do our—"

"Do you want to get it right?"

"What are you going to do? Defend Sal?"

"First I'll tell you my real name."

"Okay. It's not Tucker?"

"It's not Al. That's the tip of the vast iceberg of your wrongness."

"Meet me for lunch."

We made plans and exchanged phone numbers, which reminded me of the reason that I hadn't gotten any of Rittenhauser's calls.

I needed a new phone.

THIRTEEN

The LaBrea Tar Pits of retail buildings sits on the corner of Newbury Street and Mass Ave. It's a nifty structure with tall arching windows, canted external beams, and a matching canted roof that flares into the skyline. It has 45,000 square feet of retail space, sits on a busy corner, and has access to students and professionals alike. This attractive spot is irresistible to the mighty retail beasts that drown in its clutches.

Virgin Records, secure in the idea that everything they touch turns to gold, built the damn thing, moved in, flailed around in it, and sank from view. Then Tower Records, drawn by the smell of students, stepped into its gooey embrace, realized its mistake, panicked, struggled, and drowned. Then Best Buy dove in, made a go of it, and looked like it had developed a knack for swimming in tar, but eventually fatigued and slipped under.

MobileMaster was the latest player. A superstore for everything that could fit in your pocket and beep, it clearly believed that it had found the perfect place. I rushed over to buy myself a new phone before MobileMaster succumbed to the tar.

There was a time when manly men carried tiny phones, the smaller the better. Then Apple invented the smartphone and changed everything. Suddenly, bigger was better, and MobileMaster was riding this trend for all it was worth, providing an assortment of expensive phablets. I was considering the merits of a phone the size of a Pop-Tart when I felt a looming over my shoulder.

I turned and was looking into the chest of Oscar Sagese, a soldier in Hugh Graxton's MetroWest Mafia army. Oscar didn't worry me. Hugh Graxton and cousin Sal were friends or business partners or something, so he wouldn't hurt me. Still, he and I had an unfortunate history. I hoped that he had forgiven me for hacking his Facebook account.

"Hey, Mr. Fucking Hacker," said Oscar.

So much for forgiveness. "Hi, Oscar," I said. "Could you move a little? You're blocking the sun."

"Maybe you should show a little more respect now that Sal's put away."

Uh oh.

Oscar continued, "Sal's the only reason I haven't beat the shit out of you. But your day is coming."

"Oscar, did you come all the way into Boston to tell me that you're going to beat me up someday?"

"No, smart-ass. Mr. Graxton sent me. You're ignoring his phone calls."

"I lost my phone."

"How did you lose your phone?"

"I dropped it off a roof in the North End."

"You're a fucking idiot."

"Don't you want to know why I was on a roof in the North End?"

"No."

"I was trying to get Maria back from Joey Pupo."

This got Oscar to thinking. Thinking got Oscar to be quiet. I listened for the faint scraping sound of unused gears grinding to life.

"Got nothing to say?" I asked.

"I heard Joey Pupo got aced last night."

"He did."

"Did you do it?"

"Do you think I could do it?"

"Anyone could kill anyone."

"Just like anyone could kidnap Sal's daughter?"

"Joey didn't kidnap her. He's Sal's buddy."

"He did kidnap her. Sent a note and everything."

"That's bullshit, Mr. Hacker. Why would Joey Pupo kidnap Maria?"

"I thought you might know," I said.

Oscar grabbed my coat, bunching it up in his hand as he cocked his arm back for a punch. "You calling me a fucking kidnapper?"

I slapped at Oscar's hand, got him to loosen his grip. "No, you—no. I'm not. But I figure you might know what's going on."

"I don't know anything."

"Did Hugh have something to do with this? Is that why he wants to see me?"

"I just do what I'm told. Hugh told me to bring you to him and that's what I'm doing."

I looked around the store. Oscar and I were the only early-morning customers. Apparently nobody working at the store had noticed our little scuffle; their caffeine must not have kicked in yet.

"You're not here randomly," I said. "How did you find me?"

"I followed you from your house. Couldn't believe you didn't see me. You should pay attention. With Sal gone, things are gonna get ugly fast."

"What does Hugh want?"

"He wants to talk to you. He's pissed that you're ignoring him."

"I'm not ignoring him. I told you. My phone got lost. I'm picking a new one." I pointed at the display. "It's a tough choice."

Oscar looked at the array of smartphones, reached over my shoulder, and pointed at one on sale. "Buy that one."

"Yeah, but—"

"Buy that fucking phone right now."

I bought the phone. Oscar left while I was going through the endless activation process. Once the activation was done, the phone sprang to life, displaying a backlog of text messages.

Graxton had sent me several texts. The last one said, `Meet me at Cafe Vittoria on Hanover. Now!`

I didn't like the sound of that.

Cafe Vittoria was Sal's office.

FOURTEEN

WITH HIS BLUE BUTTON-DOWN shirt, gray sports jacket, and crisp jeans, Hugh Graxton belonged in the bowels of Starbucks in Chestnut Hill. Unfortunately, he was sitting in the window of Cafe Vittoria in the North End. His MacBook Air, instead of resting on a nice wooden desk, teetered on a little granite table. His ever-present paper Starbucks cup with a paper sleeve had been replaced by a tiny china demitasse with a little handle. When I arrived, Hugh was rooting around under the table with a power cord. He looked like a cat at a dog show.

"This place doesn't have any outlets," he said.

"This isn't Starbucks," I said.

"You're telling me. How am I supposed to get any work done?"

I pulled out a chair and sat next to Hugh. Nick, the barista, glanced over. I nodded. He started work on my cappuccino. Hugh noted the interaction.

"You're a regular, huh?"

"Sal's a regular. I visit Sal. What the hell are you doing here? Why aren't you out in Chestnut Hill?"

Hugh ignored me. Oscar lumbered in, moved to a seat a couple of tables from us, slumped in a chair, and opened his coat and jacket.

The butt end of a gun showed itself. I glared at the gun. "What the hell's going on?"

"Why don't you tell me?"

"All I know is Maria's missing."

"That's not all you know, Tucker. Not by a damned sight. Sophia's dead. Joey's dead. Sal's locked up. What did you do?"

"I didn't do anything."

Hugh looked at Oscar and back at me. "Can you believe this guy?"

Oscar sniggered.

Hugh said, "You were on the Common with his kid when he gets snagged and she gets taken. Meanwhile someone's strangling Sophia. You were right in the middle of it all."

"The newspaper didn't say she was strangled. How did you know that?"

"You think I get my news from the newspapers? They always get it wrong. Admit it, you know the whole story."

"I don't. I'm just trying to find Maria."

"Why?"

"Why? What do you mean, why? Because I don't want to see her face on a milk carton, that's why."

"It seems that grabbing Maria would give you some nice leverage over Sal."

"Why would I need leverage over Sal?"

"You tell me."

"This is—"

Nicky brought my cappuccino. A plate of biscotti sat on the table in front of Hugh. I grabbed a biscotti, crunched into it, let the almond flavor fill my mouth.

Hugh said, "Help yourself."

"Fuck you," I said. Biscotti crumbs aerosoled out of my mouth on the *F*, landing on Hugh's jacket.

Hugh brushed at the crumbs. "For Christ's sake, just tell me what you know."

"I don't know anything."

"How unusual. Did you and Sal have a falling out?"

"No, we didn't have a falling out. I was just there for Christmas dinner."

"Doesn't mean you didn't have a falling out. Christmas dinner is the best time for a good falling out."

"Well, we didn't have one. How about you? You and Sal have a falling out?"

"Sal and I are as thick as thieves—so to speak."

"Are you going to help me find Maria or not?"

Hugh said, "Good question."

"Because if you're not, then I have places to be."

"Yeah? Where would those be? Do you have any idea what to do next?"

I visualized my next steps, got a blank screen. "No."

"No surprise there."

I took a drink. Ate more of Hugh's biscotti. A couple of guys in Bruins jackets walked past the window and looked in, saw Hugh, and did a double take. Hugh gave them a nod. The guys conferred, pointing at Hugh, then walked on.

Hugh said, "This is going to be ugly."

"What's going to be ugly?"

Hugh turned to Oscar. "Oscar, you know why I trust this guy?"

Oscar said, "No, boss. He's a sneaky bastard, you ask me."

"No, Oscar, that's where you're wrong. He's not sneaky. He's clueless."

"Could you talk about me behind my back?" I said. "It's more polite."

Hugh continued, "He truly has no idea what's going on."

I asked, "What's going on?"

"See? There it is. I love this guy!"

Oscar crossed his arms. I guess he wasn't feeling the love.

I said, "I'm serious, Hugh. Why aren't you in Chestnut Hill? Why are you sitting here?"

Hugh said, "Despite your MIT education, I think you're a pretty bright guy."

"Thanks."

"How do you think succession works in this business?"

"What business?"

"Cut the shit. You know what business. Sal's business. My business. This thing, whatever it is. What happens when the king is dead?"

"Sal's not dead."

Hugh's gaze softened. "His blood's in the water, Tucker."

"But that doesn't explain—"

The door to the cafe opened. Oscar's hand moved toward his gun. A woman entered, wearing a fur coat. "Jesus, I had to come see for myself," she said.

Hugh said, "Angie, you're looking lovely."

Angie let her coat fall open, revealing a white sweater stretched tight over large breasts and blue jeans with strategically placed tears at the thighs. "Hugh, what are you doing here?"

I stood, put out my hand. "Hi. I'm Tucker."

Angie took my hand. Her fingers were warm. "Angela Morielli. You look familiar."

Hugh said, "Tucker was just leaving. Maybe he could walk you somewhere, Angie."

"Don't let the door hit me in the ass on the way out, huh?" said Angie.

My body responded to Angie in embarrassing ways. I said, "I'd be happy to walk you somewhere."

Angie looked me up and down and said, "Sure. I'm just heading to church." She pulled her coat closed and stepped out. I followed.

Hugh called to me as I left, "Tucker!"

I paused in the doorway.

"Watch your ass, not hers."

FIFTEEN

"So you're Sal's cousin," said Angie as she started down Hanover Street past Mike's Pastry toward the Prado and the Paul Revere statue.

"Yup. His little cousin."

"You don't look like Sal at all."

"I know, right? Thank God."

Angie laughed.

I asked, "How do you know Sal?"

"We went to first grade together."

"That's impossible. You're too young."

"Aren't you the sweetest thing?"

Snow piles constricted the sidewalk. Angie stepped closer, slipping her arm under mine. Her fur-covered breast nudged my triceps, making my stomach flip. The last time I'd had sex there were green leaves on the trees. I was feeling kind of... backed up.

I started to talk. Coughed, then said, "Did you hear what happened yesterday?"

"It's terrible. The *Herald* called it MOBSTER MADNESS." Angie shuddered.

"Sal didn't do that," I said.

"I know. One thing about Sal, he's got that old-school honor. He'll occasionally freak out and kill some goombah, but not Sophia."

"Did the *Herald* mention Maria?"

"It said that police are looking for her."

"They say they're looking for her, but I haven't seen it."

"That poor kid."

I sighed.

Angie stopped in front of Paul Revere's statue. Revere looked down at us, his arm extended, welcoming us to the Old North Church rising behind him.

Angie pointed across the street. "This is my stop."

"St. Stephen's, huh."

"I sing here. I have to practice. We're going to have a lot of funerals this week."

"My mother's funeral was here."

Angie stepped back. Looked me over. "That's where I know you."

"From the funeral?"

"I sang at her funeral. You gave that crazy eulogy where you swore to kill someone."

"Ah, yes. That would be me."

"Did you kill anyone?"

"Let's talk about it another time."

Angie reached into her coat, pulled out her cell phone. "What's your number?"

I told her, she dialed it. My new phone said "Droid." She hung up.

"Call me." She crossed the street and entered the church.

SIXTEEN

"Sal Rizzo is a murderous bastard," said Jerry Rittenhauser. He bit into a Dunkin' donut. Red jelly oozed from the little donut navel and dropped toward his lap, but Jerry was too quick for it, dodging out of the way. The roaches would be partying tonight.

"Where I come from, we eat our lunch before we launch into accusatory diatribes," I said.

We sat in CityPlace, the food court in the State Transportation Building. The building connected Boylston Street to the theater district. It was a big brick building with an open food court in the center. The building had no central heating system, relying upon captured heat from restaurant stoves and mammalian warmth from office workers in its battle against the cold. At over thirty years old, the Transportation Building is the hipster of architecture—it was green before green was cool.

Jerry, a thin guy like me, munched on donuts while I tackled a cheeseburger. I took a picture of our lunch and tweeted:

`Somewhere in the food court, a fat guy has to be hating on us.`

"Diatribe?" said Jerry. "Sal's a mobster. He kills people."

"Look, if you're just gonna shit on my family for the next half hour, I'll ditch the *Globe* and take my story over to the *Herald*."

"No. No. I want to hear your story."

"Because, you know, I think MOBSTER MADNESS beats the hell out of GANGLAND MASSACRE."

"Yeah, yeah. The *Herald* is much better at writing in all caps."

"Neither one of you is any good at getting the real story."

Jerry finished his first donut, slurped his coffee. I winced. Dunkin' Donuts coffee tastes like road tar filtered through a dish towel. Jerry started in on his next donut, a Boston Kreme.

I said, "You realize there are 310 calories in that thing."

"Whatever. I like them."

"And it contains titanium dioxide."

"Builds strong bones and teeth."

I took a bite of my burger. It didn't taste like a burger. It tasted like bread and mustard and lettuce and meat and cheese. I pushed it aside.

Jerry said, "Did you call me here to criticize my food choices?"

I said, "I called you because you called me five times yesterday. What did you want to know?"

"I want to know what really happened yesterday."

"My little cousin, Maria, got abducted on the Common."

"From what I heard, she left willingly."

"Where did you hear that?"

Rittenhauser bit into his Boston Kreme.

"Fine," I said, "don't tell me. She might have left willingly, but she was abducted just the same."

"I'll bet she's with an aunt or something."

"You didn't see the ransom note."

"What ransom note?"

"I got a note yesterday. It had a picture of Maria tied to a chair and it demanded that Sal plead guilty today to get her back."

"It demanded? Who wrote it?"

"Joey Pupo. It was a picture from his house."

"But Pupo's dead."

I spread my hands. *See?*

"Do you have the note?" asked Rittenhauser.

"No. The FBI has it, but I have a picture." I pulled out my phone. "Shit."

"What?"

"I had a picture, but my phone got smashed."

"A picture like that would be really useful if you're looking for Maria. Can you get it?"

"Give me a sec."

We assumed the clichéd pose of the modern meal. We ignored each other and fiddled with our phones. I called Bobby.

I asked Bobby, "Can you text me back that picture of Maria's note?"

Bobby asked, "Why?"

"I want to look at it, you know, for clues."

"You going to keep it between us?"

"Yeah. Yeah, sure."

"Awright, just a sec." Bobby's text came through my phone: `Remember, your eyes only.`

"Thanks, Bobby." I hung up.

"Who was that?" asked Rittenhauser.

"Bobby Miller at the FBI. He sent me this." Brought up the picture. Handed my phone to Rittenhauser.

Rittenhauser said, "Holy shit! Can I get a copy of this?"

"For what?"

"Front page, baby. This is front page."

"I promised to keep it to myself."

"To Miller, right?"

"Yeah."

"I thought you were looking to find Maria."

"I am."

"And you think that keeping pictures of Maria out of the papers will help you?"

"Well—"

"You know there are people desperate to get pictures of their lost kids out to as many people as possible."

"Yeah, but—"

"They plaster them on lampposts, send them out in email blasts, share them on Facebook, and try to get five seconds on the evening news."

"Right. But Bobby—"

"And so I'm offering to try to get, no promises mind you, try to get your niece's—"

"Cousin's."

"Yeah, whatever—cousin's picture on the front page of the *Boston* frigging *Globe*, and you're telling me that you don't want that?"

"You have a point."

"Of course I have a point."

I addressed the picture to Jerry. Poised my finger over the send button. "You think it will get Maria back?"

"It won't hurt."

"Because this isn't a normal missing kid. Somebody killed Joey Pupo to get her."

"Yeah, I was thinking about that. It was Sal's guys."

"Sal's guys? Why would they kidnap Maria?"

"Not kidnap. Rescue. These guys love Sal. They'd walk through fire for him. And they'd sure as hell kill anyone who threatened Sal or his family. They're going to war right now and they're probably keeping her hidden."

I held my finger over the send button, remembering Bobby. *Your eyes only.*

"If she's with Sal's guys, how will a picture in the newspaper help?"

"It will make it clear that Maria's disappearance is considered a kidnapping and the FBI is on the job. They won't want to deal with the FBI so they'll want to send her home. They need to clear the decks for the upcoming war."

"War? What war?"

"What war? The Great War of Succession. Someone has to replace Sal. People are choosing sides."

The situation clarified. I said, "Maria is leverage."

"If she's in the wrong hands. But that picture tells me that she was in the wrong hands and got rescued."

"By who?"

"That's why you put her picture on the front page. To find out."

I moved my finger over the send button, got distracted by somebody across the brick concourse. A willowy woman dressed in black entered the food court and removed her sunglasses. Looked me in the eye. Jael Navas. *Uh oh.*

Jerry looked into his phone. "Did you send the picture?"

Jael waved me over.

"Do I want this on the front page?" I asked.

"Of course you do," Rittenhauser said. "If Sal's guys have her, they'll drop her someplace or at least get word to Sal. Happy ending."

I stood. Headed for Jael.

Rittenhauser called, "Did you send it?"

I turned, waved my phone at him, pressed send. "It's yours."

The genie was out of the bottle.

SEVENTEEN

Jael Navas was tall enough to be a runway model, fit enough to be a volleyball star, and dangerous enough to be a Mossad assassin—which she had been, though I'm not sure you lose the title "assassin" once you give up the trade. She brings beauty, power, and brains to our partnership and I bring, well, I'm not sure, but it must be something good, because she chose to be my friend.

Jael wore a black leather jacket and tight black winter pants and black gloves. With her black hair and sunglasses, the only color was a light winter pink on her cheeks. We shook. I'd learned not to pull her in for a hug. The one time I tried it was one of the only times I'd seen her be anything but dead calm. It was like hugging a fence post.

"You are in danger," she said.

"And here I thought you just wanted a donut."

The corner of Jael's mouth twitched. "No."

"What makes you say I'm in danger?"

"Hugh told me."

"Hugh?"

"Hugh Graxton."

"I know who Hugh is, I've just never heard you use his first name."

"Come with me." Jael led the way back across Boylston Street and down Charles.

I asked, "What danger?"

"There are those who say you turned against your cousin Sal."

"Who?"

"And there are those who say you would never turn against Sal."

"Again, who?"

Jael stepped over a slush pile. "It does not matter. What does matter is that all sides see you as an enemy."

"Sides of what?"

"A war."

"Again with the war. Doesn't anybody want to find Maria?"

"Tell me what happened."

I pointed up at the Common. "I took her sledding on that hill. Then she got in a car, down where that guy is standing."

Jael looked. A guy in a Bruins jacket stood at the kidnapping spot, apparently considering a run across the street.

Jael said, "The rumor is that you turned on Sal. That you took Maria for leverage."

"That's ridiculous. I don't care who runs the Mafia."

"It does not matter whether you care. It only matters that dangerous men see you as a traitor or threat."

"Who?"

"All of them."

"I've taken care of that."

"How?"

I told Jael about the ransom note, the photo, and how Rittenhauser was going to put it on the front page.

Jael said, "Then I am too late."

"Too late for what?"

"Hugh Graxton told me to find you before you did something rash."

"That wasn't rash. These people will see that I'm looking for Maria."

"It was rash. You do not know what these people will do. Neither do I. We have to get off the streets." Jael quickened her pace.

I sped up to follow. "I think you're overreacting."

"What did you do that they see you as a threat?"

"I visited Sal, had coffee, went to Christmas dinner. Just normal stuff."

"Exactly!" I'd never seen Jael so agitated.

"Normal is good, right?"

"Normal is irrelevant. Whatever you do will be badly interpreted."

"So what should I do?"

"Hide. Stay out of sight. Go away for a few weeks."

We continued down Charles. The guy in the Bruins jacket stood at the curb, gazing at the Public Garden.

I changed topics. "Why would anyone take Maria? What do they want?"

"There are only three reasons for kidnapping a young girl," said Jael.

I waited.

Jael continued. "The first is to do unspeakable things to her."

I imagined the unspeakable for a second. Pushed it from my mind. "What's the next one?"

"To sell her."

"Are you shitting me?"

"It happens," said Jael.

"What's the third reason?"

Jael kept walking and said, "Be ready. We are about to be attacked."

"What?" I said.

The guy in the Bruins jacket turned and stepped in front of us.

"Hey Tucker, you fucking traitor," he said.

Jael stopped walking, stood stock still.

I stood next to her. "Do I know you?" I asked.

"I saw you in Cafe Vittoria with Graxton. You turned on your own cousin."

"I didn't turn on anyone. I'm . . . "

"Fuck you," said the guy.

"We are leaving," Jael said.

Bruins Jacket looked Jael up and down. Reached out to push her. Said, "Shut up, bitch."

There was no transition. No warm up. No delay. There was simply a change of state, snapshots of action. Bruins Jacket standing in front of me, his arm extended, his fingertips on Jael's leather jacket, his mouth showing teeth as he finished the word *bitch*. Then, Jael's gloved knuckles buried in the guy's Adam's apple. The guy reaching for his throat. Jael's boot lifting him from the pavement by the balls. The guy on the ground. Jael's heel on an elbow. The elbow popping.

The *pop* brought me back to real time. Bruins Jacket couldn't scream through his ruined throat. He gurgled instead, cradling his shattered elbow.

Jael said, "Let us go." Started walking.

The guy regained his voice. "I will fucking kill you both."

Jael stopped, turned, and was suddenly holding a black boxy gun to the guy's forehead. She looked at me. "Would it be better for me to just end this now?"

Bruins Jacket looked from Jael's gun, to me, back to the gun, and back to me.

"What's your name?" I asked.

"Pistol Salvucci."

"Do you have Maria?" I said.

Pistol said, "No."

"Do you know where I can find Maria?"

"No."

"Might as well kill him," I said to Jael.

"No!"

"No? Then tell your friends I'd never turn on Sal."

Jael's gun disappeared in a smooth motion. We turned from Pistol to head back down Charles.

And ran straight into Agent Frank Cantrell.

EIGHTEEN

CANTRELL POINTED AT JAEL, then at Pistol. “You can’t do that!”

“I cannot ask questions?” Jael said.

Cantrell said, “You can’t sucker punch our citizens, break their arms, and stick guns in their faces.”

“Sucker punch?” Jael said. “I punched him in the throat.”

“You punched him when he wasn’t ready.”

“How else would you punch a large hostile man?”

“What I mean is—”

“It would be foolish to warn him.”

“Yeah, but—”

“He touched me.”

“Well, maybe, but—”

I asked, “What do you want, Frank?”

“That’s Special Agent Cantrell to you, Tucker.”

“Oooh lah-dee-dah. Look at me, I’m *Special Agent Cantrell.*”

Pistol groaned.

“Aw jeez, Pistol,” Cantrell said. “Stay here. I’ll get help.” He pulled out a cell phone, dialed.

I said, "See you around, Frank."

Cantrell, ear to the phone, pointed to me and said, "You two stay here." Then into the phone, "No, not you. I need an ambulance."

"What do you want with us?" I asked.

Cantrell made the universal sign for "zip it." He gave the ambulance directions, hung up. Crouched next to Pistol. "Hang in there," he said.

"Hey, Pistol," I asked, "how did you know we'd be here?"

Pistol lay on his back, eyes rolling into his head.

Cantrell said, "Shit, he's going into shock. He needs a coat thrown over him." Looked at us. We looked back. It was too cold to think about sharing a coat.

I said, "How did he know we'd be here?"

Cantrell snapped his fingers at us. "C'mon, I don't have a good coat."

"I mean, it's like he was waiting for us."

Jael unzipped her leather jacket. Threw it over Pistol. Now Frank and I looked like jerks. I took off my coat, threw it over Pistol. The cold sliced through my cotton button-down and set my teeth chattering. Jael was fine, she'd dressed in layers.

Cantrell said, "Pistol wasn't waiting for you. He was waiting for me. I was going to talk to him about Maria. She got taken here."

"He doesn't know anything about Maria. I asked him."

"Before or after you broke his elbow?"

I rubbed warmth into my arms. I said, "Seriously, Frank? You're going to keep your coat?"

"I didn't cripple the guy. Serves you two right."

"Pistol was an informant?" Jael asked.

Frank said, "No! Be careful spreading that idea."

I nudged Pistol with my UGG. "That true, Pistol? You ratting out Sal?"

Pistol shook his head. "N-n-n-o."

"Pistol is loyal to Sal," Frank said.

"It doesn't look that way to me," I said. "I think Sal should know."

Pistol said, "No!" and passed out. Lay still, his body settling into the slush as his muscles lost their tone.

"Is he dead?" I asked. "Can I have my coat back?"

Frank said, "He's not dead. You scared the shit out of him."

"So if he's not an informant, why were you meeting him?"

"He was going to talk to Sal for me."

"About what?"

"They're going to arraign Sal today and the DA is going to ask for no bail. I'm pretty sure Sal's going to get killed if we leave him locked up, so I have a plan. I want Sal to turn so they'll agree to let him make bail."

I said, "Sal won't turn."

"He'd better turn."

"Agent Cantrell is right," Jael said. "Sal will die in prison."

An ambulance arrived, lights flashing, no siren. I grabbed my coat off Pistol, pulled it on, shivered in the freezing fabric. Jael waited until the paramedics handed her her coat. She was a woman of steel.

"Why will Sal die?" I asked Jael.

Frank said, "It's like with lions."

"What are you talking about?"

"The new pride leader," said Jael.

"Exactly," said Cantrell.

"What about the lions?" I asked.

Jael said, "When a new lion takes over a pride, he kills the old male."

"What's that got to do with Sal?"

The ambulance guy knelt over Pistol. "What's wrong with him?"

"He has a broken elbow," said Jael.

"And a crushed nut sack," I added.

Frank asked, "You kicked him in the nuts?"

Jael said, "No."

I kept a straight face. "He slipped on the ice," I said.

"He slipped on the ice and crushed his nut sack?" the ambulance guy asked.

"He's really clumsy," I said.

The ambulance guys bundled Pistol into a gurney, lifted him into the back of the ambulance, and took off up Beacon Street toward Massachusetts General Hospital.

I pointed after the ambulance. "They're taking him to Mass General?"

Cantrell said, "Yeah. You just cost the Commonwealth a bundle."

The ambulance disappeared around a corner.

"What's this about the lions?" I asked.

"Guys are fighting it out for Sal's turf. The winner isn't going to want Sal back."

"Maybe Sal will win."

Cantrell said, "Maybe, but he sure as hell won't win from jail."

I shivered, willing my body to heat the coat. "Sal won't turn," I said.

"I heard you," said Cantrell. "Pistol was supposed to talk some sense into him."

Jael said, "Pistol is in no shape to talk to Sal."

"Yeah, no shit."

"Now what?" I asked.

Cantrell said, "It's simple, Tucker. You do it."

"Sal won't listen to me."

"Then fuck you both." Cantrell stalked up Charles Street.

I turned to Jael. "I'm not kidding. He won't listen."

Jael shoved one arm through her coat. I reached for the coat to help, but she turned so that it was out of reach.

"What?" I said. "You're mad at me?"

Jael walked toward her Acura MDX. "You need to go home."

NINETEEN

Silence filled Jael's SUV as she navigated Commonwealth Ave, then Arlington. Her eyes darted from road to mirrors then back to road, ignoring me. I felt like a package, the source of an unpleasant errand.

I said, "You shouldn't feel bad about Pistol."

"I do not feel bad about Pistol," Jael said.

"Oh."

I looked out the window. A doorman dressed like a train conductor hailed taxis in front of the Taj hotel. The Taj had been the Ritz Carlton once, but the Ritz had moved.

"Are you mad at me?" I asked.

"I am not angry with you."

More silence, more careful driving. Traffic was slow.

"You're quiet," I said.

"I am always quiet when I am working."

"Working?"

Jael glanced at me. Annoyance slipped into the corner of her mouth.

"What?" I asked.

"Do you deliberately ignore the danger around you?"

"What danger?"

Jael shook her head.

I said, "You mean Pistol?"

Jael said, "How many factions do you believe are fighting over Sal's business?"

"I don't know," I said.

"Exactly. You don't know," said Jael. "Do you know how many of those factions consider you an enemy?"

"No."

"All of them."

"Even Hugh Graxton?"

"You are right. All but one. But Hugh does not consider you an ally."

"There you go, calling him 'Hugh' again."

Jael turned down St. James. Drove half a block, got stuck in traffic. Something beyond our view had blocked the street. She said, "This is dangerous."

I said, "You think someone will be looking for us here?"

"If someone does look for us here, we will be trapped." Jael reached beneath my seat, pulled out a black gun, and put it in my lap.

"What do I do with this?" I asked.

"Hand it to me if I need it," Jael said. "It is a precaution."

Light dawned on Marblehead. I said, "You're scared."

Jael said, "You should also be scared. There are men who want to kill you. There are probably others who want to take you hostage."

I said, "Why? I'm just Sal's cousin."

"Blood relationships are everything to these people. To them you are either Sal's ally or a turncoat."

"I only want to find Maria."

The traffic sludged its way down St. James toward the Pike. Tailpipe steam filled the road ahead of us.

Jael said, "You cannot find Maria without being murdered."

She turned at the John Hancock Tower, its blue-sky reflection filling the MDX's sunroof. The road was clear. Jael settled back in her bucket seat and picked up speed. She took the gun, slid it back under the passenger seat.

"Maria was my responsibility," I said.

Jael said, "That does not mean you can find her."

"But I thought, with your help—"

"I cannot help."

"What the hell are you taking about?"

Jael glanced at me, then back at the road. "I cannot keep you safe."

"Why not?"

"It is beyond me."

"I didn't think anything was beyond you."

"There are limits."

I digested the notion of Jael's limits. "Well, what should I do?"

Jael stopped at a red light. She had right on red but didn't take it. She looked up and down Columbus, peering around snow piles. She asked, "Do you like the winter?"

"The winter?" *What the hell?* "No. I don't like the winter."

"We don't have this weather in Israel. It is never this cold."

"But you have terrorism."

"Every place has terrorism."

"You think I would be safer in Israel?"

"Yes. Or any warm climate you choose. Perhaps you can find computer work in California."

The MDX rolled down the slushy street. The sun had come out and warmed the pavement enough to create a sheen of water. It would ice over in a couple of hours. I thought about sitting under a palm tree in Union Square, drinking a coffee and musing about some coding problem at a hip startup. No family, new friends, nobody trying to kill me.

"I'd hate myself," I said, "for running away."

"You'd rather die?"

"I was hoping that you could help me avoid that."

"I wish I could."

Silence refilled the SUV as we rolled down Columbus Ave. Red brick buildings hunkered against the cold on either side of us, their color an antidote to the weak light and black slush. Dormant trees dropped bits of snow as the sun finished its work for the day and started to slope toward its four o'clock bedtime.

Enemies or not, I could not run away to California. Maria was in Boston somewhere with no one to protect her. Or, who knew? Maybe she was being protected by one of the factions in the Sal war. Or maybe she'd be a hostage again. Maybe there was, at this moment, another note on my door—or worse, a pinkie or some other evidence.

I didn't know how to find Maria, but I also didn't know how to stop looking. One thing was sure, though: I'd need to do it without Jael. It was one thing to tilt at a windmill; it was another completely to get your friend killed while you were doing it.

"Okay," I said. "Let me out here."

"What?" Jael asked.

"You're right. I shouldn't be dragging you into this. Just let me out here. I can walk home."

"That is a terrible idea."

"Why?"

"There could be somebody in your apartment. I will check it with you."

"And then what? I sit in it for a month? Get groceries delivered by Peapod?"

"That would be safe."

"You and I both know that I'm not going to sit in my apartment while Maria is out there."

"When you are killed, there will be nobody for Maria."

"I'm not sitting this out," I said. "C'mon. Stop the car."

Jael's eyes flicked to the mirror, back to me. "It seems I have no choice."

"What's that mean?"

A bullhorn blared behind us. "Pull it over."

Red and blue lights flashed in the side view mirror. Jael stopped the SUV. I thought about the gun. Had Jael shoved it all the way under the seat?

A fat cop hoisted himself out of his car and moved alongside the SUV, his hand resting on his revolver. Jael rolled down her window.

"Please step out of the car," he said.

TWENTY

BLUE JEANS ARE, PERHAPS, the worst invention in the history of winter. My jeans proved the point as they greedily sucked up every drop of ice water on the curbstone. Jael's pants appeared to be waterproof.

The cop looked into the car windows and went to try the door. I reached for the key fob in Jael's hand and pressed the locking button. The car blooped.

"Miss, would you unlock this door?" asked the cop.

"We do not consent to searches," I said.

"Why not?"

"It's against the law."

"What law?"

"My law. You want to search the car, get a warrant."

The cop retreated from the car and stood in front of us. His belly loomed overhead. I had a better view of his crotch than he'd had in ten years.

"What are you?" he asked. "A lawyer?"

"I'm just a guy with a wet ass who's getting a little cranky."

"Really," said the cop. "You'll be a little more cranky in a second. Get on your feet."

I stood.

The cop pulled out his baton, pointed it at Jael. "Please stay there, Miss."

Jael looked him in the eye and ignored him at the same time.

"Okay, you," the cop said. "Over here. Put your palms on the car, lean forward, spread your legs."

As I leaned on the car, another police car pulled up next to us. Lieutenant Lee climbed out and waved the car away.

The cop said, "We have a troublemaker here, Detective."

"What's the problem"—Lee looked at the guy's nameplate—"Officer Denton?"

"He thinks he's a lawyer. Won't let me search the car."

"Did anyone ask you to search the car?"

"Um, no."

"Why is Ms. Navas sitting on the curbstone?"

"Safety, sir."

"Whose safety?"

"My safety."

"Your safety?" Lee smiled. "You do realize that the only reason you're still standing is that Ms. Navas is a gentle soul."

"You know her?"

"Of course I know her."

Lee stepped around me and extended a hand to Jael, who took it and stood.

"Perhaps we should ask Pistol Salvucci?" Lee said to Jael. "Would Pistol be able to enlighten Officer Denton, Ms. Navas?"

Jael brushed off her backside. Said nothing.

I was still stuck in the position I had assumed. "Mind if I stop leaning on this car?"

Lee said, "Not at all, Tucker."

I stood. Tried to brush the snow off my butt, but it had melted into the cotton.

"Officer Denton," said Lee, "thank you for your help. You can go."

"But there was a BOLO out on this car," said Denton.

"Yes, I know," said Lee. "I issued it. Good-bye now."

Denton muttered his way back to his car, threw it in gear, and left.

Lieutenant Lee said, "Would you two mind giving me a ride to police headquarters? It's down the street."

"Certainly," Jael said.

We negotiated the game of oh-no-you-sit-in-front until Jael was driving, I was sitting next to her, and Lee was sitting behind us.

Lee said, "Jael, I heard that you had a run-in with Pistol Salvucci."

"Where did you hear that?" I asked.

"Agent Cantrell."

Jael said, "He touched me."

"He also called her a bitch," I said.

"Whether the rock touches the pot or the pot touches the rock, it always goes badly for the pot," Lee said.

I twisted in my seat to face Lee. "Pistol is the pot, right?"

"Yes, Tucker, Pistol would be the pot."

"Good."

"Still, I don't see how touching Jael justifies a broken elbow."

"And a crushed nut sack."

"Oh," said Lee. "I hadn't heard about that."

"Are we under arrest?" asked Jael.

"Oh, no," Lee said. "I wouldn't bother to arrest you for beating up Pistol Salvucci. I believe Pistol gets beaten up at least once a year, and deserves it every time."

"Huh," I said.

"Of course," continued Lee, "he is one of Sal's most loyal soldiers."

"I got that impression," I said.

"Really? I have to wonder why one of Sal's most loyal soldiers would try to attack Sal's cousin."

The police station had literally been down the street from us. Jael pulled into the driveway. She said, "Pistol was convinced that Tucker had turned on Sal."

"Why would he think that?" asked Lee.

Now that the car had stopped moving, I turned to face Lee. He held a gun.

"A gun?" I said. "I thought you weren't arresting us."

Lee said, "It slid out from under the seat."

"Please put it back," Jael said.

"Certainly," said Lee as he put the gun away. "I am not worried about you, Ms. Navas."

Jael looked at Lee through the rearview mirror.

"On the other hand, Tucker, you worry me," Lee continued.

"Why should I worry you?"

Lee opened his car door, stepping out into a long shadow from the setting sun. He tapped on my window. I lowered it. Lee flipped open a little spiral-bound notepad. "Let me just run some facts by you, Tucker."

"Okay."

"You had Maria to the park at the same time as her mother was being murdered, yes?"

"But I didn't—"

Lee held up his hand. "Please, just humor me with yes/no answers."

"Yes."

Lee made a check mark in his book. "You called Agent Miller because you possessed a ransom note."

"Someone drop—"

Lee held up his hand again.

"Yes."

Another check mark. "The ransom note showed you where to find Maria."

"Yes."

Check mark. "You were the first person to enter the apartment, having failed to call Agent Miller?"

"My phone—"

The hand again.

"Yes."

Check. "And Joey Pupo was murdered just moments before Miller arrived."

"Yes."

Check. "And you did consulting work for a company called PassHack."

"Yes. Wait. What?"

Big check mark. Lee said, "I thought as much."

"What does PassHack have to do with this?"

Lee closed his book. "Could it be that Pistol Salvucci is smarter than he looks?"

"I don't thi—"

The hand. "Just a rhetorical question, Tucker." Lee pulled his overcoat closed. "Do me a favor."

"What?"

"Don't leave town. I'd hate to have to chase you around when I'm ready with a warrant." He headed into police headquarters, leaving Jael and me sitting in the car.

I raised the window. "Well so much for me visiting a warmer climate."

Jael watched Lee enter the building and said nothing.

I said, "Didn't you tell me that Sal would be a dead man if we left him in jail?"

"Yes," she said.

"How long do you think I would last?"

"Not as long as Sal."

"So you're telling me that I'm a dead man if I'm in jail *and* if I'm out of jail."

Jael said nothing.

"Those are pretty much my only two options."

"We have no allies," said Jael.

She had let the *we* slip out. I let it linger in the air.

"We have one," I said. "But he's locked up."

"Essentially no allies. Turn on your phone's GPS."

I touched the app, turned on my GPS signal for Jael, and thought of Bobby. "So that would make two of you tracking me."

"Who is the other one?"

"The FBI."

"Good."

"Maybe. If they convinced a judge that I was a suspect."

"Better to be a suspect than to be dead."

I fiddled with my phone. "We could make Sal a more useful ally. Cantrell offered us a deal."

"Do you think Sal will take the deal?"

I started dialing Sal's lawyer, Caroline Quinn. "There's only one way to find out."

TWENTY-ONE

Caroline Quinn's black business suit, with its deep, cleavagy V, added life to the FBI conference room. Sal, sitting at the round conference table in prison scrubs, did not. Sal's beard had grown since yesterday, deepening the gray and black across his face. His eyes had sunk another notch into their sockets. His dry lips were flaked despite his tongue's unconscious attempts to keep them moist. A bruise darkened his eye.

"What happened to your eye?" I asked.

"Nothing," said Sal.

"A fight?"

"Nothing happened. What do you want?"

"I want to get you out of here," I said. "They're going to kill you."

"So they kill me. So what?" Sal said.

"So what?" I said. "You've got a daughter, that's what."

"She'd be better off without me."

Caroline said, "Let's cut the fucking drama."

Sal turned. "What did you say?"

"You heard me."

"You work for me."

"Not for long."

"What's that supposed to mean?"

"It means I'm not going to sit here and listen to this 'poor me' crap. I play to win. If you want to sit here and play baby boo-boo, then you need to get someone else to represent you."

"Don't you think that's a little harsh?" I asked.

"Oh, great," Caroline said. "Another quarter heard from."

"I mean, Sal just lost Sophia. On top of that, Maria's missing."

"I know that, Tucker. And I know you're trying to help, but self-pity will get him nowhere. We're going to be in the fight of our lives here, and I need Sal to have some spunk in him. Which brings me—" Caroline leaned forward as she scolded me, her jacket falling open a notch.

Despite the circumstances, my focus drifted to the bare skin of Caroline's chest, the line of her neck.

Caroline snapped her fingers. "Well?" she asked, still leaning forward.

"Well what?"

"Why are we here?"

"Um," I said.

Caroline sat back. "You know, you're looking pretty bad yourself. You okay?"

I ran through several possible responses. "I'm fine," I said. "I'm just here to get Sal out of jail."

"You have any ideas on how to do that?"

"Frank Cantrell told me—"

"Why the fuck are you talking to Cantrell?" Sal asked.

"He was getting an ambulance for Pistol."

"An ambulance? Why did Pistol need an ambulance?"

"Because Jael broke his arm."

"What?"

"He was going to beat me up, and he went to push—"

"Why was Pistol going to beat you up?"

"Because he says I turned on you."

"Why would he say that?"

"He saw me with Hugh Graxton in Cafe Vittoria?"

"Graxton's in my spot? What the fuck is going on out there?"

"That's the point, Sal. It's all going to hell. They're fighting over your turf. Half of them think that I'm with you, so they want to kill me. The other half think that I'm against you, so they want to kill me too. Lieutenant Lee just wants to arrest me."

"Arrest you?" Caroline asked. "What for?"

Sal said, "You mind not finding new work while I'm paying you?"

"I'm not finding new work," Caroline said. "I just want to know why Lee would arrest Tucker."

"He thinks I've got something to do with Sophia's murder."

"Why?"

"I don't know. It's got something to do with the work I did for PassHack."

"PassHack?" Sal said.

Something in the room changed, became poisonous.

"Um—yeah," I said. "PassHack. It was a startup."

Sal said, "I know it was a fucking startup. You didn't think to mention to me that you worked there?"

"Why would I tell you? Computer stuff bores you."

"Sal, what's this about PassHack?" Caroline asked.

Sal ignored her. "So you're buddies with David Anderson?"

"I don't know any David Anderson," I said. "I just know that Cantrell mentioned him."

Sal pounded the table. "Again with fucking Cantrell! Why are you hanging around with Cantrell talking about David Anderson? What did Frank tell you?"

"He told me that you and Anderson had a problem getting along."

"What kind of problem?"

I glanced at Caroline. She sat with her arms crossed, staring at the table, clearly bullshit at being ignored.

"A ten-thousand-dollar problem," I said.

Sal stood over me and pointed. "You worked for a guy who stole from me and killed Sophia?"

I would not be loomed over. I stood. "I didn't work for anybody."

"You took his fucking money."

"I was a consultant. How do I know where that money came from?"

"You think David Anderson killed Sophia?" Caroline asked Sal.

"He wouldn't do it himself," Sal said. "He'd have help." Sal looked me straight in the eye. "He'd have *someone* get Maria out of the house, then—"

I don't know how the brain works: how sounds enter the ear, get converted to thoughts, and processed into insights. I don't know how those insights mix with the vagaries of personality and puddles of neurosis to create a conclusion, nor do I know how that conclusion converts itself into action or how the nerve impulses travel down the spinal column, out to the arm, and into the hand. I don't know why the hand chooses to form itself into a club, nor how the eyes coordinate with it to aim the strike.

I just know that I saw my fist, balled up and pale, smashing itself into Sal's bruised eye, scraping its knuckles across his brow while his eyes squinted shut and his head snapped to the side. Sal, my big older cousin, the man whose size and violence always scared me, rocked back, tripped on his chair, and sat.

Next, I was standing over Sal and chewing my sore knuckles as something close to a sob ground its way up my chest.

I'd lied to Caroline. I was not fine.

Sal rubbed his cheek. "Get out, you Judas," he said.

"Fuck you," I managed as I turned for the door. I needed to get out before Sal could see the tears. I was out the door and down the hall when I heard my name.

"Tucker!" Caroline called.

I stopped in the empty hallway. Caroline followed, limping slightly on her baroque metallic leg.

I pointed past her down the hall. "I'm done with that asshole."

Caroline said, "He doesn't mean it."

I focused on suppressing the sob, but my eyes started leaking. *Aw, shit.*

"Maria is out there," I said. The sob broke through, and then another. "Aw, Jesus, I'm sorry."

Caroline reached out, wrapped her arms around me, pulled me close. "Shhh."

I breathed in Caroline's perfume, felt her body against mine, reached back and pulled her toward me.

Caroline said, "You're a good man."

"How do you know?" I asked.

"Sal told me."

The hug worked. Distracted by Caroline's perfume, wool suit, and body beneath the suit, my emotions stabilized. I loosened my hug. She gave me an extra squeeze and let me go. Took a step back.

"Wow," I said. "You're not so tough after all."

"Sal needs me to be tough," Caroline said.

"And me?"

"You just needed a hug."

"I need more than a hug. I need a miracle and a bazooka."

Caroline smiled and rested her hand on my chest. "You'll find her."

I covered her hand with mine. "Checking my heart rate?"

"No," said Caroline. "I just wanted to know how your chest felt."

"And?"

Caroline never answered because my new Droid interrupted us.

"You'd better take that," Caroline said. She turned and went back down the hallway to the conference room.

I made a mental note not to mess with Caroline and looked at my phone. The number wasn't one I recognized. "Hello?"

"Tucker, it's me—Angie. I'm shopping in Back Bay. You want to get dinner?"

Angie. Huh.

"Sure," I said. "Meet me in front of the Capital Grille in an hour."

Angie made a happy squealing noise and hung up.

I was suddenly awash in women.

TWENTY-TWO

IT WAS NEARLY SIX o'clock. Midwinter night squatted over City Hall Plaza. Rush hour was in full swing as office workers scuttled from warm offices to a warm train to a warm house, minimizing their time in the cold. I pulled my coat tight around me, dodged across Cambridge Street, and mashed myself into the crowd jamming Government Center Station.

I ran across the platform at the bottom of the escalators and wormed my way into a waiting Green Line train, achieving a toe-hold in the stairwell leading to the door. I squeezed in as the door folded shut. Unable to achieve the top of the steps, I got my head crushed against some guy's ass. They say people in Boston are rude because they ignore each other, but when your head is crammed into some guy's ass, the only polite response is for you and he to ignore each other. I took a selfie and tweeted:

`Stuck on the train wearing an asshat #commuting`

I sighed, happy to stop moving for the first time all day.

When the moving stops, the thinking starts.

Sal had said, *Get out, you Judas.*

I imagined a big white board with two lists: "People who want to kill me for betraying Sal" and "People who want to kill me for supporting Sal." I mentally wrote Sal's name under "betraying." The third column, "People who want to keep me alive," had one name, Jael Navas, partially erased. I let my mind drift away from Sal and into technical musing.

As the trolley squealed through the tunnel at Boylston Street, I let myself focus on classifying Angie. Which list would she go on? That depended upon the results of our date. I could add a fourth list: "People who want to sleep with me." That would also put Angie in the "People who want to keep me alive" list. It would be inefficient to write Angie's name down twice. I could make the "sleep with me" list a sublist of the "keep me alive" list.

Copley Station slid into view. As the last guy into the train, I was the first one pushed out when the crowd made a break for it. I should have waited for the crowd to empty and climbed back on board, but I lost patience with the whole thing and ran upstairs to Boylston Street. Leaving Angie to fend for herself on a street corner would be no way to make a good first impression.

I hustled down the street, dodging left and right around pedestrians who strolled as if they had all the time in the world. Perhaps they did. I didn't.

I saw Angie before she saw me. She wore the same fur coat and was doing a fantastic impression of an angry woman who had been stood up: walking in little circles, arms crossed, looking up and down Boylston Street, checking her watch, and shaking her head.

"Angie!" I called.

She turned and transformed from a menacing harpy into a welcoming angel. She gave me a big smile, reached out, hugged me close, and kissed me on the cheek. Her perfume floated around us, turning knobs in my stomach.

"I thought you were going to turn out to be a jerk," she said.

"There's still time," I said.

"Let's go in." Angie took my arm and stepped toward the Capital Grille.

I hesitated.

Angie stopped tugging. "We're not eating at the Capital Grille?"

Actually, I had been thinking Bukowski Tavern—burgers and beer from a bartender. The Capital Grille was steaks and wine from a sommelier. I had told Angie to meet me here because it was an obvious landmark. My brain jammed as I adjusted to the change in plans.

Angie pulled herself close. "I wore my new dress. You'll want to see it."

"Um—"

"We can go somewhere else," she said, "if it's too expensive."

Too expensive? Of course it was too expensive. No food was worth that much money. But that didn't mean that I couldn't afford it. I had plenty of money, an eight-digit souvenir of a truly horrific separation with a previous employer. I decided to defend my financial honor and rationalize it by noting that I had been late for our date. It was time to stop disappointing the lady.

"Let's go," I said. "I haven't eaten here in years."

"Why not?"

"There's been a shortage of beautiful women in my life."

Angie rewarded me with another brilliant smile. We entered the restaurant, and she rewarded me further by taking off her fur coat. Red, short, and satiny, her dress clung to her curves, giving me views of breast and thigh that encouraged my imagination to paint a picture of the rest. My eyes widened, my heart skipped. Other parts of my body did awful, wonderful things. Her dress alone was worth every penny.

I took off my coat and handed it to the coat checker. I wore blue jeans and a cotton button-down. At least it had a collar.

Angie said, "Oh honey, you really weren't planning to come here, were you?"

I looked down at my shirt and jeans. "I'll be fine. They'll just think I'm a dot-com whiz kid."

Angie looked at my shoes. "Do dot-com whiz kids wear UGGs?"

"Tom Brady wears UGGs."

"Don't feel bad. They're cute."

The pretty girl behind the maître d' station ignored my UGGs and said, "Right this way." I put my hand on the small of Angie's back to guide her, but she slid toward me so that my hand wound up around her waist, resting on her hip.

"This day is looking up," I said.

Angie snuggled closer.

TWENTY-THREE

The Capital Grille exists to allow men and women to show off their finest assets. The women show off their bodies, the men show off their money. It's a win-win. The maître d' sat us in a dark corner. We ordered our drinks, white wine for the lady, Lagavulin scotch for me. The scotch was $20, but what the hell. If I was going to show off my wealth, I was going to drink good scotch.

"Have you heard anything about Maria?" Angie asked.

"No." I stared into Angie's brown eyes to avoid staring at her generous décolletage.

Angie said, "That poor kid."

"On top of it, some guy named Pistol Salvucci tried to give me a beating."

"Pistol? What for?"

"He thought I was siding with Hugh over Sal."

"But you are siding with Hugh, right? I saw you guys."

"I'm not siding with anyone. I'm just looking for Maria."

Our drinks arrived. We clinked glasses. "Cheers," I said.

"*Salud*," Angie said.

The Lagavulin's smoky warmth settled in my stomach and flowed into my brain.

"Pistol's an asshole," said Angie, "but he's pretty tough. You don't look beat up."

"I have a friend who—but screw Pistol. How long have you known Sal?"

"Aw, hell. We grew up together, went to high school together. But now look, you've got me talking about my age. Where were you in 1976?"

"Well—ahh—"

"Were you even born?"

"No. I was born in '78."

"You are the cutest thing. You don't even remember Bucky Dent."

"I read about him."

Angie pointed her wineglass at me. "I'm robbing the cradle."

"You want to see my cradle?"

Angie slapped my hand. "Fresh."

Our salads arrived. Angie had a Caesar with anchovies, I had an iceberg wedge served with bleu cheese dressing and bacon. Ah, the wedge... you have to love a salad that you eat with a steak knife.

Angie asked, "How will you find Maria?"

"I don't know. I'm digging into Sal's relationship with a guy named David Anderson."

Angie said nothing.

"Have you heard of David Anderson?"

"Nope."

"I'm probably not even looking at the right one. There are tons of David Andersons."

"Which one are you looking at?"

"The private equity guy."

"What's a private equity guy?"

"He's a guy who makes money buying and selling companies."

"What would a guy like that have to do with Maria?"

"I don't know. But Sal hates his guts."

Angie sipped her wine. "What would you do if you found Maria?"

I drained my Scotch. "I have no idea."

"Would you let her live with you?"

"She wouldn't want to live with me. Maybe her Aunt Bianca would take her."

"Sal's Jewish sister? She lives on Long Island."

"Adriana, then?"

"The gay one?"

"That's the one."

Angie stood. "I need to find the ladies' room."

"It's that way," I said, pointing.

Angie turned and left.

I should have stood when she stood. Or should I? Do people still do that? Was I resisting the patriarchy? Either way, it was too late. I finished my salad, scooping the last bits of applewood bacon onto my fork. Around me, rich men in business suits entertained beautiful women. My cotton button-down made me feel like a kid sitting at the adult table. Nobody would mistake me for Mark Zuckerberg; I'm too old. The restaurant clinked around me, muted conversations forming a background hum.

My Droid chirped. I despise the default sounds on a phone, but I hadn't gotten around to replacing them.

It was a text message from Caroline. `Lunch tomorrow?`

`Is this about Sal?` I texted.

`No.`

`What then?`

`It's about you and me. The 617 Restaurant. 1 PM. My treat.`

What was I going to say? `OK`

"Boys and their toys," Angie said.

I looked up from the screen and Angie was sitting across from me. I had missed my chance to stand again.

"Who were you texting?"

"Sal's lawyer."

"You know what?" said Angie. "Enough with Sal. Let's just enjoy ourselves."

The waiter arrived with plates of food, and we did just that. I ate a steak that was worth every one of the $45 I would pay for it. Angie tucked into a broiled lobster that had been gently dissected so that she didn't have to use nutcrackers to break the claws. We talked about my views on the Celtics, what it was like to grow up in Wellesley, my house, my job, my thoughts about what it took to make a happy life. It was all me, me, me. Angie was an outstanding conversationalist.

After dinner, we had more drinks: a Courvoisier VSOP for the lady and a glass of port for the gentleman. I paid the check, promising myself that I would expunge the price from my memory. We rose, went back to the coat check, and prepared ourselves for the cold December night. Angie's fur coat enveloped her dress. I donned my ski jacket. We exited and stood on the corner of Boylston.

On the sidewalk, I pulled Angie close and gave her a test kiss. She responded, but with some resistance.

"Would you like to come back to my house for a drink?" I asked.

Angie gave me a peck on the cheek. "On our first date? What kind of girl would that make me?"

"A lucky one?"

"You're a sweetie pie. I'm going home."

I hailed a cab. It pulled up and I put Angie inside, giving the cabbie twenty dollars. "Take the lady home, please."

Angie kissed me softly, her tongue feathering my lips. "I'd like to see you again," she said.

"Same here."

The cab pulled away. Angie's feathery kiss had me all discombobulated. I considered getting a beer at Bukowski Tavern, but decided that I'd rather go home and take a cold shower. I walked back to the South End, unlocked the door to my building, climbed the steps. Frank Cantrell sat in front of my door.

"We need to talk," he said.

TWENTY-FOUR

CANTRELL SAT AT MY kitchen counter, tapping on Click and Clack's aquarium glass.

"Please do not tap the glass," I said.

Cantrell said, "Huh?"

"It disturbs the animals."

"I thought they were dead."

"They're resting."

Cantrell spread his hands on the counter. Looked at me.

I said, "Yes?"

"You gonna offer me something to drink?"

"No. What do you want?"

"I heard you screwed the pooch."

"What's that supposed to mean?"

"That means you were supposed to use an FBI conference room to get Sal to turn, and instead you punched him in the face."

"He accused me of helping David Anderson kill Sophia."

"Did you help David Anderson kill Sophia?"

"I can punch you in the face too."

Cantrell stood, hands still on the counter. "Let's not go there."

"You done? You want to leave now?"

Cantrell just stood, staring at me, heavy eyelids over five o'clock shadow. "I didn't sit outside your door for a half hour just to leave."

"Then get to the point."

"Are you sure you don't want to offer me a drink? Get one for yourself too?"

I hesitated, looked Cantrell up and down. "You aren't here because of Sal?"

Cantrell shook his head. "No."

"Why did you sit outside my door for a half hour?"

"I wanted to tell you something face-to-face, figured you'd come home eventually."

"What do you need to tell me?"

"You got scotch? You're gonna need it."

I opened the cabinet over the fridge. I had scotch, but I wasn't in the mood for it. I like ice in my scotch, and it was too cold for ice. Instead I pulled down some Bully Boy white whiskey. Distilled in Boston, it was all the rage: whiskey that had never sat in a barrel.

"What's that, vodka?" Cantrell asked.

I slid a rocks glass to Cantrell. "Moonshine." I poured Cantrell an ounce and made mine a double.

Cantrell sniffed at the white liquor, then took a sip. Winced. "Jesus, it tastes like tequila mixed with whiskey."

"I know, right?" I said. "The good stuff."

Cantrell pushed the glass to one side, pulled out his phone, and started screwing with it. "I got a call today."

I revolved my index finger: *C'mon, get on with it.*

"It was from a *Globe* reporter, Jerry Rittenhauser."

I drank half my whiskey. Took Cantrell's glass, poured it into mine.

Cantrell brought up a picture. "He sent me this."

It was the picture of Maria's ransom note. I said nothing.

"Rittenhauser wanted me to confirm that this was a real ransom note. I asked him how he got it. Naturally, he wouldn't tell me."

"Maybe Bobby sent it to him?" I said.

Cantrell said, "Sure. Try again. Bobby and I didn't want this note out there. We didn't want people to know that Maria was in play."

"In play?"

Cantrell put the phone away. "Oh, for Christ's sake, Tucker. Don't be a fucking idiot. If people know that Maria is out there, that somebody grabbed her, then they're going realize that she could be used as leverage."

My stomach clenched. The whiskey wasn't helping. "Leverage," I said.

Cantrell said, "When you were a kid, did you ever play Smear the Queer?"

"What?"

"You know, that game where you kill the guy with the ball."

"We didn't call it that in Wellesley."

"Well, Mr. Fancy Ass, once this picture gets out, Maria's the ball."

I drained my whiskey, wishing for the alcohol to find the pain and wash it away. It only made me dizzy. "Did you do it?" I asked.

"Did I do what?"

"Did you confirm that photo to Rittenhauser?"

Cantrell said, "I told him that the FBI refuses to comment on ongoing investigations."

"So you didn't confirm it."

"No. I didn't want Maria's blood on my hands." Cantrell stood from the breakfast nook, shrugged on his winter coat. "I thought I'd leave that to you. I'll let myself out." He opened the front door to leave.

I called to him, "Cantrell."

He paused. "Yeah?"

"Couldn't you have told me this over the phone?"

"Sure. But then I wouldn't know what I know now from looking at you."

"What do you know now?"

"That you gave Rittenhauser the picture, and that you never thought any of this through."

I said nothing.

"Buck up, Tucker," Cantrell said. "At least you're not a suspect. You're too stupid to be a suspect." He closed the door behind him and clomped down the stairs.

I locked it behind him.

He was right. I thought making that picture public was going to help me find Maria, but the only people who would see any significance in it were more likely to hurt her than to help her. I grabbed my phone and called Rittenhauser.

"Hey!" said Rittenhauser. Bar noise reverberated behind him. "How you doing, Mr. Front Page?"

I winced. "Yeah about that, Jerry. I need to apologize."

Pause. "What do you mean you need to apologize?"

"You can't publish that picture."

"Aw, shit. It's a fake? How could it be a fake?"

"No, it's not a fake. I just can't let you print it. It could put Maria in danger. So I have to take it back."

"Are you shitting me?"

"No. Sorry, but I can't let you print it."

"Wait a second. I need to get someplace quiet."

A pause. The bar noises disappeared. A siren whirred by in the background. Rittenhauser had moved to the street. "Say that again."

"You can't print it?"

"My City editor is going to love this."

"Yeah, I know—"

"He's standing out here in the cold with me. Why don't you tell him yourself?"

"Can't you tell him?"

"Tell him what? That he needs to stop the presses because you got cold feet?"

"That he needs to stop them because—"

"There's nothing happening here that you didn't ask for."

"I know. I didn't think it through."

"Screw this. Talk to him yourself." Muffled murmuring told me that Jerry was explaining the situation.

A new voice introduced itself. "Max Black, City editor."

"So Jerry explained the situation to you?" I said.

"Yes, Mr. Tucker."

"And?"

"Fuck you."

The phone went dead.

TWENTY-FIVE

If there is a hell, it will not be fire or ice. It will be a disheveled bed in a dark room lit by a digital clock that says 3:30 a.m.

I don't know what it is about 3:30 a.m. Perhaps it's got something to do with circadian rhythms getting mangled by alcohol, or some deeply hidden instinct that remembers when the saber-toothed tigers started hunting. Perhaps it's coincidence, or maybe black magic. All I know is that whenever I'm about to head into a bout of alcohol-induced insomnia, I wake up, turn to my digital clock, and see the numbers 3-3-0.

I lay on my back, stared at the dark ceiling, and focused on my breath, trying to keep a simmering pot of thoughts from boiling over. Once the lid cracked, once the first thought slipped out, sleep would be gone.

What will Bobby say?

Aww crap, here come the regrets.

I played the scene with Rittenhauser over in my mind, looking for different things I could have said that would have delivered a different result. It wasn't hard. It started with not calling Bobby or asking him to text me the picture of the ransom note. It progressed to not asking Rittenhauser for his email address, or typing in the email address correctly, or pressing send.

Perhaps it started earlier. Perhaps it really started with not calling Rittenhauser, not getting upset with his article, not reading the newspaper. Well—at the limit, not buying Maria a sled.

But where would that have gotten me? So I didn't buy a sled, that meant that Maria would have been home with Sophia when the murderer came. Would they have found two bodies, Sophia and Maria strangled side-by-side? Would Maria have called 911? Would Sal have been home?

Was Sal at home?

I pushed the thought away. Sal did not kill Sophia. If he had, he would not have blamed me for my part in Sophia's murder. Wouldn't have guessed that I was selling him out for some guy, this David Anderson.

I climbed out of bed, used the bathroom, took some Advil for the hangover, drank some water, stared at a sleeping Click and Clack. Listened to nothing. The city was quiet, not even any sirens. Activity was out there, though. Beyond my street, someone was bundling freshly printed newspapers. Throwing them into trucks, carrying the dead-tree edition of the *Boston Globe* to street corners. Meanwhile the electronic edition was coalescing into the bits that would fly to laptops, tablets, and smartphones. The picture was probably already on the web, probably already had comments.

I considered firing up my computer, heading over to the website, seeing my handiwork. Decided against it. Once I touched a mouse, sleep would never return. I'd be done. I went back to my bedroom. Lay down.

The clock glowed 4:30 a.m.

Maybe I was overreacting to the thing with Bobby. Hell, I'd probably be dead tomorrow, shot by some Mafia vigilante. That would show Bobby. *I'm fighting for my life out here doing his job and he's got the nerve to be angry because I shared a friggin' ransom note? Screw him.*

And screw David Anderson, whoever the hell he is. And screw Jarrod Cooper for calling me up and asking me to work on his startup. Why do I even bother? I don't need the money. I just needed to do some work. I didn't even do much for Jarrod. A little architecture work, a little debugging.

Debugging was my favorite part, finding out what was wrong and working your way back to the cause. At least that's how the good debuggers work. The bad ones just try random shit. Well, to be fair, the good ones do too when they're stumped. They come up with improbable theories and take desperate action just to see what happens.

Like I did with Rittenhauser. I tossed him the picture because I didn't know what else to do. I didn't even know about the gang war then. Hadn't met Pistol. Would I have given Rittenhauser the picture after Pistol tried to give me a beating?

I rolled my head toward the clock: 5:00 a.m. Must have dozed.

In the summer I'd be completely screwed by now. The sun would be rising and I'd give up on sleep. But it was winter; there'd be no sun for hours. It was time to break out my secret weapon.

I padded into the living room, fired up my Internet TV, and found a documentary about astronomy. I lay on the couch, closed my eyes, and let a sonorous voice tell me things I already knew.

The narrator droned: "Out beyond the edge of the solar system. Beyond mighty Jupiter, beyond Saturn, with its gossamer rings, beyond Uranus, rolling along its orbit, beyond mysterious Neptune, beyond even Pluto, the ex-planet, lies the Kuiper Belt—"

I woke to my television's logo bouncing around the screen. Gray light filtered through my windows. Sunlight. I had managed to sleep, and in sleeping had come to a decision. I climbed to my feet, making an old-man noise as my back complained about the lumpy couch.

Stumbled to my cell phone. Bobby must not have seen the paper yet. He'd call soon enough.

I dialed the phone. Called a guy who I knew would be on a elliptical trainer at this time of day. The guy answered.

"Jarrod," I said. "We need to talk."

TWENTY-SIX

I SAT ACROSS FROM Jarrod Cooper in Zaftigs Delicatessen on Harvard Street, staring in horrified fascination at a large portrait of the deli's logo: an obese woman in a red nightgown posing seductively, one hand behind her beehive hairdo, the other caressing a meaty thigh.

Jarrod looked over his shoulder at the portrait. "Looks like my mother," he said.

"Is your mother Jewish?" I asked.

"No. She's fat."

High-tech people love to tell stories about turning down opportunities at startups that hit it big: "I was employee 13 at Microsoft, but I quit." "I had an offer at Facebook, but Zuckerberg pissed me off." "I told Jeff Bezos that Amazon would never make it." These stories have the double allure that the teller gets to describe a brush with greatness, while the listener enjoys the schadenfreude of knowing people who have missed out on high-tech riches.

My story with Jarrod was more typical. A dewy-eyed entrepreneur came to me with nothing but a dream and a term sheet. I told him that it was a bad idea, but he persisted, chugging along like The Little Engine That Could—except that he couldn't.

The check arrived. Jarrod reached for it, but I grabbed it first.

"Didn't you lose all your money in PassHack?" I asked.

"Yeah," said Jarrod. "Thanks for the reminder."

I pulled out my credit card, threw it on the check. "Let me get this."

"Well, not *all* of my money," Jarrod said. "I can still afford an omelet."

"Tell you what: let's pretend I'm spending the money you paid me."

Jarrod popped an egg-encrusted mushroom into his mouth. "Yeah, you were a cash drain."

"Hey. I helped you debug your code. You needed me."

"Turned out that I needed cash more."

I chewed some bagel, letting the whitefish's vinegary goodness waft through my nose.

"Who is David Anderson?" I asked.

Jarrod said, "If you know to ask, then you know who he is."

I considered another angle to this conversation, but I had no idea what I wanted to ask. The guy at the table next to ours took off and left the *Boston Globe* behind. I grabbed the paper. Maria's ransom note took up the center of the paper above the fold.

Rittenhauser had done good work on the story. He wrote about Maria, but he also covered the power struggle in Sal's territory. He said the odds-on succession favorite was Hugh Graxton. Rittenhauser listed off Marco Esposito, Joey Pupo, and Pistol Salvucci as victims of an internecine Mafia war. He wrote of knife fights, jilted courtesans, stolen iPhones, prostitution, and drug dealing. Apparently Sal had done it all, and now Hugh wanted to do it in his place.

I showed the paper to Jarrod. "You know about this?"

"What? Mobsters are killing each other or something?"

I pointed at the picture. "That's my cousin's daughter."

Jarrod read the caption. "Your cousin is Sal Rizzo?"

"Yeah. How do you know Sal?"

"Hah! The paper used your first name, Aloysius."

"You said that you know Sal?"

Jarrod read from the article. "'*I'm just trying to find Maria,' said Aloysius Tucker, who has since been questioned by the police.*"

"Yeah. I know what it says."

"Questioned by the police? That's not good."

"It happens when you find a body. What is this about you and Sal?"

"Man, you are a tire biter. Once you grab that tire you just ride the rim." Jarrod dug into his omelet, brought egg to his lips.

I slapped my hand on the table. Egg splashed as Jarrod jumped, knocking his fork to the floor.

Jarrod said, "Jesus, Tucker. Calm down."

A waitress brought Jarrod another fork and gave me the bill with my credit card. "Is there a problem?" she asked.

"No," I said, scribbling a 50 percent tip onto the sheet. "Sorry. Won't happen again."

"What the hell is wrong with you?" Jarrod asked.

"What's wrong is that when Sal heard that I had worked for you at PassHack, he accused me of killing his wife for David Anderson."

"Worked for me? You consulted for two weeks."

"Sal isn't good at subtlety. He just hears that I worked there."

"Sorry."

"That's not the point. The point is that something happened at PassHack. Something that has him enraged."

Jarrod spread his hands. "What can I tell you? We went belly up. Ran out of cash."

"His cash?"

"Yeah. Some of it must have been his. Sal took David and me out to dinner in the North End when we started up. We walked right past the line at Giacomo's. It was pretty cool."

"So then what happened?"

"You know what happened. We wrote software, got some customers, and started hacking passwords."

"And you went out of business because you couldn't hack them?"

"Shit, no. We went out of business because it was so easy. You can download all the hacking software you want right off the web. Between that and the stuff we wrote, we were cracking passwords like nobody's business."

"Scared the shit out of people, didn't you?"

"Hell, yeah. That's when they all started canceling their contracts. One guy told me that he felt like he had invited the devil into his bank vault."

"I told you that would happen."

"I told you that would happen," Jarrod mimicked. He picked at his omelet.

I took another bite of my bagel. "What about the end?" I asked.

"What do you mean?" asked Jarrod.

"How did the company shut down? Did you go to work and find the doors locked?"

"What are you, a ghoul?"

"It's a simple question. Did you have to sell off the computers?"

"We shut the thing down and called it a day. What does it matter about the computers?"

"I'm just trying to figure out if Sal got anything back."

Jarrod poked at his omelet. "I don't want to talk about this anymore."

I drank some coffee. "Fine, let's change the subject."

"Good."

"What are you doing now?"

"Now? Now I'm 'consulting.'" Jarrod punctuated the word with air quotes.

"You mean unempl—"

Jarrod's eyes shot over my shoulder, looked up, widened.

I started to follow his gaze when a hand grabbed me by the shirt, pulled me up.

I was eye to eye with Bobby Miller in his FBI flak jacket.

Bobby said, "Let's go."

I grabbed my coat as he dragged me out of the restaurant.

TWENTY-SEVEN

Bobby dragged me down the sidewalk and into a playground next to Zaftigs. Strangely, we were the only ones standing among spring-loaded rocking horses and a fire truck–shaped jungle gym all covered in a layer of snow.

I shrugged my arm free. "Get off me!" I pulled on my coat as Bobby waved the *Globe* at me.

"What the fuck is this?"

"It's the *Globe*."

Bobby wound up for a backhand with the newspaper. He threw it at my chest instead, pointed at the paper once it hit the ground. Maria looked up at us from the front-page picture. "I trusted you," he said.

I looked down at Maria crying under the headline: MAFIA MARIA MISSING.

Bobby continued, "Then you gave the picture to that hack Rittenhauser."

Mafia Maria? Seriously?

I said, "You don't know I gave it to him."

Bobby grabbed me by the front of my coat, cocked his fist. "Don't you fucking lie to me. Not any more!"

I winced and waited for the punch, resigned to taking my beating. The punch never came. I opened one eye. "What was I supposed to do?"

Bobby released my jacket. "*Supposed* to do? You were supposed to go home. You were supposed to let the FBI handle it. You were supposed to keep the picture secret. It's going to be a feeding frenzy. Everyone's going to be after her."

"I know," I said. "Frank told me."

"Frank?" said Bobby. "Cantrell?"

"Yeah, yeah. Cantrell told me what would happen. I called Rittenhauser and—"

"When were you talking to Frank?"

"Last night."

"And he knew about the picture?"

"Yeah. He told me that you two decided to keep it secret."

"He's not even on the case."

I said nothing. What did I know about FBI office politics?

Bobby looked down at the paper on the ground. "This hurt me, Tucker."

"Politically?"

"No, personally. I trusted you with this picture. I told you to keep it to yourself."

"I didn't know what else to do," I said. "Maria is out there, nobody knows where, and I'm the only one looking for her."

"You're not the only looking for her."

"The FBI is ignoring Maria."

"The FBI is not ignoring Maria. It's my case. I'm looking for Maria."

"You're looking for her? Since when?"

"Since she was taken, you idiot. I'm an FBI agent. We handle kidnappings."

"Okay, you're looking for her. How?"

"I'm chasing down my leads."

A schism rippled through my brain. Something was off, some set of facts that didn't add up. Little errors hide big errors. Inconsistent behaviors mean something's not working the way you think it should. I sifted and churned the information, panning for the piece that stuck out.

Bobby continued, "I'm looking for Maria and I wanted to keep this picture secret."

Looked at Bobby standing in the park. I'd never seen him in Brookline before. I'd found gold in my clue pan.

Bobby pointed at the ransom note. "Those are some weird deman—"

"How did you find me?" I asked.

"What?"

"How did you find me? How did you know that I was in Zaftigs?"

"What's that got to do with anything?"

I said, "You come here all gussied up in your FBI gear and drag me out of Zaftigs—which reminds me, how did you know where to find me?"

Bobby bent over, picked up the newspaper. "This is going to—"

I said, "You tracked my credit card."

Bobby looked at the sky.

"Or you're tracking my phone."

Nothing.

"Or both? You're doing both?"

Bobby said, "Look, this is pointless."

"You can't track my phone without a warrant, right? You need a judge's permission."

"I was just mad over this."

It all fell together. "You son of a bitch."

"Look, Tucker—"

"You think I did it. You think I killed Pupo and took Maria."

"No. Look. I don't know—"

"That's why I didn't know you were looking for Maria, because you were really investigating me. You froze me out."

Bobby's eyes slithered, not meeting mine. "I can't let—"

"*Et tu*, fatso?"

"Hey!"

I moved to walk past Bobby. He stepped to block me. I moved the other way. Blocked again.

"Are you arresting me?" I said.

"What?" Bobby said. "No."

"Then get out of my way."

"Calm down."

"You drag me out of a restaurant, scream at me in the street, then tell me to calm down?"

"Let me explain."

I took a step around Bobby. He moved to block. "Either arrest me or get out of the way," I said.

Bobby relented.

I crunched through the snow back to the playground fence, turned, pointed at Bobby. "This is bullshit. I'll find her without you."

"No, wait!"

I was gone, down Harvard, back to the T. It was time to visit this David Anderson guy.

I pulled out my phone, called Jael. "I'm heading into the North End and I'm worried that someone will try to kill me."

"Someone will try to kill you," said Jael.

"I know. I know."
"But still, you are going."
"Want to come?"

TWENTY-EIGHT

THE NORTH END HAD fully recovered from the snowstorm. Hanover Street pulsed with double-parked madness as cars, trucks, and pedestrians vied for control.

"It is not safe here," Jael said.

I watched a hipster on a bike navigate around an unloading truck. "Is it ever?"

"For you, rarely."

We passed Cafe Vittoria on the way to Battery Street. Hugh Graxton sat in the window, engrossed in his MacBook Air.

"Let's touch base with Hugh," I said.

We stepped into Cafe Vittoria. Hugh looked up, alarmed. Oscar reached under his jacket. Jael unzipped her purse. I patted the air. *Let's all calm down.*

Hugh waved at Oscar to put away his gun. Turned to me. "If it isn't the newsmaker."

Nick caught my eye from behind the espresso machine.

I shook my head. I wouldn't be here long. "It looks like you made the news yourself," I said.

"Rittenhauser's an asshole," said Hugh.

"No doubt," I said. "Still, is it true that you're trying to take Sal's spot?"

Hugh looked at Jael. "Is Tucker wearing a wire?"

"No," said Jael.

I said, "You could have asked me. Don't you trust me?"

"I asked who I asked. Don't get your panties in a wad."

"You haven't answered the question."

"You noticed. Well done."

"Why are you even here? You have a nice thing going in the suburbs."

"You're playing checkers when you should be playing chess, Mr. MIT."

"What's that mean?"

Hugh looked at Jael. "I'm really going to have to explain it?"

"Please explain it quickly," said Jael. "We are exposed in this window."

Hugh said, "Sal and I were partners, of sorts. For one thing, we stayed out of each other's way. More importantly, we had each other's back."

"I can see how that would work."

"It's like the Army. I covered Sal's flank, he covered my flank."

"Okay."

"The rest is left as an exercise to the reader."

"If Pistol runs Boston, you're worried that he'll roll on you."

"Not just Pistol. Sal has a whole crew with delusions of grandeur, and there's two things I can tell you about those guys. First, they'll get arrested on some bullshit within two weeks. Second, they hate me."

"Why?"

"Why? Why not? I'm the kind of guy who made them feel stupid as kids, except now I make them feel stupid as adults."

"How?"

"I wear a jacket and sometimes I use big words."

"You didn't make Sal feel stupid?"

"Sal's smarter than you and me combined, and he knows it. He understood about the flanks. Pistol, on the other hand, is a shithead. He'll throw me under the bus first chance he gets."

Silence.

Jael said, "We are going to see David Anderson."

"You be careful around that bastard, okay?" Hugh said.

"Careful? Why should I be careful?" I asked.

"I was talking to Jael. You don't need to be careful. You can do what you want. Just don't get her killed."

I looked from Hugh to Jael and back. "Is anybody going to tell me—"

"Here's the deal," Hugh said. "Sal and I were in business with David Anderson. We wanted to move our money out of... its current place."

"How?"

"We made some investments in a startup."

"PassHack."

Hugh's eyes narrowed. "How do you know about that?"

"Maybe Mr. MIT can play chess after all."

"Sal told you, didn't he?"

"He's pretty pissed about it."

"I'm pretty pissed too."

"Why? I talked to the CEO, I didn't hear about any of this."

"That little shit Jarrod?"

"Yeah. He told me that Sal was an investor."

"Is there something about this you don't know?"

"I didn't know you were involved, until now."

"So what's your plan now that you know?"

"Jael and I are headed over to—"

The floor-to-ceiling glass that fronted Cafe Vittoria blasted open in a shower of crystals. Two guys stood on the sidewalk. One dropped the red sledgehammer he had used to smash the glass. The other was Pistol Salvucci, one arm in a sling, the other holding a gun.

Jael, Hugh, and I sprang into action. Jael went high, leaping onto Hugh's table in one long stride. Hugh went low, diving beneath the same table. I stood stock still, my mind frozen between options.

Pistol couldn't decide whether to shoot high or shoot low, so he decided to shoot me. Aimed the gun at me and pulled the trigger. I flinched. The bullet tore goose down out of my ski jacket. I dove for the floor. Rolled away and looked behind me.

Oscar stood in the middle of Cafe Vittoria. A red stain grew on his chest. He dropped to his knees, then onto his face.

Jael sailed above Pistol. She fired straight down, blasting red spray from the top of his head. The guy who had smashed the window had produced a gun of his own. He tracked Jael in her arc. His gun rose as he aimed at the spot where she'd have to land now that gravity had turned her into a target.

"No!" I shouted.

Jael landed, rolled, and smashed against a parked car. The pile of snow trapped her on her back in the gutter. The guy fired and blew out a tire. Hugh Graxton shot him twice in the middle of the back. The guy went down as Jael rolled away from the settling car.

Hugh scrambled out from under the table, jumped down to the sidewalk, and helped Jael to her feet.

"Are you okay?" he asked.

"Yes," said Jael.

I climbed to my feet and looked around. Oscar was dead, a sheet of blood spreading from his chest. Nick the barista was gone, probably hiding.

Hugh called from the sidewalk, "Tucker, grab my laptop."

Typical Mac guy. He would have climbed back into a burning building for the thing.

I grabbed the Mac and hopped onto the sidewalk, handed it to Hugh. "What now?"

"Now we scatter and lose the guns."

Jael said, "Agreed."

"See you guys around." He looked at Jael. "And thank you. I owe you."

"We are even," said Jael.

Hugh set off toward Government Center.

I asked Jael, "Where do you want to scatter?"

"We will go to your meeting with David Anderson and act as if nothing had happened."

Jael and I walked down Hanover, deeper into the North End, deeper into enemy territory.

TWENTY-NINE

WE HUSTLED DOWN HANOVER Street as police sirens started wailing. I was having trouble acting as if nothing had happened. I held my gloved hand out in front of me. It bounced and trembled like a captured rabbit.

"Is this normal?" I asked.

Jael said, "Yes."

"What should I do about it?"

"Keep walking. You must burn off the adrenaline."

"Okay."

"Also try deep breathing and prayer."

"Prayer helps?"

"It does not hurt."

I walked, breathing deeply and replacing prayer with the lineup of the 2013 Red Sox: *Ellsbury, Victorino, Pedroia, Ortiz*... "Why aren't you shaking?" I asked.

"I have been trained."

"Who trained you?"

Jael ignored the question. Instead, she disassembled her gun, pulling out a tiny piece and throwing it in the snowbank, then putting the barrel into her pocket.

"What did you just do?" I asked.

"Ballistics is based on the gun barrel and the firing pin. I will replace them and my weapon will be clean."

"What will you tell the police if they find pieces of the gun on you?"

"I will tell them nothing."

"Right. Silence. I always forget silence."

Battery Street had rung a bell when I had looked up Anderson's address. As we neared the street, I realized that it was one of the three streets that framed Joey Pupo's triangular block. Sal's street ran parallel.

"Anderson lives near Sal and Joey," I said.

Jael said, "It is not a surprise."

We turned down Battery and followed it until Commercial cut in half. We ran across Commercial, skirting the snow piles that blocked the sidewalk, and walked toward the water and David Anderson's building at the end of the street.

I had called David Anderson's office expecting to deal with a receptionist. Instead, Anderson himself had answered the phone. I explained that I was Sal Rizzo's cousin and that I was looking for Maria.

"I don't see how I can help you," said Anderson. His voice resonated, deep without being deep.

"I'd just like to talk," I said. "There's no telling what could help me find Maria."

"I read about that this morning. It's tragic."

"It's not tragic yet. I'd like to keep it that way."

"Sure," said Anderson. "Come on by." He had given me directions and hung up.

Now Jael and I stood at the base of a long four-story building that jutted into the gray ocean. A stiff breeze came off the water, chilling me, blowing goose down from my ski jacket's new bullet hole. We walked around the building, leaned on a railing, and looked out into the harbor.

Jael dropped the gun barrel into the sea right in front of us.

"Wouldn't you want to throw it deeper?" I asked.

"A longer throw would allow witnesses to see the shape," she said.

"Good thinking."

"It is my profession."

We entered the lobby, two city folk walking amidst the deep mahogany and cream marble of luxury. A few questions and phone calls later, and David Anderson was inviting us into his condominium.

To say that Anderson and I both owned condominiums would be like saying that Han Solo and Darth Vader both owned star ships. He had a kitchenette like mine, with a breakfast bar and stools, but the similarity ended there. My little shotgun condo would have fit in Anderson's living room, a living room that overlooked a snow-covered terrace and a view of Boston Harbor—Coast Guard ships in the fore, the Tobin Bridge in the background.

Anderson had a couple of inches on me, which put him at six-two. He was fit and wore a V-neck wool sweater over a white button-down shirt tucked into dark blue jeans, a working-from-home-and-might-have-to-Skype look. We made introductions all around.

"I just brewed some coffee," he said. "Can I get you a cup?"

"Sure," I said. "Black."

"No, thank you," said Jael.

"Tea?"

"No, thank you."

Our condos were also similar in that they both lacked a woman's touch, or even a gay friend's touch. Anderson's living room featured black leather couches, a huge television, and a black granite coffee table.

Anderson brought the coffee in a large French press, pressed the plunger, poured the coffee into two big mugs, and sat across from us. The coffee was excellent.

Anderson asked, "Is this conversation being recorded?"

I said, "What?"

"I'm sorry. It's a formality my lawyers insist upon."

"You're the second person who's asked me that today."

"You must lead an interesting life."

"You have no idea."

Silence. "Is it being recorded?" he repeated.

"No," I said, "it's not."

"Well, that's good. I've never had someone say yes. It would lead to some awkward moments."

"I imagine it would."

"How can I help?"

"To be honest, I don't know. I'm looking for Maria Rizzo and I'm grasping at straws."

"How would any straw lead you to me?"

"I only know that Sal Rizzo did some business with you and lost his money."

"Told you that, did he?"

"Yup," I lied.

"Called me a thief?"

Interesting. "He made mention of it," I lied again.

Anderson rubbed his nose and looked out toward the Tobin Bridge. "Sal Rizzo is an idiot."

"Really?"

"He thought his investment was some sort of a loan. Wanted his money back. Of course I didn't give it to him. He's a big boy. He can take his lumps like the rest of us."

"How much did he lose?"

"All of it. Just like me."

"How much was that?"

Anderson drank more coffee. "It's my own fault, I suppose."

"Why do you say that?"

"I didn't vet Sal properly. I let Hugh vouch for him."

"How do you know Hugh?"

"Undergrad at UMass, business school."

"Another UMass guy."

"We're everywhere."

"Hugh invested with you too?"

"Yes, but Hugh understood the rules of venture investment. I figured that he'd told Sal, but he hadn't. So we had misalignment."

"Misalignment?"

"Sal thought he was making a loan, when he was really making an investment. He thought he had no risk, but he did. He was misaligned with reality."

"I'm surprised you didn't wind up paying him back."

"Why would I pay him back?"

I had more of the wonderful coffee. "Sal can be pretty persuasive."

"You mean because he's a Mafioso?"

Well, that was direct. "Yeah. I guess that's what I'm saying."

"Are you a Mafioso?"

"No. I'm just Sal's cousin."

Anderson looked at Jael, who was sitting on the sofa next to me, the black leather of her outfit acting as sofa camouflage. "If you're not a Mafioso," he said, "then where did you get your hired muscle?"

Jael said, "I am not hired muscle. I am Tucker's friend."

"But you could be hired," Anderson said. "Am I right?"

Jael said nothing.

Anderson pressed, "You do provide security services, don't you? You have the look."

Jael said, "Yes."

"How much do you charge?"

Jael told him.

"You could be making much more, afford better equipment—a Kevlar vest."

"I am fine."

"I'm sure you are." Anderson turned back to me. "Tucker, last year I cleared eleven million dollars. It's not Mitt Romney money, but it's still good money. I use it to hire security personnel such as Jael here."

I had never thought of Jael as "security personnel."

"Believe me when I tell you that Sal was never a threat to me," Anderson said.

I said, "Okay."

"I'm not threatened by a two-bit hood with a crappy business model."

"Crappy business model?"

"Prostitution? Drugs? Really?" Anderson scowled. "Prostitution isn't scalable. Drugs have supply problems. You need to fight for street corners, and half your sales force is stoned."

"I'd never thought of it that way."

"The fact that Sal noticed a loss of two hundred thousand dollars tells me that he doesn't make very much money. Those poor assholes have to scrape for every penny."

"Have you told this to Hugh?"

"Oh, he agrees with me, but he loves the thrill. He's nuts."

"I see."

Anderson poured more coffee from the French press. "Have you had any luck tracking Maria down?"

"No. I was hoping to discover some thread from you."

"No threads here."

I downed my coffee. "Sorry I bothered you."

"Not a problem."

We stood and headed for the foyer. Anderson noticed the hole in my jacket. "Catch it on a fence?" he asked.

"Yeah. Stupid fences." I let Jael through the door ahead of me. *Ladies first.* I started to leave, but turned. "Oh, one last question."

"Okay," said Anderson.

"What happened to Jarrod's technology?"

"Hmm?"

"Jarrod Cooper is a frigging genius, and his technology alone should have recovered some of the investment. But you said you lost all of it."

"We did."

"So you didn't sell Jarrod's technology."

Anderson's cheeks turned a light shade of anime pink. "Turns out it was unsellable."

"Why?"

"It was all just derived from open source software. Jarrod hadn't invented anything new."

"Huh."

"That deal went bad every possible way."

I shook Anderson's soft hand. "Thank you for your help."

"Anytime." He closed the door.

I was silent as we rode the elevator down and walked through the lobby. Once we were down the street and at the corner, Jael spoke up.

"Did you learn anything?" she asked.

"Yeah," I said. "I learned that David Anderson is a big fat liar."

"Why do you say that?"

"I worked on Jarrod's stuff. It was original. He could have—hey look, it's Angie."

Angie Morielli, resplendent in a long fur coat, hustled down Battery Street carrying shopping bags.

I headed for the curb. “Let’s go say hello.”

THIRTY

THE IDEA THAT YOU could get a traffic citation for crossing a street is more than foreign to native Bostonians; it's laughable, a prank pulled by tourists. "A ticket? Seriously?" On the other hand, drivers consider stopping for someone in the street to be a merciful act, worthy of note and praise. Streets are for cars, not people.

Seeing no cars, I ran diagonally across the intersection. Jael was right behind me. "Angie!"

Angie looked up from scanning the sidewalk for ice patches. Her expression moved from neutral to happy to irritated as her eyes moved from the sidewalk to me to Jael. We met at the corner.

"You're gonna get killed, you know," said Angie.

"Why does everyone keep telling me that?" I said.

"Because you cross streets like an idiot."

"Oh, you mean *accidentally* killed. I thought you meant shot or something."

"You mean like Pistol?"

News travels fast.

Angie flicked her eyes over Jael and pursed her lips. "Who's your friend?"

Jael stuck out her hand. "I am Jael."

Angie stared at the hand a moment, put down her groceries, and shook. She turned back to me. "I didn't know you had a girlfriend."

"I wish," I said, laughing. Jael looked at me. Cocked an eyebrow. I said to her, "I mean, I wish I had a girlfriend, not I wish *you* were my girlfriend."

Jael blinked at me.

I said, "Well—I mean—it's never been—"

"That's not very nice," Angie said. "You owe her an apology."

"Yeah, but—"

"She's very pretty."

"Thank you," said Jael.

"I know she's pretty," I said. "It's just that—you know."

"So you guys aren't dating?" Angie asked Jael.

"No," said Jael. "We are friends."

I pointed. "Yeah. Yeah. We're just friends."

Jael said, "I am helping him find Maria Rizzo."

"That poor kid," Angie said. "I saw her picture in the paper today."

"Yes," said Jael.

"What kind of idiot puts that kind of picture on the front page?"

"Idiot?" I asked.

"Yeah," said Angie. "With all this shit—oh, sorry, Jael—with all this stuff that's happening, you think they wouldn't take Maria? Try to use her? It's obvious."

"Obvious," I said.

"And they're a bunch of animals. Pistol and Dan just got killed right up the street. Them and some other guy. I mean, who does that? Over what?"

"Maybe the picture will help find her."

Angie took a step closer, draped her arms over my shoulders. "Tucker, you're sweet."

"Well, you know—"

Angie pulled me close and planted a kiss: first a touch of the lips, then something deeper. I flailed my arms a bit, then wrapped them around her fur-clad body while part of me floated outside, watching Jael watch me.

Angie whispered in my ear, "I should have taken you up on your offer last night."

I said, "That's okay."

Angie stepped back. "That's okay?"

"Um, yeah."

Angie reached for her groceries.

"Let me get those," I said.

"No," said Angie, picking up the bag. "That's okay."

"You sure I can't help?"

"No, I'm fine. I'll see you." With that, Angie turned and strode off down Commercial Street.

Jael and I headed off in the other direction.

"I'm confused," I said.

Jael said, "Clearly."

I looked at my watch. "I'm supposed to have lunch with Caroline. Do you have any advice to make that go better?"

"Yes."

"What?"

"Wash the lipstick off your face."

THIRTY-ONE

A LITTLE TREE STANDS in front of the 617 restaurant. A larger tree had stood in that spot until Dzhokhar Tsarnaev planted a bomb next to it and blew a hole in the Boston Marathon.

The little tree got a lot of attention soon after it was planted. People festooned it with flowers, ribbons, and Boston Marathon runners' numbers. Time passed, the shrine was cleared, the Red Sox won the World Series, and people largely forgot how the little tree got its start.

Today the tree stood leafless, covered in snow, waiting for April when its leaves would bud and new people would stand next to it watching their friends and neighbors run the final block to the finish line. I tapped the tree's bark for luck and entered the restaurant.

The hostess, a brunette in a tight black turtleneck, led me back past the bar to an elevated booth with a script *Reserved* sign on it. She took the sign, laid out two menus, and headed back to the front.

Reserved?

I glanced at my watch. I was a little early, battling pre-date jitters. If this was a date. Perhaps it wasn't a date. Maybe it was a strategy session. Perhaps Caroline knew something I didn't know about my impending arrest. Caroline said it was "about you and me." Maybe she meant "you the defendant and me the lawyer." That made more sense than "you the man and me the wo—"

The turtlenecked hostess reappeared, with Caroline close behind in a luscious green knit dress that covered her from neck to knee, yet showed every curve from breast to thigh. I slid from the booth, sticking my hand out to shake but wishing I could touch that dress. Caroline ignored my hand and, apparently reading my mind, stepped in close for a hug. Best hug ever.

As we slid into the booth, I noticed that Caroline had a different prosthetic: gold instead of silver, with a different curlicue design running up her shin.

She caught my glance and said, "The gold goes better with green."

"And the green goes with your red hair," I said.

"Why, thank you for noticing, sir."

"And thank you for inviting me to lunch. I was thinking that this might be a business lunch, but that doesn't seem to be a business lunch dress."

"This is my date-with-Tucker dress."

Well, at least that was clarified.

Caroline continued, "That's okay with you, I hope."

"Oh, yes."

"You don't have a girlfriend?"

"Nope."

"Or a wife? Because if it turns out you have a wife—well, let's just say I know people."

"I'm a widower."

"Oh. I'm sorry."

Way to bring the party down, genius.

I said, "It's been a couple of years now."

"You're so young. Was it cancer?"

"No. Murder."

Deer-in-the-headlights look from Caroline. The server, a blond girl with a long ponytail and some chin acne, saved the day. "Would you like something to drink?"

Caroline ordered Jameson on the rocks. Good, not an ice tea lunch.

"Woodford Reserve," I said. "Neat."

The server left.

Caroline said, "That conversation got pretty intense pretty fast."

"Yeah, sorry. Too much sharing?"

"No. No. I want to know about you. That's why I invited you out."

I looked around the restaurant. The place had once been named, The Forum, but they had closed and 617 opened in its place. Tsarnaev's bomb had blown in its windows and shredded the interior, but there was no sign of that anymore. A bustling lunch crowd boiled around us.

I knew why we were eating at the 617, and why Caroline rated a reserved booth. "Do you eat here often?" I asked, knowing the answer.

"Yes, I come here all the time."

"You were standing out by the little tree, huh?"

"Why—?"

The server arrived with the drinks. Caroline and I clinked glasses.

"Cheers," I said.

"To answer your question," Caroline said, "yes. I was standing out front. How did you know?"

"You seem like the kind of person who would get back on the horse."

"Exactly. You're the first one to get that without me having to explain it."

"Why were you out there?"

"Why was anyone out there? I was watching the marathon, waiting for my boyfriend to cross the finish line."

"Boyfriend?"

"Well, then-boyfriend. Turned out he didn't have the stomach for the whole in-sickness-and-in-health thing."

"Ahh."

Caroline downed her Jameson. I followed with my Woodford.

"Aren't we a cheery couple?" Caroline said.

"There's plenty of time to be cheery," I said. "This way we don't use it up all at once."

That got me a bright smile, white teeth, red hair, green dress. It would be easy to get cheery.

The server came, took our lunch order. Caroline reloaded her drink. I followed.

"Are you trying to get me drunk?" I asked. "Or maybe cheerful?"

"Is it working?" Caroline asked.

"It's getting there."

"Seemed to me that you could use a drink or two."

"Does it show?"

"Oh, yeah. I felt your shoulders when we hugged. They're like rocks."

"That's from all the weightlifting."

"You sure it wasn't stress?"

"Could be stress."

"Stress from what?"

"Getting shot at."

"You were shot at?"

"Yeah, but he missed."

"In the North End?"

Time to change the subject. "How are things going with Sal's bail?" I asked.

Caroline said, "Not talking, eh? I can respect that. But you brought it up."

I waited.

"Sal's bail was denied this morning," she said. "The DA is being a hard-ass and the judge went along with him."

"Why?"

"'The defendant killed his best friend and his wife,'" Caroline said in a whiny singsong. "'His daughter is gone. He has no reason to stay here and face trial.'"

"The judge agreed?"

"Oh yeah. The fucker doodled on his legal pad while I made my pitch."

"That leaves Sal stuck in there until trial?"

"Yup."

"I don't think he'll survive in there."

"He's a tough guy."

"But still."

"I'm working on something that might get him out."

"What's that?"

"Too early to say."

I remembered Cantrell's offer. "You know, I was talking—"

The server arrived with our lunches and our whiskey reloads. We got all the business sorted out with who ordered what and who had a napkin and the wrong salad dressing. We had more water brought, glasses filled. We placed our napkins in our laps. All part of the lunch dance.

"You know, I'm tired of talking about Sal," Caroline said. "I asked you out. Let's talk about you. What do you do?"

"I'm pretty much a lovable wastrel," I said. "I do some computer security consulting, but mostly I live off a severance package."

"A severance package? What kind of severance package sets you up for life?"

"A we're-so-sorry-we-got-your-wife-killed severance package."

"Holy shit."

"Indeed."

Caroline reached out, rested her hand on mine. "How am I doing getting you drunk?"

I gulped. "You're doing okay."

"You know, because we don't really need to stay for dessert."

"Um—sure. Skipping dessert would be good."

"Only good?" Caroline pouted.

"Well, no—ah—"

"Because I'm thinking—"

"Ah! Just the two people I was looking for." Frank Cantrell stood over our table like a rumpled busboy.

I looked up at Frank, scowled. Caroline followed my gaze, scowled.

"You two don't look happy to see me," Frank said.

I said, "You are a master of deduction."

"Yeah. Scooch over," Frank said. He climbed up into the booth next to me.

Caroline said, "We're having a private conversation, Agent Cantrell."

"Yeah, well," said Frank, "I needed to talk to Tucker here, but this is even better."

"How did you find—aw shit," I said. "Are you guys still tracking me?"

"Tracking?" Caroline asked.

Frank said, "Yeah. Tucker's a person of interest."

"It takes more than that to get a warrant to track him."

"Well, we're real interested. But that's not why I'm here."

"Why are you here, Frank?" I asked.

"Did you tell her about my offer?"

Caroline asked, "What offer are you talking about?"

"I told Tucker that I could get Sal a deal on bail if he'd turn," Frank said.

Caroline turned to me. "And you didn't think to mention this?"

"I was going to, but then lunch came, and—"

She stood in that magnificent dress, opened her purse, threw three hundred-dollar bills onto the table. Benjamin Franklin scowled at me.

"I want to see you both in my office at four," Caroline said. She turned and strode from the restaurant, her prosthetic limb not slowing her down one bit.

Frank followed her out with a low whistle. "Jesus, she's hot, even with the leg."

"Shut up, Frank," I said.

My Droid beeped. Caroline's text: `Idiot.`

She was right.

THIRTY-TWO

I WALKED DOWN BOYLSTON Street, my down-spouting ski jacket wrapped tightly against the weather. It was cold, 10 degrees. It had been cold yesterday. It would be cold tomorrow. Then it was supposed to warm up a bit—and snow. Then it would be cold again. The sun shone in the clear blue sky. It had started its descent and would be gone in a couple of hours, and then we'd be back in darkness. I headed down Dalton, back to the South End, hoping the red brick buildings would add some color to the unremitting gray.

Shit. I was sick of winter and it wasn't even January.

A police car squatted in front of my house, exhaust curling from its tailpipe. The passenger door opened and Lieutenant Lee climbed out. He was eating a Fudgsicle.

"Jesus, Lee, it's freezing," I said. "How can you eat that?"

Lee said, "You shouldn't swear all the time."

I raised my hands in contrition. "Sorry."

"Are you still trying to find Maria Rizzo?"

"Yeah. Of course."

"I have some information that might help."

"Great. What is it?"

Lee bit into the Fudgsicle, leaving a bite-shaped gap. He talked around the chunk of ice cream. "I want to trade information."

"What do you need to know?"

"I need to know what happened on Hanover Street."

Uh-oh. "What are you talking about?"

"Three men died in and around Cafe Vittoria."

"Espresso poisoning?"

"You know how they died. You were there."

I said nothing.

"One of the deceased was Pistol Salvucci," Lee continued. "His elbow was broken. I know your friend Jael did that."

Saying nothing remained my best option.

"Witnesses say that there was a gunfight, and three people walked away. One matches Hugh Graxton's description. The other two match you and Jael." Lee took another bite out of his Fudgsicle.

I shivered, imagining the cold ice cream sliding down his throat.

Lee said, "If you tell me what happened, I'll tell you what I learned about Maria Rizzo."

"Why tell me?" I asked.

"What?"

"Why not find Maria Rizzo yourself?" I asked.

"Because that is not my job. My job is to find out who killed those three men on Hanover Street. I am a homicide detective. We have others who look for missing people."

"Why not tell them?"

"Oh, I will. But they have so many cases. I understood that you had a special interest in finding her."

"Lee, this is bullshit. If you have something on Maria, just tell me."

"And if you know something about Hanover Street, you just tell me."

"I don't know what you're talking about."

"I never lie to you, Tucker. Do me the same courtesy."

"Sorry. I meant to say that I have nothing to say to you."

"Ah, well," said Lee. "Suffer the little children."

"Screw you, Lee."

"What did you say?"

"You should be ashamed of yourself, you self-righteous bastard. How dare you quote scripture at me?"

"I had no idea that scripture had become important to you."

"Maria is important to me. You're playing a game with her life. Would Jesus do that?"

Lee's lips thinned. He looked at the Fudgsicle, started to take a bite, then threw it toward the gutter. He missed, and it splatted on the granite curbstone.

"Jesus," he said, "would approve of me finding the person who killed those men."

"Even if it was self-defense?"

"Are you saying it was self-defense?"

Oops. Dammit. "I'm not saying anything. I'm just asking."

"It's not my job to decide whether it was self-defense. It's my job to bring the killers to trial."

"Well, good luck with that."

"I have enough probable cause to arrest you."

"Arrest me, then," I said. "Then nobody would be looking for Maria."

"That's not true."

"Oh, right. Bobby Miller is on the case."

"That's not what I mean. Someone else is looking for Maria."

"Who?"

"Who was with you on Hanover?"

I reached down, picked up Lee's Fudgsicle by the stick, and handed it to him.

"Please don't litter in front of my house."

Lee took the Fudgsicle.

I said, "I have to go." Turned and walked up my front steps.

"Tucker," Lee said.

I stood at the top of the steps, looking down at Lee's greasy wind-blown hair. "Yeah?"

Lee climbed the steps, stood next to me. It was so cold that the Fudgsicle didn't even drip in his grasp.

"That night when you found Pupo's body, there were Boston cops at the end of Holden Court. They were having a discussion with Bobby Miller about shoving Boston's citizens."

"Okay."

"Nobody ever came out of those buildings."

"So whoever shot Joey disappeared with Maria?"

"Or he was dead before you got there. You were the only one who claimed to have heard a shot."

"What are you saying?"

"Did you kill Pupo too?"

"Thanks for the help, Lee."

I slipped through my door and shut it in his face. He probably threw the Fudgsicle into my bushes.

THIRTY-THREE

CAROLINE HAD CHANGED INTO call-them-on-the-carpet clothes, replacing her fantastic green dress with a severe black business suit. She sat behind her desk, glowering at Bobby Miller, Frank Cantrell, and me as we sat in a line like naughty schoolboys.

"When are you fucking morons going to get your act together?" she asked.

I said, "What did I do?"

"You shut up."

I crossed my arms and pouted.

Caroline pointed at Bobby. "I thought we had a deal."

Bobby said, "We do have a deal."

"Then why is Frank Cantrell trying to get a different deal?"

Bobby looked at Frank. "Jesus, Frank. You could have told me."

"I don't work for you," Frank said.

"It's a little thing called teamwork."

Caroline said, "This is like the Three Stooges."

"I didn't do anything," I said.

"Shut up."

I crossed my arms again.

Caroline said to Bobby, "Sal's more valuable to you out than in. Make it happen."

"I can't just make it happen," Bobby said. "The DA thinks we have Sal on an airtight murder charge."

Caroline said, "Well you don't."

"She's right," Frank said. "We don't have a case against Sal."

"Why not?"

"Because our star witness, Pupo, is dead."

"Yeah, probably because one of Sal's guys killed him."

Caroline said, "Idle speculation. Do you still want to keep your deal with Sal?"

"What deal?" I asked.

"Shut up, Tucker," Bobby said.

"Screw you, Bobby. What deal?"

"Sal has been informing against David Anderson," said Caroline.

Frank turned to Bobby. "What? You could have told me."

Bobby said, "Shut up, Frank."

"You know? Teamwork?"

"Sal told me he'd never turn," I said.

"He'd never turn against his guys," Caroline said. "Anderson isn't one of his guys, and Sal hates Anderson's guts."

"I think Anderson figured it out on his own," Bobby said.

"Just fucking great," said Caroline.

Frank asked, "Then why didn't he just kill Sal?"

"Because that would be too easy," I said.

"What?"

"Those private equity guys are ruthless."

"Anderson wants to destroy Sal as a warning to others," Bobby said. "Kill his wife, take his daughter, show that he'll play dirtier than any of them."

I said, "I think the plan was to kill Maria too."

"Jesus," Frank said. "That's cold."

I said, "It's just lucky I had taken her to the Common."

"So who took her from you?" Frank asked.

"Must have been Pupo," I said.

"Who has her now?"

Silence hung in the room.

I asked, "How did Anderson find out Sal was an informant?"

"Pupo," Frank said.

"What?" Bobby asked.

"Pupo had turned on Sal. He told us that Sal killed Marco."

Caroline said, "Pupo was a lying piece of shit."

"Yeah," Frank said. "But I think he was a lying piece of shit who worked for us and David Anderson."

"He was playing all sides?" Bobby asked.

"Yeah. If Sal said it, Pupo blabbed it."

"And you think that Sal told him about our Anderson deal?"

"Why not? Sal and Pupo were friends, at least until the end."

"What do you mean, *until the end?*" Caroline asked.

Frank said, "The Boston cops tell us that they had an argument at Marco's funeral. Sal walked out."

"I don't see how this changes anything," I said. "I still need to find Maria."

"I don't think we're going to find Maria." Bobby said.

"You still think Anderson killed her?"

"Anderson has people for that."

I thought back to Anderson's comment about "security services." "Why not just arrest him?" I asked.

"Because we have less on him than anyone else in this thing." Bobby nodded at Caroline. "This one would have him out in a day."

Caroline said, "Screw you, Miller."

"You saying you wouldn't take the case?" Bobby asked.

"That's got nothing to do with this. Let's focus on Sal."

"That's your job, Caroline. It's not mine. Sal probably didn't kill his best friend and his wife, but he sure as hell has killed someone somewhere."

I had watched Sal kill someone. It was the day he saved my life. I stood.

Caroline said, "Where are you going?"

"It seems to me that Anderson is the crux to this whole thing," I said. "I'm going to find out what he's doing."

"The hell you are," said Bobby. "I'm running this investigation."

"Really?" I asked. "You still wasting time tracking my GPS?"

Frank Cantrell chortled.

Caroline, Bobby, and I said in unison, "Shut up, Frank."

"Fuck you all," Frank said.

Caroline said, "The three of you, get out of my office."

We gathered our winter coats and left.

Outside Bobby said, "I'm serious, Tucker, don't mess with Anderson. You'll get yourself killed."

"Well, then, you'll just have to use your GPS tracker to find my body," I said.

"You don't know who Anderson's got working for him."

"Do you?"

"No."

"When I find out, I'll let you know."

THIRTY-FOUR

After two days of getting dragged into tablecloth restaurants, I had finally found my way to Bukowski Tavern, a place where I could sit at the bar, eat a burger, and snigger at the boob jokes in the menu. I have simple needs.

Those needs didn't include sitting next to a backstabbing scumbag from the *Boston Globe*, but there he was: Jerry Rittenhauser, enjoying a spiced winter ale and eating a gigantic hot dog. I tweeted:

`Don't you have some place to be? #imaginedbartalk @bukowskiboston`

"This bar is outstanding," said Rittenhauser.

"It's my happy place," I said.

"You get happy often?"

"Not lately." I pulled up the Maria article on my phone. "I read your story. Good list of gangland warriors. I know most of these guys: Hugh, Oscar, Pistol—"

"Well, Oscar and Pistol are out of the running."

"Who is this guy Vince Ferrari?"

"Great name, huh? Love to have him win the war."

"How did you find out about him?"

"Um ... a source."

"I see."

"Seriously, you don't want to know."

"I do want to know."

"Well, I'm not going to tell you."

"I'm looking for guys who might have grabbed Maria."

"I can't help you."

"Right. That's what they all say."

We sat for a moment, eating comfort food and drinking beer. Actually, come to think of it, a good stout is a comfort food. Hell, if monks could live off it ... my beer was empty.

Mikey the bartender pointed at the empty glass. "Dude?"

"Sure," I said.

"That's your third," Rittenhauser noted.

"My mother's dead. You want the job?"

Rittenhauser went back to his beer. "Don't be a dick."

I let the question of Rittenhauser's source rattle around in my head. The answer fell out like a gumball.

"What else did David Anderson tell you?" I asked.

"Who's David Anderson?"

"He's your source."

"You mean the one at Battery Street Private Capital?"

"I thought you didn't know him."

"He's not my source."

"Of course he is. He's the only guy who's in this fight but not on your list."

Rittenhauser said nothing. Drank his beer.

I said, "Okay, that's settled. What can you tell me about him?"

"I can tell you that he's a private equity guy who lives on Battery Street."

"Yeah, I knew that."

"Well, there you go."

"You must have something else."

"Apparently, he picks a lot of losers."

"I only know about one. You ever hear of PassHack or Jarrod Cooper?"

"Yeah, I heard of him. What a horrible idea. I don't want my passwords hacked."

"What you're probably saying is that you don't want to know it's possible."

Jerry took a big swig of beer. "Is it possible?"

"Of course it's possible. Somebody steals a database of encrypted passwords, cranks at them for a few days with a fast computer to pull the passwords out."

"They can decrypt the passwords?"

"No, they can't. But they guess and encrypt the guesses. Then they compare their encrypted guess to your encrypted password. If they match, then you're cracked."

"Does guessing work?"

"Depends on your password. It's like cracking a safe. Richard Feynman, the physicist, used to crack a lot of safes at Los Alamos."

"What did he do?"

"He'd come into a guy's office with a stethoscope and go to work."

"He'd use the stethoscope to listen to the tumblers?"

"No, he'd use the stethoscope to look cool. It had nothing to do with safe cracking."

"Then how would he crack it?"

"First he'd try the default combination that shipped with the safe. That worked a lot."

"Oh."

"Then he'd try variants of the owner's birthday."

"That seems obvious."

"If those didn't work, then he'd just try all the combinations. There were a lot fewer than you'd think because the safes back then weren't precise. They were like the combination lock you use for your gym locker. You could be off by one number and they'd still open, so there were fewer real combinations. Feynman could get through them all pretty quickly. Jarrod was doing the same sort of thing at PassHack."

"Yeah, but guessing my password would take millions of years, right?"

"If your password is only six digits long, Jarrod wouldn't have to guess. He could crank through all the combinations in two minutes."

"But mine is longer than six digits."

"Good for you. So then Jarrod would start guessing. First he'd see if someone else in the world had used your password. Then he'd use words in the dictionary, then combinations of words."

"He wouldn't use my birthday?"

"He wouldn't know your birthday, or your kids' names, or where you went to school. That stuff's ridiculous. He just uses words. But, you know, *Boston* and *Globe* are words, right?"

Mikey brought my new beer. "Thanks, man." I turned back to Rittenhauser, who had stopped eating. "Hitting close to home, right?"

Rittenhauser said, "But he probably doesn't have a database with my password, right?"

"You got a LinkedIn account?"

"Yeah. Everyone does."

"Then he's got it. Or at least an old one. They got hacked a year ago. Have you changed your passwords this year?"

"Oh, shit. What would Jarrod do if he cracked my password?"

"If Jarrod cracked your password, he'd call you and tell you that it was crackable. That was the whole point of PassHack. If someone else cracked your password ... well."

"Well, what?"

"It depends on whether you use the same password on all your websites."

Rittenhauser pushed his plate away.

"You didn't do that, did you?" I asked. "Tell me you didn't use the same password for LinkedIn as you did for your bank."

"Well, Jesus! How am I supposed to remember a bunch of different passwords?"

I drank my stout, smiled a beer-mustache smile. "They have software for that."

"I have to go." Rittenhauser got up and threw a twenty on the bar. He shrugged on his coat and turned to leave.

I called after Rittenhauser, "Remember! Don't use real words, throw in some numbers and an exclamation point or two."

He didn't turn back. Instead he charged out into the cold, racing an imagined hacker to his bank account.

THIRTY-FIVE

THE LIGHT FROM MY monitor splashed through my office and spilled into the dark apartment. Click and Clack were asleep. The Bruins weren't playing. Nothing was left for me to do but poke around on the web and do research on PassHack. My screen displayed some old PassHack advertising, nothing recent; the company had dropped off the face of the earth. Tweeted:

`Trapped in the dark midnight of the Internet #sleepwhereareyou`

I stopped typing and listened to my silent condo. In the distance, a siren spoke of someone else's emergency. A door closed. A mother yelled at her kid, "For the last time, go to bed!" I leaned back. My chair creaked. Silence. Darkness. Time for a drink.

I padded into the kitchen by the light of my monitor. Reached up over the fridge and pulled down a bottle of WhistlePig Rye, distilled in Vermont. Poured a triple or so of WhistlePig into a rocks glass, didn't add any ice. Took a slug of rye, felt the burn of the attack, and let the strong rye esters travel through my nose. The alcohol nibbled at my consciousness, rounding the harsh edges.

I slumped in front of the computer. Old PassHack information glowed on the screen. Jarrod started it, Anderson invested, he invested again, then it crapped out. I saw no mention of selling the assets. No product discussions. No news stories. Nothing.

Well, that wasn't quite true. There was an address, PassHack's last known location. I copied the address into Evernote, decided to visit it the next day, and gave up for the night.

I sat in front of my browser, doing the random clicking that has replaced mindless TV watching. Clicked on Gmail: nothing. Clicked on Stumbleupon: nothing. Considered joining Facebook again, decided against it again. Went over to Twitter and found a random article retweeted by a celebrity, read it while ignoring it—something about a movie star who had sworn off drinking. *The fool.*

I considered World of Warcraft, decided against it. I didn't want to be that guy, sitting alone in his apartment, drinking rye whiskey and killing orcs. Opened the holiday pictures I had taken with my old phone. Watched a movie of Maria unwrapping her sled. "Finally!" she had said.

The rye dug into my brain, slipping between the folds, creating fuzz. I watched Maria open the sled again. Sophia sat on the couch, cradled in Sal's gigantic arm. Sal's hand covered Sophia's thigh, her hand rested over his. They grimaced in unison as the sled emerged from the wrapping.

I flipped through other pictures. Sal raising a glass of wine. Sophia, in an apron, serving the lasagna that had followed the soup and would be followed by the ham. An old crèche sitting at the base of a Christmas tree, Jesus lying in his bassinet, Mary praying next to him. Joseph lying on his side, having been knocked over by a large gift. Maria horsing around on an iPad, Sal yelling at her to put that damn thing away and be social.

The video had it all: the food, the gifts, the uncles and aunts. It was A Child's Christmas in Boston. No videos of me, of course. I was behind the camera, reveling in the chance to be part of a family again. Recording all so we could look at it in the future. I hadn't realized that I was capturing Maria's last Christmas with her mom, that the family was about to be blown apart. If I had known, I'd have taken better videos.

I poured myself more rye and looked for something technical to do, something to occupy my hands before I drank myself into a coma. My Droid lay on the counter. It still had its stupid "Droid" ringtone. Picked up the phone, poked around in Settings, surfed the web, bought a ring tone: the Bruins' foghorn. Whenever the Bruins score a goal, the Garden blasts a foghorn. It's one of the world's best noises and it made a great ringtone.

My ringtone foghorned. It was as if the gods themselves wanted to test my phone. I answered: Angie.

"Hello."

Nothing.

"Hello."

Snuffling sounds, maybe breathing.

"Hellooooo?"

Pocket dialed.

I broke the connection.

The rye whiskey worked its magic, slowing my thinking, calming my stomach, giving me the chemical illusion that all was right with the world. I knocked back the rest of the liquor and padded off to bed.

THIRTY-SIX

Riverside Station is the westernmost outpost of civilization. It's the last stop on the Green Line; after that, you have to drive or take the commuter rail. I walked down the station's ramp, holding an empty Wired Puppy cup and looking for an address, the last known location of PassHack.

I tossed the cup in the trash, pulled on my gloves, and followed my Droid's walking directions. It led me to the end of the driveway and down the sidewalk. The day was brilliantly cold, just as predicted. My nose hairs stiffened in the bitter air, a sign that the temperature was in the single digits. Sadly, I was wearing a leather bomber jacket instead of my punctured ski jacket. The cold lanced right through the leather.

Hard snow crunched under my UGGs as I made my way into the office building's lobby and batted my arms to warm myself. I exited the elevator on the third floor, looking for a sign that said PassHack. There was none. There was a desk. Behind the desk sat a dapper young man with blond hair and braces. He wore a blue button-down shirt, a repp tie, and a navy jacket. He looked like a Young Republican on a job interview.

"I'm looking for PassHack," I said.

"Certainly, sir," Repp Tie said. He looked at his iMac, tapped some keys, and talked on the phone.

"Your name?"

"Tucker."

Repp Tie spoke into the phone. "Mr. Tucker is here." He hung up and gestured to a coffee area. "Please make yourself comfortable. Mr. Kane will be here momentarily."

"Mr. Kane?"

"Yes."

"Of PassHack?"

"Yes."

I'd never heard of him. I wandered into the coffee area and confronted a contraption that claimed to make coffee from one of a dozen little packets hanging like tiny sides of beef. I suspected the coffee would taste the same no matter which packet I chose. I picked a Kona blend, hoping that thoughts of Hawaii would warm me. Stuck the packet in the slot, pushed the button, watched the machine gurgle out a cup of coffee. Tasted the coffee. It tasted like coffee made by a machine using a packet. No images of Hawaii sprang to mind.

A short guy wearing a tight black polo shirt and jeans walked toward me. He crossed his arms, looked at me.

I said, "Mr. Kane?"

"Yup."

I stuck out my hand. "Tucker."

Kane looked at my hand. "Yeah?"

I dropped my hand. "I came by to talk about PassHack. I thought they were out of business, but this address popped up on the web."

Kane said, "There's nothing to talk about."

"Hmm. I'm not so sure—"

We were interrupted by a bunch of guys engaging in post-meeting good-byes. They shook hands, slapped shoulders, laughed, and stopped for coffee. "One for the road," one joked. The others laughed; clearly Mr. One-for-the-Road was the boss. The jovial band of business brothers hung around the coffee machine, agreeing with their boss about the superiority of packets when it came to coffee-making. Kane and I waited for them to leave. I tweeted:

`If I ever get a real job, please kill me.`

I said to Kane, "Can we go somewhere?"

Kane turned, beckoned, and walked down the hall. I followed him to a small office with a desk, a phone, and a window. There were no decorations, no pictures, no Red Sox posters, no sign that this guy had any life beyond this small room. Kane sat, pointed at a chair. I sat.

"Shut the door," Kane said.

I reached back and swung the door shut.

Kane asked, "What?"

I said, "I just came by to learn what happened to the PassHack technology."

"Do I look like a guy who would know what happened to PassHack's technology?"

"You're not wearing a tie, so yeah, you do."

"Well, I don't."

"Then why are you sitting in an office for PassHack?"

"Look, Tucker, I don't know where you got your information."

"The web."

"Well, the web is wrong. It's possible that PassHack was in this office, but they're not now. I use this space."

"Do you pay for this space?"

Kane blushed—honest to God blushed—then narrowed his eyes.

"Why do you ask?"

"I wondered if David Anderson paid for it."

More blushing, a twitch in the cheek. Mr. Poker Face. "I've never heard of David Anderson."

"You suck."

"I suck?"

"At lying. You suck at lying. You're the worst."

"You're an asshole."

"At least you really believe that. What's your relationship with David Anderson?"

Kane stood. "Get out."

I appraised Kane again. Small guy, tight clothes, buzz cut. Reminded me of Jael.

"Holy shit," I said. "You're David Anderson's security guy."

"Get out."

"I've heard that you make a shitload of money."

Kane came around the desk and grabbed my leather jacket—which he had not offered to take before—and pulled me to my feet. He was a strong little bastard.

"Get the fuck out of here!" Kane pulled open the office door, threw me into the wall across the hallway, and slammed the door shut behind me.

A massively perfumed woman carrying a manila folder stopped in the hallway and stared at me.

I said, "Apparently, there's no soliciting."

She shook her head. "Um. No."

I asked, "Do you purchase office supplies for your company?"

She looked at the manila folders, looked back at me, and shook her head again.

"Well, then," I said, straightening my bomber jacket. "Good day, madam."

I walked past her, the coffee machine, and Repp Tie, into the elevator and back into the cold.

THIRTY-SEVEN

Riverside Station is the best place to catch the T in the winter because the warm trains sit and wait for their scheduled departure time. I found a seat farthest from an open door. Somewhere under my clothes, my Droid vibrated and played the Bruins foghorn. I fumbled my gloves off, dug into the folds of my jacket, and saw that David Anderson wanted to talk to me.

"Tucker, why are you bothering Jack Kane?" asked David Anderson.

"I didn't think saying hello would bother him, but it turns out he's a touchy guy," I said.

"What did you want from him?"

"Information about PassHack's technology. He doesn't have any."

"Of course he doesn't have any."

"Seeing as he's your security guy."

Silence. The train started moving.

I asked, "You still there?"

"What do you want?" Anderson said.

"I want to find Maria Rizzo."

"What does that have to do with PassHack?"

"You said it yourself," I said. "You and Sal had a falling out over PassHack, seems relevant."

"You think I kidnapped his daughter? Are you fucking crazy?"

"I'm just following up on everything I can find."

"Listen, you asshole—"

"Asshole?"

"Leave me alone. Don't bother my employees. Don't investigate my businesses."

"Or?"

"Look. It's logic. Either I destroyed Sal or I didn't. If I didn't, then you have no reason to harass me."

"Okay."

"And if I did, then I'm obviously not to be fucked with."

"Are you threatening me?"

"Threatening you? No. Threats are useless."

"I'm glad we agree."

"I'm promising you. If you talk to my employees, investigate my businesses, or even Google my name, I will kill you."

The connection died.

I called Bobby Miller and was surprised when he picked up.

"David Anderson just threatened to kill me," I said.

Bobby said, "You have that effect on people."

"Just thought you'd like the heads-up."

"Is Jael sitting next to you?"

"No."

"Is she watching you?"

"No."

"Does she know that you were threatened?"

"No."

"Idiot."

"Nice."

"The war for Sal's turf just got bigger."

"How?"

"When you guys killed Pistol Salvucci—"

"Us guys? What's that supposed to mean?"

"Don't fuck with me. There were witnesses."

"Really? What did they see?"

"A tall woman dressed in black leapt over a table and killed a guy, then a guy in a suit jacket shot the other one. There was a third guy who didn't do any thing useful. That would be you."

I said nothing.

"Then the guy in the jacket took his MacBook Air and walked off down the street. Do I have to go on with this?"

"I don't see how this makes Sal's turf war bigger."

"Pistol was running a crew of ten guys."

"Okay."

"Now you got ten guys trying to take over his spot."

"It's like the Hydra."

"What?"

"You cut off a head and it grows back two."

"Yeah. So you decided to go poke one of the heads in the eye."

"I suppose."

"I figured after yesterday you'd lie low. Instead you made another enemy."

"There's got to be some connection between Anderson and Maria."

"What did you do, ask Anderson where he hid her?"

"I met a guy named Jack Kane."

A keyboard's clacking came through the phone. Bobby said, "Shit."

"What?"

"Jack Kane is in my database."

"Okay."

"My potential terrorist database."

"Oh."

"He's an ex-SEAL. Dishonorable discharge. Accused of shooting his squad leader."

"Friendly fire?"

"Bar fight."

The train rattled into Newton Center. I watched the diner in the Newton Center station pass by. They served an excellent Bloody Mary. I considered jumping off the streetcar and ordering a drink. The doors opened, they closed, I stayed put.

"Do you think he could have killed Sophia?" I asked.

Bobby said, "These are not people you should be fucking with."

"Thanks for the advice."

"At least call Jael."

"I will."

I closed the connection and waited for the train to take me home.

THIRTY-EIGHT

I STOOD ON THE sidewalk outside Hynes Station, looking for Maria. I looked up Mass Ave. Maria wasn't there. I looked down Mass Ave. Still didn't see her. Okay. Now what?

The single-digit cold chewed my earlobes. I should have worn a hat, something knit, with earflaps. That's what I'd do. I'd buy a hat. I turned down Boylston, heading for the Prudential Center.

The Pru, beyond being the skyscraper that uses its office lights to write the phrase "GO SOX" every few years, is a part of a terrible story featuring the unholy combination of petty rivalry and modern engineering. Prudential Insurance built the Prudential Center back in 1964, so as to have a taller building than the John Hancock Insurance tower. John Hancock, not being content with having a nice tower topped by a nifty weather-predicting light, put up another building—the new, mirrored John Hancock tower. The new John Hancock tower demonstrated the fact that an engineer's life is nothing but a list of problems.

Problem One: The Hancock's face was made of mirrored sheets of glass—mirrored sheets of glass that had a tendency to fire themselves into space and knife down onto the streets below. Police cleared the sidewalks, workers covered the window holes with plywood, and the John Hancock became the world's tallest plywood building. Engineers finally figured out that two-pane glass couldn't handle wind or temperature changes. They developed a new, bendy glass, and replaced all the tower's windows.

Problem Two: The tower injected a fresh new hell into the lives of cubicle dwellers—motion sickness. It swayed in the breeze. People threw up. Engineers went to work again. They installed two 300-ton weights to the 58th floor to limit swaying. It was like forcing the building to carry a couple of full shopping bags for stability. The vomiting stopped.

Problem Three: The analysis for the swaying showed that the damn thing could, honest to God, fall over like a gigantic vertical Tacoma Narrows bridge. It would have either smashed Trinity Church, destroyed the Public Library, or knocked over the old John Hancock tower. Engineers added 1,500 tons of structural steel to keep that from happening.

At the end of all this, the John Hancock company was the proud owner of a building that was 51 feet taller than its rival. A full 7 percent (if you round up).

Despite the wonderful splendiferousness of the mirrored Hancock building, the Pru has a mall. I headed there to buy a cap. My ears were transitioning from howling pain to frightening numbness. A nice warm hat and a cappuccino might make up for a death threat.

They couldn't hurt.

Once in the mall, I bought myself a stylish fleece beanie, black with an orange athletic logo. The sign next to the beanies said that the logo would show that I "meant business." I considered hopping on a train and heading back out to Riverside to show Jack Kane my beanie, let him know that I meant business.

Instead I grabbed lunch at Boston Chowda, the name an homage to the accent we adopt to delight the tourists. I'm not normally a chowder guy, but something about the way winter creeps into the deepest parts of your body makes the thought of a steaming bowl of anything the highlight of your day.

Afterward, I wandered over to the Microsoft Store to engage in some retail therapy. Men relate to technology stores the way women relate to clothing stores. We go in, fondle the merchandise, and drop into a Zen-like state where the gadget in front of us becomes a portal into thoughts of who we are, how such a gadget would fit into our lives, and what has become of our childhood fantasies.

The gadget in front of me at the moment was a Surface tablet that someone had left logged into their Facebook page. Mikey Jones had written, "I'm at the Microsoft Store" as his status. Debbie Holt had liked the fact that Mikey was at the Microsoft store. I sent Debbie a private message that said, "I love you, Debbie, please bear my children and make me sandwiches." Then I wrote Mikey's status, "I'm a big stupid-head who smells like feet" and logged him out of Facebook, having taught him a lesson about computer security.

Things could have gotten a lot worse for Mikey. I could have poked around his account, discovered his mother's maiden name, learned his email address, and perhaps even gotten his credit card numbers. Then I would have—

Maria was on Facebook.

The thought flashed into my mind like a billboard as I remembered Christmas.

Maria had been puttering around on Twitter when Sal yelled at her to put her tablet away and come to dinner. She said she would, but she didn't, so he yelled at her some more, then she turned off the iPad and came to dinner.

I like Twitter. Few people can deliver more than 140 characters of content. Facebook gives people enough space to hang themselves, as they do regularly.

That said, Maria's list of followers would give me a new place to start. Some new people to talk to. All I needed to do was get into Sal's apartment and find Maria's tablet. I'd need some help with that. I pulled out my Droid and dialed Lieutenant Lee to see if he could be useful for once.

THIRTY-NINE

"You realize that you're a murder suspect," said Lieutenant Lee in front of Sal's apartment door.

"Are you going to open the door or not, Lee?" I asked.

"Are you going to tell me what happened on Hanover Street or not?"

"Nothing happened on Hanover Street."

Lee pursed his lips, scowled. "Proverbs 19:5."

I waited. He just stood there.

I said, "Are you going to make me ask?"

Lee waited, silent.

"You know, I have a smartphone. I could just look it up."

"A false witness shall not be unpunished, and he that speaketh lies shall not escape."

"Open the damn door."

"Must you always swear?" Lee asked.

"I think you've got a Heisenberg problem, Lee."

"What's a Heisenberg problem?"

"There, now you look that up."

Lee pocketed the keys. "This was a mistake."

I raised my hands. "Okay. Okay. Heisenberg said that the observer always affects the experiment."

Lee reached into his pocket, pondering my wisdom. Pulled out the keys, pushed the key into the lock. "Are you saying that you only swear around me?"

My turn to be silent.

"Did you swear around Maria?" Lee asked.

I mentally flipped through my interactions with Maria. "Now that you mention it, no."

"Well, at least you've got some control over it."

"Can we just go in?"

Lee swung the door open. The familiar smell of burnt coffee wafted out, stale and greasy.

"Nobody cleaned the coffeemaker?" I asked.

"Nobody touched anything. At least not since we finished with the crime scene."

"Sal's going to come home to this."

"God willing, Sal will stay in prison."

"Nice thing to say about my cousin," I said, stepping into the apartment.

Lee followed. "You've never admitted it to yourself, have you?"

I skirted the fully extended dining room table that filled the small living room. Crunched through some discarded wrapping paper and headed for Maria's room. "Admitted what?"

"That your cousin is a criminal. A murderer."

I ignored the dig, pushed open Maria's door. Looked around.

"No comment?" Lee said.

I said, "There's something different in this room."

Lee stood next to me, peering into the room. "I've got pictures." Lee produced an iPhone and pulled up a panoramic view of Maria's room from the day after Christmas. We stood, heads together, comparing the photograph to a new reality.

"The iPad was on the dresser," I said.

"It's gone now."

"And that drawer was closed."

The dresser's top drawer kicked out a bit where an errant piece of underwear had lodged. I stepped into the room.

Lee grabbed my arm. "Don't touch anything," he said. "If someone was in here, we may be able to get new prints."

Lee stood next to me as I pulled on my winter gloves, padded to the dresser, gripped the bottom of the drawer, and slid it out. The underwear fell back into an empty drawer.

"Cleaned out," I said. "Someone took all her underwear."

Lee said, "And her iPad."

So much for Twitter.

I reached for another drawer, but Lee shook his head. "There's no way to open it without destroying prints."

"Sure there is."

I lay on my back, reached my hand under the dresser, and hooked my fingers around the underside of the bottom drawer. Jiggled at it until the drawer was a couple of inches open, then slid it open the rest of the way from the front. The bottom drawer was empty.

"What was in here?" Lee asked.

I thought back to the pandemonium of getting ready for the sledding trip. "Sweaters. They took her sweaters?"

The closet door hung open, Lee swung it open the rest of the way. "How many winter coats did she have?"

"She got one for Christmas, so at least two," I said.

"I don't see any here."

We backed out of the corrupted room, moved through the apartment. The kitchen was as Sophia had left it. A Bialetti full of rancid coffee sat in the sink. The bedroom was the same, except that crime scene markings had replaced Sophia's body. The living room had been tromped through to reach the other rooms. No telling what had happened in there.

Lee said, "They took only Maria's things."

"Why would a kidnapper come back for clothes and her iPad?" I asked.

"Let's go." Lee headed for the door. "Before we contaminate things further."

I followed Lee out into the hall. As he locked the door, I picked at the implications of the missing clothes. Remembered George Carlin talking about stuff, about how you had all this stuff, but when you went away for a vacation you took along a subset of your stuff, and then an even smaller subset for a weekend.

Lee headed down the stairs.

I followed. "Somebody came for her stuff."

"Her stuff?" Lee asked.

"Yeah. Like for a vacation. Except they took it all."

"Why would kidnappers take all her clothes?"

My Droid chirped its text message noise. I looked at the screen: Angie. `RU there?`

"Do you mind not texting when I am talking to you?" Lee said.

I said, "Mmmhmm" while texting. `Yes. Got a weird clue about Maria.`

`LOL`

LOL?

Lee said, "I don't have time for this."

My phone rang. It was Angie.

"Can I see you?" she asked.

"I'm glad you called. I'm at Sal's house. I've got a question for you."

"Could you meet me at the bocce courts in ten minutes?"

"Sure."

I looked up. Lee had left me standing in the hallway. I headed out Sal's front door, pulled my jacket closed and my hat down against the cold. Looked up and down Salutation Street. Lee was long gone. Must have driven off in a self-righteous, anti-texting snit.

I was alone in the North End.

FORTY

WIND WHIPPED OFF THE ocean and charged across the baseball diamonds and swimming pools that the North End had gotten as compensation for a polluted beach. The bocce courts were at the other end of the park. They'd be empty now, filled with snow. The Bruins foghorn on my phone echoed across the frozen ball fields.

I pulled off a glove so that the touch screen would recognize me as human, and swiped at the phone.

It was Jael. "Where are you going?" she asked.

"I'm going to—"

"This computer says you are in the North End."

"I am in the North End."

"It says you are walking down Commercial Street."

"I am walking down Commercial Street."

"Are you alone?"

"Yeah."

"You are walking alone there after someone tried to kill you?"

"Well, not me, really. They wanted Hugh."

"I told you not go back to the North End without me."

"Lieutenant Lee drove me."

"He is not with you now?"

"No. He dumped me."

"Stay where you are. I will meet you."

"But it's freezing here."

She hung up.

I shoved my phone back into my pocket and pulled on my glove. My aching hand chilled the interior of the glove. I'd said I'd wait here, but "here" included the park, and the park included the bocce courts. I could still meet Angie.

A car pulled up next to me and two guys got out. They wore Bruins jackets, jeans, and sneakers. They started toward me, eyeing me the way a dog eyes a rat. I wanted none of that. I climbed over a snowbank and ran.

One of them yelled, "Hey!" Not sure why that was supposed to make me stop.

Snow and parked cars blocked my way to the far sidewalk, so I ran down Commercial the wrong way, counting on drivers to do the right thing. A big Lincoln pulled out of a side street. The driver saw me and swerved—toward me. He clipped me with his bumper, knocking me up onto his hood. I hit my head on his windshield and rolled off to the side. The two guys who had been chasing me grabbed me up off the street and shoved me into the back seat of the Lincoln.

Once they had me inside, one of them shoved a gun in my neck. "Give me your fucking phone."

"Wha—?" I said.

He hit me with the gun. Lights flashed across my vision. "Your fucking cell phone. Give it to me."

I reached into my coat and pulled out the phone. The guy opened it, pulled out the battery, shoved it in his pocket. Then another smash across the back of the head, and blackness.

FORTY-ONE

COLD SLAPPED ME AWAKE as a guy in a Bruins jacket dragged me out of the car by the ankle, my coat scraping across concrete.

I shook my ankle loose. "Get off me." I flipped over onto my stomach, rose to hands and knees, and spewed my chowder across the frozen ground. The vomit spread in a steaming white puddle.

"That's fucking gross," one of the guys said.

"It doesn't matter," said another. "Get him up."

They pulled me to my feet. I was standing on a concrete plain. Flatbed shipping containers rested in stacks around us, forming streets and alleys. The sun had just given up on another winter's day. Purple clouds smeared across the sky. Two guys held my arms. Another stood in front of us with a gun.

"Sal's going to be pissed," I said.

The guy with the gun wore a torn knit Red Sox beanie. He pulled it off, tossed it aside, and smiled at me with a black-gapped grin. He stepped close and pulled off my new beanie. The cold was even worse than before. It had a gnawing marine quality. The guy pulled my hat onto his head.

"This is a good fucking hat," he said.

"I'm serious about Sal," I said, pushing on my only leverage.

"Fuck Sal," the guy said. "I worked for that guy for five years; he couldn't tell you my fucking name. He called me Gappy. He'd tell Pistol, 'Get Gappy to do it.' and Pistol would tell me, 'You heard him.' Fucking guys. I'm the boss now."

"So what's your real name?" I asked.

"Vince," he said.

"Vince Ferrari?"

"Yeah. How did you know?"

"You were in the paper. You're famous."

Vince smiled his gap grin at the two guys holding my arms. "You hear that? I'm famous."

"You don't have to kill me, Vince," I said.

"Well, I sure as fuck do now, right? Kidnapped you and all that shit. Like the paper said, there's a new boss in town."

"Who?" I asked. "Hugh Graxton?"

Vince slapped my face. The two guys holding my arms snickered.

"Fucking Graxton? You think I'd work for that faggot? He's next. I'm the new boss."

My stomach twisted. I pictured a bullet cracking through my skull. A gun held to my forehead. Then nothing. Bad time to be agnostic. I pulled at my arms and twisted, but the two goons held firmly.

"Don't kill me, Vince," I begged. "I've got nothing to do with any of this. I'm just Sal's cousin. That's all."

Vince punched me in the nose. Warm blood spurted down my face, steaming.

"Shut the fuck up," he said, then to the others, "let's get this over with."

Vince led the way as the guys dragged me down a street of shipping containers. I kicked and scrambled. It made no difference. We turned down a shipping-container alley and reached the end of it. There was a blue container secured with a padlock. Vince produced a key and worked the lock. The container would mute gunshots and screams.

"Don't do this, Vince," I said.

Vince pulled the chain off the door and opened it. Beyond the maw of a door, the container was pitch black. The two guys dragged me inside. Vince followed. He pulled the door shut behind him, blocking out the last rays of dying, purple sunlight.

"Get the light, Vince," said one of the guys holding me.

"Hold your fucking horses," said Vince. "I got it."

A bare incandescent bulb glared yellow. Sal stood beneath the bulb, gun in hand.

He shot Vince through the leg. Vince's guys let go of my arms. I dropped to the floor and scrabbled away. Gunshots boomed behind me. The blasts echoed in the shipping container, knocking me to the floor.

I got to the wall, turned. One guy lay on the ground and Sal was shooting the other one: two shots in the chest. Sal turned to Vince, kicked Vince's gun away, and pointed his own gun at Vince's nose. Vince lay on the floor, pressing his hand against a wound in his thigh.

"Fucking Vince," said Sal. Apparently he *did* know the guy's name. "What happened to Pistol?"

Vince pointed at me. "That guy killed him."

Sal looked at me. Looked back at Vince. "Yeah, right."

"Honest to God, Sal. It wasn't my fault."

"And now Tucker's here. That's not your fault?"

Vince whimpered.

"What's that?"

"I'm sorry. You were gone, Sal, I'm sorry."

"You're sorry? You're sorry for what?"

"For taking Tucker here."

"What, you're sorry for showing him the place? Is that why you brought him here, to fucking show him around?"

Vince averted his eyes. "I'm sorry."

Sal said, "You know why I'm going to let you live, Vince?"

"No," Vince said.

Sal shot him in the face. "Neither do I." Sal pulled me to my feet, his giant hand engulfing mine. "C'mon. Let's go."

"Wait a sec." I walked over to Vince, checked out my beanie. It had brain flecks on it. Vince could keep it. Took my phone from his pocket. Reassembled it. "Now we can go."

Sal turned out the light. We stepped out into the dark night. He locked the door behind us. Sodium lights buzzed, flooding us with orange light, turning our skin gray.

"Don't we have to clean up or something?" I asked.

"Why do you ask shit like that?" Sal said. "You want to get subpoenaed?"

"I just want to help."

"It's a shipping crate. It's gonna get shipped somewhere."

"That's genius."

"Shut up."

The Tobin Bridge arched above us. A black lump lay in the orange sodium lights. Sal made for it. Stood over it. "What's that?" he pointed.

"That's Vince's Red Sox hat," I said. "He got rid of it when he took mine."

Sal picked up the cap, put it in his pocket. "Guy wants to take over from me and can't do a simple job."

"You mean killing me is a simple job?"

Sal said nothing. We walked on.

"How did you get out of jail?" I asked.

"Bail."

"You agreed to help them with David Anderson, huh?"

Sal grimaced. "Why can't you just leave shit alone? Is it so fucking hard?"

We continued in silence along the black Mystic River.

"Thank you for saving me."

"You're my cousin," Sal said. His mouth twisted. He stifled something. "You're family."

I touched his shoulder. "Not your only family. You've got sisters, and we'll find Maria."

"Maria's dead," said Sal.

"No, she's not," I said.

"Yeah? How do you know?"

"She texted me," I said.

"What? Let me see the text."

I showed it to him.

Sal pointed at the text. "That's Angie."

"You ever text with Angie?"

"Text? I don't fucking text. I want to call you, I call you."

"Angie ever say LOL?"

"What the fuck is LOL?"

"Exactly. People your age don't text."

"My age? What's that supposed to mean? Angie hears you talking like that, she'll shoot you herself."

"What I mean is that Angie didn't text me. Maria texted me with Angie's phone, then Angie took it away from her and called me."

"Angie rescued Maria?" said Sal. "Then they're both as good as dead."

"Not if we get to them first," I said. We had reached Sal's Buick Regal. "You drive."

FORTY-TWO

Sal spun his wheels, turned hard, and rocketed down a long straight road with the Tobin rising on one side and the low buildings of the Charlestown Navy Yard sitting on the other.

I gripped the panic handle over the passenger door and asked, "How did you find me?"

"When I got out, I called some guys, loyal guys. They heard that Vince was going to take you out. Prove he was in charge."

"Yeah, but how did you know he'd go there?"

"Because he's got no fucking imagination. He just did what he was taught. Except I never taught him to leave a fucking DNA beanie behind."

Taught? The truth hit. I wasn't the first guy dragged into a crate. I was the first one to walk out. I rolled the revelation around in my head. Killing guys in a disposable murder scene. It was a business process, a competitive advantage, a trade secret. It was freaking patentable! It required planning, coordination, training, bribes, and guys to pick up the crate and put it on some ship. There had to be guys across the world who got the dirty crates and—what, dumped them? Cleaned them? The system required foresight and genius. Evil genius.

I had been keeping Sal in a little compartment. He was Sophia's husband, Maria's father, my first cousin, and maybe a guy who did a little crime. That was as far as I had let myself go. Now I saw that he was a guy who owned, and probably invented, a murder processing facility. I glanced at Sal as he drove, pulling up to the end of the street, turning hard, and firing us across the Charlestown Bridge.

Sal said, "So you're finally quiet."

"I'm thinking," I said.

"You're new to this stuff, baby cousin. So take my advice."

"Yeah?"

"Don't think too much."

"Easy for you to say."

"What's that supposed to mean?"

"You know how to handle yourself. I don't know what to do. Ever since I got into this, everyone wants to either kill me or arrest me."

"Welcome to my world," said Sal. We drove in silence down slushy gray streets, through scattershot intersections, and over the Charlestown Bridge into the North End.

Sal said, "I'm glad you got into this."

"Why?"

"You're the only friend I got."

I had nothing to say. Sal navigated the narrow roads in the North End, turning down smaller and smaller streets until he turned at a sign that said CLEVELAND PL and stopped in what was essentially a canyon cut between brick buildings.

"We're here," Sal said.

"Where?"

"Angie's condo."

Sal reached beneath my seat and pulled out a small gun. Handed it to me. "Be fucking careful with this."

I took the gun. "Okay."

Sal pointed at my gun hand. "Take your fucking finger off the trigger, unless you want to shoot someone."

My finger had slipped beneath the trigger guard. I pulled it out, rested it alongside the gun. My hand shook and I watched it dance. Looked at Sal. "Maybe I shouldn't have a gun."

Sal gripped my shoulder. "Stay behind me." He climbed out of the car.

Sal walked to a door, jingled through his key chain, produced a key, and unlocked the door.

"You've got a key to Angie's place?" I asked.

He put his finger to his lips, opened the door to the hallway, and whispered, "She's on the second floor."

The staircase corkscrewed up to the second floor, the steps flaring wide against the wall and narrow against the railing. We climbed, the old boards creaking with each step. This wasn't going to be a surprise. Angie's closed door slid into view.

Sal knelt in front of the door, put his ear to it, stood, and put his hand on the knob.

"You're not going to knock?" I whispered.

Sal shook his head. He pushed at me, getting me to move back down the stairs, around the corner. If there were bullets, he'd be taking them. I gripped the railing and waited. My finger had found its way under the trigger guard again. I slid it out, resting it on the side of the gun. I peeked around the corner as Sal tried the knob. It turned, and the door swung open to a dark apartment.

We waited, listened. Not a sound. Cooking smells from the apartment downstairs wafted up. Tomato gravy. I remembered my mother and her gravy, my mind drifting from this place to a different time. A dining room table. My father serving spaghetti. My mother fussing over something imperfect.

Sal took a step into the apartment. Still no sound, no light. I moved to the top of the stairs. Light from the hallway spilled into the apartment. Sal motioned for me to enter and close the door. Finger back to his lips, and a downward patting motion. *Stay here.* We weren't surprising anyone in this place. The door and the hallway light took care of that. A living room opened to one side of the door; a hallway with two bedrooms off it led to the kitchen.

Sal worked his way down that hallway, peeking into each bedroom as he slipped past. He reached the kitchen, stepped past it into another room. Turned on the kitchen light.

I stepped inside, locked the door behind me, and joined Sal in an oak-paneled kitchen with an office and bathroom off it. Apartment envy wormed its way into my thoughts. I pushed it aside and focused.

"Why was the door unlocked?" I asked.

"Good question," said Sal. "Check the office and bathroom. I'll check the rest."

I glanced through the small bathroom, peeked into the shower. No place to hide. Checked out the sink. Something was missing. Took an inventory: bar of soap, hand cream, a tube of some ointment best left alone.

No toothbrushes. No toothpaste.

The office would take longer. I surveyed the layout.

Sal called, "Tucker, come look at this."

"What did you find?"

"Come look."

I walked back down the hall and entered a girly bedroom with light pink wallpaper and a floral bedspread. Sal had opened a drawer in the dresser. It was full of little clothes.

"These are Maria's," Sal said.

"So she is with Angie."

"Yeah, but where are they?"

We stood, thinking. Not talking. If we had been talking, we wouldn't have heard it.

A footstep squeaked on the hallway stairs.

Sal slammed his hand across the light switch. "Kill the kitchen light!" he hissed. "Stay there!"

I hustled into the kitchen. Killed the light and crouched by the refrigerator, peering around the corner at the front door. Sal crouched in the hallway in front of me, aimed his gun at the door, waited.

The door lock rattled, banged as something slammed into it, then spun, moving the dead bolt. Then nothing. I slid forward down the hall, next to Sal.

"What's going on?" I whispered.

"Shh. The fucker is waiting for us to make a sound."

Silence stretched: a minute, two minutes. Sal lowered his gun.

"Damn thing is heavy," he whispered.

Three minutes. Four minutes. Five minutes.

"Did he leave?" I whispered.

Sal shook his head. "He's—"

The door kicked open. An explosion and a ball of light knocked me on my ass. I couldn't see. My ears rang. I scrambled around on the floor. Got to my knees. Looked up. A black gun bore into my face. Gloved hands held the gun steady, unmoving. I followed the line of arm. Black sleeves. Black jacket. Black hair. Beautiful eyes.

Jael Navas had the drop on us.

FORTY-THREE

Fading tinnitus rang through my ears, but I could still hear Sal say, "What the fuck, Jael?"

We stood. Jael's gun slid from view. She turned on the light and locked the door. Said to me, "I heard you were taken in the street."

"I was taken in the street," I said.

Jael said to Sal, "I thought you were in jail."

"I was in jail," Sal said.

"So our situation has improved." Jael, master of the understatement.

I said, "The guys who took me were going to kill me. They had me"—Sal shot me a look—"in Charlestown. Sal saved me."

"How did you find Tucker?" Jael asked. "His GPS was offline."

"I knew where to look," Sal said. "What are you doing here?"

"Tucker's GPS came back online. I thought he was being held."

"By Angie?" asked Sal.

"Angie?"

"This is Angie's house."

"The records say this apartment is yours."

"Yeah, well, it's Angie's."

"Tucker was taken just around the corner."

"This is the North End," Sal said. "Everything is just around the corner."

"Who told you about me being taken?" I asked.

"A friend."

"Who?"

"It is not important."

"How is that not important?"

Sal said, "Can't you see she doesn't want to tell you?"

"Yeah, I can see that," I said. "I just want to know why."

"Well, you do have a big mouth," Sal said.

You never expect the last straw to actually break the camel's back. It's a friggin' camel, for God's sake. It should be able to handle one more straw. Just like I should have been able to handle one more jibe, some cousin-to-cousin banter. A little joke with maybe a tiny kernel of truth. But this camel had been kicked, punched, knocked unconscious, shot at, flash-banged, and shoved face first against his own mortality. I had nothing left.

"Who do you think you are?" I asked Sal.

"What?" Sal said.

"Who do you think you are to talk to me like that? Like I'm a stooge. An idiot." I advanced on Sal. He took a step back.

"You hit me again, Tucker, and I swear—"

"You swear? What do you swear, Sal? You swear you're going to beat me up? Then who's going to look for Maria? You? Mr. She's Better Off Without Me? Mr.—"

"Tucker," Jael said. "This is not helping."

"What? What? You're defending him? You won't even tell me who sent you, and you're going to defend him and his fucking secrets? His lies?"

"Hey, I never lied to you," said Sal.

"No. Just don't tell me what's going on. Don't tell me what I need to know to—"

"To what?"

"To save your daughter, you shithead. To save your daughter from whatever secret bullshit deal you're pulling."

"I'm not pulling any deal."

"Oh, and the contract on Anderson? What's that?"

"You shut your mouth about that."

"Why? You think it's a big secret? The FBI told me about it. Frank Cantrell knows, Sal. The FBI already knows."

"I said shut up! You want to make Jael an accomplice?"

Jael said, "It makes no difference."

"Why not?" I asked.

"Because none of us is innocent."

"That thing on Hanover Street? That was self-defense."

Sal asked, "What exactly happened on Hanover Street?"

"Wouldn't you like to know?" I said.

"Yeah," said Sal, "I would like to know, and you're gonna tell me."

"Or else what?"

Sal cocked his fist. "Or else I swear to God—"

"Enough!" said Jael. It was the first time I'd ever heard her raise her voice. "Enough of this foolishness." Jael pointed at me. "You are lucky to be alive after your recklessness." She pointed at Sal. "You are lucky to have someone who risks his life for your daughter." She pointed between us. "Apologize."

Sal and I looked at our shoes. I chanced a peek at Sal as he was doing the same. Our eyes met. We stuck out our hands to shake. Sal grabbed my hand, pulled me in close for a bear hug.

"I'm sorry," I said.

"I know," Sal said. "It's okay."

I called it a win.

"C'mon, let's have some coffee," Sal said. "It's freezing in here." He turned and headed for the kitchen.

Jael and I followed. In the kitchen Sal bustled around like a short order cook. He took a Bialetti coffeemaker off the stove, unscrewed it, and filled the lower reservoir with water. Reached up into a cabinet, pulled down a can of coffee, popped the plastic cover off, scooped out some black coffee.

"You look like you know your way around this kitchen," I said.

"I should," said Sal. "I own it."

"I thought you said Angie lives here."

"She does live here."

"So how do you know the kitchen so well?"

"Figure it out, college boy."

Ah. Well. Time for a subject change. "What happened with you and Anderson?" I asked.

Sal screwed the Bialetti together, put it on the smallest gas burner, and turned up the fire.

"I needed a place to put cash," Sal said.

"You mean launder?"

"No. The cash was clean. I needed an investment."

"What happened?"

"He took a half mil from me, then—"

The front door rattled. A key scraped in the lock, turned. The door creaked open.

"Hello?" I called out.

"Shhh," said Jael. But she was too late. The door slammed shut.

The three of us bolted down the hallway. Pulled the door open in time to hear the downstairs door close. I ran down the stairs.

I scrambled out through the front door, looked down the alley, saw nothing, looked down the other way.

Saw a little girl in an orange pom-pom hat turning the corner.

FORTY-FOUR

Jael and Sal clambered through the door and into the street next to me. They had winter coats. The cold blew through my sweater.

I pointed. "It's Maria."

We ran down the alley, reached the end, and looked down the street. No pom-pom. She must have been running.

Like the maze from the old Adventure game, the North End was a twisty maze of passages all alike. One set of abutted brick buildings led you to another. Alleys, courts, parks provided plenty of hiding to a person with home field advantage. Fortunately, we had Sal.

I reached the end of the street. I looked both ways, didn't see a little girl or an orange pom-pom. Sal caught up to me, turned without hesitation. I followed with Jael.

"Why are we going this way?" I asked.

"If it's Maria, she'll be heading home. This way is home."

We slipped and skidded our way to Salem Street. Stopped for a look. The Old North Church towered nearby. A moving van blocked the roadway. An old man walked a thin and shivering dog down the sidewalk. A mother hustled a two-year-old past us. A car glided past, headlights battling the impending twilight. The clock on the building across the street told us that it was four. The sun would set in twenty minutes.

No orange pom-pom, no little girl.

"Are you sure you saw her?" Sal asked.

I said, "Of course I'm sure. It was her."

Jael asked Sal, "Which way is your house?"

Sal pointed through the school building, the angle of his arm indicating the middle distance. "It's over that way."

"How could she get there?"

"I don't know, a hundred different ways."

"Can't be a hundred," I said.

"Okay, math genius. It's a lot."

Jael said, "We must take different routes. Tucker, you follow this street to the end, Sal you go through the Old North Church courtyard. I will take that road."

"What if she went that way?" I pointed at another.

"There are only three of us. We must gamble."

We bolted down the street. Jael peeled off down her street, Sal ran into the Old North Church's courtyard, and I kept on straight. The moving van blocked my view and a good chunk of the street. A car came up behind me, forcing me off the road and behind the van. I climbed a snowbank, ducked under a ramp bridging the distance from the van to a stairwell, and popped up. Saw the orange pom-pom hat turn the corner.

"Maria!" I called, but the pom-pom had vanished.

Adrenaline and joy sloshed together in my gut. This was so close to being over. I ran down the street, reached the end of Salem, turned the corner, and ran into a lady carrying shopping bags. Groceries fell to the ground.

"Watch where you're going, you animal!" she said.

"Sorry. Sorry." I craned my neck around her.

"You going to help me with this?"

"I gotta go."

"Grab that can."

A can of tomatoes had rolled into the gutter. I reached for it, had it slip out of my fingers, grabbed at it again. I still didn't have a coat, and the cold was starting to get to me. Grabbed the freezing metal can, shoved it at the lady, looked down the street.

No pom-pom.

The narrow street split. One road curved out of sight. The other, called Henchmen, split away. I ran to the intersection, my teeth starting to chatter.

Henchmen Street? Seriously?

I looked down Henchmen. No Maria. Either she hadn't taken it or I'd spent too much time with Grocery Lady. I continued around the bend. The buildings formed steep walls around more twisty side streets, all alike.

I stopped at an intersection, wrapped my arms around myself, and looked down another street. Looked the other way into a park. If I were Maria, would I have taken that street? No. It led back toward where I had just come from, and I didn't see Maria pulling any sort of double-back trick. She was running somewhere. Hopefully to her house; we'd all meet there. I decided to go through the park.

It's almost impossible to shovel snow on cobblestones, and nobody had really given it a try. I crunched down a path beaten down by shortcut-takers before me. Didn't see any little footprints in the path. A concrete seal statue waited for the spring, when kids would start climbing him again. The park narrowed ahead into an alley between two buildings. I peered down the alley onto Commercial Street. Saw the orange pom-pom hat flash past. *Finally.*

I ran down the alley into Commercial, turned to chase the little girl under that hat.

Nature in Boston is, for the most part, benign. Nobody's ever seen a rattlesnake, though they're said to live in Massachusetts; the black bears content themselves with eating from bird feeders in the Berkshires; and the great white sharks that glide off our coast have never bitten anyone north of the Cape. Still, one killer lurks in our city.

I don't remember hitting the patch of black ice. Nobody ever does. One second you're going about your business, the next you're lying on the ground, perhaps with a concussion, definitely with some part of your body worse for having slammed into concrete coated by a transparent layer of invisible death.

I sat up from where I had fallen. An old guy came out of a nearby entry carrying a bucket of rock salt.

"Oh, Jesus, are you okay?" he asked.

Was I okay? I felt the back of my head. No bump, no blood. Felt my hip, no break. My shoulder? Fine. My elbow. *Holy crap!* Yup. My elbow had smashed into the concrete. Probably saved my head.

"A little help?" I said.

The guy scattered rock salt around me. I got my feet under me, and the guy gave me a pull to my feet.

"You sure you're okay?" he asked.

I flexed my arm. No grinding. No unbearable pain. A bruise.

"Yeah, I'm okay."

"Where's your coat?"

"I was only supposed to be out for a minute."

"Yeah, I know how that goes. Never go out without my coat anymore. When I was young, yeah, then it was something—"

"Thanks. I gotta get inside." I needed to find Maria. I left the guy standing on the sidewalk, throwing more rock salt, and headed down Commercial toward Sal's house. Walked past Holden Court where I had run along the roof so long ago. Mr. Follicle Disorder was walking up to his door. He wore a Follica knit hat instead of a Follica t-shirt.

"Hey," I said. "Have you seen a little girl in an orange pom-pom hat?"

"Aren't you that guy who wanted to get on my roof?" he asked.

"Yeah."

"With the fat, bald FBI agent?"

"Yeah."

"I ought to sue you and him."

"Why?"

"He pushed—"

"So you haven't seen her?"

"Who?"

"The girl in the orange pom-pom hat."

"Who?"

Idiot. "Thanks," I said. Walked on past Battery. Looked across Commercial to David Anderson's condo/lair. Would he consider that a provocation? Send Kane out to kill me? I moved on to Salutation. Turned back to Sal's place, climbed the steps. Reached his door. Knocked. No answer. Knocked again. Nothing.

Maria wasn't here.

Sal wasn't here.

Jael wasn't here.

I had no coat and no plan. Settled myself down on the top step to wait, then my cell rang. Jael. I answered, listened.

"Sal's where?" *I'll be damned.*

FORTY-FIVE

THE SUN HAD SAID, "Screw this," and set at 4:30. The cold dug its fingers into my unprotected back and shoulders, crushing my trapezius into my spine as I hustled down the street, wishing I had taken a moment to grab my coat before running after Maria. My elbow throbbed, the frigid air grinding away at its black-ice bruise. I dodged around slow-moving pedestrians on Hanover, glanced across the street at the Paul Revere statue, and pulled open the door to St. Stephen's Church.

Charles Bulfinch designed St. Stephen's in 1802 for a Congregationalist parish. Its simple square interior had always struck me as a place where one would attend a town meeting with God rather than a Mass. My mother's family had come to this church since I was little, christening, marrying, and burying a long line of Rizzos.

Sal sat alone in a pew halfway down the church. Jael sat by the door. I stopped next to her.

"I am worried about him," Jael said.

"What did he say?" I asked.

"Nothing. He just sits there."

I moved down the center aisle toward Sal. He had flipped down the kneeling bench and rested against the pew in front of him. I knelt next to him and said nothing. He'd talk when he was ready.

The cold that had sliced into my joints kept up its pressure. The church was heated, but winter cold finds you no matter where you go. I rubbed my elbow, feeling around for the knot.

"What happened to you?" Sal asked.

"Black ice," I said.

"Jesus. You okay?"

"Nailed my elbow."

"You're lucky."

"Yeah."

Silence.

I looked around the church, my eyes floating over the Corinthian columns that held up a second-level balcony. Twisted in my seat to look at the organ that had played a dirge for my mother at her funeral. Sal followed my eyes.

"Angie sings up there," he said.

"I know. She sang at my mother's funeral."

"Sang at Marco's funeral too."

Was this the right time? There'd never be a right time. "What happened at Marco's funeral?"

"What do you mean?"

"Frank Cantrell told me that you had a fight with Joey Pupo and walked out of it."

"I gotta have a talk with Frank Cantrell."

"What happened?"

"I fucked up. That's what happened."

"How?"

"You get that Joey, Marco, and I were friends since we were kids?"

"Yeah."

"I mean, Joey was always sucking hind tit, but still, we were friends."

"Right."

"Then one day Joey comes over and kills Marco."

"How do you know?"

"I saw him. Marco and I were watching the Bruins game in Marco's man cave. Joey knocks on the door and says that he told Marco to stay away from Angie. Then he shot him." Sal tapped my chest twice, then my forehead. "Two in the chest, one in the head. Then he went home. I should have killed Joey then, but Marco wasn't dead. I held that fucking guy in my arms. Watched him die."

"What did you do then?" I asked.

"I got stupid. Came to Marco's funeral, listened to the priest, thought about forgiveness, gave Joey a chance to turn himself in."

"It was the right thing to do."

"Yeah, sure, the right thing to do." Sal twisted on his knees to face me. "What did it get me? If I had just killed Joey, just gone over to his apartment and did the same to him that he did to Marco, none of this would have happened."

"You don't know that."

Sal turned to face the altar. "It's all my fault. I should just shoot myself."

Oh for Christ's sake, here we go. "Don't say that," I said.

"What do you know about it?"

"I know you can't talk that way."

"What do I got to live for?"

Screw this. I said, "You know, you're right."

"What?"

"You should just go shoot yourself. We'd all be better off."

"What the fuck's wrong with you?"

"Except maybe Angie, she'd lose that sweet apartment."

"All right, that's enough."

"Seriously, you and Angie?"

Sal said, low and quiet, "You stay away from that."

"Beautiful wife like Sophia, and you're fucking a *putana* like Angie?"

Sal grabbed my shirtfront. "It's none of your business."

"I thought you loved Sophia."

Sal pulled a hand back, ready to slap me. I stuck my chin out, ready to take it.

"Of course I loved her."

"Then why Angie?"

The hand came in, tapped my cheek. "I know what you're doing, little cousin," he said. He released my shirtfront and turned to face the altar.

"Did it work?" I asked. "Or are you still going to shoot yourself?"

Silence.

I faced the altar. Took a deep breath.

Sal said, "Why don't you go?"

"I can't go," I said.

"Why not?"

"I don't have a coat."

Sal looked at me out of the corner of his eye, a little smile tugging at his face.

He said, "You're a fucking idiot, you know that?"

I shrugged. "What can you do?"

Sal stood, pulled off his black greatcoat, rested it over my shoulders, and wrapped it around me like a blanket, still warm from his back. The warmth seeped through my shoulders.

"You're right," he said. "I'm not going to shoot myself."

"Good," I said.

"But I'm going to shoot someone, that's for damn sure."

"Jesus, Sal we're in a church."

"Jesus would agree with me." Sal called out to the altar, "Right, Jesus?"

Jesus had nothing to say.

We stood, walked back down the aisle. Jael joined us as we pushed the doors open. The cold buffeted us, but Sal's coat kept me warm.

FORTY-SIX

SAL POURED BLACK COFFEE from the Bialetti coffeemaker into a small coffee cup and slid it in front of me, then he poured two more for himself and Jael.

It was bitter as hell. "Wow," I said. "Did you burn this?"

"No," said Sal. "I turned off the fire before I ran out. Didn't want to torch the house."

"Why is it so bitter?"

"It's always like that," Sal said.

"It is an acquired taste," said Jael. "It is the only coffee I've had in America that tastes like coffee."

Angie's kitchen made mine look like a kid's toy set. Where I had a nook separated from the rest of my condo by a countertop, Angie had room for an entire wooden table. We sat around the table and drank black coffee.

"How is it that Angie lives here?"

"What do you mean *how*?"

"How is it that you gave Angie a place to live?"

"It's none of your fucking business, that's how."

"Oh, I'm sorry. I thought that seeing as it looks like Angie has Maria, this was all relevant."

Sal picked up his coffee cup. "I don't think that girl you saw was Maria."

"What are you talking about? She was wearing Maria's hat."

"I never saw the girl in the hat," Jael said.

"Neither did I," said Sal.

I said, "So you guys think I'm lying."

"No," said Jael.

"I imagined it?"

Silence.

"Really," I said. "You guys think I imagined a girl in an orange pom-pom?"

Jael gave me a look: *It's happened before.*

"That was a long time ago," I said.

More silence.

I said, "Totally different situation."

Sal looked from one of us to the other. "What? What are you talking about?"

"Now it's none of your fucking business," I said.

"What's none of my fucking business?" Sal said. Then to Jael, "What's he talking about?"

"Tucker will have to tell you," Jael said.

I stood and pulled on my coat. "I don't want to talk about it."

"Tell me what?" Sal asked.

"You haven't earned it." I headed for the door.

"Earned what?"

"You start trusting me with your secrets and I'll start trusting you with mine." I banged through the front door, down the steps, and into the street.

It was dark and I was starving. Fortunately I was in the right place. Boston's North End has literally hundreds of restaurants, but I only had eyes for one.

I headed toward home, zigging down one street and zagging down another until reached my goal: 11½ Thatcher Street, or Regina Pizzeria. I have no idea how you get an address like 11½; it probably comes from being on the corner of one of those Boston intersections that made sense for horses, but not for cars.

I walked past a line of people waiting for tables, climbed the steps, pulled open the door, and allowed myself to be enveloped by the aroma of bread and tomato sauce. Stopped, took a deep breath, and got hit by someone coming in behind me.

"Jesus, buddy, move it."

Happy holidays to you too.

The bar was full, but a lone surface was crammed behind the coat rack, a little table that faced straight into the wall and a poster sharing Boston's many firsts: first public park, first sewing machine, first college, the list goes on. I settled into the nook and turned to catch the bartender's attention. Police Department patches festooned the wooden shelving and a neon sign declared that Peroni was "Italy's #1 Beer." I ordered a Peroni and a slice of pepperoni. Tweeted:

`Calling Peroni Italy's #1 Beer is like calling someone America's #1 Soccer player #beersnobbing`

They arrived and I tasted the Peroni. Turned out that Italy's #1 beer is pretty good, probably like America's #1 soccer player. I relaxed into my dinner, happy to stop moving for the first time all day.

It was a bad idea, because that was when the thinking started.

Maria had not been a figment of my imagination. Sure, there was a time when I'd had long conversations—arguments, really—with my dead wife, Carol. But Carol would appear in front of me, wearing her funeral dress and taunting me. She'd never led me on a chase through the city. No. The girl in the orange pom-pom was real, and she was Maria. Maria was safe somewhere in the North End with Angie.

Which raised a simple solution to the problem: I called Angie.

Her phone rang five times, then went to voicemail. "Hey Angie, it's me, Tucker. Call me."

That should do it: one whiff of the old Tucker charm brings them right out of the woodwork. Tried calling her again, just in case. Went to voicemail immediately. Angie had looked at my name and chosen not to take the call. So much for the charm; she probably hadn't heard the voicemail.

I'd give the charm one last try. Made a phone call. Caroline picked up on the first ring.

"Where are you?" she asked.

"Regina Pizzeria, why?"

"I just heard some things. I was worried."

"If you heard what I think you heard, then you were right to worry."

"What happened?"

"I'm in a public place. Let's just say that you saved my life today by getting Sal out on bail."

"Oh my God."

"And how was your day?"

"You're going to act like nothing happened?"

"For as long as I can. I've gotten pretty good at repressing things, though I could use a hug."

"You're going to need more than a hug."

"You have a bazooka?"

Caroline switched subjects on me. "Where's Sal?"

"I left him at Angie's place, or his place, or something," I said.

"What's that mean?"

"Long story."

"You left him there?" Caroline asked.

"With Jael, though she'll probably head out soon."

"Tucker, don't leave him alone. He didn't look so good today."

"Really? You want me to go back there?"

"Could you?"

I blew out a heavy sigh.

Caroline said, "He trusts you."

"Oh, that's why he never tells me anything?"

"He's protecting you. He never wants you to get subpoenaed."

"He's a big pain in the ass."

"Tell me something I don't know."

"So you see my point."

"He needs you."

I chewed some pizza, washed it down with Peroni. "Yeah, I'll go back over there."

"Thanks."

"So, that lunch we had yesterday," I said. "Was that a date?"

"Do you want it to be a date?"

"Absolutely."

"Then it was a date."

"When could we have a second date? Or is that forward and creepy?"

"I'm busy tonight, but soon."

"How soon?"

"Go help your cousin," Caroline said and hung up.

Go help my cousin. I drank my beer, tore at my pizza. Thought about Sal screwing Angie, shook my head. *The shit catches up with you eventually. Love to know the story that led to Angie getting an apartment.*

My phone rang.

It was Sal. "You want me to trust you?" he asked.

"Yeah."

"I'm trusting you. We've got a meeting, I'm gonna clear some shit up. You in?"

"Yeah, I'm in."

Subpoena, here I come.

FORTY-SEVEN

THERE IS NO CLEARER sky than the one overarching a frigid winter night. I hunched into my coat as I stared up at bright stars punching their way through light pollution over Commonwealth Avenue. Sal, Jael, and I formed a small circle within the arms of a memorial to nineteen firefighters killed in the Hotel Vendome fire. The snow had slipped off the memorial's low granite wall, exposing quotes from the firefighters. My eye followed the line of stone to a firefighter's helmet and coat, seemingly left by an owner who would return for it, though we knew he wouldn't. Beyond the hat was the spot where the hotel had collapsed.

"Jesus, it's cold," I said. "Why are we out here?"

"Because nobody else is here, and I have to meet someone," said Sal.

"Who?"

"Here he comes."

Frank Cantrell joined us in the circle. "Hi, Sal."

Sal punched him in the stomach.

Cantrell doubled over, wrapping his arms across his gut.

I said, "What the hell are you doing?"

"Payback," said Sal.

Jael watched, relaxed but ready for action.

"Urrgggh," Cantrell said.

"You fucking asshole," Sal told him. "I paid you twenty thousand a month to keep me the fuck out of jail." He stepped forward.

Cantrell, still bent over, stepped back. Put out his hand in a placating gesture. "I did my best, Sal. Miller kept me out of the loop."

"Because you blew it," Sal said. "He suspects something, doesn't he?"

"Hey, I got you out."

"After—"

Sal's argument with Cantrell drifted away as I processed what I was hearing. I was no longer straddling two worlds. Until today, until this moment, I had told myself that I had nothing to do with Sal's profession. To others he might be a gangster, maybe even a murderer, but to me he was Cousin Sal. And me? I was just the guy who came over for Christmas dinner and took Maria sledding.

Now I was an accomplice. I'd watched Sal kill Vince and his crew. The shipping crate was going someplace where they didn't care about crime scenes. I was standing next to Jael, who had killed the guy on Hanover Street, and I had watched Hugh Graxton kill the other. This was the final coffin nail. Frank Cantrell was a dirty FBI agent, and Sal had been running him.

I was dirty too.

I heard the name "Caroline" and rejoined the conversation.

"Caroline?" Frank said.

"That's right." Sal poked Cantrell in the chest. "Caroline got me out of jail, and now I'm a fucking snitch."

"Well, you shouldn't have strangled your wife!" said Cantrell.

"You cocksucker, I will fucking kill you!" Sal took a step forward. Jael moved to intercept him.

Cantrell held up a finger. "Don't you touch me again." He stepped back. Straightened his coat. "I'm still an FBI officer."

"He is right," Jael said. "Also, it would be hard to explain his beating if you left marks."

"I didn't kill Sophia," Sal said to Cantrell. "Why would I kill Sophia?"

"Word has it that she was fucking Marco."

Cantrell was standing too close. Sal's right fist smashed him in the nose. Cantrell spun, blood spraying across the snow from his shattered nose.

Sal grabbed Cantrell by the jacket, blood splashing onto both of them. He cocked his fist. "She's the mother of my kid!"

Cantrell covered his face. "Okay. Okay. I'm sorry."

Sal pushed Cantrell, who staggered back and wound up sitting on the memorial wall. "Get the fuck out of here, you useless piece of shit."

Jael tugged on my arm. "We should leave."

Blood drops dotted the snow around the monument. Cantrell leaned against the wall, catching his breath. Sal turned away and started down Commonwealth Ave toward the Public Garden. Jael and I started toward Kenmore Square. We walked through the cold, single-digit snow crunching under our feet. I was too cold to shiver; I hunched my shoulders instead. My bare head radiated my body heat into the night. My ears were beyond aching.

"Israel is warm, right?" I asked.

Jael said, "Yes."

"Even in the winter?"

"The winters are pleasant."

"How do you deal with this weather?"

"I wear a hat."

"Why did you move to Boston? It's so cold."

"The snow can be beautiful."

"But Bostonians are rude."

"You have not been to Israel."

"And there are people shooting each other!"

Jael stopped in front of a statue of a guy sitting on a rock. He looked over us, holding binoculars. He looked as if he had been watching Sal beat up an FBI agent. He had a stack of books next to him, covered in ice. I stood in front of Jael. We were the same height. She looked at me, into my eyes. What did she see there? She took the black knit cap from her head and pulled it down over my ears. It was warm from her body heat. A little twitch took hold of the corner of my mouth. My throat tightened. Jael pulled me close in a sisterly hug, her chin on my shoulder. She gave me a squeeze and said, "You are safe now."

I touched the spot on my face where Vince had hit me. Three guys had dragged me into a shipping crate. I felt the fear again. I'd stuffed it down in front of Sal, forgotten about it when I was chasing Maria, and thought I had washed it away with a Peroni and a slice of pepperoni. But I hadn't. Jael's hug cracked me open. I wrapped my arms around her and sobbed. "They were going to kill me."

"I know."

"Sal saved me. He knew where they'd take me."

"He loves you very much."

My sobbing deepened. "But he's a crook," I said.

"Shhh."

We stood that way for I don't know how long, Jael holding me tight as I sobbed it out.

FORTY-EIGHT

I WAVED TO JAEL as she pulled her Acura MDX onto Newbury Street, toward the Pike. The woman had a genius for finding parking. I turned toward home. My chest felt hollow, a side effect of uncontrollable sobbing. It's supposed to make you feel better. I just felt empty.

And then I was standing in front of Bukowski Tavern, trying to remember how I got there and why I had stopped. It was on the way home. I considered walking past the bar, going home. I could feed the hermit crabs, take a shower, and sleep. I took a step, then stopped. Remained rooted to the spot. Pictured myself sitting alone in a dark house, guzzling rye whiskey and talking to two crustaceans. Imagined the ticking sounds of a cooling apartment, the blue glow of a computer screen, and a little pool of light where I could replay the events of the day in my head until—until when? Until I passed out, I guessed. I didn't see how sleep would happen.

Cars zoomed under Dalton Street, following the Mass Pike toward the airport. Cold reached down my coat's collar. My head had been so cold that I hadn't noticed my neck. I needed a scarf. Needed to warm up a bit. Took a step into the Tavern, worked the ATM, got fifty dollars of cash. Sat at the bar.

Bridgette, tall, toned, and broad-shouldered, greeted me with a nod. Unlike most female bartenders, she made no pretense of flirting with her male customers—no come-hither eyes, brilliant smiles, or chest-thrusting poses. She exuded confidence and power. I'd once tried to imagine sleeping with Bridgette. Nothing had come to mind.

Bridgette pushed the beer list toward me.

I pushed it aside. "Knob Creek, neat. A double, please."

An arched eyebrow. "Really?"

She came back with an on-the-rocks glass half-filled with bourbon. Slid it in front of me. I picked it up, knocked it back, let the bourbon burn my throat, placed it on the bar.

Bridgette pursed her lips. "I've never seen you do that."

"Been a big day. Refill, please."

Bridgette refilled the glass and stepped away. I closed my eyes, felt the alcohol slip into my blood stream, climb to my brain, and knock on my pleasure center. *Hello, who is it? Knob Creek. Why HELLO, Mr. Creek.*

I giggled.

A meaty hand slammed me on the shoulder, startling me out of my conversation with my whiskey.

Bobby Miller said, "Look at that. You *are* here."

I blinked. "Yeah. Why wouldn't I be here? What are you doing here?"

Bobby dropped his iPhone on the bar and pointed at a map with two little dots overlapping each other. Bobby's FBI map. "Your dot was here, my dot was passing by, thought I'd drop in."

"You were following me today?"

Bobby continued to point. "Well, following your dot. It's been on the move. Even disappeared for a while."

My dot. Bobby had been tracking my phone, a phone that had travelled to hell and back.

"It's probably just as well," I said, "because—"

"Because?"

Because mobsters abducted me, but Sal shot them in their secret killing crate, and then Sal punched your dirty colleague, Frank, in the face. Because I can't tell you any of this. I shot back my bourbon. "Because you were able to find me. Have a drink!"

"You're awfully happy."

"I just did a shot."

"You never do shots."

I motioned to Bridgette for a refill.

She refilled me. "You're not driving, right?"

"No, ma'am."

"What's wrong with you?" Bobby asked.

Bridgette said, "It's been a big day."

I pointed at Bridgette and winked. "Exactly."

"Honey, would you get me whatever's in the cask?" Bobby said.

"Honey?" said Bridgette.

Uh oh.

Bridgette pointed at Bobby with her thumb. "Can you believe he called me 'Honey'?"

Bobby said, "What?"

"She hates that," I said.

"Hates what?"

"Guys thinking I'm their honey," said Bridgette.

"Could I just have a beer, please?"

"Yes," said Bridgette.

"And hold the spit."

If laser beams could shoot from a woman's eyes, Bobby's bald head would have exploded right there.

Bobby turned to me. "What were you doing on Commonwealth?"

"Whaa—?"

"Commonwealth. You were just on Commonwealth Ave."

It was decision time. Bobby needed to know his colleague was dirty. But then Sal was going back to jail. Once the truth started to escape, it would rush out until the whole mess lay at our feet. But Bobby was my best friend, and he was in danger.

"I was looking at the statues." I needed more time. Couldn't give Sal up yet.

"The statues," Bobby said.

"The one with the firefighters."

"In the dark?"

"It's beautiful at night."

I knocked back my third double, nodded. Made eye contact with Bridgette, pointed at the glass.

Bridgette said, "Maybe a beer?"

"I'd rather not," I said.

"I really think you should try a beer," Bridgette said. She handed me Bobby's beer. "It's on the house."

"What about me?" Bobby said.

Bridgette ignored him.

"Aw, c'mon!" Bobby said.

I took Bobby's beer. "Probably shouldn't have made the spit joke."

"What were you doing in Charlestown today?"

I pulled my phone out, showed Bobby the text. "I got this today."

"*LOL?*"

"I think it's Maria using Angie's phone. Angie would never type LOL."

"Maria's with Angela Morielli?"

"Also, I think I saw Maria today in the North End, but there's no way to figure out where they're hiding."

"Good God, Tucker," Bobby said. "You have a lead. You have an honest to God lead."

"Yeah, but how do I find Angie?"

"We use her GPS."

"She's not running a GPS app."

"The FBI doesn't use a GPS app." Bobby took out his phone, made a call. "Yeah. I need to know the location of a phone."

There followed a discussion of warrants, probable cause, endangerment of a minor, and calling in old favors. At the end of it Bobby recited Angie's phone number. Waited. Got a text that held the picture of a map.

Bobby looked at the picture and shook his head.

"What?" I asked. "Where's Angie's phone?"

Bobby showed me his phone. "This isn't good."

FORTY-NINE

"A CELL PHONE ON a river is never a good sign," said Bobby.

"Beats *in* the river," I said.

"Aren't you a ray of sunshine?"

We stood on the edge of the Charles River next to Harvard Bridge. Traffic buzzed above us, following the bridge into Cambridge.

Angie's cell phone GPS had led us to this spot. Apparently the phone was out there, broadcasting its GPS signal. I peered into the night, but couldn't see it despite the snow reflecting the city lights.

"We should wait until tomorrow," said Bobby. "Come back and find it when we have some light."

"The battery will probably be dead by then," I said.

"Well, we can't find it in the dark, and I'm not walking on the ice."

I took out my Droid, found Angie's number, and pressed dial. A lonely simulated bell rang out across the ice.

"I'll get it," I said. Headed toward the river.

Bobby grabbed my arm. "Don't be an idiot. What do you think this is, Moscow? That ice won't hold you."

I took a tentative step onto the ice. Listened for cracking. Heard nothing.

"It's fine," I said. "It's been really cold lately."

Bobby took a step onto the ice. I stopped him with a gesture. "Let's not press our luck, big fella."

"Are you shitting me? You're going out alone?"

I rang Angie's phone again. It was about fifty feet out. It had to have been thrown there, either off the bridge or from the shore. Either way, landing in the snow had kept it from shattering. Took another step. No cracking sounds.

Bobby placed a call. "We'll need a ladder truck down here. Get an ice rescue team. No. Nobody's in the river ... yet."

I took another step, then another, walking toward the spot where I'd heard the phone. Dialed the number again. Nothing. Tried again. Nothing. Looked at my phone. Five bars. Angie's phone battery had died.

"The battery just died," I called back.

"Then get back here!"

I kept my eyes fixed on the spot in the snow where I'd heard the last ring. I saw a little gray speck in the white. An indentation? A hole? A spot where a phone might have splashed onto a drift? Kept walking, stepping, listening. No cracking. Well—maybe that was cracking. Maybe that was just my shoe scraping on the ice.

The river ice had frozen, been snowed upon, then shone upon by a cold sun. It was hard to tell which of those processes had won. Was the ice thicker or thinner? The snow on it had melted and refrozen into a crunchy pack. I didn't slip as I walked on it, but I couldn't hear through it. If the ice started cracking, I'd have to feel it in my feet. If I felt it in my feet, it was probably too late.

I reached the spot where I thought I'd heard the ringer. Tried it again. Nothing. I'd killed it. Surveyed the snow pile looking for a disturbance, some disturbance that hadn't been created by the wind. Couldn't see a thing. Despite the lights of Boston all around me, the snow in front of me was a smooth, undifferentiated gray. It held no sharp shadows. No way to see a slice in the snow where a phone might have landed.

"Can you see anything?" Bobby called.

"No, it's too dark."

"Okay. Then get back here."

"Just a second."

I used my Droid's LED as a flashlight. Directed it across the snow, was greeted by the curves and swoops of windblown snow. No phone. No hole.

"Jesus, Tucker, get the fuck back here!" Bobby shouted. "It could be anywhere!"

It couldn't be anywhere. It needed to be somewhere within five feet of me. I broadened my search, sweeping the light out and across a broader patch of snow. The light dimmed quickly with distance, so I began to walk in a small circle, shuffling my feet to avoid crushing the phone. Shuffled parallel to the shore, turned, headed out toward the middle of the river. No phone. No phone. Smooth snow. Nothing. Nothing.

Clunk.

Looked down and saw the damn phone leaning up against my Tom Brady-approved UGGs. Bent over, picked it up.

Fell through the ice.

It turns out that ice doesn't crack all that loudly when it goes. A little crinkle, a whooshing sound, and I was falling.

I tossed Angie's phone and my Droid toward the shore and grabbed onto the ice with gloved hands while the river tried to rip me away.

On a warm summer's day, with the sun shining, and kids cavorting in sailboats, the Charles River looks like a lake. The water drifts toward the sea, its current hidden by its width and placidity. This is an optical illusion.

The river churned past my ass. Heavy frozen water pulled at me, trying to get my center of gravity below the waterline. Then it would be able to take me away.

"Hold on, Tucker!" Bobby charged onto the ice.

"No!" I shouted. "It won't hold you."

Bobby didn't stop. He skidded out, picking up speed. My ass slid lower and my chest tilted up as the balance shifted. I lost another five inches to the water rushing under the hole. Ten feet away, Bobby launched himself in a slide, lay out across the ice, and grabbed my wrists. I grabbed his.

"Just hold on," he said. "They're coming for us."

Bobby's weight gave me the purchase I needed. The water was frigid. My toes went numb first, then my legs. My grip was loosening. If I went under, Bobby wouldn't know about Frank Cantrell, and Cantrell would probably get him killed.

"Bobby," I said.

"Just hold on."

"I need to tell you something. Something important."

Bobby grunted. "Can't you just wait? This is a lot of work."

"But I have to tell you that Frank—"

"Remain calm!" A bullhorned voice boomed from the shoreline, where a group of firefighters carried a ladder and ropes.

"You think I should wave to them?" Bobby said.

I gripped his wrist harder. Bobby grinned.

"Asshole," I said.

"And you're a stupid fuck," he said, "but you're safe."

Later I sat in Bobby's car, blankets wrapped around my frozen legs, a cup of coffee steaming in my hand.

Bobby handed me my phone, attached Angie's phone to his car charger.

"Let's see what's on this thing," said Bobby.

I shivered, drank my coffee. I needed to tell him that his colleague was a dirty bastard, that Bobby couldn't trust him. I needed to tell him that Sal had been running Cantrell for years. But telling Bobby about Cantrell would finish Sal, put him away. Maria wouldn't have a mother or a father. Sal was family. He'd saved my life.

"What were you saying about Frank?" asked Bobby.

"I was going to say—"

The phone blooped to life. Bobby poked at it with a meaty finger. "How do you get the text messages?"

"Give it here." I took the phone. The screen looked like a Mondrian painting, with icons sitting in tiled boxes, a consequence of someone avoiding Apple's patent-happy lawyers. I muttered a quiet prayer of thanks that Apple hadn't invented the car; we'd be stuck with three different kinds of steering wheels. Found the text message app and opened it. There was Maria's text to me:

"LOL"

Bobby said, "Check the email."

I fiddled with the Mondrian squares, pulled up the email. It was connected to Angie's Gmail account. Apparently she was a deleter, one of those people who think that an empty inbox is a happy inbox. There was only one message, sent while Sal was punching Frank Cantrell.

You're in danger. Meet me at the Mass Ave Bridge. Bring Maria.

Hugh

Bobby and I read the email, looked at each other, and said in unison, "Motherfucker."

FIFTY

HUGH GRAXTON'S NEWTON HOME towered above us, its assortment of stucco walls, wooden beams, and gables creating spiky shadows against the night sky.

"Great," I said. "He lives in a haunted house."

"It's a Tudor Revival," said Bobby. "They were popular during the Depression."

"How do you know that?"

"I always knew it."

We climbed the three steps in front of the house, approached the front door, rang the bell. The house was dark, silent, except for the simple *bing-bong* of the bell. Bobby *bing-bonged* it again. Waited. Then pressed it rapidly: *bing-bong-bing-bong-bing-bong-bing-bong.*

"You are just the master at making an entrance," I said.

A light came on in an upper window.

"I am," said Bobby.

"Making an entrance and making friends."

"I'm not here to make friends. Neither are you. I'll bet you Angie's in there."

"Doubt it."

"Really, smart guy? Why?"

"Makes no sense. What would Hugh want with Angie, and why would he hide her in his house?"

"Who knows? All we know is that Angie got an email from Hugh, and Angie's phone was thrown off the bridge."

"Something's—"

The door cracked open.

"FBI," Bobby said. "We'd like to speak to Hugh."

A just-woken voice said, "Hugh isn't here."

"We'd like to ask you some questions. It's official." Bobby waved his credentials at the door crack.

A young woman's face appeared in the crack, looked at the credentials, and disappeared. The door closed, then swung open.

A girl in a Boston College t-shirt turned on the hall light. She had blond hair, long legs, and nipples that poked out from the words *Boston* and *College*. We stepped in and closed the door behind us, keeping out the cold.

"I'm Special Agent Miller," Bobby said. "This is Mr. Tucker."

"You can call me Tucker."

"I'm Sandy Cameron."

"We need to ask you a few questions," said Bobby.

"Hugh told me to never talk to the cops or let them in the house," she said.

"Yet you let us in," Bobby said. "Why?"

"Hugh's missing."

"What do you mean, missing?"

"He went out to work yesterday morning and never came back."

"Did you try calling him?"

"His cell phone is dead."

Bobby scribbled into his book. "What's your relationship to Hugh?"

"I rent a room here."

Bobby cocked an eyebrow. Looked at me. "You're a boarder?"

"Yeah."

"You pay to live here?"

Sandy looked away. I wondered what Hugh considered payment.

"It's easy to get to classes," she said. "I go to BC."

"What's your major?"

"Biochem."

"You mean with the Krebs cycle and stuff like that?" I asked.

"More like splicing DNA. Protein replication. Stuff like that."

Bobby asked, "Did Hugh say anything? Did he seem nervous."

"Yes," Sandy said. "He said that things were heating up in Boston."

Bobby asked, "What things?"

"I don't know. He didn't tell me."

"We think that Hugh was involved in a shooting on Hanover Street yesterday."

"Oh God. Is he hurt?"

"When he left he was fine," I said.

Bobby turned to me. "How would you know?"

"Or so I am told," I said.

"By who?"

Dammit. Trapped!

I said to Bobby, "Let's talk about this later."

"No," Bobby said. "Let's talk about this now."

"I can't go into it now."

"You can't go into it? What the fuck does that mean?"

Sandy crossed her arms, hunched up. "Can you guys do this somewhere else? It's cold."

"Sorry to disturb you, miss." Bobby handed Sandy a business card. "Call me if Hugh shows up, okay?"

In front of the house, Bobby said, "How did you know what happened to Hugh yesterday?"

"Um—"

"Don't you fucking lie to me. You were there, weren't you?"

I saw Jael, launching herself off the tabletop, firing down onto Pistol Salvucci as he shot at me. She didn't have to be there. None of this was her fight. She didn't deserve an arrest, a jail term, deportation. *What will you tell the police? I will tell them nothing.*

"I was there," I said.

"Who else was there?"

"Hugh, another guy."

"The witnesses said there was a woman."

"The witnesses were mistaken." I worked to control my thoughts, tell myself that this was the truth, keep the deception off my face.

"You're fucking lying to me," said Bobby.

"I'm not."

"You just did it again! It's all over your face."

"Stop it."

"It was Jael, wasn't it?"

My eyes pulled wide. "No, it wasn't."

"I pulled your ass out of the fucking river, and this is how you repay me?"

"Look, can we just go?"

"*We?* What's this fucking *we?* You're actually going to stand there, fucking lie to my face, and then expect a fucking ride home? There is no *we*."

Bobby walked around his car. Worked the fob once, unlocking the driver's door. He pointed. "The fucking T stop is that way. Newton Center. Get walking."

He slid into his car, slammed the door, and drove away, his tires kicking up rock salt and road sand.

I didn't blame him one bit. I turned, freezing in my damp cotton jeans, and started for the T station.

At one in the morning I finally dropped into bed. Had hyperrealistic dreams in which I shot Bobby dead with Frank Cantrell's gun.

FIFTY-ONE

The Boston Bruins foghorn blared. Screaming fans jumped to their feet. The Jumbotron screen in the center of the Garden showed the replay of my one-timer blasting past a Bobby Miller goalie. The foghorn blared again, and a third time. I opened my eyes, pulling myself out of the dream. My phone rang a fourth time, foghorning me into action.

"Tucker? It's Caroline."

"Whaa?" The sky outside showed the slightest gray hint of dawn. "What time is it?"

"Seven. Did I wake you?"

I nearly wept. "Seven?"

"Would you like to have breakfast?"

"Yeah. Sure. When?"

My doorbell rang.

"Now."

The call ended. My doorbell rang again. I untwisted my sheets, stumbled out of bed, pressed the intercom.

"Hullo," I said.

Caroline's voice crackled through the intercom. "It's me, sleepyhead."

"C'mon up."

I pressed the buzzer, opened my apartment door, and heard the street door open below. Looked down at myself, saw nothing but boxers. Stumbled back into my room, found sweatpants and a t-shirt that read *Code Monkey.*

When I returned, Caroline stood in in my apartment, wearing a big green peacoat. She carried a bag of bagels and a cardboard tray with two gigantic Starbucks coffees. At least it wasn't Dunkin' Donuts.

"You don't have a problem with gluten, do you?" she asked.

My brain clanked and groaned. "Gluten?"

"The bagels have gluten."

"No. No. I like gluten."

"Good."

"What brings you here?"

Caroline put the bagels on the counter and walked toward me, unbuttoning her peacoat. The coat fell open to reveal black yoga pants, a red prosthetic, a green sports bra, and a bare midriff. Caroline followed my eyes down to her red prosthetic.

"It goes with the green bra," she said. "For Christmas."

I felt my sweatpants start to reveal something, Caroline's outfit exacerbating my typical morning stiffness. I needed to put a counter between us or things would get obvious. Stepped around Caroline, behind the breakfast nook, and started to unload the bagels.

Caroline removed her peacoat. I would have taken it from her, but that would have required coming out from behind the breakfast counter. "You can just toss that into my office," I said.

Caroline turned to stash the coat and I got to see the backside of her outfit. The person who invented yoga pants deserves a Nobel Prize. My sweatpants bumped the breakfast counter. A tiny groan escaped.

Caroline returned. "Did you say something?"

"No," I said. "Are you dressed for exercise?" *Stupid question.*

"Yup. Yoga."

"Do you do yoga often?" I arranged the six bagels Caroline had brought on a plate.

Caroline sat on one of the kitchen stools. "Every day."

"What kind?"

"Bikram hot yoga."

"Ah," I said, cutting the first bagel. "What does it do for you?"

"It makes me hot."

I swallowed. "You mean like 'boy, it's hot out' hot or 'you look hot' hot?"

"Every kind of hot."

I arranged the bagel so that the halves were slightly offset, then started on the second bagel. "Are you going to yoga or coming from yoga?"

"I rarely come from yoga."

I gave a goofy spasmodic laugh. I think I snorted. Continued cutting bagels and arranging them in a circle. The Starbucks coffee had the generic burnt flavor that had made them famous. "Good coffee!"

"It's the Christmas Blend."

"Festive."

I turned to my cabinets, grabbed a little glass bowl, turned back and started scooping the cream cheese from its paper container into the bowl.

"What are you doing?" Caroline asked.

"Who, me? Nothing. I'm just making things look nice."

"You really don't have to do that."

"I just hate eating out of paper." I placed the cream cheese in the center of the circle of bagels, found a butter knife, stuck it in the cream cheese, reached into the spice rack, and pulled down some dried chives. Sprinkled them on top. Presented it to Caroline. "Ta-da."

"It's pretty," she said.

I turned to grab two big coffee mugs that read KEEP CALM AND CARRY ON and poured our coffees into the mugs.

"I hate drinking out of paper," I said.

"Who wouldn't," Caroline responded.

Took a big gulp of burnt Starbucks Christmas cheer. Said, "Mmm."

Caroline cocked her head to one side, looking at me.

I pulled down a pair of plates. Chose a bagel. Smeared some cream cheese on one half, offered it to Caroline who shook her head. Put the dry half on her plate, put the smeared half on mine, and set them in front of us.

Caroline nodded to herself. "Shit. I should have known."

"Known?" I asked. "Known what?"

"That you're gay."

The coffee went down the wrong pipe, hit my trachea, and launched me into a fit of coughing. I spun and spit coffee all over the back of my kitchen nook, mostly in the sink.

Caroline said, "Not that there's anything wrong with it."

I tried to speak through a coffee-paralyzed larynx. "Grk—gg—"

Caroline looked concerned. "Are you choking?"

"Gaaak—"

Caroline came around the table, stood behind me, wrapped her arms around me. "If you need the Heimlich, make the universal sign for choking."

Universal sign for choking?

"Grrkk?" I said.

"Yeah, you're choking." Caroline balled her fist, shoved it under my ribs, squeezed hard, and jabbed her fist into my spine. Knocked the wind straight out of me.

Now I couldn't talk because I had no air. "Hhunnh! Hhunnh!"

"Another? Okay."

No, dear God, not another.

I spun in Caroline's grasp. Putting myself chest to chest with that amazing sports bra. Did the only thing that I knew would save me. Pulled her tight against me. Kissed her. My sweatpants said the rest.

Caroline reached down and patted my buddy. "Oh—so you're *not* gay."

I shook my head. Sucked in a lungful of air.

Caroline rubbed her hand around. "You seem happy to see me."

I kissed her again, softly, as my hands slipped down her yoga-slicked skin to her waistband. I lingered there, tracing my fingers across the small of her back. I smelled Caroline's clean sweat as I kissed her just behind the ear, my tongue tasting salt as it tickled the base of her neck. My fingers stopped stroking and switched to massaging the toned muscles of her spine.

Caroline let slip a tiny gasp, traced her fingers down my belly, undid my drawstring, and slipped her hand inside my boxers. It was my turn to gasp.

"I don't know the universal sign for choking," I said.

Caroline said, "I'll show you later." She took my hand and led the way to my bedroom.

We fell on the bed. The yoga pants, sweatpants, t-shirt, sports bra, panties, and boxers found their way to the floor. I ran my hand down Caroline's belly, over to her thigh, where I reached the sleeve of her prosthetic.

"Let's get rid of that," she said, guiding my hands down her leg and showing me what to do. Soon the bedsheets were tangled and heaped on the floor as our bodies tangled and rocked together. We pet and panted, kissed and cuddled, surrendered and strove. No matter how things went, Caroline always wound up on top.

Who was I to argue?

FIFTY-TWO

I slipped from the bed as Caroline snoozed, placed my robe on the bed for her, and padded out into the kitchen. The bagels sat on the cutting board, forgotten. The Starbucks coffee was cold. *Good.* I dumped the Starbucks down the drain, its burned smell filling the room. Grabbed some Colombian from Wired Puppy, set up Mr. Coffee, and let him do his thing.

I was feeding Click and Clack when the door opened and Caroline peeked out, her red prosthetic peeking out from under the robe. She gave me a sleepy smile, waved, and limped into the bathroom. The bathwater ran. I considered asking if she needed help, decided that she was the type who would have asked.

I poured myself a cup of coffee, put the rest of the coffee into a thermos, carried the bagels and thermos out to the dining room table, and waited.

My mind, left to its own devices, drifted back to yesterday and the impossibility of my situation. Bobby, Sal, Hugh, Jael—how many people were relying on me to tell, or not to tell, the truth about the past week? If I admitted that I was on Hanover Street, Jael would go to jail. If I didn't, Bobby would rightfully shun me. He probably wouldn't even listen to me if I told him about Cantrell's deal with Sal—a deal that could get him killed.

Maybe I just tell everybody everything. Bobby would learn about Jael and about Cantrell. Sal would deal with the consequences. Maybe there was no proof, and Sal would walk. Maybe they'd arrest Hugh Graxton for murder. Maybe Bobby would ignore Jael and focus on Cantrell. The amazing thing was that nothing would happen to me, regardless. I didn't shoot, bribe, or hurt anyone. I'd walk, live a long life as a traitor. A traitor and a loser who let a little girl get kidnapped, killed, or worse.

The bathroom door opened and Caroline stepped out. Limped lightly down the hallway. Stood in front of me, undid the robe. My hand reached unbidden for the first thing in reach: Caroline's toned thigh.

I caressed her just above the prosthetic sleeve, then offered her my hand for support. "Sit?"

Caroline accepted the offer, sat next to me, left the robe as it was. "So it doesn't bother you?" she asked.

"What?"

She lifted her leg, flexed the knee to wave the red prosthetic. "This."

"Why would it bother me?"

"It bothered my ex-fiancé."

I took Caroline's hand, kissed the back. "He was a schmuck."

"You say the nicest things."

I reached into the robe, rested my hand across Caroline's hip, kissed her again. "Let's have some bagels."

Caroline rewarded me with a brilliant smile, closed the robe, and chose a sesame bagel. I poured her some coffee. We leaned back. Caroline threw her leg across mine. I massaged her foot in the instant intimacy created by sex.

"What were you thinking about earlier?" she asked.

"When earlier?"

"When I walked down the hall. You looked sad."

"Oh, nothing."

Intimacy was one thing. Truthfulness might take more time.

"Oh, okay. Nothing," said Caroline. "That was a whole lot of nothing."

"I don't even know what I could tell you."

"Anything you want."

"But you're an officer of the court or something, aren't you?"

"I'll just invoke attorney-client privilege."

"Don't I need to pay you a dollar or something as a fee?"

Caroline patted my crotch. "Consider it paid."

"Really? I was worth a whole dollar?"

"No. No. At least five dollars."

"Can I ask you something?"

"Sure."

"What just happened—before, in bed?"

"I'm pretty sure you were there."

"Yeah, but—I didn't know we were at that point," I said.

"I went a little fast for you?"

"I'm not complaining."

"There was a time I would have waited the customary three dates," Caroline said over her coffee mug.

I worked the sole of Caroline's foot. "You mean a time before the bombing?"

"A few feet closer ... I don't know. It's hard to explain, being so close to getting killed."

Vince Ferrari and the shipping crate flashed into my head. "Yeah. I know."

"How would you know?"

"Long story."

"Oh, you mean the whole lot of nothing you were thinking about before?"

I said nothing.

Caroline slipped her foot away, sat next to me on the couch. She said, "Anyway, I took the initiative and came over for a booty call."

"Ahh."

"I wanted to get in your pants. You are sexy as hell."

"Oh, pshaw. I'll bet you say that to all the nerds."

"You want to get dinner tonight?"

"Like a second date? Sure."

Caroline shifted on the sofa, leaned into me, her leg and flank pressed against mine. She took my arm, wrapped it around herself, settled in.

"So tell me why you're sad," she said.

This was good. It was the first good I'd felt in a long time. The first time I'd felt that I could trust someone. So I took the plunge and told Caroline everything. Almost everything. Told her about Hanover Street, about Cantrell. About chasing Maria in the North End, about falling through the ice and Graxton's email. I didn't tell her about the shipping crate. That was between Sal and me. He could tell her.

When I was finished, Caroline said, "Damn!"

"Damn indeed."

"Have you told anyone about all this?"

"You're the first one."

"You'd better keep me the only one. If you start talking, it will just keep you from your top priority."

"And what's that?"

"Finding Maria."

"Right. But I have no idea what to do next. It's all dead ends."

"Not all dead ends," said Caroline.

"No?"

"You can still talk to Hugh Graxton."

"Yeah, but he's hiding or something. I don't know where to find him."

"I know where he likes to hide," Caroline said.

"Aren't you talking outside attorney-client privilege?"

"I don't think this counts as privileged information."

"So where is he?"

Caroline smiled a little. "You wouldn't believe me if I told you."

"Try me."

So she told me, and she was right: I didn't believe it.

FIFTY-THREE

Poor Chelsea, Massachusetts, is kind of like Boston's appendix: a small protuberance jutting from the city that everyone ignores until it flares up and requires intervention. The last intervention was in 1991, when the state disbanded Chelsea's corrupt government and installed a new one. The city consists almost entirely of triple-decker houses, three-family structures with apartments stacked like Lego blocks.

My Zipcar rolled down Marlboro Street as I looked for Graxton's hiding place. The address pointed me to a brown triple-decker with open porches running up its face. Fresh paint shone in the pale winter sun, a contrast to the peeling faces of the houses next door. I climbed the steps and found the name next to a painted-over doorbell: Graxton. Pressed the button. A buzzer sounded on the first floor. An inner apartment door opened, then the door in front of me.

An old woman looked up at me. Her translucent skin stretched over a pinched face. "Yes?"

"I'm here to see Hugh," I said.

"Well, come on in and shut the door. All the heat's getting out."

She turned and led me into the apartment. "Hugh!" she called, then plunked herself down in a recliner, reclined, and picked up a remote. *Wheel of Fortune* resumed.

I stood by the front door. A long hallway ran down the length of the house, bedroom doors breaking the wall on one side. I could see a refrigerator in the kitchen at the end of the hallway.

Hugh Graxton appeared around the refrigerator, yelling, "What is it, Ma?" He saw me and ducked back behind the fridge. I looked at Hugh's mom, pointed down the hall. *May I?* She motioned me along with a wave of her remote. I walked down the hallway, noting the fresh paint and clean bedrooms. Reached the kitchen, peeked around the refrigerator to find a closed door.

Knocked on the door. "Hugh?"

Nothing.

Knocked again. "C'mon Hugh, I know you're in there."

Nothing.

"If you don't open this door, I'm going to tell your mom."

"Go away!"

"I swear I'll do it, I'll interrupt her show."

"She's got a DVR."

"All right, you asked for it." I called out, "Mrs. Grax—"

Hugh pulled the door open. "You're a bastard."

"Hugh!" Hugh's mom called from the easy chair. "Do I have to come down there?"

"No, Ma, no! Tucker was just being a jerk."

"You boys play nice."

Hugh was wearing a gray UMass sweatshirt with flannel Snoopy-dancing-with-Woodstock pajama pants. I arched an eyebrow at him.

Hugh said, "What? You've never seen a guy relaxing around the house?"

"Woodstock?"

"Woodstock is cool. You leave Woodstock alone."

"Hugh, what are you doing here? Where's Angie?"

"How should I know?"

"Because you emailed her, met her at the Harvard Bridge, and threw her cell phone onto the river."

"That's crazy." Hugh stepped past me and grabbed a teapot off the stove. He ran water into it. "How did you find me here?"

I ignored the question. "Where's Angie—and Maria?"

Hugh ignored me back, placed the teapot over a gas flame. "You going to tell me how you found me?" he asked.

"No."

"Then screw you."

"Why should I tell you? You're the one who kidnapped Angie and Maria."

"I don't know anything about Angie." Hugh pulled two mugs from the pantry. "Nobody's supposed to know I'm here. That's the whole point of hiding. Does anyone else know I'm here?"

"Nobody knows. I was just guessing."

"Hmmph. Lucky guess."

"Where's Angie?"

"I don't know. I've got enough problems without dealing with that crazy bitch."

"What are you talking about?"

The teapot whistled on the stove. Hugh shut off the gas, pulled tea bags out of a box, threw them in the mugs, poured water over them.

I read the box. "Earl Grey," I said. "Hot."

"Yes, nerd," said Hugh, "just like Picard drinks."

"I thought you were a coffee guy."

"I'm off coffee for a while."

"What makes Angie a crazy bitch?" I asked.

Hugh said, "Well, first, she's a woman."

"Oh, nice."

"But more specifically, she can become—possessive."

"Possessive?"

"Once you sleep with her."

"You've slept with her?"

"Shhh!" Hugh looked over his shoulder. His mother was watching somebody buy a vowel. Hissed, "Yes, I slept with her. She's—enthusiastic."

"Did she become possessive afterwards?"

"Oh, yeah."

"What did she do?"

"Kept following me around, emailing me, getting in my way. Finally asked me to marry her."

"What did you say?"

"I told her, 'Hell no!' She threatened to tell Sal about us, and I told her to go ahead."

"Was Sal pissed off?"

"Why would he be pissed off? Angie is kind of like the Common. A shared resource."

"That's terrible."

"Angie just keeps trying to get one of us to marry her. Me, Sal, Marco, Joey. Well, not Joey so much, though he probably got some action. She hasn't fucked you?"

"No."

"Man, you're even lower than Joey. That's sad."

"If she's so common, why would Sal buy her a condo?"

"Sal didn't buy it for her. He had it for a couple of years. He called it his fuck pad, said he got the idea from Marco. Of course, Marco had a little more class. He called his a man cave."

"So how did Angie get it?"

"Well, she probably had a key, made it easy for her to be there. Anyway, when the time came, Sal just told her to live in it."

"When the time came? What time?"

Pause. "You'll have to ask Sal."

My tea was finally cool enough to drink. I got back to the point. "Why did you email Angie? Get her to the Harvard Bridge?"

"What is it with you and this email? I didn't email her."

I drank some tea, maybe Picard was onto something. "I saw the email, Hugh. On Angie's phone. From your Yahoo account."

Hugh got up, went into his room, closed the door. Came back out having replaced his pajamas with jeans, and carrying his MacBook Air. He sat. Gestured at the Mac Vanna White style, opened it, and clicked on a link.

"I haven't sent her an email," said Hugh. "I haven't even been on this account this week. I don't use email."

"Why?"

"It's like a friggin' evidence vault. I don't want to see my emails at a trial."

Hugh typed in his username and password. Got it wrong. Typed it in again. Got it wrong again. "Dammit," he said. He typed his email a third time.

The website switched to a helpful page: Forgot your Password?

"No," said Hugh to the computer, "I didn't forget my password. You did." He clicked on the "Reset your Password" link.

I had a bad feeling about this.

Five minutes later, Hugh was still waiting for the reset email to arrive.

"You've been hacked," I said.

Hugh said, "Jarrod, you little shit."

FIFTY-FOUR

DEAD WINTER IVY CLUNG to the archways in Columbus Park, its brown vines frozen to the latticework that covered the park's walkways. The city had compensated by encrusting the arches in purple lights, but the lights were off in the middle of the afternoon. A fishy wind blew off the harbor, chilling our faces.

We stood at the base of Columbus's statue. Columbus gazed across the harbor toward Logan Airport, clearly thinking that his life would have been much easier if he had air travel in 1492. I followed Columbus's gaze, not wanting to make eye contact with Sal, who glared at Hugh.

"You killed fucking Pistol?" asked Sal.

"Well, to be fair," said Hugh, "he started it."

"Let me get this straight. My wife is dead. Maria is missing. You killed Pistol—"

"Not just Pistol. Jael killed another one."

"Whatever, so you killed two of my guys and I killed three. That's all of them."

"Yup."

"As I was saying: my wife's dead, my crew's dead, my daughter's missing, I'm under indictment, and you're bitching to me that Jarrod Cooper hacked your email account? Do I have that right?"

"Cooper works for David Anderson," Hugh said.

"What are you talking about?" I asked. "PassHack went under. Jarrod doesn't have a job."

Hugh turned on me. "Wake up, Tucker. You think we ever expected PassHack to succeed?"

"You didn't?"

"With a name like PassHack? Seriously?"

"Why would you want it to go under?"

"Because the money in PassHack doesn't come from selling the service to idiots, and it won't come from selling PassHack to Google. It comes from hacking into businesses and—" Hugh looked to Sal. "Should I tell him?"

Sal said, "Go ahead. Tell him. He's in up to his neck anyway."

Graxton said, "Anderson and Jarrod use the technology to hack into businesses and rob their bank accounts."

"Oh my God. And you knew about this?"

"Knew about this? Of course we knew about this. That was the point."

"Tucker, you worked there," said Sal.

"Yeah, I helped Jarrod set up a hacking system, but that was for a good cause."

"Yeah," said Sal. "The good cause of making us some dough."

I was going to be sick. "It's illegal!"

Hugh said, "It's called organized crime for a reason, dipshit. Or did you forget the crime part?"

"No, I didn't forget the crime part," I said. "So what happened with you three?"

Sal said, "We caught Anderson stealing from us."

I said, "He told me that you lost your money when PassHack went under."

"Yeah, he fucking lied to you."

"He was skimming," Hugh said. "Jarrod got drunk with us once and let it slip."

"Anderson called it a fucking—fucking—" Sal snapped his fingers at Hugh. "What did he call it?"

Hugh said, "Management fee."

"Yeah, a fucking management fee. Cocksucker. Told him I wanted every penny back. He told me no, so I put a hit on him."

"When was this?" I asked.

"Two weeks ago."

"That's when it all went to hell," I said.

"Yeah."

Cold wind blew in from Boston Harbor. A Southwest Airlines jet traced an arc into the sky, flying away from Boston, probably toward some place warmer, or at least less dangerous.

"So what's this shit about your email account getting hacked?" Sal asked Hugh.

"It looks like Angie got an email from my hacked account," Hugh said. "Somebody emailed her in my name and took her, and probably Maria."

Sal asked, "Why you?"

"What do you mean?" Hugh asked.

"Why would Jarrod hack your account?"

"Why not?"

"Why would Angie trust you? She doesn't know you. You live in Newton."

Hugh crossed his arms.

"You're shitting me," Sal said. "You too?"

Hugh said nothing.

Sal turned to me, pointing at Hugh. "Was he fucking Angie?"

"Umm," I said.

Sal said, "He was fucking Angie!"

"What of it?" Hugh asked.

"What of it? Is there nothing I own that you won't try to take from me?"

"What are you talking about?"

"I'm gone one day and I hear that you're sitting in my spot. I get back, my place is covered in plywood because you had to come out here and play king."

"I was keeping the peace."

"Great fucking job." Sal's hot breath blew steam around Hugh's head. "Now I hear you were screwing Angie."

"You don't own Angie. You're married to Sophia."

"What the fuck does that have to do with it? Did you fuck her in that condo I bought her?"

"C'mon, Sal. Marco was fucking her too. So was Joey, for all I know."

"So you thought you'd pile on. What was she doing, pulling the train?"

"Don't be an asshole."

"An asshole? I buy her a condo, pay for her fucking abortion, listen to Sophia's bullshit for years, and you guys get to fuck her?" Sal turned to me. "You fuck her too?"

I said, "What? Me? No. We just had dinner."

"Dinner? You mean you were *trying* to fuck her?"

Hugh made a placating gesture, both hands out. "Look, Sal, this is getting us nowhere. Anderson's got Maria."

Sal kept yelling at me. "And whose fucking fault is that? Fucking sled."

I turned.

"Don't you turn your back on me!"

I shouted over my shoulder, walking toward the Aquarium. "Fuck you, Sal." Took out my cell phone, dialed. "Jarrod, we need to talk. Sal's going to kill you."

FIFTY-FIVE

An angular pile of poured concrete, the New England Aquarium adorns the waterfront. The bad news is that it blocks the ocean view. The bright side is that it features a three-story ocean tank, once the largest such tank in the world. A spiral walkway carries one around the tank, down into a deepening abyss of water and concrete, while a series of windows provide a view of the fish who choose to inhabit each depth.

I stood next to a window, halfway down the tank, watching Myrtle the Turtle cruise past with stately strokes of her flippers. The concrete and darkness gave me the serene feeling of standing underwater. A nurse shark followed the green turtle. I waited, and Myrtle came around again. I envied her routine and considered spending the rest of the day next to this tank, protected from the elements, from family, from enemies, from guilt. Just me and Myrtle, whiling away the afternoon.

"There you are."

I looked at the reflection in the glass. Jarrod Cooper stood behind me. Concrete pillars framed each window, supporting the tank and providing a little alcove protected from the stream of people walking past.

Jarrod slipped in and stood next to me at the window. "Great idea coming here. It's private," said Jarrod.

"Thanks."

"What do you mean that Sal is going to kill me?"

"Right to the point, eh?"

"Is there a more important point?"

"I suppose not," I said.

"So why am I in trouble?"

"Hugh Graxton is convinced that you hacked his email account."

"I don't know what you're talking about."

"Don't lie to me. I'm trying to save you."

"I'm not lying."

"What do you think, Myrtle? Is he lying?" I called through the glass. "Wave your flipper for yes."

Myrtle waved her flipper.

"The jury's in, Jarrod. You're a liar."

Jarrod pointed at the turtle. "That's ridiculous!"

"Should I ask the nurse shark?"

Jarrod crossed his arms, looked at the fish.

I said, "Lying to me really doesn't help your cause. I'm not here gathering information for Sal or Hugh. They believe what they believe, and they're looking for you."

"This is completely unfair."

"Did you hack the account?"

"It was Hugh's own fault."

"How did you get his password?"

"I can't discuss it."

"Proprietary hacking algorithms?"

Jarrod said nothing. Another head duck.

"Jesus, Jarrod, what happened to you?"

"What?"

"*What?* You know what."

Jarrod crossed his arms again. Actually pouted. I couldn't believe it.

I said, "You're the Bernie Madoff of computer science."

"Shut up, Tucker."

"And a disgrace to MIT."

"Oh, the hell with MIT!"

"Keep your voice down."

Mothers pushed strollers past us. Kids Maria's age ran up and down the ramp. The Aquarium was busy during the Christmas school vacation.

"How did this happen?" I asked.

"How did what happen?"

"How did you become a crook?"

"I'm no crook."

"By what definition are you not a crook?"

Jarrod stared at me.

"I know all about PassHack," I said. "What it really was. What you tricked me into developing."

"I didn't trick you. I really wanted to make PassHack."

"Oh, I see."

"It started as an investment."

"What?"

"An angel investment in PassHack. Anderson, Sal, and Hugh offered me half a million to get started."

"You took their money?"

"Of course I took their money. I had been pitching venture capitalists for months. I must have made fifty pitches. That was my first bite."

I could see the way this had played out. "You burned through the angel round," I said.

"I never got the chance. Those guys took me to the North End to celebrate, sat around a table in a little restaurant, and told me how it was going to be. How I was going to hack passwords for them."

My curiosity got the better of me. "How? Some cracking algorithm?"

"No. You know, the usual. You send some executive an email with a link, and get them to click on it."

"Phishing."

"Well, more like spear phishing. You send an executive a real-looking email from someone they know, get them to click on a plausible link."

"Executives still fall for that?"

"They're cautious, but you can trick them once you know who their friends are."

"Facebook?"

"Yeah. And LinkedIn. You just gather every bit of data and use it to get that one click."

"So then why the hacking servers you had me make?"

"I'd also try to get the executive's personal passwords. You wouldn't believe how many of these guys use the same password for both."

"Is that all you guys do?"

"No, we just throw everything at them. You can get people's credit card number, or parts of their credit card numbers, then you call the website and see if you can trick them into emailing you a password reset link. You find one website that thinks the last four digits of the credit card are the Holy Grail of security, and another that thinks that the last four digits are public domain knowledge. You put it all together and you hack the account."

"A holistic approach."

"Exactly!" Jarrod was getting excited, giving off a weird passionate vibe. "Then there's the key logging. We record their keystrokes."

"You do key logging?"

"If the spear phishing works, you install a key logger first thing."

"Is that how you got Hugh's password?"

Jarrod rolled his eyes. "Hugh's an idiot. He came over to the office to get his weekly cash and asked to use my computer. He logged into webmail and told the browser to save his password. He must have clicked the box automatically, didn't even notice."

"So you just had his account all this time?"

"Yup."

"What's this weekly cash?"

Jarrod's lips clamped shut.

I said, "Sal and Hugh tell me that Anderson was skimming."

Nothing.

"Jarrod, talk to me. I'm Sal's cousin. I can put in a good word for you. I can save you."

"You actually think you're going to save me by talking to Sal? I don't give a shit about Sal. If he's lucky, he's out of business; if he's not, he's a dead man. I'm not afraid of Sal or Hugh. I'm afraid of Anderson and Kane."

"Did Kane tell you to hack Hugh's account?"

"He just made me send the email. I don't know what he did after that."

"He kidnapped Sal's daughter."

Jarrod looked into the tank, watched a tarpon flash past. "I'm sorry."

I left him there and spiraled down the ramp, picking up speed. Bundled myself into the cold, considered my next move. According to Jarrod, Angie and Maria were being held by a highly trained killer and his supervillain boss. Right. Nothing I shouldn't be able to handle with a little help.

I whipped out my Droid and called Sal. "Hi, Sal."

"Fuck you." Connection broken.

I called Bobby. "Hey, listen—"

"Bite me." Connection broken.

Called Hugh. "Hugh—"

"Don't call me." Connection broken.

I called Jael. "Please don't hang up on me."

FIFTY-SIX

THE LEGAL SEAFOOD RESTAURANT on Long Wharf sits across from the Aquarium, a warning to aquarium fish that refuse to toe the line. I sat at the bar amidst wood and blue glass, slurping a bowl of clam chowder and drinking a Harpoon IPA. Jael sat next to me, eschewing the clams and opting instead for a dinner roll and spring water.

"You should not be drinking at this time of day," she said. "It will slow you down."

I said, "It doesn't matter. I'm going home. I can't do this alone. I quit."

Jael reached over to me, grabbed the beer, and dumped it behind the bar into the sink. The bartender walked over.

"Something wrong with the beer?" he asked.

"He should not be drinking," said Jael. "He needs water."

Bartender gave me a look. *You gonna let her run your life?* I shrugged. He poured me the water. I pulled out a twenty, made a *keep the change* motion.

I turned to Jael. "What was that about?"

"It is ridiculous that you should quit," she said.

"I thought you'd be happy. You're the one who told me not to get involved."

"That was before you were involved."

"Well, there's nothing I can do now. Kane has Maria and Angie. I can't rescue them alone. Sal's mad at me. Bobby's mad at me. Hugh's mad at me. Lee just wants to arrest me. It's a clusterfuck."

Jael reached for my hand. Grabbed it. Bore into me with her gray eyes. "You are not alone," she said.

Shame sloshed around my gut. "I know, but—"

"You are doing a good thing," Jael said.

"Yeah, doing it badly."

"But still."

"I have no idea what's going on. I'm just going to get somebody killed."

"Tell me what you know."

"You know what I know."

"Just do it."

So I told her everything, starting with losing Maria, almost getting her back, losing her again in Pupo's. Told her about Victor trying to kill me in a shipping crate. Told her about Angie's phone and the ice and how I still hadn't warned Bobby about Cantrell. About how everyone was after me about Hanover Street and about Angie's reputation. I even told her about Caroline's booty call. It was the only thing that shocked Jael.

"She is an aggressive woman," Jael said.

"You're telling me."

"Why would she do that?"

"Because she thinks I'm sexy?"

"It is possible, but unlikely."

"Oh, thanks. That was the bright spot in my day."

"I am just saying that you should not let your guard down."

"I am so tired of having my guard up."

"Still."

"I just want this to end. I want to stop hurting people."

"You are not hurting people."

"Oh, c'mon. Everything I touch turns to shit."

"And you think it would be different if you were not involved?"

"Of course it would be different."

"Would Sal still have been arrested?"

"Well, yeah."

"Would Hugh have sat in Sal's spot and started a war?"

"Sure."

"What would have happened to Maria?"

"I guess that she would have been taken."

"Or killed with her mother."

"Well, probably not. Pupo knew where to find her."

"And someone would still have killed Joey Pupo. Taken Maria from him."

"Either way."

"Correct. Either with you or without you."

I drank water. Cold water on a cold day. "You're saying that I've accomplished nothing and that I might as well go home?"

"*Yet the righteous holdeth on his way, and he that hath clean hands waxeth stronger and stronger.*"

"Is that the Bible? Why does everybody quote me the Bible?"

"It is from the Book of Job."

"Am I supposed to be the guy with the clean hands?"

"You have worked hard to reach this point. You are getting strong enough to turn the tide, and yet you want to quit."

"I don't have clean hands."

"You have the cleanest hands of any of us."

I had nothing to say to that. Stared off at rows and rows of delicious whiskey behind the bar, drank my water. Poked at my congealed clam chowder. I could still quit, head home, and—and what? Set up a Google alert for "Maria Rizzo"? Wait for the body to turn up?

"What if we assume that David Anderson has taken Maria and Angie?" I asked.

Jael said, "It is a good assumption."

"What will he do with them? You said there were three options: kill them, do unspeakable things to them, or use them for leverage."

Jael did not answer, looked into her water glass instead.

I said, "It's pretty clear he's going to use them for leverage to get Sal off his back."

"He will probably do three things," said Jael.

"Which three things?"

"Use them as leverage to get Sal into a vulnerable position. Then kill Sal. Then kill them."

"He'd kill Maria?"

"And Angie," said Jael. "They are all witnesses."

"So what do we do? Confront Anderson?"

"I do not think that would help. In fact, it would hurt. It would give him information."

"Do we break into his apartment?"

"Probably not possible."

"Maybe we get some evidence somehow. You know. Hack his email?"

"I do not know how to do that."

"No," I said, "but I do."

I dialed my phone. Got an answer. "This is David Anderson."

"Dave, this is Tucker. We need to talk."

"My name is David. You want to talk? Talk."

"I'd rather meet on neutral ground."

"Oh," said Anderson. "It's that kind of talk."

"I was thinking of the Ritz Bar."

"You buying?"

These guys. Always with the negotiations. "It was down to either calling you or my friends in the FBI, Dave," I said. "Want me to call them instead?"

"It's David. I think you know I have something you want."

"Yeah."

"We'll split the bar bill."

"Okay."

FIFTY-SEVEN

There was a time when the Ritz Carlton lived in a stately brick building overlooking the Public Garden. This building was sold and the hotel renamed Taj Boston (a case of Indian insourcing). The new Ritz Carlton hid behind a movie theater and overlooked what had once been the Combat Zone, the porn center of the city. The Combat Zone was destroyed by technology, as VHS, DVD, and the ability to Google "boobs" had replaced its core business.

I sat at the white marble horseshoe of the Ritz Carlton's bar, waiting for David Anderson and watching some schmucks on TV prattling about whether tomorrow's New Year's Eve festivities (called First Night) were to be doomed by snow.

Anderson walked through the front door, searched the room, saw me. I waved. He sat next to me, shaking my hand while looking at the bourbon bottles. His hand was cold.

"You don't believe in gloves?" I asked.

"Gloves are for the weak," he said.

Anderson ordered a Booker's Manhattan, twist instead of a cherry. I got an Allagash White, Maine's best Belgian beer.

Anderson said, "So, what you got?"

"I got Angie's cell phone off the Charles River."

"Good for you. You should return it. You were going to call the FBI for that?"

"I'll do that once I find her—and Maria."

Anderson looked me up and down. "What's your game?" he asked.

"I don't have a game."

"Everybody has a game."

"I don't."

Another long look. "Are you wearing a wire?"

"No."

"Because if you're wearing a wire—you don't want to be wearing a wire."

"I'm not. I won't."

"Why not?"

I didn't answer. The drinks arrived.

Anderson took a sip of his Manhattan. "Oh, I get it," he said. "That whole *omerta* thing."

"The what?"

"The Mafia code of silence."

"I don't know what you're talking about," I lied.

Anderson clapped my shoulder. "Rule One: There is no *omerta*."

I drank my beer. Anderson was just as smart as he looked.

"Here's what I don't get. What the hell are you doing in the Mafia?"

"I'm not in the Mafia."

"Yeah, whatever. You're a young guy. Educated. Intelligent. Where did you go to school? BU?"

"MIT."

"Even better. So you've got a worldview that's bigger than the North End."

I took another swig of Allagash, thinking back to the Peroni I'd drunk in the North End. Anderson was right. Allagash was definitely not a beer you'd find in the North End.

"What's your point?" I asked.

"My point is that you could do better than a has-been like Sal."

Family pride kicked in. "Sal is at the top of the heap."

"The top of what heap? The drugging, whoring, robbing, numbers heap?"

I said nothing.

"Sure, don't confirm it," Anderson said. "But for a second, look at it like a private equity guy."

"Private equity? I'm more comfortable with the drugging and whoring."

"Yeah, sure. Funny. Just think about it for a second. What kind of businesses are those? They suck!"

"What are you talking about?"

"From a business perspective, they suck. They don't scale. Take whoring." Anderson grabbed a napkin off the bartender's pile. Took out a green plastic pen from a local bank.

"Cheap pen," I said.

"Mont Blanc is for suckers," said Anderson. He drew a stick figure on the napkin, two circles for boobs, two lines made a road next to her. "Your average street whore can turn five tricks a night. Oh, they'll tell you ten, but that's ridiculous. There's only about six hours of prime pickup time, like eight p.m. to two a.m. The whore stands on the corner with her friends. Cars drive by, pick up her hotter friends first—remember, I said average—then they take her. Assuming a car every five minutes, that takes 15 minutes." Anderson wrote 0:15 on the napkin with the word *Marketing* next to it.

"She gets in the car, collects the money, and either takes him to a room or they park the car," he continued. "That takes another fifteen minutes." He wrote 0:15 and *Sales* next to it.

"At worst, fifteen minutes to blow the guy or screw him, and fifteen back." Anderson wrote 0:30 and the word *Operations*.

"So you add these up and every trick takes at least an hour. Take into account slow guys, bad weather, peeing, maybe doing drugs, and you don't get a trick an hour. So maybe you get five at an average of $75 each. That's what?" Anderson wrote 75 and a 5 under it. He opened the calculator app on his phone.

"$375," I said.

Anderson tapped at the phone. Showed me the number: 375. "Wow," he said, "good job. You did go to MIT. So there you have it: 375 dollars a night revenue per employee. And there's no way to get more money without hiring more girls. You got to feed them and their manager—"

"Pimp."

"Whatever. Titles are unimportant. So, say half of that $375 is profit, about $180."

"$187.50," I said.

"Precision really doesn't matter here. Call it $200 to make the math easy, she works 350 nights a year, each employee makes me $70,000, maximum."

"Seems like a good deal."

"It's mouse nuts," Anderson said. "And for each of these women I get one more person for the police to flip, one more chance of a murder to cover up, and don't forget legal fees when she gets caught. You have to be a hard worker to run this business."

"Probably why Sal was good at it."

"Right tense there. *Was*."

I hadn't noticed my tense. Shit.

Anderson asked, "Do you know how much you can make by reading an internal document and shorting a stock?"

"More than $70,000?"

"Millions—in one deal. I can do one of those deals a month, sometimes two. A girl would have to work fourteen years to make me a million bucks."

"And how do you get the inside documents?"

Anderson smiled. Finished his Manhattan. "I think you know."

"How would I know?"

"Because Jarrod Cooper is loyal to no man."

"Huh?"

"Called me from the Aquarium. Confessed that he had spilled it all. Begged me to not kill him."

"You make a decision on that?"

"No." Anderson waved to the bartender for the check.

The check arrived. I took out my phone and my wallet. "A card each?"

Anderson said, "Sure." Threw down a Visa card decorated with George Washington from the dollar bill. I threw down my card, undecorated. The bartender took them both.

I fiddled with my phone and brought up the camera. Took a picture of the bar and tweeted it:

`The new modern, fancy Ritz Bar #nowIfeelsad`

"Oh, right," said Anderson. "Got to feed the followers."

"It's sort of a diary," I said.

"So Jarrod tells me that you know about PassHack."

I continued to snap pictures. "Yeah," I said. "I had already figured it out."

"He tells me that you believe I have Maria."

"I do."

"You're right."

I lowered the camera. The bar slipped from my view. There was Anderson and me, and Maria, somewhere.

"Where is she?"

"Unsafe," said Anderson. "Quite unsafe. She probably needs rescuing."

"What does that mean? *Unsafe?*"

"It means that she's with an unstable person who'll probably wind up killing her one way or another."

"What do you want with her?"

"I don't want anything with her," said Anderson. "She's a burden. A bad risk, really. But I want something from Sal."

"What?"

"I want him to back off."

The checks arrived on two little trays. I took a picture of the trays.

"Receipt?" Anderson said. "Really? For this."

"Habit," I said.

Anderson pointed at his eyes. "Focus here, Tucker. Right here. I want Sal to call off the hit, forget my manager's fee. He learned a lesson, so just call it tuition."

"Why not just pay him back?"

"Because now it's not about the money."

"Okay. If you say so."

"I'm going to text you some instructions tomorrow, and you and Sal are going to follow them. If you don't, I'm going to kill Angie and Maria and leave them on Hanover Street." Anderson held me with a stare.

I averted my eyes.

"You got it?" he asked.

"Yeah," I said.

"Good." Anderson stood, turned, and left.

I opened the photo app on my phone. I had what I needed.

FIFTY-EIGHT

Jael Navas sat across the kitchen counter from me, holding a mug of Bitches Brew while eyeing Click and Clack. Elevator music echoed from my cell phone's speaker. We were on hold, waiting for a live customer support person at Anderson's email provider. Clack climbed a sponge. Jael's nose crinkled in an unusual display of emotion.

"You really don't like them, do you?" I asked.

"They are disgusting," said Jael.

"Cover your ears, boys. She doesn't mean it."

Jael shuddered, moved across the room, drank her coffee. "I will not eat near those insects."

"Okay. That's a—"

The customer support person interrupted. A perky female voice said, "Thank you for calling, this is Gretchen. To whom am I speaking?"

To whom? Gretchen was one classy lady.

"This is David Anderson," I said. "I need to reset my password for my email account." I told her Anderson's email address.

"I can help you with that, Mr. Anderson. Can you give me your mother's maiden name?"

“I can,” I said, “but that won’t help. I never write down her real name on those things.”

“Oh.”

“Unless I did. It’s McGillicuddy.”

“No sir, you didn’t give us that name.”

“Yeah, figures. I should keep a list of my passwords.”

“How about the make and model of your first car?”

“I think I wrote *Nissan Sentra.*”

“No, sir, that’s not it.”

“This is why I had to call. I’m really stuck, Gretchen.”

Jael watched me lie with a new look in her eye.

I pushed mute. “How am I doing?”

“You are a much better liar than I would have guessed.”

“Why, thank you.”

“It is not a compliment.”

Gretchen broke in. “Sir, without your security questions there is only one thing we can do. Do you know which credit card you used to create this account?”

When I took the picture of my receipt in the Ritz Bar, I also got David Anderson’s credit card in the shot. I had copied that information off the picture. Now came the big test. Did David Anderson use the same credit card for drinking as for his data services?

I said, “I do have the credit card.”

“Could you give me your billing address and that number?”

“Sure.” I gave Anderson’s address.

“Thank you, sir. Where should I email the reset link?”

I knew this question was coming. I had set up a onetime email address on Hotmail in preparation. I gave Gretchen the email address.

She said, “I’ve emailed you a reset link.”

I watched Hotmail on my laptop. The email popped up.

“Got it.”

"Great! Is there anything else I can help you with today?"

"No, Gretchen, I'm good."

"Because you are such an excellent customer, we have an offer for you to get a new credit card."

"No thank you, Gretchen."

"When you sign up, you get five more gigabytes of disk space." Gretchen pronounced gigabytes as "jigabytes."

I said, "No, thank you, Gretchen. I have all the jigabytes I need."

"Okay, thank you, Mr. Anderson. Please remain on hold."

"On hold, why?" Stalling? Were the police on their way?

"For a short survey on your experience at this ti—"

I hung up on Gretchen. Let her think David Anderson was a jerk. She'd be right.

"God, I hate the phone," I said.

Jael said, "You would prefer to trick people by email?"

"As a matter of fact, yes. Do you have a problem with this?"

"It is . . . unsettling."

"What?"

"That you were able to get into Anderson's account so easily."

"I know, right?"

"Anyone with a picture of his credit card could do that."

"Well, they'd need to know his address too."

"Didn't you originally find David Anderson's address on the web?"

"Yes."

"So anyone could take a credit card and break in?"

"Depends on the service."

Jael crossed her arms, shuddered.

I said, "What's gotten into you? I've watched you shoot a guy in the face and go on your way."

"That was a different situation," she said.

"Well, yeah, but—"

"He could see me. He could shoot back."

"And why was that good?"

Jael was silent. Glanced at Click and Clack, took her coffee into the living room. I followed. We sat at the dining room table.

"What's wrong?" I asked.

"It was very easy," she said.

"Hacking Anderson?"

"Yes." Jael pulled her smartphone from her purse, looked at the email application. "Who else could be reading these?" she asked.

"Probably nobody but you," I said.

"Probably." Her voice trailed off. I'd never seen her rattled.

I took her mug into the kitchen. Poured us both more coffee. Came back.

"How do we live in a world like this?" Jael asked.

"Like what?"

"Where it is easy to see ..."

"You mean see our secrets?"

She glanced at me, surprised. "Yes. Our secrets."

"Welcome to my world," I said.

"The computer world?"

"No. The world of being afraid."

"Why would you be afraid?"

"Pistol Salvucci almost shot me. Then Vince."

"Yes, but—"

"I've almost died twice this week."

"I know."

"And it would have been so easy for them. They don't need my credit card number and address to blow my head off."

"No."

"So I have to ask you ..."

"Yes?"

"How do you live in a world like that?"

Jael sat, silent.

"I'm serious," I said. "How do you live in a world where anyone could kill you?"

She said, "I trust."

"Trust? Trust what?"

"I trust that people are not killers. I trust that they will not randomly attack me."

I nodded. "So do I. If I didn't, then I'd never leave the house."

"But this is different."

"No," I said, "it's not different. It's the same. Trust makes it livable."

Silence.

"Besides," I said, "it's getting harder all the time to do these hacks. I'm going to tell Rittenhauser about this one. He'll run a story and these guys will close their hole. But guns, they'll always be just as easy to use."

"I see your point," Jael said.

"Now, let's read Anderson's email."

FIFTY-NINE

THIS HACK WAS ONLY going to last until David Anderson checked his email and discovered that he was locked out. I needed a warning. I set up his account to send password-reset emails to my Hotmail account so that I'd get a warning when he clicked on the "Forgot My Password" link. Then I went to work.

I launched the Thunderbird email reader on my laptop, typed in Anderson's account information, and started downloading the most recent emails first. I had run for ten minutes, downloading a couple of years of emails, when the Hotmail account told me I had new mail. Anderson wanted back in. I changed the reset email back to his original and logged off. I had not forgotten Anderson's warning about Googling his name; he'd probably be pretty pissed about my stealing his email.

"Do you want to look these emails over with me?" I asked Jael.

"No," she said, "I do not."

I couldn't blame her. Fishing through Anderson's emails made me feel like a particularly nasty form of voyeur. There were emails from his sister wishing him a happy birthday, a realtor pitching new condos in the North End, a Tesla store saying "Happy New Year" to one of its favorite customers, and Anderson's brother, who wrote about their mother's dementia: *She almost recognized me yesterday.*

I felt like a shit.

Then I got to an email unlike all the others. It started with a single line:

-----BEGIN PGP MESSAGE-----

Followed by a blob of textual gobbledygook and then the final message:

-----END PGP MESSAGE-----

"Son of a bitch," I said.

"What is it?" asked Jael.

"David Anderson is using Pretty Good Privacy email encryption. We can't read his emails if he's using PGP."

"Is all of his email encrypted?"

"No, just some of it."

I checked the header. It read kane23223@gmail.com. That made sense. You an only use Pretty Good Protection if both people in the conversation have the software.

"He's encrypting his emails with Kane," I said.

Jael said, "So your hacking was worthless."

"Oh no," I said. "We still have the metadata."

"Metadata?"

The word *metadata* became all the rage back when Edward Snowden leaked the fact that the NSA was spying all over us by storing our metadata. It's data about the data. It tells you who emailed whom, but not what they said. Metadata was all I had when it came to Anderson's encrypted emails.

Of course, his encrypting created its own security leak. It allowed me to ignore emails about Anderson's mother, shopping habits, and, perhaps, embarrassing health issues. The encrypted emails were the only ones that mattered.

"I'm going to write a script and extract the list of people Anderson has been emailing with PGP," I said, and settled into some nice quality coding time.

We're told that we have to get out of our comfort zone, push ourselves to try new things, and stop doing what makes us feel fat, dumb, and happy. But after a week of being chased, shot at, and abused, I was ready for a little comfort. Writing a script would be the perfect way to unwind.

I opened an editor on my laptop, thought a little about what I wanted to do, then slipped into the warm embrace of a programming flow state. The cold, the danger, the urgency, and the fear all slipped into a small place in the back of my mind while I wrote a script that found all the PGP-encrypted emails, scanned them for email addresses, put the email addresses into a database, and presented the information to me in a nice sorted table that contained ten names. Five of the names were strangers. Five were not. Of the five I knew, three were expected: Kane, Jarrod, and Hugh.

But two were surprises: Frank Cantrell and, lo and behold, Caroline Quinn.

"Sonovabitch," I said.

"Who?" asked Jael.

"Oh, no one in particular. Just the situation."

I went back to coding. Added in a bit that showed me the dates of the oldest and most recent emails from all of the encrypted folks, then made a histogram of their communication frequency by month and year. Of the five I knew, Hugh had the longest relationship with Anderson. I had managed to capture two years' worth of data from Anderson, and Hugh's emails were littered throughout all the way back in time. They had emailed at least once a month.

Next came Kane, whose emails started infrequently about a year ago. Jarrod's emails started about eight months ago and continuously picked up in frequency. There was even one today from after the time Jarrod and I had watched Myrtle circle her tank. That must have been when he told Anderson about our meeting.

The surprising fourth name on my list started emailing using PGP ten days ago, when Hugh had received his first encrypted email from Frank Cantrell. PGP doesn't encrypt subjects, and Cantrell's first encrypted email said, *What do I Need to Do?* I had to wonder why Cantrell was talking to Anderson, but it could have been for many reasons.

This left me with the last surprise person to be emailing Cantrell using PGP: Caroline Quinn. She had sent Anderson only one email, while I was driving around Chelsea looking for Hugh Graxton's mother.

Which secrets had I divulged to Caroline?

Oh, yeah. All of them.

The timestamp showed that Caroline Quinn had left my bedroom, gone to her computer, and emailed David Anderson.

I looked at the clock. I was supposed to have dinner with her in an hour.

"What do you boys think?" I asked Click and Clack.

They did their best hermit crab impression of Admiral Ackbar: *It's a trap!*

SIXTY

The famous New England phrase "You can't get there from here" is really a paraphrase of the more common situation in Boston: you can get there from here, but it is a major pain in the ass. Which was why I was sitting in a cab next to Jael, letting a cabbie try to figure out how to get to Fan Pier from the South End. You'd think it would be easy. Both neighborhoods are south of the downtown; you can practically see Fan Pier from my rooftop. Yet the cabbie was swearing, swerving, and diving into tunnels as he yelled into his cell phone in what I assumed was Arabic, but could have been Portuguese.

"I told her everything," I said.

"Including Hanover Street?" asked Jael.

"Yeah."

"This is not your finest moment."

"I trusted her."

"Sex is a good way to create trust."

Instant intimacy.

"But it is not clear that your trust was misplaced. The message was short, correct?"

I looked at the printed message in my hand, the one I would use to confront Caroline:

```
From: Caroline Quinn
To: David Anderson
-----BEGIN PGP MESSAGE-----
Version: GnuPG/MacGPG2 v2.0.22 (Darwin)
Comment: GPGTools - https://gpgtools.org
jA0EAwMCsyIpOFIfzMLPySLTw4/7pbmVUl5JyHwYBeVNAoU
F1+vAfe3ahvM7Qdhj
x7bF
=cmUN
-----END PGP MESSAGE-----
```

"Yeah," I said. "It's pretty short."

"So it was not a full report."

"No. It might just say 'Mission Accomplished.'"

"We do not know what it says. It does not help to assume."

The cab burrowed farther into a tunnel, then stalled in traffic. The weather reports were talking about a big snowstorm tomorrow. People seemed to be getting a jump on their panicking.

I fiddled with the printed page, folded it, stuck it in my pocket. "So what now?"

Jael said, "Your original reason for reading Anderson's email was to gain leverage on him and avoid a meeting."

"Yeah."

"Did you accomplish that?"

"I don't know. I mean, Anderson must know that something is up, but I didn't really learn anything."

"What does Anderson know?"

"That he was locked out of his email."

"Can you use that?"

The cab driver had fallen into a sullen stupor as traffic inched its way through the tunnel. Simple logic dictated that the cars in this tunnel would eventually make it to the surface and go home, but I saw little evidence of that. I had given us about an hour to make a ten-minute drive across town, and it looked as if we were going to use every minute of it.

"This traffic is ridiculous," I said.

Jael said, "The traffic is irrelevant. You must find a way to regain the initiative against Anderson. He is dictating to you."

"I could call him now."

"And say what?"

"You'll see." I started dialing, then stopped. "He said he'd kill me if I kept bothering him."

"Everyone has threatened to kill you."

"Yeah, you're right. What's one more?"

Anderson picked up immediately. "Tucker, you hacking son of a bitch."

"And a Merry Christmas to you too, sir. Oh, I'm sorry. Do your people celebrate Christmas?"

"What people?"

"Dickless assholes."

Jael rolled her eyes.

Anderson ignored the insult. "Did you hack my email account?"

"And what if I did?"

"We'd have a problem."

"You sure that you don't want to send that to me in an email? I could send you my PGP key."

Silence.

"Yeah, Dave, I hacked your email," I said. "Turnabout is fair play."

"Well, as you say, it is encrypted."

"For now."

"What's that mean?"

"It means I'm decrypting it on my computer as we speak."

"Decrypting it? How are you decrypting it?"

"Why do you think it's called Pretty Good Privacy and not Fucking Great Privacy? It's like hiding your house key under your doormat. They assign hacking PGP as a homework assignment in computer science classes."

This was a great big lie. Nobody has ever successfully decrypted PGP. It is, in fact, Fucking Great Privacy. But Anderson wouldn't know that. Like most of the public, he'd assume that hackers are invincible and unstoppable.

Anderson said, "You are a dead man."

"Oh, very dramatic, Dave. But I don't think so. My whole stash of email goes to the FBI if something happens to me." That was an excellent idea. I should set that up. "They'll crack PGP even faster than me."

Silence at the other end.

"Hello, Dave?" I said. "Can you hear me now?"

"What do you want?" Anderson asked.

"I want you to give me Maria without a meeting tomorrow. I want you to call off your ambush and not kill Sal or me."

"Kill Sal? I was never going to kill Sal."

"Then what's the purpose of the meeting? What do you want for Maria?"

"I want Sal to call off his $10,000 hit on me, that's what I want. Then I want to go back to the way we were before he and I ever got involved."

"You going to give him his money back?"

"I'm going to give him his daughter back."

"You don't need a meeting for that."

"Yes, Tucker, I do. If I'm going to get Maria back to Sal, there has to be a meeting. A face-to-face meeting. That's the way it's gotta be."

What the hell?

"And Tucker," Anderson continued, "all that email crap doesn't mean squat if there isn't someone to testify as to how it was gathered. It would all get thrown out in court. So you enjoy your computational masturbation. Decrypt it all, because I don't care."

I was negotiating on fumes. "You're not gonna like the distraction, Dave."

"I swear to God, Tucker, if you call me Dave one more time—"

"You'll what? Kill me twice?"

"Wait for my call tomorrow," Anderson said. "As for today, watch the news and think about if you really want to threaten me."

He hung up.

I turned to Jael. "He doesn't care about the emails. He still wants to meet."

"Don't worry," Jael said. "I will—"

The cabbie interrupted us. "Here you go, sir."

The Whiskey Priest squatted in the darkness. Caroline was inside. She knew everything about me, and had been emailing Anderson.

It was time for some truth.

SIXTY-ONE

Caroline Quinn sat alone along the back window of the Whiskey Priest, the nighttime lights of Boston Harbor twinkling behind her as she read emails on her phone. Three rocks glasses sat on the table in front of her, two with an amber liquid, one with ice. It looked like she was waiting for me.

"Would you wait by the bar?" I asked Jael.

"You think this interrogation will go better without me?" Jael asked.

"I think that I'm not sure it should be an interrogation."

"You have not shown good judgment when it comes to—"

Caroline looked up, saw us, smiled, and waved us over. She stood as we approached. She wore a black turtleneck under a black cable sweater. Whatever prosthetic she had chosen today was hidden beneath an outstanding pair of sleek navy jeans.

Caroline hugged me and shook Jael's hand. "I'm Caroline Quinn."

Jael shook the hand. "I am Jael Navas."

"You were with Tucker on Hanover Street, right?"

"I am his bodyguard."

Caroline gave Jael an up-and-down appraisal. "Well, let's sit."

We sat. Caroline sat across from me next to the window. Jael sat next to Caroline, hemming her in.

Caroline glanced at Jael but turned her attention to me. "I ordered you one of my favorite bourbons, Tucker. It's called Blanton's," said Caroline. "Jael, would you like some whiskey?"

"No, thank you. I am working."

"Should I be worried? Are we going to get attacked?"

"Not to my knowledge."

I tried my bourbon. "It's good," I said. "Thank you."

We sat. Looked out into the harbor. There was nothing to see. The sun had pulled its disappearing act hours ago. I looked over the dark water. Random lights twinkled across the harbor. Caroline reached out. Touched my hand. I pulled it back without thinking. Caroline sat back. Crossed her arms.

"Well, this is awkward," she said.

"What's awkward?" I asked.

"This whole thing. The two of you. A bodyguard. What the hell is going on?"

"How was your day?" I asked.

"Oh, it was peachy. How was yours?"

"Funny you should ask. I hacked David Anderson's email account today."

"You realize that's a felony," said Caroline.

The Blanton's warmth rode through me. "You going to turn me in?"

"Of course not. Don't be ridiculous."

"I mean, if you didn't turn me in after what I told you today, then why turn me in for this, right?"

"Okay. Let's do a reset. I need to go to the ladies' room." Caroline stood. "Excuse me, Jael."

Jael remained in place.

Caroline tapped Jael on the arm. "Excuse me."

Jael said, "Tucker has a question for you."

"Well," said Caroline, "Tucker and his question will just have to wait. Now get the hell out of my way."

This was going badly. I nodded. Jael stood. Caroline slipped around the table and locked her gaze on me. "You had better have figured out a fucking great explanation for all this by the time I get back."

I watched Caroline stride to the ladies' room.

Jael asked, "Why didn't you ask her about the email?"

"I'm working up to it," I said.

"She knows everything."

"I know. I know."

We looked out the window until Caroline returned. She made an ushering motion to Jael. "Do you mind?"

"Do I mind?" asked Jael.

"Do you mind waiting at the bar? I want to talk to this chucklehead alone. I promise to guard his body for you while you're gone."

Jael slipped out of the booth. Strode to the bar, arranged herself where she could keep an eye on us.

Caroline sat, knocked the rest of her bourbon back, and thunked the glass onto the wooden table. "Explanations," she said. "Now."

I pulled the printed email out of my pocket, spread it out on the table. "I found this email."

Caroline looked at the sheet. "It's an email from me to David Anderson."

"Yeah."

"So?"

"What do you mean, 'So?' You sent it today, right after our—"

"Assignation?"

"Yeah, our assignation."

"Do you demand an email embargo from everyone you fuck?"

"No."

"Then what the hell?"

"David Anderson has threatened to kill me."

"I don't blame him."

"I'm serious."

"So am I."

"Why did you email him?"

"It's none of your goddamn business."

"Well—"

"But I'll tell you anyway."

"You will?"

"Yes. You know why?"

"No."

Caroline took both my hands in hers. She was warm and her hands were soft. She leaned forward, bore in. "Because it's clear to me that you're scared shitless."

My breath caught in my throat. She had named it. I started to talk, got stuck, tried again.

"Shh," Caroline said. "Don't say anything. I know you're scared, Tucker. It's why I came to see you this morning."

"Wha—?"

"Sal had told me what happened in Charlestown."

"He did?"

"You know why you're terrified? Because you know this could get you killed, but you also won't leave that little girl out there on her own."

I drained my glass, hoping the buzz would hit immediately.

Caroline continued, "And I thought, here's a guy who's got what it takes to stick with Maria. He'll have what it takes to stick with me."

"Stick with you?"

"Despite my job and my leg and my personality."

"I love your personality."

"Clearly, you have a mental condition."

I laughed. First laugh I'd had all day.

Caroline nudged the email. "David Anderson wanted to put me on retainer to be his advisor. If you decrypt that email you'll see that it reads 'No means no.'"

"You turned him down? He must have offered you millions."

"I don't need millions. I need self-respect. If he gets arrested, I'll make sure the state proves its case and he'll pay me for my time. But I'm not—"

"Excuse me." Bobby Miller stood above us, Jael next to him. "I need you with me, Tucker," he said.

"What?"

"Here's your coat. We're going."

Caroline said, "We're talking."

"Sorry, Counselor," said Bobby. He threw my coat in my lap. "Let's go."

"But—where?"

Bobby turned, headed for the door.

I stood to follow, but Caroline caught me. Kissed my cheek. "Be safe," she said.

Safety? That would be sweet.

SIXTY-TWO

BOBBY'S CHEVY IMPALA STEAMED exhaust in a double-parked spot on Northern Ave. As we climbed over a shoveled-out fire hydrant to reach the car, Bobby said, "You can sit in the back with Jael."

"I would love to sit in the back with Jael, but I have something you need to know," I said.

"You can tell me from the back."

"It's hard to talk from the back."

"Good. Then for once in your life, don't talk."

I slumped in the back seat, directly behind Bobby. Jael slid in next to me.

I typed out a message on my phone, showed it to her: `I need to talk about Hanover Street. You OK with it?`

Jael pursed her lips. She was most likely not okay with it.

`Trust me.`

Jael nodded, crossed her arms, and looked out the window.

I called forward, "So, as I was saying."

"Yeah, Tucker, tell me what you were saying," Bobby said.

"I was saying that you are a big fat pussy."

Bobby nearly spun the car trying to turn and get a look at me. "Fuck you."

"Hey, pussy, you wanted me to sit back here. Now you deal with it."

Bobby caught my eye in the rearview mirror. "How am I a pussy?"

"All this bullshit about how I lied to you."

"You did lie to me."

"How?"

"You kept Hanover Street from me."

"What do you think happened on Hanover Street?"

"I think you and Jael were talking to Hugh Graxton and Oscar Sagese when Pistol Salvucci and his buddy smashed the window and tried to shoot you."

"That's what you think."

"Yeah, it's obvious. Ten witnesses place you there."

"Then what do you need me for, Bobby? You want me to pat you on the head and tell you how smart you are?"

"I want you to be honest with me."

"And that makes you a pussy," I said. "'Oh, Tucker, it hurts my feelings when you don't share.'"

"This has nothing to do with sharing. It has to do with trust."

"Trust? You've still got your GPS tracker on my phone. What do you know about trust? You've got no idea who to trust."

"Oh, fuck you."

"Jael here is the most trustworthy person on the planet, and yet you trust that piece of shit Frank Cantrell over her."

"Frank is a good agent," Bobby said. "What are you trying to do?"

"What am I trying to do? I'm trying to save your friggin' life, you moron."

"Why would you say that about Frank?"

I paused. Could I do this without betraying Sal? The impossibilities of my situation hadn't changed. I had done nothing but wedge myself in tighter between a rock and a hard place.

Bobby said, "Well?"

I caught Bobby's eye in the rearview mirror. "You promise not to arrest me if I tell you this?"

"Of course I don't promise not to arrest you. What did you do?"

"It's a felony."

"For Christ's sake. Just tell me."

"I hacked David Anderson's email today, downloaded a bunch of his messages."

"And?"

"Frank Cantrell sent an email to David Anderson this afternoon."

"What did it say?"

"I don't know. It was encrypted."

"Seriously? What do you want me to do with that?"

"Well, isn't it suspicious?"

"I don't know," said Bobby. "There are a thousand reasons that Frank could be emailing Anderson."

"Name one."

"Undercover operation."

"Wouldn't you know about it?"

"No. That's what makes it an undercover operation." Bobby pulled to a stop next to Columbus Park, where Sal, Hugh, and I had argued a day ago.

Jael said, "There is more."

"You think Frank's dirty too?" Bobby asked.

"Agent Cantrell is dirty," said Jael. "I am sure of it. I have seen it myself."

"What did he do?"

Jael said to me, "There is only one way forward."

"I don't want to betray him," I said.

Bobby asked, "Who?"

"Anyone," I said. "I don't want to betray anyone."

"Will you just tell me what's going on?"

Jael said, "It is time for the truth, Tucker."

"Are you going to tell him?" I asked.

"You should do it."

I took a deep breath. "Bobby, a couple of days ago I was on the Commonwealth Ave Mall with Jael and S—"

Someone rapped on the window. We looked out to see Frank Cantrell shout through the glass: "You guys going to get out here or what?"

SIXTY-THREE

THE TWINKLING LIGHTS UNDER the Columbus Park arbor were pulling their weight now that the sun was gone, turning an archway of desiccated vines into a fairy tunnel. I'd have stopped to gape at them if I wasn't being hustled along to a spot beyond the park where a fence made of thick black chains kept people from accidentally pitching into the harbor.

The chains did nothing, however, to keep a body from being intentionally pitched into the harbor. The body at the bottom of the rock harbor rested on a pile of frozen seawater chunks.

"Who is it?" I asked.

"You mean who *was* it," said Frank Cantrell.

"Yeah, who was it?"

"Jarrod Cooper."

Jarrod's body was splayed across the chunks, his neck bent at an impossible angle, his legs floating in the water.

"Did somebody throw him down there?"

"We figure he got shot and then thrown into the water farther away from shore. But the currents are crazy, and he must have drifted in here at high tide."

"The tide is going out now," Jael said.

Frank said, "Yeah. But he got hung up on the ice."

I asked Bobby, "Why did you bring me here?"

"I wanted to know if you had any ideas about who did this," Bobby said. "Give you a chance to tell us what might have happened."

"Why would I know anything?"

"Oh, c'mon, Tucker," Frank said. "You're right in the middle of all of this. You're a hacker. He was a hacker. Your cousin was mad at him. You worked for him. Why wouldn't we ask you some questions about him?"

"Why blame Sal for this?"

Bobby said, "We're not blaming Sal, but we're sure interested in Sal."

"Sal had issues with Jarrod Cooper," Frank said.

"Sal had issues with a lot of people," I said. "Did they all wind up in the harbor?"

Bobby said, "We don't know where they wound up."

I knew where they wound up: a shipping container someplace in Asia. I looked down at Jarrod floating in the water. Guys in black wetsuits were wrapping a rope around his chest, getting ready to hoist him onto shore. I didn't want to see that.

I said to Jael, "We should be going."

She nodded and we turned from the harbor. Walked back toward the Impala.

Bobby followed. "Where are you going?"

"Why wasn't there any blood?" I asked.

"Blood? Where?"

"On the ice. Why wasn't there any blood?"

"Bodies don't bleed when they're dead, and Jarrod had been dead for a while."

"You think he died instantly, or do you think he drowned?"

"Depends where he was shot. We'll know when we get him out of the water."

We reached the Impala.

I looked over Bobby's shoulder. Frank Cantrell had stopped watching the body retrieval and was striding toward us.

"Cantrell is dirty," I said. "What will it take to convince you?"

Bobby said, "A lot more than just your word."

"I'm telling you that he's going to get you killed."

"Smearing Frank Cantrell is not going to help Sal."

"I'm not trying—"

Frank caught up. "Hey Tucker," he said, "you'd better watch your ass. Looks like it's open season on hackers."

"What are you talking about, Frank?" I asked.

"I'm just saying that hackers like Jarrod over there, guys who can steal passwords, think they're real smart until they get caught up in something that's bigger than them."

"Is that what happened here?"

"You tell me. Why would someone kill Jarrod?"

"Shit, I don't know, Frank. If you're so smart, why don't you tell me?"

Cantrell stepped close. "I think Jarrod pissed off the wrong guy."

"Who? You?"

Cantrell shoved me. I bounced off the car hood. "I've had enough of your shit, Tucker."

Bobby stepped between us. "C'mon, guys, this is ridiculous. Frank, go direct things over there."

Frank said, "This asshole is pissing me off."

"Yeah, he's pissing me off too, but I still want you to let me handle him."

Cantrell gave me the finger and stalked off.

I called after him, "Happy New Year to you too, Frank."

"Will you just shut up for once?" Bobby asked.

"You've gotta start listening to me."

"Yeah, well, not today."

"Fine. Whatever. C'mon, Jael, let's go." I started walking.

"Where are you going?" called Bobby.

I ignored Bobby, dialed my phone instead. Sal picked up. "Can I come over?" I asked.

"Yeah."

Jael and I walked down Commercial toward Salutation and Sal's place. I tried to formulate a plan as we went, because I was pretty certain of what had happened to Jarrod Cooper. I needed to make Bobby see it.

SIXTY-FOUR

I KNOCKED ON SAL'S door, expecting to be blown away by the combined odors of stale food, pine needles, and prison sweat. I was wrong.

Sal opened the door onto a pristine apartment.

"C'mon in," he said.

The Christmas tree was gone, its place of honor taken by an easel holding a large, framed photo of Sal and Sophia on their wedding day. Sal's hair had been jet black before it took on today's silver highlights. Sophia sat in Sal's tuxedoed lap, wearing a tight wedding dress whose strapless décolletage raised questions about whether the laws of physics applied to boobs.

The dining room stood empty, its holiday table having been stored wherever dining room tables went after the holidays. Maria's room had been straightened to within an inch of its life. The closet and drawers were shut tight, the bed made, the floor cleared down to the hardwood.

"Holy crap, Sal, did you do all this?" I asked.

"Yeah. It was time to get my shit together."

"There might have been evidence," said Jael.

"Fuck that," said Sal. "The cops took all the evidence they wanted when they were trying to prove that I stran—was the one."

Jael said, "I meant evidence for finding Maria."

"There's nothing here that's gonna help," said Sal. "I believe Tucker now. I think Maria's still in the North End."

"Why would you think that?"

In answer, Sal pressed the button on an old answering machine.

Maria said, "Daddy. I don't want you to worry. I'm hiding with Angie—"

"Wow," I said.

Sal held up his hand. Maria wasn't finished. "—so Tucker won't get me."

"What?" I said.

"So you won't get her?" Sal said. "What the fuck is that about? Did you say something?"

I had played and replayed the day of sledding on the Common. Well, not so much replayed it as reconstructed it. There's little more repetitive than watching a kid go up and down a hill on a sled. All our conversations were the same.

I would say, "Are you cold yet?" Because I was cold.

Maria would say, "I want to go again." She would go again, and I would stand at the top of the hill and do jumping jacks trying to generate heat.

"No idea," I told Sal. "You were there at the end."

"How about you?" Sal asked Jael. "Any idea why Maria should be afraid of Tucker?"

"No," said Jael.

"It explains why she ran when she heard your voice," said Sal.

I said, "Yeah, but it doesn't explain why she's afraid of me."

"Where did she call from?" Jael asked.

"I don't know," said Sal. "I couldn't hear anything in the background."

"Do you have caller ID?" I asked.

"No," said Sal. "I never bought the box."

"Do you have star sixty-nine?"

"What's that?"

"You dial star sixty-nine and it calls back someone who just called you."

Sal picked up the phone, dialed *69. My phone rang.

Sal said, "Look at that. It works. You're a genius."

"Well, how was I supposed to know you had another call?" I asked.

"This does not help," said Jael.

Sal asked, "Tucker, did you talk to Joey Pupo?"

"I had never heard of Joey Pupo until that day."

"Then how did he know to go to the Common to get Maria?"

"Well, how did you know?"

"I knew because Frank Cantrell called me. He said that he'd heard some, you know, chatter or something, about someone kidnapping Maria. Told me to get over there."

Jael said, "The police were waiting for you there."

"Yeah," said Sal. "Now that you mention it, they were."

"Do you think it was just a ploy to get you out into the open?" I asked.

Jael said, "If it were only a ploy, nobody would have taken Maria."

"Oh, Jesus," I said. "It's worse than I thought."

"What?" asked Sal.

"Think about it. Somebody set things up so that you, Sophia, and Maria were all separated."

Jael said, "A coordinated attack."

"Exactly. Maria gets taken at the same time that Sal gets arrested and Sophia gets—"

"Murdered," Sal said.

"Yeah," I said. "At the same time that Sophia gets murdered."

Jael said, "There is a connecting thread."

"Right. Frank Cantrell set it all in motion with his phone calls."

"And he wasn't there when I got arrested," Sal said.

"Right."

"So he killed Sophia? Why would he do that?"

I said, "It made no sense to me until just now. Jarrod Cooper's murder pulled it together."

"Jarrod Cooper got murdered?" Sal asked. "The PassHack guy?"

"His body is over by Columbus Park. Cantrell says you shot him."

"I got nothing to do with that."

"No, of course not."

Jael said, "David Anderson is cleaning up loose ends."

"Jarrod Cooper was floating facedown in freezing water," I said to Jael. "Did you see any sign of how he died?"

"No," said Jael. "There were no wounds."

"So then, how did Frank Cantrell know that Jarrod Cooper had been shot?"

The answer was finally obvious. The pieces: Sal getting arrested just as Maria was kidnapped, Sal arriving at the Common just in time for the kidnapping, Joey Pupo being an informant, the ransom note appearing at my apartment. Cantrell had done it all. Shit, he even showed up at the scene of the crime when he pulled me away from Lieutenant Lee.

"Ah, shit," I said. "We should have seen it at the start."

"Frank Cantrell did it all," Jael said.

"He's been working for David Anderson."

"And he put this whole thing in motion because Anderson wanted to make a lesson of you."

"Fucking Frank," said Sal.

"I tried to tell Bobby that Frank was dirty, but he won't listen to me," I said.

"So how do we get him to see it?"

"I know how to do it." I outlined my plan.

Sal and Jael looked at each other, said nothing.

"It'll be okay," I said.

Famous last words.

SIXTY-FIVE

THERE ARE UNINHABITED PLACES in this world, places where one can be sure that nobody will see you, places where you can get away with murder. A cornfield in Kansas will do. Death Valley affords solitude. The backwoods of Maine swallow screams and gunshots.

None of these places were within easy driving distance of Boston, so Jael, Sal, and I stood at the base of a high seawall on Revere Beach, in the winter, at eleven o'clock at night. Nobody was out on the water. Nobody was on the beach. Nobody was peeking over the concrete seawall. We could do what we needed to do unseen.

Jael said, "This could go very badly."

The silent ocean lay at the edge of a hundred feet of tidal flat. Low tide. Chunks of ice clung to the breakers where the salt water had congealed in the cold. A wet ocean breeze froze my face and found the chinks in my jacket.

I shivered. "Do we have a better plan?" I asked.

"Now you ask?" Sal said. "This was your fucking idea."

"I know, but I can't think of anything else."

Jael said, "Bobby is my friend."

"Mine too," I said.
"This is wrong."
"We're doing it for the right reasons."
Sal said, "Why don't you two shut up?"
The seawall towered ten feet behind us, but the beach farther down rose to meet the wall, making it only two feet high for most of its length. A hundred yards away, a solitary figure climbed over the seawall and jumped onto the snow-covered sand. The figure put hand to forehead, peering around the beach, a useless gesture with no sun to block. He couldn't see us anyway. We stood in shadow. The figure shrugged and trudged toward us. We stood among rocks on wet sand that had been scrubbed clean of snow by the ocean. Barnacles clung to the rocks like frost, waiting for the tide to rise and feed them.
The figure crunched through the snow, then over the wet sand. It was Frank Cantrell, right on schedule. Cantrell saw us against the seawall and veered to join the group.
"What the hell, Sal?" Cantrell said. "Why meet here?"
Sal said, "It's private here."
"Guy could get killed on these rocks."
"Guy could get killed a lot of ways."
Cantrell unbuttoned his coat. "What's that supposed to mean?"
I asked, "Where did you learn to use PGP encryption, Frank?"
Cantrell said, "What are you talking about?"
"You sent David Anderson encrypted emails. What was that about?"
Sal said, "You turning on me, Frank? You playing both sides?"
Jael edged behind Cantrell. He turned to keep her in view. "That's plenty far," he told her.
"I want to know," said Sal. "You throw in with Anderson now?"
"How did you see that email?" Cantrell asked me.
"Elves," I said. "I've got magic email elves."
"Don't fuck with me, you hacker son of a bitch."

Sal said, "Fuck with you? He's not fucking with you. You're fucking with me. I paid you twenty thousand this month and got nothing for it. Now I hear you're buddies with Anderson?"

"I'm not buddies with Anderson," said Cantrell. "I'm investigating. I gotta ask him some questions."

"That's bullshit," I said. "You weren't using an FBI account."

Jael slid closer to me. She stood next to me and I stood next to Sal. Cantrell faced the three of us, his back to the footprints he had left in the snow. A hundred yards away, another figure jumped down from the seawall.

"Of course I wasn't using an FBI account," said Cantrell. "It's a back channel thing."

The figure, large and round, found Cantrell's footsteps, started following them.

Sal said, "What do you mean, *back channel?*"

The figure was Bobby Miller, still more than half a football field away. I focused on Cantrell's face.

Cantrell said, "I'm trying to gain his trust. To gather data."

"By killing Sophia?" I asked.

"What? I didn't kill Sophia. I don't know who killed her."

"How about Jarrod Cooper?"

A pause. "What are you talking about? You saying I shot Jarrod?"

"How did you know he was shot?"

"Listen—"

"Cut the shit, you two. Frank, if you're switching sides, tell me to my face," said Sal.

"I'm not switching sides," said Cantrell.

"He would not tell you if he were," said Jael.

"Don't believe him," I said.

Cantrell said, "Don't listen to this hacker, Sal. We've been friends for years. I'm your guy."

Bobby had fifty yards to go.

Sal said to me, "He did get me out on bail."

Cantrell said, "Yeah, I made that deal with Caroline Quinn. Got you out."

I shook my head. "That would have happened anyway."

"He will tell you what you want to hear," said Jael.

"I swear that I'm telling the truth, Sal."

Twenty-five yards.

Sal asked, "You're my guy?"

Cantrell said, "Absolutely."

"Okay," said Sal. "Prove it."

Behind Cantrell, Bobby Miller said, "Aloysius Tucker, Jael Navas, and Sal Rizzo, you are under arrest."

SIXTY-SIX

CANTRELL WHIRLED. SAW BOBBY Miller standing behind him. Bobby nodded at Cantrell.

"Good job, Frank," Bobby said as he stood next to Cantrell.

"What are you doing here?"

"Got a tip."

I said, "This is bullshit, Bobby."

"No," said Bobby. "What was bullshit was you hiding Hanover Street from me."

"I wasn't on Hanover Street," said Sal.

"Shut up, Sal," Bobby said. "The three of you. On your knees."

"Oh, for Christ's sake," I said. "I'm not getting on my knees. It's freezing here."

Bobby unbuttoned his coat. "Don't make me draw on you, Tucker. You were my friend."

"Were?"

Jael said, "You were my friend too, Agent Miller." She drew her gun and pointed it between Bobby's eyes.

Bobby flinched. Raised his hands in front of his face, as if to catch the bullet before it killed him. "Jesus, Jael. What the hell?"

Cantrell said, "Cut that shit out."

Jael said, "On your knees, Agent Miller."

Bobby dropped onto the wet sand. Sal drew his gun. Cantrell remained standing.

"What are you doing?" asked Bobby.

"I am not going to your American prison," said Jael. "Hands behind your head."

Bobby slid his hands behind his head, interlocking the fingers. "Don't shoot me, Jael. Please, God!"

Cold water glittered in the tidal pools. The seawall rose above us, concrete and implacable, hiding evidence of the civilized world. Sweat gleamed on Bobby's bald head despite the cold. Sal and Jael stood, weapons drawn, pointing them at Bobby. Both had the same blank stare, mouths set in an impartial line, their souls turning inward to hide from what had to be done. I envied them. I looked at Bobby kneeling in the sand, tried to snuff out the notion that he was my friend.

I said to Jael, "What about Cantrell?"

Jael said, "We will have to kill him too, unless he proves himself."

Cantrell asked, "What the fuck is this, Sal?"

"Time for you to choose, Frank," Sal said. "Either you prove you're my guy and kill Miller, or we kill you both."

Short puffs of steam obscured Cantrell's face. He looked from Sal to Jael to me to Bobby. Bobby looked up at Cantrell, his fingers interlocked behind his head. He said, "Frank?"

Cantrell pulled his gun from its holster. It was big and black. He slid the top of it back. It clicked.

Cantrell said, "I'm sorry, Bobby."

Bobby said, "What are you talking about?"

"Come on, isn't it obvious?" Cantrell said.

"What?"

"I'm dirty. This whole charade proves it." Cantrell pointed his gun at Bobby.

Bobby said, "Killing me won't help, Frank."

Cantrell said, "Killing you? Why would I kill you?" Cantrell's gun moved. The black hole of its barrel slid up, away from Bobby.

Bobby said, "No!"

The hole pointed, like a deadly finger, at open space. Then at Sal.

Bobby reached into his jacket.

The gun slid past Sal, pointed to the rocks beyond him, then onto Jael. Her lips pulled back into a grimace, her hand tightened.

Bobby held a gun.

Cantrell's gun slid past Jael, into the space between her and me, and rested on my chest. I gasped.

Cantrell said, "Two hackers in one day."

The trigger slid, responding to the tightening of Cantrell's ungloved hand. I froze. Bobby raised his gun. I fixated on Bobby's knees, imagined them getting wet and cold. Heard Cantrell's gun *click*. It *boomed* at the same time as Bobby's. I was thrown to the ground. But the bullet hadn't knocked me down.

Jael had.

My head hit a barnacled rock with a scraping blow. I lay on the sand for a second, orienting myself. I rolled, sat up, and looked across a black shape to see Cantrell lying in the sand, his head misshapen, a chunk of it gone. Bobby, still on his knees, lowered his gun.

Sal rushed toward the black shape as I crawled, my head spinning. Jael Navas lay on her back, her teeth gritted, her eyes staring. She seemed to be concentrating on breathing, getting air in and out. A wet hole glistened in her chest, whistling with each breath.

SIXTY-SEVEN

HOSPITALS SMELL LIKE SADNESS.

The odor is always there, just under the cover of antiseptics, floor cleaners, and ubiquitous hand sanitizer. It worms its way into your nostrils, your hair, your skin, reminding you that staph germs are everywhere, poking, prodding, searching for a pimple or overripe hair follicle, hoping to deliver the yellow spot of infection. My hands, after touching the doors, the chairs, and the coffee machine, felt coated by an invisible and permanent layer of filth.

I'd sent Sal home. He'd offered to stay. Insisted. I told him to go. He was threadbare and gray, a beaten gorilla who had been shocked into submission by the zookeeper's cattle prod and could do nothing but sit in the corner of a bare glass tank and rock. He needed sleep. He needed time in a dark room, alone and safe on his couch. He hadn't slept in his bed since they found Sophia on it.

Bobby never made it to the hospital. He'd killed a fellow agent. There were debriefings, interrogations, and inquiries. He never asked me to come with him to support his story. He told me to be here when Jael came back to us. I was alone.

Then I wasn't. A pair of gray ASICS sneakers appeared in front of me. I looked up.

It was Hugh Graxton. Unshaven. Wearing jeans under a maroon UMass sweatshirt.

Hugh pointed down at me. "What did you do?"

What did I do? Nothing. I had stared down the barrel of a gun and waited for it to kill me while Jael jumped in front of me.

What did I do? Everything. I had set a trap to get Frank Cantrell to incriminate himself to Bobby. A trap so stupid and transparent that he had recognized it immediately, had recognized the naive mind that had conceived it, and had acted to take revenge before the trap closed.

Jael had warned me. *This could go very badly.* It had.

Graxton was still there. "I asked you a question."

What to say? Nothing. I averted my gaze. "Have a seat."

"I don't want a seat. I want to know what happened."

Shook my head. Small arcs. "She took a bullet for me."

"Why?"

Looked up. "Couldn't tell you." Looked back at Hugh's shoes.

"Aw, shit," said Hugh, slumping into a nearby seat, leaving a gap between us. "Well, what did the doctor say?"

"He didn't say anything."

"Why not?"

"Privacy. They'll tell me when she's been moved to a room."

"So she's going to be okay?"

I shrugged. "How did you know I'd be here?"

"Sal called. Told me everything."

Silence. I pulled out my phone, played solitaire, mindlessly losing game after game. Hugh stared into space.

I said, "I didn't realize you and Jael were friends."

Hugh said, "She's a special lady."

"I know."

More solitaire.

"Frank Cantrell killed Jarrod Cooper," I said. "I think Anderson is cleaning house."

"Anderson's a tool."

"Yeah."

"Frank Cantrell is worse. He's a weasel."

"Was a weasel."

"Was?"

"Bobby killed him."

"No shit."

"Just after Frank shot Jael."

"Good for Bobby."

"You think Frank was working for Anderson?"

"Sure, why not? He was a bigger whore than Angie."

"You would know," I said.

"You didn't even get a blow job? What's wrong with you?"

"I've got some standards," I said. It was a mean thing to say, but there you have it.

"More like you messed up somehow," said Hugh. He crossed his arms, stared at the door to the waiting room.

I played more solitaire, played my date with Angie over in my mind. What did I do wrong? Probably it was not being ready to go to Capital Grille.

"Here we go," said Hugh.

A doctor had slipped through the waiting room door. He was a small Indian man, looked to be in his twenties. We made eye contact. Hugh and I stood.

"How is she?" I asked.

The doctor said, "She's in intensive care."

"And?"

"I really can't share more than that."

Hugh said, "You can tell me, doc."

"No. I can't."

Hugh reached into his jeans, pulled out a sheet of paper. "I'm her health care proxy."

Good one.

"Ah," said the doctor, reviewing the paper. "Thank you, Mr. Graxton." The doctor looked at me.

Hugh said, "He's cool. Just tell us."

"She had a collapsed lung. Broken ribs. Lots of bleeding."

"How is she?"

"We repaired the lung, removed the bullet, and have her on a ventilator as a precaution. She's sedated."

It was like talking to Microsoft technical support. The guy was spewing facts that were true and useless at the same time. I asked, "Will she live?"

The doctor glanced at me, addressed Hugh. "Guarded optimism for a full recovery. She should be able to take visitors tomorrow."

Hugh said, "Thanks, Doc."

They shook hands. The doctor slipped back into his netherworld.

Hugh said, "Well, that's that."

"Good thinking on the health care proxy," I said.

"What are you talking about?"

"It wouldn't have occurred to me to lie to the doctor."

"I wasn't lying."

Right. "It's late," I said. "Don't screw with me."

"I *am* her health care proxy."

I stared at Hugh. Tried to fit the pieces together. They didn't fit. "Really," I said. "She appointed you as her guardian in a hospital?"

Hugh brandished the paper. "Yeah. Why so surprised?"

"Why you?" I asked.

"Why not me?"

"I don't know. I just would have thought—"

"It's not all about you, Tucker."

An image flashed in my mind: Jael and Hugh, in bed. A handsome couple, yet still a disturbing thought.

I asked, "Does Jael know about Sandy?"

"Sandy?"

"The girl you've got living with you."

Hugh folded the proxy once, twice, making a clean rectangle. He slipped it into his back pocket, crossed his arms across his UMass logo, and faced me square on. He was a little bit taller, a little bit older, a little bit grayer.

"It's none of your business," he said.

"What is?"

Hugh made a stirring motion with his finger. "This whole thing. Me, Jael, Sandy. It's none of your business."

"So you're saying there's something there?"

"No. I'm saying it's none of your business. Don't ask me about Jael. Don't ask me about Sandy."

I said, "It's not right."

My phone chirped. I had a message.

Hugh said, "You'd better check that."

He turned, walked away. Stopped at the door. Turned. "You know why Jael trusts me with her privacy?"

"Why?"

"Because I can keep a secret."

Hugh left.

I can keep a secret. I fiddled with the phone, brought up the message.

It was from Caroline.

`Caroline: Awake?`

`Me: Oh yeah.`

Caroline: Sal told me what happened. How is Jael?

Me: They're optimistic, but she's still sedated.

Caroline: Sal said that thing that happened was your idea.

Me: Yeah. Another great idea.

Caroline: You need to talk? I could come over.

Me: Really?

Caroline: Yes.

Me: That would be great. But why would you come over?

Caroline: See you in an hour.

Now there was someone who could keep a secret.

SIXTY-EIGHT

I TELL MYSELF THAT I shouldn't drink so much, that a booze assortment that consisted partially of WhistlePig rye, Lagavulin scotch, Bully Boy whiskey, Tito's vodka, 1792 bourbon, Hendrick's gin, and Jack's Abby beer was perhaps too much for a man who lived alone with two hermit crabs.

But then I tell myself to shut up and pour something.

I had arrived at my apartment before Caroline, checked on the hermit crabs, and, scanning the bottles in my cabinet, pulled out the Black Maple Hill Kentucky bourbon. A lady was coming to visit.

Caroline arrived around one in the morning, looking a little worse for wear. Her eyes had lost their normal flash and sparkle, settling for a sort of tired crinkle. She was back in jeans, a turtleneck, and a big sweater.

I said, "Wow, you look great."

"You're a big liar," Caroline said. "You pouring that?"

I poured us each a rocks glass of bourbon and we took them into the living room, sat on the couch.

"It's not that I'm not grateful for the company—"

"But?"

"It's so late. I don't get why you're here."

Caroline drank bourbon. "You know what I do for a living, Tucker?"

"Yeah. You defend Mafia guys."

"Well, not just the Mafia, though they make up a good portion of my business. There's also the Bratva, the Triad, the Irish Mob, and seven-figure white guys who got their hand caught in the cookie jar."

"That's a hell of a portfolio."

"Yeah, it is. And do you know who is not in that portfolio?"

"No, who?"

Caroline slipped closer to me on the couch, put her hand on my shoulder, touching my neck and bringing me closer. "A nice guy who wants to do the right thing."

"And that would be me?"

"Yeah."

"Because I feel more like an idiot who got his friend shot."

Caroline sat back with her drink. "You could see it that way."

"But this didn't really answer my question. Why are you here?"

"I'm here because I'd like to have a friend."

"A friend?"

"Well, a friend with benefits."

"Ahh."

"You're pretty good with the benefits there, pal."

"Why, thank you." I drank, gestured to Caroline. "What do you think?"

She sipped hers. "Nice. Sorry I can't say more. I can never do that 'I get hints of vanilla' thing."

"Me neither," I said. I went back to my original point. "But I would have thought you'd have lots of friends."

"Why would I?" Caroline asked. "I'm a one-legged Mafia lawyer."

"Oh, that's unkind," I said. "I distinctly remember being between two very nice legs. I think you're great."

Caroline shot back her bourbon. "You see why I like you?"

I followed suit, rose, walked to the cabinet, got the bottle, gave us each another splash, flopped on the couch.

Caroline said, "You know that you were doing your best tonight, right?"

"Yeah, sure. My best."

"You went up against a crooked FBI agent. That's pretty hairy. So yeah, you did the best you could."

"Is that what Sal told you?"

"No. Sal was not as kind. He said you were an idiot."

"You know, screw Sal. I got him a meeting with David Anderson to get Maria back."

"When?"

"Tomorrow sometime. Anderson is going to call me with details."

"And you're going?"

"Sure. Sal's going. Why not me?"

"Because it's probably a trap."

"'All in the valley of Death, rode the six hundred.'"

"Oh my God," said Caroline. "You're quoting Tennyson. You're officially drunk."

And I was. I was gloriously drunk. The alcohol had washed it all away: the guilt, the fear, the dead certain knowledge that I had no idea what I was doing, the dismay at being killed tomorrow next to Sal. All gone.

I looked at Caroline. "Hey, pretty lady. How about some of those benefits?"

Caroline said, "I think benefits would kill you."

"Oh no, oh no. I'll rally."

"Let me enjoy the rest of my drink."

"Okay," I said and poured myself a little more. Caroline put her hand on mine. Took the bottle and brought it across the room. I watched her hips sway there and her front sway back. I no longer noticed the limp.

Caroline leaned into me. A thought popped into my head and slipped through my lips before I could stop it.

"So why did you email Anderson?" I asked.

Caroline sat up, shifted away from me. "Again with that?"

Aw, crap. "Well—it was just niggling in my brain."

Big sigh from Caroline. "I told you, he wants me to work for him."

"And, if I remember correctly, you said, 'No.'"

"Exactly. Actually it was closer to 'Hell, no.'"

"So he wants you to defend him?"

"No," said Caroline. "He wants me to help him keep from getting arrested."

"And you don't want to do that?"

"That's where I draw the line."

I raised my glass. "Bully for you."

Caroline rolled her eyes. "Okay. Time to get you to bed." She pulled on my hand.

I stood, and we walked to the bedroom together. Once inside, Caroline helped me take off my shirt and pants. She kissed my chest, slipped her tongue across my nipple. I groaned and pulled her close.

"Do you have something I could wear to bed?" she asked.

"I was thinking nothing," I said.

"For after," she said.

I fumbled over to my chest of drawers, pulled out a long t-shirt with a bottle of Harpoon IPA down the front. "How's this?"

"Good," said Caroline. "I need to use the bathroom."

Caroline left for the bathroom. I pulled open the polar fleece sheets, slipped into bed, fluffed Caroline's pillow, then mine, and lay back to wait for her.

And fell asleep.

SIXTY-NINE

THE BRUINS FOGHORN CUT into my dreams, transitioning me to a hockey game, then a Patriots game, then to a combination of both in which I was executing a goal-line penalty kick. The foghorn stopped, then started again. My eyes popped open as my ringtone blasted in the dark.

Caroline lay snuggled against me, snoring softly in the long t-shirt. I pawed through my memories, trying to dredge up what we did together last night. I guessed we slept, just slept. *Huh.*

The foghorn blasted again. Somebody wanted to talk to me. Caroline stirred and moaned. I silenced the phone and slipped from the bed. The phone hadn't woken her, but a bouncing mattress would. I closed the bedroom door behind me, taking the phone with me.

"Hello," I croaked.

"Did I wake you?" It was David Anderson. "Early to bed, et cetera, et cetera."

"What do you want?"

"Today's the big day, remember? Sal gets Maria back."

"I remember."

"I picked a meeting place. We'll meet there at noon."

"How dramatic."

"I try. It's simple. I'll give Sal my message, and you guys leave with Maria."

"What about Angie?"

"Angie will be there. She insists. I don't need to tell you to come alone, right?"

"Not alone. You mean with Sal."

"You engineers are worse than accountants. Yes, the plural *you*. *Youse, y'all,* whatever."

"Is that why you killed Jarrod Cooper? Excessive precision?"

"I didn't kill Jarrod Cooper."

"No, you had Cantrell do it for you."

Silence.

I said, "Yeah, I know Cantrell did it, and I know he was working for you."

"Cantrell was hoping to work for me," Anderson said. "I mentioned being concerned about Jarrod's resolve and apparently Cantrell decided to show initiative. It was a Thomas Becket problem."

"You mean Josh Beckett."

"No, not the pitcher. The priest."

"What priest?"

"Jesus, Tucker. You *are* an engineer. Didn't you ever take—forget it. Just be there."

"Where?"

He told me.

"That's ridiculous," I said.

"It's perfect." He hung up.

I called Sal, got voicemail, hung up, texted him: `Call me. We get Maria today.`

I made coffee, remembered the guest sleeping in my bedroom, and broke out the Kitchen-Aid. I assembled raisin muffins and put them in the oven to cook. My phone rang. It was Sal.

"Where the fuck are you?" he asked.

I said, "I'm home. Where are you?"

"I'm at the hospital."

"Mass General?"

"Of course Mass General. I'm visiting Jael."

"Well, that's nice of you."

"Why the fuck aren't you here?"

Sal was playing the holier-than-thou game. I said, "They're not even open yet."

"Of course they're open. They're always open. They're a fucking hospital."

"Okay. Okay. I'm having breakfast with—I'm having breakfast. I'm heading over after."

"The woman took a bullet for you, asshole. The least you can do is be here."

"Is she awake?"

"No. You should still be here."

"Look. Fine. I'm a horrible person. That's not why I called you."

Caroline peeked out of my bedroom and slipped into the bathroom. I told Sal what David Anderson had told me.

Sal said, "He wants to meet there at noon? What the fuck?"

"Tell me about it."

"What did you tell him?"

"That we'd be there at noon."

Silence on the line.

"Sal?" I asked. "You there?"

"He's going to kill us."

"That's what Jael said."

"She's right."

"Maybe you could call Hugh. See if he can help."

"I'll ask him."

"Where is he?"

"He's sitting next to me."

"Oh."

"Get your ass down here." He hung up.

There it was. The high point of my day: ceding the moral high ground to two gangsters.

SEVENTY

A BOUQUET OF FLOWERS adorned the nightstand next to Jael's hospital bed. Another sat on the dresser. The flowers had come in with the two visitors: Hugh in a plastic easy chair, and Sal, who stood by the bed looking at an unconscious Jael.

Sal turned, looked me up and down. "Where are your fucking flowers?"

Hugh said, "Jesus, Tucker, you've got no class."

"You mind if I just see how she is?" I said.

"She's unconscious," Sal said. "Get your ass downstairs and buy her some fucking flowers."

"Big ones," said Hugh.

I turned, went back to the elevators, pushed the button. They were assholes, but they were right. How hard would it have been to stop by the gift shop on the way up? I added a little more guilt to the fear churning in my gut. It made for a putrid smoothie.

Buying flowers in the hospital gift shop would have made me feel even worse than having forgotten them. Google on my phone told me about a flower place across the street from the hospital. I pushed through the revolving doors and back into the street.

The cold wasn't so bad. We had swapped it for low gray clouds. The frozen ozone smell of snow hung in the air. I brought up my phone's weather app. Yup. Snow. People scurried through the city, heads bent by the pressure of impending snow. They wanted to get their work done and be home before the storm engulfed us. Boston's psyche has never recovered from the storm of '78, a blizzard that trapped hundreds of cars on the 128 beltway, closed schools for weeks, and destroyed homes along the coast.

Bostonians fear nor'easters more than hurricanes. A hurricane blows through, topples trees, kills the electricity, and floods the coast. A nor'easter does all that and also immobilizes the city in snow, trapping people in unheated houses, halting repair crews, stalling emergency vehicles, and making the apocalyptic survivalist who owns a stash of meals-ready-to-eat look like a genius. Another nor'easter was almost upon us.

I pulled my coat tight against the damp cold and ran across Cambridge Street. The flower store had just opened. I pushed through the door, pulling it tight behind me to keep the cold out. A pudgy Asian girl stood behind the counter, pulling a pink sweater tightly around her shoulders.

"Thanks for closing the door," she said. "Gonna snow."

"Yeah," I said. "Any idea how much?"

"The television guy says two feet."

"So a foot, then."

She eyed me, clearly uncomfortable with someone who doubted the omniscience of a New England television meteorologist.

"I need flowers," I said. "For a woman. At the hospital."

"What's she like?"

"She's loyal and good with a gun. She's dangerous. Kicks ass. She's saved my life more than once."

"I meant, what kind of flowers does she like."

"Oh. I have no idea."

"Makes it tough to pick flowers, then."

"It's the first time I've bought her flowers."

The girl twisted her mouth, giving me the I-don't-buy-it face. "The next time a girl saves your life, you should buy her flowers."

Great. Another judgy opinion. I said, "I'll just look around."

I circled the small shop. Sprays of baby's breath, mounds of chrysanthemums, and wads of geraniums failed to impress me. None of these foofy things reminded me of Jael. They were conventional, boring, typical—exactly what Sal would buy.

"Don't see what you like?" the girl asked.

"I want something unusual."

"Does she like roses?"

"Roses aren't unusual."

"These are," she said, pointing at a tall, rectangular vase. River rocks adorned the bottom three inches. Water covered them, filling the vase halfway. Twelve orange roses stood in the vase, their stems held in place by the river rocks, their crowns forming a flat flowered surface at the top. The combination of orange flowers, straight stems, and sturdy rocks were exactly right.

"Perfect."

I carried the vase back across Cambridge Street. A few snowflakes drifted onto the traffic, early scouts for the coming storm. Pedestrians waited for traffic lights, glancing at the flakes as if they were radioactive ash. This was going to be a big storm. Maybe two feet was a good estimate.

In Jael's room I unwrapped the vase and placed it on the dresser next to Hugh's spray of carnations.

Sal said, "What the hell is that?"

"What?" I said. "They're flowers."

"Those aren't flowers for a sick person. They look like art or something."

"They're pretty," I said.

"Orange? Orange isn't pretty."

"Will you two assholes shut up?" Hugh said. "She's sleeping."

Jael shifted in her bed, her eyes still closed. "I am awake."

We moved to the bed, forming a semicircle around Jael. Her eyes opened, moved from face to face.

I had a dream. And you were there. And you. And you.

"Sorry you couldn't wake up to better-looking guys," I said.

Hugh said, "Speak for yourself."

A smile tugged at Jael's mouth.

"How are you feeling?" Sal asked.

Jael said, "Drugged."

"They've given you a lot of painkillers," Hugh said. "You should sleep."

"What happened after I was shot?"

Sal said, "Bobby blew Cantrell's head off."

"Jesus, could you leave out the details?" I said.

"Why don't you shut up?" said Hugh to me.

"Maria?" Jael asked. "Have you found Maria?"

I didn't want to tell Jael that Sal and I were planning to walk into a trap. Said nothing instead.

Jael repeated, "Tucker? Is Maria dead?"

"No," I said. "She's—"

Sal said, "She's fine. We're gonna get her back today."

Jael said, "You are not meeting with Anderson, then."

"No," Sal lied.

"That is good." Jael's eyes slipped closed, her lips parted. She slept.

Hugh motioned us outside the room. We closed the door.

"You're actually going to meet with that bastard?" Hugh said.

Sal said, "We're going to get Maria back."

"How?"

Silence.

Hugh turned to me. "Tucker. How are you going to get Maria back?"

"I have no idea," I said.

"Where are you meeting Anderson?"

I told him.

"Well," said Hugh, "at least you'll be in the right place for a miracle."

SEVENTY-ONE

SNOW HAD ACCUMULATED ON the Wise Man's head, as well as on the camel's hump, the sheep's rump, and the cow's back. A manger-like awning protected the Baby Jesus, as well as Joseph and Mary. They presented their child to the assembled. Behind the Christmas crèche, an adult Jesus floated suspended in front of a cross, his arms raised in blessing rather than stretched in agony. An enormous statue of the Madonna loomed over all of them, gazing across East Boston.

Sal, hatless in the falling snow, ignored the crèche and crucifix. He moved to stand directly in front of the Madonna. She towered above us, 35 feet tall (it said so on the road sign). Her bronze face and hands shone. They had been polished clean. Her draped garment was the copper-oxide green of the Statue of Liberty. One bronze hand pointed above, to heaven, while the other gestured beyond her. A gray void dominated the space behind her. On a clear day we would have seen a vista that included houses, wetlands, airports, and the earthly realm of Boston. Today, the falling snow blocked it all.

Sal genuflected, stood, and said to me, "Show some respect."

I took off my Red Sox knit cap. Snow melted on my ears. "What are we doing here, Sal?"

I had seen David Anderson's East Boston meeting place from the highway, and Sal had turned off 1A to reach it. We wound our way through snow-clogged streets, ignoring the recalculations of my GPS app until Sal said, "Shut the fucking thing off."

He slushed our car past the cookie-cutter buildings of a housing project, on into the bowels of the working-class neighborhood. Clouds of swirling snow had obliterated the sun. Gray light diffused over the neighborhood. There were no shadows. Sal crept past triple-deckers, studded with south-facing DIRECTV dishes, and the odd, small single-family house.

Christmas lights dominated the street. Most houses sported strings of red, green, blue, and yellow lights. These weren't the tiny white bulbs of Wellesley, tastefully appointed and lovingly draped across a dogwood. These were colorful expressions of the happy season, following the lines of porches, rooflines, and doors. The inflatable Christmas monstrosities that breathed across the suburban landscape didn't fit in the snug confines of Orient Ave. Instead, hard plastic Santas waved their greetings—holiday lawn gnomes.

It was noon. Most of the Christmas lights were dark, saving electricity for nighttime. But some had been turned on, perhaps in an effort to ward off the nor'easter's gloom. Sal parked on Orient Ave, in front of the Don Orione nursing home. Got out. I had followed him across the street into the Madonna shrine.

Sal pointed at the Madonna. "She was the one who made the real sacrifice."

"What?"

He motioned at the low concrete lean-to that framed the courtyard. "In the story." Fourteen mosaics surrounded us, protected by the low roof.

I said, "The Stations of the Cross."

"Yeah," Sal said. "You learned something in Sunday school after all."

"What do you mean, she made the real sacrifice?"

Sal looked up at the Madonna's bronze face. "Didn't you see it back there?"

"What?"

"In the manger scene."

"I saw the wise men, the animals."

"She was a mother. She had just given birth to Jesus. She suffered to bring him into the world."

"You think God let her suffer?"

"He says that she will in the Garden of Eden story, right?"

I had no idea what he was talking about. "You mean the apple?"

"Yes, because of the apple. Eve ate the apple and gave it to Adam, so God told her that she'd suffer in childbirth. Mary must have suffered too."

I said, "It doesn't seem right."

Sal raised his hand in a dismissive wave. "Ah, what can you do?"

We stood in the snow.

I said, "We're going to be late."

"She has this kid, raises him," Sal said. "Probably gave him a fucking bar mitzvah."

"We should get going. It's noon."

"Joseph, God bless him, gives Jesus a skill. Made him a carpenter. And then—" Snow melted on Sal's face as he looked up at the statue. Those probably weren't tears.

"Then?"

"And then Jesus decides to let the Pharisees kill him."

"Wasn't that the point?"

"The fucking point? You think Mary raised that kid so he could be killed?" Sal grabbed me by the arm, pulled me across the courtyard in front of one of the mosaics. Mary stood in front of Jesus, bent by his cross.

"What do you think she's saying?" asked Sal.

"What?"

"She's telling him that he's the Son of God. He should save himself."

I was helpless. I had no idea what to say.

Sal said, "She didn't ask for any of it. She didn't ask to be the Mother of God. She didn't ask to have her kid killed. Jesus got what he wanted. God got what he wanted. Hell, I get what I want. Jesus died for my sins. I go to Heaven. You think I don't appreciate that?"

"I—I guess."

"But Mary didn't agree to lose her kid for my sins. Mary would have told me to go to hell. And she'd have been right. Who would even ask her to watch her son die?" Sal still had my arm. He was squeezing it. Starting to shake it.

"Sal, we gotta go," I said.

Sal released my arm. Patted it. "You mean I gotta go."

"What do you mean?"

"I'm not losing you, little cousin. You don't know what you're getting into."

"Neither do you. It's even more reason I should go."

"What, so he can kill you too?"

"My mother's dead, Sal. She's not going to suffer. I lost Maria. I'll get her back."

Mary stood before us, frozen in tile, weeping before her condemned son.

Sal reached into his pocket, pulled out a gun, and handed it to me. "Keep your fucking finger off the trigger."

I slid my finger out of the trigger guard.

"And put it in your pocket. We don't want people to see it."

"Right," I said.

Sal pulled me close, kissed my forehead. "I love you, little cousin. If Maria's there, you take her and you run, no matter what. You hear?"

"We'll see."

"Fuck no, we will not see. You grab her and take her to Adriana. She'll take care of her."

"You'll take care of her yourself."

Sal turned, I followed.

SEVENTY-TWO

I WALKED TO THE car, started brushing snow. The back window already had an inch of new accumulation. Sal shuffled past me. Kept going. I jogged after him, slipping on slush.

"We're walking?" I said.

"They won't be expecting us to walk. Gives us a chance to scope things."

I brushed snow off my hair, pulled my hat on before more could accumulate. We continued down the street, enveloped in a gray swirl of flakes. Big driving snowflakes landed silently around us, drifting against tires. There's no quieter bad weather than a snowstorm. Trees rustle in wind, rain splashes, lightning and thunder deliver a booming show. Snow accumulates without a sound, growing like a white mold over every surface.

I peered through the flakes. "If it's a trap, shouldn't we have gotten here a couple of hours early?"

"Eh. Early or late. I like late. Makes them nervous. Also, I didn't want to stand in the fucking cold for two hours. Let them do that."

"Maria too?"

"If she's there."

"You don't think she'll be there?"

"You just remember what I said. If she is, you grab her and run."

Snow stuck to my lashes and started to cover Sal's bare hair. He swiped at it. We crested a small rise in the road and saw the top of Anderson's meeting place: "Under the cross in Orient Heights." The directions had been clear.

Route 1A shoots north out of Boston, past the airport, through Revere, and on up the coast. But first it passes Orient Heights, a hundred-foot hill stuck next to the road. At the tip of Orient Heights, looking out over 1A, Chelsea, Boston, and Revere, is a gigantic cross. Anderson could have meant only one place. The top of that hill, under that cross.

"Anderson is a dick," I said.

Sal said nothing.

"Who does this under a cross?"

More nothing.

We trudged down the street. A plow pushed past, forcing snow into parking spaces that had been shoveled out and reserved with garbage barrels. People were going to have to shovel again. Winter sucks.

The cross was still too far away for us to see its base. The thing grew as we walked, black against the snow. Orient Ave would have driven straight off the hill and down onto 1A if it didn't make a sharp U-turn before it reached the cross. Sal stopped walking before we reached the U-turn. Scrubby snow-laden trees lined the road. They hid us from anyone down there, while hiding them from us.

Sal pulled out his gun and held it by his side, gripping it with a black Thinsulate glove. "Yours too."

I pulled the gun from my pocket, holding it in my puffy ski glove.

Sal looked at my glove. "You can't work it like that."

"If I hold it in my bare hand, I'll freeze," I said, holding it up. "It'll be fine."

"Keep the fucking thing pointed that way." He motioned away from him.

We pushed on to the end of the narrow street, where small homes closed in on the U-turn. The neighborhood had that North End feel: intimate, working-class, forbidding to outsiders, including high-tech nerds wearing Tom Brady UGGs. I hunched my shoulders as if I were walking through these people's living rooms rather than down their barely plowed street.

We reached the U-turn. The cross loomed ahead. Plows had pushed a dike of snow against the U-turn's curve. We'd have to climb over it.

"Keep your head down," said Sal. He bent and crab-walked up the snow, finding purchase for his rubber-covered shoes on chunks of gritty ice. I followed. At the top, we could see over the trees. A rolling field of snow bumped its way toward the edge of the hill. A fence framed a square at the edge of the hill, protecting the cross. Three figures stood in front of the fence, all adults.

"No Maria," I said.

"Good," whispered Sal.

As Sal predicted, they were looking for us in the wrong place. We skidded down the snow pile and slogged through a foot of snow left over from the last storm, weaving between scrub trees until we were fifty feet from the cross. We'd be visible now. Sal stepped out from behind a shrub, gun raised. I followed, gun by my side.

David Anderson, Jake Kane, and Angie Morielli turned. Saw us. Kane reached for his gun.

"Don't be fucking stupid, Kane!" Sal called. Kane raised his hands away from the gun.

Anderson called across the snow, "Why the gun, Sal?"

"You know why, asshole."

"Sure I know why. You want to kill me."

"You fucking stole from me."

"It was a management fee, Sal."

Sal and I moved toward the cross. Rocks, bushes, pits, and a metal retaining wall formed a hidden obstacle course under the snow. Sal dropped to his knee at a sudden drop off, his gun dipping into the snow. Kane reached for his gun. I raised mine, my finger outside the trigger guard. Sal was right. I couldn't shove my finger in there without firing.

Sal regained his footing. We progressed slowly, with Anderson, Kane, and Angie watching.

Sal was ten feet away when Anderson said, "Unless you're going to kiss me, that's close enough."

I stood next to Sal, gun at my side. The huge black cross rose behind Anderson. It was an industrial-strength cross, built of I-beams with square white lights running up them. With its lights off, the cross looked like a dead Christmas tree.

Sal pointed his gun at Anderson and his chin at Angie. "What's she doing here?"

"Fuck you too, Sal," said Angie.

"She insisted," said Anderson.

"Where's Maria?" asked Sal.

"Ask her."

"You brought me all the way out here and you don't have Maria?"

"She wouldn't bring her."

"And you couldn't make her?"

"What am I going to do, torture her?"

Sal turned to Angie. "Where's Maria?"

"No hello, no nothing, huh?" said Angie.

"Yeah, cut the shit. Where's Maria?"

"She's safe."

"Where?"

"Safe."

Sal turned to me. "Do you fucking believe this?"

I said to Angie, "You lied to me, at dinner. You had her then and didn't tell me."

"I didn't trust you," said Angie. "And I was right."

"Right how?"

"You killed Pistol the very next day. You're just an animal like the rest of them."

"Pistol tried to—"

David Anderson interrupted. "Can we get this done?"

"What do you want?" asked Sal.

"I want some consideration," said Anderson. "I bring the woman who has Maria, you agree to call it even on the money."

"Consideration? You don't even know if she has Maria."

Angie said, "I have Maria. I saved her for us, Sal."

"Us?" said Sal. "There is no us."

David Anderson said, "C'mon, Angie, just tell him. I'm freezing out here."

Angie ignored him. "Of course there's an us, Sal. You've always wanted me."

"I didn't always want you. I wanted to fuck you. See the difference?"

"You son of a bitch!"

Anderson grabbed Angie's arm. "Just tell him, for Christ's sake!"

Angie pulled her arm loose. "Don't touch me!"

Disasters start with the little things. An O-ring freezes and a shuttle explodes. A cement tube fails and an oil rig floods the Gulf. A bad sensor light starts Three Mile Island. For want of a nail…

My little thing was that I moved my foot, just a little step. I don't know why I did it. Perhaps to get a better view of Angie, who was blocked by Anderson and Kane, perhaps to see Sal's face? I don't know why I stepped. But I did.

The step took me into a hole, hidden by snow, its shadow invisible in the diffuse gray light of the snowstorm. I fell, my arms pinwheeling instinctively. My puffy glove caught the trigger, firing my gun. The gunshot blasted across Orient Heights, the bullet ricocheting off the iron cross and into the storm. That was all it took.

Kane reached for his gun. An instinct? Pulled it out. Raised it.

Sal shot him in the chest.

Kane toppled backward, his gun flying free from his hand and landing at Angie's feet, poofing into the snow.

Angie reached into the snow, pulled out the gun, and pointed it toward Anderson.

"I'm not your whore!" she yelled as she fired two shots.

They missed.

Behind Anderson, Sal took a step back, looked at his chest. Blood gushed from Sal's shirt in a spurting flood. He sank to his knees. Steam rose off the blood spewing from Sal's chest. He fell back to his heels. Kane stood; he'd been wearing a vest. He tackled Angie, taking his gun back.

I flopped over to Sal just as he fell to his back, his legs bent beneath him. I pushed my hands into his chest, trying to stop the bleeding. Steaming blood rivered out of Sal's back, melting its way through the snow.

His eyes wandered up to me. His gloved hand rose, red with his blood, he patted my cheek. "Little cousin." Sal looked over my shoulder. His eyes rested on the cross.

I pulled off my glove, grabbed his hand. "Hold on. Just stay here."

Sal's breath shuddered out. "Sophia," he mouthed. His gaze moved beyond the cross, through it, and he was gone.

SEVENTY-THREE

Snowflakes drifted onto Sal's face, stuck there. I brushed at them, looked up at the cross, obscured by blowing snow. Anderson, Kane and Angie had tugged at my arm, yelled at me to leave, then thrown up their hands and gone. I had stayed, sitting on my haunches staring out in the gray monochromatic blur of the storm, replaying events in my mind.

It had been a slip, just a slip. I hadn't even shot anyone.

I looked down at Sal, brushed another bit of snow off him. "Why did you give me a gun?"

Sal said nothing, staring up into the clouds, not blinking when snow caught itself in his eyelashes as it grew silently around me, piling on the cross's arms. Still, I could hear him. *I told you this would happen. Now you have to find Maria.*

What about Maria? Angie said she was safe, Anderson had said that she wasn't safe, had said that she was with an unstable person. Someone who would kill her in a—

"Tucker!" Bobby's hand clamped down on my shoulder. I started.

Bobby said, "Didn't mean to scare you." He looked down at Sal. "Jesus."

I stood and started to compose an edited series of events, concocting a plausible chain of lies that would explain what Bobby saw in front of him but would keep Sal—I grabbed Bobby, pulled him close. "He's dead."

"What happened?" Bobby repeated.

And the truth tumbled out. The whole unedited truth, nothing redacted, nothing polished, nothing sculpted—just the truth. I hugged Bobby and spewed truth into his ear. About the times that Sal had saved me, about the things I'd overheard, about the lies I'd told to protect my cousin. I told him about Sal's gift of the Bialetti, about Christmas, about Angie's apartment, about Sal's being in Jael's hospital room this morning while I slept.

Bobby said nothing, just pulled me close.

"It's my fault," I said. "I got him killed."

Bobby stepped back. "What?"

"I slipped, my gun went off, all hell broke loose. Sal shot Kane, Angie took Kane's gun, tried to shoot Anderson, shot Sal instead."

"Where's Kane's body?"

"He was fine. He had a vest."

"And Angie and Anderson?"

Aw, shit.

"I missed it," I said.

"What?"

"So stupid. I was so stupid."

"Stupid how?"

"Stupid to think that Angie was trying to kill Anderson."

"What?"

"Angie wasn't shooting at Anderson."

"How do you know?"

"Someone tries to kill you, do you offer them a lift back into the city?"

"Well, no. That would be crazy."

"And Anderson isn't crazy."

"He's not that."

"Angie's crazy."

"You think he wanted Angie to kill Sal?"

"Oh my God. Angie is the unstable person."

"What unstable person?"

"The one Anderson told me about."

"Today?"

"It's all a mess."

The temperature had dropped and the snow had shifted from large puffy flakes to small driving crystals. I looked down to where cars had been running just an hour or so ago. The traffic was gone. Probably a state of emergency.

"You're still tracking me, aren't you?" I asked Bobby.

"When your dot stopped moving, I thought I'd find you dead."

The snow had covered Sal. I crouched next to him and brushed snow off. "Why did he even trust me?" I asked.

"Same reason that I trust you," said Bobby.

"Oh, you trust me now?"

"I always trusted you. I just forgot sometimes."

"Yeah, well, you forgot pretty good."

"I never thought you were a crook, Tucker. I just thought you could use some backup."

"And lead you to Sal."

"If that's where it led. But I still trusted you."

"Hmmph."

"You think I'd have come out to Revere Beach and let Frank take a shot at me if I didn't trust you?"

"Well, you shouldn't have, and Jael shouldn't have trusted me either. I almost got her killed too."

Bobby squatted next to me, helped brush at the snow. "You never pulled a trigger, Tucker. You've never done anything but try to find Maria."

I stood. The wind fired ice crystals against my cheeks. "She's an orphan now."

"She's got family. Adriana Rizzo," said Bobby. "Now that this is over, Angie will bring her back."

The thought of Angie returning Maria jammed in my head like a square peg grinding at a round hole. I turned it and examined it from all sides. I pictured Angie walking up to Adriana's house, Maria in tow, knocking on the door, sad hugs all around. Maria the orphan, back with her aunt.

I couldn't see it. The scene wouldn't resolve properly. What would Adriana say? She'd ask Angie why she had kept Maria for so long, and Angie would answer—she wouldn't really have an answer. She'd say she was keeping Maria safe, but Maria would have been safer with her relatives. She would have been more comfortable in a house she knew.

Adriana would ask Maria, "Where were you?" and Maria would answer—what? Where would she say she had hidden?

I said to Bobby, "She's not bringing her back."

"What?"

"If Angie were going to return Maria, she would have brought her to this meeting. Hell, she drove out here with Anderson, and Anderson wanted to get Sal off his back. Anderson would have wanted to bring Maria to clean this up and let Sal see what a good guy he was."

"So why wasn't Maria here?"

"Aw, shit. We need to talk to Hugh."

SEVENTY-FOUR

MANKIND HAS YET TO invent a hospital room that holds enough chairs. There's always one big chair, then a bed, then—nothing. Next thing you know, you're leaning on the beeping monitoring equipment, and that is generally frowned upon.

The situation was worse in Jael's room because she had taken the big chair, and none of the men wanted to sit on the hospital bed. Bobby, Hugh, and I formed a semicircle around Jael, who was looking surprisingly comfortable in her hospital pajamas.

"How are you?" I asked.

"I am enjoying the pain medication," said Jael.

"Yeah, she's a trouper," said Hugh.

My mind saw an escape route from thinking about Sal and took it, engaging in the calculations and permutations that would explain this relationship between Hugh and Jael in terms that I could understand. Mutual professional admiration? Mutual personal admiration? Mutual personal—

"What happened at the meeting?" asked Jael, dragging me back.

"Sal's dead," I said.

"Aw, Jesus," said Hugh. He sat on the bed. Clutched his face with his palm. "Aw, hell."

Jael said, "I am sorry to hear it."

"Thanks," Hugh and I said in unison.

"How did it happen?" Jael asked.

I said, "Angie shot him."

"Angie?" asked Hugh. "Who the hell gave that crazy bitch a gun?"

"Long story."

"Yeah, with you at the center of it, no doubt."

"Ease up on him," said Bobby. "He just lost his cousin."

"And I just lost my friend, Miller. What the hell are you doing here, anyway?"

"Bobby drove me back from East Boston."

"The roads are closed to traffic," said Bobby.

Jael said, "I am sorry that I was not there to help."

"Didn't you do enough?" asked Hugh. "He almost got you killed once."

"Hey, Hugh," said Bobby, "that's not what I mean by *go easy on him*."

Hugh stood. "Why don't you mind your own business?"

Bobby stepped close. "It looks like you're gonna be all in my business, Hugh."

"What's that supposed to mean?"

"Oh, don't give me that shit. You're the last one standing."

Hugh looked from Bobby to Jael to me. Sat back on the bed. "Yeah," he said. "I'm the sole survivor."

"I hear the espresso is excellent at Cafe Vittoria," said Bobby.

"You'll never see me there," said Hugh. "That was Sal's spot."

"You mean I'll never see you there *again*," said Bobby. "It's pretty clear you were there already."

"Do we have to do this now?" I asked.

Jael said, "I do not understand why Anderson would kill Sal."

"He didn't kill him," Hugh said. "Angie did."

"Anderson brought Angie to the meeting?" asked Jael.

"I still don't see why he did that," said Bobby. "If he wanted to make up with Sal, he should have just brought Maria."

I remembered why we were here. I asked Hugh, "Why did you call Angie a crazy bitch?"

"Because she's a crazy bitch."

"But what makes you say that?"

"The fact that all the crazy in her head spills out sometimes."

"When did that happen last?"

"You probably just saw when it happened last."

"She's, like, murderous crazy?"

"Ever since the abortion, something has been wrong with her."

"What abortion?"

"Sal never told you this?"

"He said something in passing once."

"He got Angie pregnant."

"Oh, no."

"He paid Angie off to get an abortion. Gave her an apartment."

"Up on Cleveland Place."

"That's the one."

"That's a hell of a payoff."

"But she's never been quite right since. Even more desperate and needy than before. Started sleeping with everyone."

"Even—" I started. Got a warning look from Hugh. Didn't need to finish the question.

Jael said, "We have known that Angie was protecting Maria."

"And we assumed that when Anderson took Angie with that email trick, he took Maria too," I said.

"Yes. That was a bad assumption."

"Anderson doesn't know where Maria is," I said. "He just had Angie."

Bobby said, "If he still has Angie, we have a way to get to Maria." Bobby grabbed his coat. I grabbed mine and gave Jael a quick peck on the cheek. We had to go back into the storm.

SEVENTY-FIVE

WHETHER THE CAUSE IS zombie apocalypse, bomber manhunt, or nor'easter, being the lone car on the streets of Boston is creepy as hell. Bobby's SUV crept down Causeway Street, past the TD Bank Garden. The crowds that normally throng around the Garden were gone, replaced by deepening snow, tinted a sick orange by sodium streetlights. I thought about tweeting a picture, then remembered Facebook.

Texted Adriana.

Me: Do you have power?

Adriana: Yeah

Me: Get on Facebook and look at Maria's last status.

Adriana: The one where she says she's going sledding with you?

Me: Yeah, did anyone like that status or comment on it?

A delay.

Adriana: I liked it, Angie liked it, some of Maria's friends liked it.

Me: Angie liked it?

Adriana: Yeah.

Me: Thanks. I gotta go.

Night had taken the city, and the storm clouds were now illuminated from below as the lights of Boston struggled against the darkness. The storm had worsened. Tiny, cold-shriveled flakes canted down the street, driven by a relentless wind. The occasional plow clattered past, pushing snow against the curb and tossing salt into the road. Despite the plowing and salting, the snow continued to win the battle of the pavement, growing faster than the plows could push it aside.

"You sure that Anderson can help us?" Bobby asked.

"He's definitely the last person to see Angie. If Angie has Maria, then Anderson can point us to her. That is, if he'll talk to us."

"Oh, he'll talk to us," said Bobby. "I'm not driving through this shit just to get stonewalled."

Causeway Street dumped into Commercial. I gazed at the spot where Vince Ferrari had smashed me with his car and taken me to Charlestown for a good murdering. Sal had been there to save the day, killing three guys. The complications of Sal never ended: savior, murderer, father, cousin. His tantrums, violence, embraces, cheek taps, and incongruous Catholic faith bumped and jostled for top spot in my image of him. Fear him, love him, punch him, help him—what should I do?

It didn't matter. He was dead.

Bobby said, "You okay?"

"Huh?"

"You're kind of sniffling there."

"Aw, shit." I pulled off the stupid poofy glove that couldn't hold a gun and rubbed my cheeks dry as Bobby slid the SUV in a slow arc onto Battery Street. Pulled up in front of Anderson's place.

"Let's do it," said Bobby.

We climbed out of the car and pushed through the unshoveled walkway that led to the warm lobby, where we stood in front of a bank of doorbells. I pushed Anderson's.

"Yes?" said the intercom. It sounded like Kane.

I shushed Bobby and said, "Kane, it's me, Tucker."

No answer. I pushed the doorbell again.

Nothing.

Pushed it again and employed Bobby's trick, leaning into the bell far too long.

"What?" said the intercom. That was Anderson.

"Dave, we have to talk."

"We've got nothing to talk about."

"The hell we don't."

"Are you alone?"

"Why wouldn't I be alone?" It wasn't quite a lie.

The door buzzed.

Anderson said, "Get up here before someone sees you."

Ridiculous elevator music accompanied us to Anderson's floor. Warm-toned carpets and wood paneling hid any notion of the storm outside. I knocked on Anderson's door. He opened it, looked at Bobby, frowned.

"I thought you said you were alone," Anderson said.

"I didn't lie and I didn't not lie," I said. "We need to talk."

"I've got nothing to—"

Bobby rushed the door, knocking Anderson back and bulling his way inside. I followed in his wake, closed the door behind me. Kane ran out of a back room, gun drawn.

Bobby pointed at Kane, then Kane's gun, then his holster. "Do it."

Kane holstered his gun.

Anderson asked, "Do you have a warrant?"

"Why would I have a warrant?" Bobby said. "I'm not even here."

"What's that supposed to mean?"

I said, "It means we just want to ask you about Angie."

"Who?"

"Don't be ridiculous."

"I'm not talking about any of this."

Bobby took a step forward and punched Anderson right in the nose. Blood spurted down Anderson's shirtfront. Bobby wheeled on Kane and said, "Don't even think about it."

Kane grabbed a towel from the kitchen, walked over, and handed it to Anderson. "Do you need me to do anything?" he asked Anderson.

"No. Leave me with these guys," Anderson said. "One less variable."

Kane walked off into the nether reaches of the gigantic condo.

Anderson said to Bobby, "I'm going to sue the shit out of you."

"Who, me?" Bobby said. "I wasn't even here—right, Tucker?"

I said, "Can we all just cut the crap?"

"What the hell do you want, Tucker?" Anderson asked.

"What do I want? Well, considering that you gave Sal's murderer a lift home, I thought you might tell us where you dropped her off. Maybe where she lives. Maybe even where she has Maria."

"I don't know what—" Anderson looked at Bobby, who was absentmindedly making a fist.

"What I don't get is why Angie didn't have a gun," I said. "If it was her job to kill Sal, then why did she need Kane's?"

"Oh, don't be an idiot, Tucker. Angie wasn't supposed to kill Sal. She was supposed to bring Maria, but then she showed up without her."

"And you didn't ask her where Maria was?"

"Of course I asked her. But she wouldn't tell me. I offered her money, I threatened her, I tried to talk reason. She wouldn't tell me."

Bobby said, "Didn't try torture?"

"I'm not an animal, Miller. Unlike you."

"Like to keep your hands clean, eh?"

"So you meant to bring Maria to the meeting?" I asked.

"Yeah," Anderson said. "I was going to pay Angie a hundred grand to bring Maria to the meeting. She showed up without Maria and told me to shove the money up my ass."

"And you still brought her?"

"There was no point in me going alone, and I was hoping that Sal could talk some sense into her. Apparently, they were almost married once."

"What?"

"Yeah, she told me that he got her pregnant and promised to marry her, but then he was too chickenshit to tell Sophia."

The horrible puzzle fell into place. "Oh my God," I said.

"What?" asked Anderson.

"This all makes sense now."

"Well, good. Glad I could help."

Bobby said, "You haven't done shit. Where does Angie live?"

"I told you that I don't know. She calls, we make a plan, she comes over. She can't be far."

I remembered Angie kissing me in front of Jael. She'd been carrying groceries. Where was she taking them? Her apartment was blocks away.

"Where does she call from? Do you have caller ID?"

Anderson walked over to his desk, grabbed a handset. Stared at it and beeped through a list. "That's the weird part," he said. "She called from this number." Anderson handed me the phone.

The caller ID said *Marco Esposito.*

"But Marco's dead," I said.

"I know that."

"This must be Marco's wife's house."

Bobby said, "That makes no sense. Angie can't be there, Marco's wife wouldn't put up with that."

The man cave.

I said, "Sal told me that he and Marco were sitting in Marco's man cave, and that Joey came over and killed Marco. I had assumed that Marco's man cave was in his house—"

Bobby said, "Marco wasn't killed in his house."

"Well, where was he killed?"

Bobby got onto his phone. "Lieutenant Lee? Yeah. Yeah. Storm's fuckin' terrible. Listen. Do you remember the address where Marco Esposito got murdered?" Bobby paused, held up a *wait a second* finger. "You're shittin' me. Seriously? Sonovabitch. I gotta go. Yeah. Yeah. You drive safe too. Yeah. Yeah. God bless."

"So where was Marco's man cave?"

"You're not going to believe it."

SEVENTY-SIX

Holden Court, rather than protecting us from the northeast wind, channeled and intensified it. Snow swirled through the court as the windchill gnawed at my face.

"Sonovabitch," said Bobby.

"Yeah, you said that," I said.

"She was here all along."

Joey Pupo's apartment, or ex-apartment, still stood at the end of Holden Court. I looked up at the roof that I had travelled so long ago, looked around in the snow beneath me.

"What are you looking for?" Bobby asked.

"My cell phone. I dropped it here off the roof."

"You'll never find it."

"Yeah, I know. I just wanted some closure."

"We're going to get all the closure we can handle in a couple of minutes."

We stood in front of another door off the court.

Joey came over and killed Marco. "Came over" as in "Mrs. Pupo, can Joey come over and play?" You say that when you live in an apartment building, in a neighborhood, or in a tiny court with entrances on both sides. You say it when the guy who came over to kill your best friend lived three doors away.

"Angie never left Holden Court," I said.

"That's why I never saw her," Bobby said.

"Let's get this over with."

Bobby reached to lean on the bell to the first floor apartment, but I decided to try the front door instead. It was unlocked, either an oversight or an acknowledgement that you wouldn't want to leave someone out here in the storm fumbling for their keys.

We climbed yet another spiral box of stairs, again to the third floor, the top. I hazarded a guess that the people on the first and second floors would have some idea about a little girl who had come to live in the apartment. A little girl who, a few days ago, had run breathlessly up these stairs while I recovered from a battle with black ice.

We reached the door. Bobby and I exchanged a glance. Bobby made an *after you* gesture. I knocked.

Angie's voice floated out. "Who is it?"

Bobby said, "It's the FBI, ma'am. Please open up."

The door opened. Angie looked at Bobby, then with surprise at me. "Come in."

Maria sat at the kitchen table, holding playing cards. We had interrupted a game of cribbage. When Maria saw me she dropped the playing cards, jumped off her chair, and ran behind Angie, hiding behind her skirt.

I said, "Hi, Maria."

Nothing.

"I've been looking all over for you," I said.

Maria clutched herself tighter into the skirt.

"Tucker, leave Maria alone," Angie said. "You terrify her."

Bobby said, "Why is that, ma'am?"

"Call me Angie."

"Why is that, Angie?"

Maria pointed at me. "He killed Ma, with the necktie I gave Daddy."

"No, I didn't," I said. "I was with—"

Bobby shushed me. Squatted. "Why do you say that, honey?"

Maria wouldn't make eye contact.

"Nobody is going to hurt you."

Nothing.

Angie said, "Maria, why don't you go to your room and I'll tell these men to go home."

Maria fled, dodging from behind Angie's skirt, sliding along the cabinets, and bolting out of the room.

"What did you tell her?" I asked Angie.

Angie said, "I don't know what you're talking about."

"How did she know about the necktie? How did you know about it?"

"Get out."

"You friended Maria on Facebook, used her status to tell Joey where to get her."

"Shut up."

"Then you killed Sophia."

"Shut up!"

"Did Maria see you kill Joey Pupo too?"

Angie's face twitched as a spasm of loathing shot across it.

"C'mon, Angie. Did she watch you shoot the guy when you rescued her?"

Angie said, "Of course she did. He still had her tied to that chair. Sick bastard."

"For how long?" I asked.

"I don't know," said Angie. "Long enough for me to—" She paused.

"Drop that envelope at my front door," I finished. "He had her tied to that chair for an hour?"

"At least an hour!"

"Liar."

"You're the liar!"

"Maria ran through the blood after you shot Joey. She couldn't have done that if she were tied to the chair."

"So you shot him and ran," said Bobby. "Took Maria here."

Another spasm across Angie's face. The mask was fragile. I decided to see how fragile.

I said to Bobby, "She realized that Joey was going to want more than blow jobs."

Bobby blinked at me.

"You shut your mouth," Angie said.

"Oh c'mon, Angie, it's obvious. You blew Joey so he'd kill Marco."

"Shut up."

"You led him around by his little dick."

"You're filthy."

"And you're a whore. You even got Sal to give you his apartment."

Angie's eyes filled. The mask was slipping. "You don't know what you're talking about. Sal loved me."

"Sal loved Sophia."

"Sophia? Don't you mention that name in my house."

"It's not your house. It's Marco's house. Did Marco give you the key so you could come up here and fuck him?"

"Shut up!"

"You know, he'd call, you'd come up and let yourself in so that he wouldn't have to get up from his Barcalounger. Then you could bring him a beer and blow him."

Angie said, "Stop it. Maria is right in the other room!"

"And you thought you had Sal wrapped right around your finger."

"He loved me!" said Angie, eyes streaming. "He gave me a baby. He was going to marry me, except for that bitch Sophia. Sophia made him—made him—made him do what he did."

She was at the edge and I had my thumb on the jagged cut in her mind, the place that would hurt the most if I pushed down.

I could have stopped.

If I had stopped right there, Bobby would have had enough to arrest her. He'd arrest her, we'd take Maria and be on our way. That was all we had to do to wrap this up.

I could have stopped, but Angie had killed Sal right in front of me.

"Made you do what, Angie?" I asked. "Made you kill your baby?"

"He had a name!" shrieked Angie. "Antonio! He was Antonio, named after Sal's father."

"But Sal didn't want to marry you. He didn't want a little Antonio."

"He did! He told me. He'd finally have a son. Sophia made him do it. Made him force me to get an abortion, lose my womb, lose my baby. I wasn't a woman anymore."

"Oh, you still had parts left." I hated her so much. "And you sure knew how to use them."

The gun was small and round and fit smoothly into Angie's hand as she slid it from her pocket.

Bobby shouted, "Gun!" and started to unzip his winter coat. His gloved fingers fumbled at the zipper, pulling it down.

Angie screamed, "You filthy bastard, you shut your filthy mouth!" She raised the gun at me.

The little kitchen had no space, no place to move or dodge. I was crammed between a cabinet and the sink. There was no place to get away from the gun. I could only move toward it, so I did. Took a step, reached. Was too slow.

The gun *boomed* in the little kitchen as I reached for it. Angie took a step back. It *boomed* again, then began to track toward Bobby.

I turned to see that he had pulled off his glove and unzipped his coat. He reached for his gun.

Angie's gun *boomed* again. She was just emptying it at us. Bobby pulled out his black boxy gun, aimed it at Angie. The two guns *boomed* together. Blood flew through the kitchen. I don't know whose. I rushed forward to tackle Angie, but wound up catching her instead, my hands getting tangled in bloody shards of a housecoat.

I turned to look at Bobby. He slid down the refrigerator, leaving a bloody trail from his shoulder.

And then Maria ran into the room. Maria, wearing a cotton t-shirt, pajama bottoms, and Keds sneakers, ran into the room, made straight for the front door, opened it, and was gone down the steps. I prayed that a neighbor would grab her, that somebody would see her and pull her inside. I heard her sneakers slapping against the steps.

I called, "Maria! Don't go outside!"

The sneakers kept slapping.

I stood, took a step. "NO!"

The door at the bottom of the stairs opened, closed. Maria was in the storm.

Bobby, sitting on the floor, his hand pressed to his bleeding shoulder looked up at me.

"Go!"

SEVENTY-SEVEN

I POUNDED DOWN THE stairs, praying that Maria would stop moving as soon as snow filled her canvas sneakers, that I'd be able to grab her up and get her inside. Pulled open the front door and jumped out onto the snow-covered pavement.

She was gone. Little sneaker footprints ran to the end of the court. I started to run after her, slipped, fell, got up, slipped again, and finally got myself under control. Trotted down the court to the snow pile and saw the little footprints climb up and over. Maria was in the street with the plows.

The pile was still soft. Tiny icy flakes stung my eyes. Tiny snow is cold snow. I figured the temperature to be in the teens. Maria wouldn't last long in this. I half climbed, half sloshed through the pile and into the street. Looked up and down the street through the swirling snow. Didn't see Maria. I took few steps in one direction, then backtracked.

That was when I saw the blood in the snow. It was black in the orange sodium light, steaming as it cooled. Did Maria get shot? I followed the trail. It led back to the snow pile and over.

Oh no.

I looked down at my Tom Brady UGG. Blood steamed over my ankle and onto the street. I felt around, found the hole in my jacket, reached in, and got hit with the burning pain as my finger came away covered in black blood. I didn't have much time. I needed to make a guess. I guessed that Maria would run home.

Sal had been living only two streets from Maria this whole time. I ran down Commercial toward his house, wishing that I had never discovered the gunshot wound. It was starting to hurt, hot knitting needles in my side with every step. Reached Salutation, turned up it. I knew what I'd find. I'd find Maria, huddled against the front door, ringing the bell to an empty apartment. She'd be cold, and I'd pull her into my coat and dial 911.

I ran down alley-like Salutation and was rewarded with a tiny Keds print in the snow. Maria had come this way. I called out "Maria!" but the snow suffocated my call.

"Maria!"

I reached Sal's apartment. I was wrong. The storm had drifted tiny flakes up against the front door. You couldn't see the front steps anymore; they were covered and would remain covered until somebody shoveled them out. The pristine snowdrift told me that Maria had not even attempted to reach her apartment. One tiny print in the plowed snow pile told me that she'd given up almost immediately. More prints told me that she'd run on. Now I knew where she was going: St. Stephen's Church or the fire station. She had to figure that someone would help her there.

I ran on down Salutation. I called "Maria!" again, but a wave of dizziness and burning told me to stop. Yelling wasn't helping my gunshot wound. *Friggin' Angie.* At the corner of Salutation and Hanover, I stopped, hands on knees, catching my breath. This wasn't normal. I could run five miles a day—a sunny, warm day. But today, the blood loss, boots, and sliding snow were sapping my strength.

Looked down Hanover.

"Maria." No oomph. Couldn't even yell anymore.

I started down Hanover with a shuffling gate, leaned forward, and let gravity carry me into a run. The story ran every few years: a kid gets out into the storm and they find him or her dead in a snowdrift, ten feet from the front door. Hell of a headline for Rittenhauser: THE FALL OF RIZZO—DEATH OF A FAMILY. Visions of the *Boston Globe* swam in front of me as I shuffled on, looking through it for Maria. Footprints told me that she'd ignored the fire station. I made for the front door of St. Stephen's Church. The empty street beckoned me on; brick buildings on either side housed the people of the North End, all safe from the cold, plows, and driving snow. All but one.

St. Stephen's loomed up from the snow, but one look told me that I had been wrong again. No footprints. No break in the drifts. No evidence that Maria had stopped here.

Hands back on knees, I scrutinized the packed snow in the street. Saw one sneaker print leading onward. She might lead me, but I wasn't certain how far I'd be able to follow. Blood ran down my UGG, flowing faster than before. I left a puddle a hand's width across before I got myself moving again. Shuffling. Picturing a final goal, and the last place where Maria might have felt some comfort, where a frozen girl would think to go just before the storm snuffed out the last of her fire.

The North End, with its brick buildings, Italian posters, and narrow streets fell away behind a blackout tunnel. I kept myself shuffling forward, swinging my tunnel vision to the snow in front of doorways on either side. It occurred to me that I might just die doing this, wandering in a nor'easter with a gunshot wound until I passed out and got plowed. Why not? Sounded the right way for me to go. Shit, I might even win a Darwin award.

My legs kept going and I left them to their task. I couldn't afford a stumble. I had one last idea, one last place. A place that I thought Maria could find and that I could find, and in which we'd both find some comfort.

And there they were, the tiny footprints fording the plow-piled snow. I followed, churning through the dirty snow and tripping on the curbstone. I fell into a foot of snow on the sidewalk. Footprints marked the snow. Tiny fresh sneaker prints, each one of them filling a little girl's shoe with melting snow that sucked the heat out of that tiny body.

There couldn't be more. I tried to stand, watched the world spin around me, found myself falling back into the snow. Not enough blood to stand. I crawled through the snow following the prints, finding a spot where Maria, wearing a cotton shirt and pajamas, had also fallen, then gotten up and shuffled on until she reached her destination.

The doorway of Cafe Vittoria.

Maria huddled against the doorway, leaning up against the plywood that covered the shattered glass, pawing at the door. I climbed the steps. Grabbed her.

"Maria."

Maria stared into my eyes, struggled to get away, but I had her. I opened my coat front. Pulled her inside. She squirmed.

"No!" she said.

"Shh. Shh."

"No! No!"

But as little as I had left, Maria had even less. Her tiny body pulled heat from me, leading me to shiver. She squirmed and got a finger in my bullet hole. I screamed, and she went stock still. I fumbled around in my pockets. So many pockets. Too many pockets.

Maria said, "Angie said you killed Ma."

I tried to answer, stuttered. Just said, "Shh." Found my phone, dialed 911.

The operator answered.

"Cafe Vittoria on Hanover," I said. "We're dying."

I guess they came and got us. I don't remember.

SEVENTY-EIGHT

I SAT IN A pew in St. Stephen's Church. Jael sat to my right, having insisted upon coming. Hugh Graxton was next to her. Maria sat down front with her aunt—her new family.

A hymn filled the church.

For He is thy health and salvation…

Sal and Sophia's caskets lay in front of the altar. I had helped push Sal's down the aisle, though to be honest I had used the casket as support. I figured Sal wouldn't have minded, but even if he did…

I don't know if it was the blood loss or the blunt force trauma of the past two weeks, but either way I couldn't focus on the proceedings. I watched them from a faraway place, my mind turning the simplicity of Maria's kidnapping over in my mind. Such a simple idea: kill Sophia, marry Sal, raise Maria.

Was this all there was to evil? Was it just a simple cocktail of revenge and delusion? Angie had taken revenge for an aborted baby and a shattered uterus and had coddled the illusion that Sal would marry her, that they'd raise Maria together.

It had been easy for Angie to seduce a guy like Joey Pupo, the guy who had always tagged along, run behind. The guy tolerated by the cool kids, Sal and Marco. How simple for her to convince him to kill Marco, blame Sal, take Maria while Angie killed Sophia.

Of course, Joey didn't realize he was just a cog to Angie. Maria had told me the story after we had recovered from the storm. Angie had burst into the apartment, shot the idiot Joey, and "rescued" Maria. They'd run down the steps from Joey's and up the steps into Marco's while I floundered around on the roof and Bobby argued with the Boston cops, a couple of morons in the snow.

"My brother was a good man." Sal's sister Bianca was giving the eulogy, reminding me of the one I had given for my mother. Good? I guess he was good. A good husband, a good father, a good cousin. A deadly enemy.

The dark mahogany of Sal's casket peeked out from under its shroud. I looked away, shielding myself from the image of Sal's eyes gazing upon a gigantic iron cross and losing focus. Thought about complexity theory instead. The power function. The notion that a single grain of sand, dropped on the right spot of a dune, can cause an avalanche. The right stock collapse can cascade through the stock market; the right slip on a tectonic plate can launch an earthquake that rips a city to shreds. Little things lead to the unexpected. Angie tries to steal Maria, and a gang war tears through the North End. Pistol Salvucci dies, a shipping container full of gore sails overseas. Jael takes a bullet in the chest, Cantrell gets one in the head. Sal dies under a cross in Orient Heights and Maria is an orphan.

Does evil always work this way? Does it always crawl into someone's mind, sit in their brain, spin havoc and death in the name of justice? Did it all make sense to Angie? Did she think she'd earned the right because she let Sal get her pregnant? Was it even an accident? She'd chosen the abortion and the condo. Apparently the condo wasn't enough.

The service ground on. We stood. We sat. We knelt. I let words and prayers and music and whimpering and tears and emotions pass through me, leaving me untouched. I didn't want to be touched anymore.

Next I knew I was standing at the graveside, alone in a crowd. A ring of trampled snow separated me from the others. Graxton had taken Jael home to rest. Sal and Sophia's family didn't trust me and were huddled together in grief. Sal's friends didn't know me and stayed away. A spray of flowers graced the two caskets sitting next to a hole that had been chiseled through the frozen earth.

The family circle broke. Maria stepped out. Maria had overheard my fight with Angie in the kitchen. Left with nothing to believe and no adult protectors, she had run. But she was safe now, living with her aunt, still in the North End. Maria reached for my hand, pulled me across the circle of snow and among her family members, who made room for the interloper. I picked her up. She hugged my neck. Cried into my shoulder.

"Shhh."

It was cold. It was always cold. Every friggin' day was colder and darker and snowier than the one before. Piles of snow consumed us, pushed by plows, lifted by front-end loaders, dropped by trucks. Still the piles grew, turning black in the polluted, exhaust-filled air.

Sal didn't care. This was one winter he'd miss.

SEVENTY-NINE

MARIA AND I STOOD at the top of a hill after a snowstorm. A bright blue March sky blazed above us. The sun had rediscovered warmth and snow plopped to the ground around us as it fell from the bare branches of the trees that graced the cemetery.

"Auntie Adriana says that it's not right for it to snow in March," said Maria.

"She's right," I said.

The past two months had brought changes to the North End. Adriana had taken in Maria and had, in a nice turn of justice, upgraded her living situation by moving into what had been Angie's condo. She had set up a dumpster outside the condo and had hired guys to "get rid of that bitch's shit." Then she'd moved in with her wife, Catherine, plus Maria.

Caroline and I were still friends, but the benefits were off the table since Caroline had taken over Angie's legal defense. I had tried to start a fight with her about it, but she would have none of it.

"You're defending the woman who killed Sal," I said as we sat in Zaftigs.

"Do you want lox on your bagel?" asked Caroline.

"She doesn't deserve someone as good as you."

"You know, it's early, but I'm thinking that it would be fun to have a mimosa."

"Are you listening to any of this?"

"It's better for you that I'm not. So lox, or just straight up?"

"Seriously?" I asked.

Caroline gave me a raised eyebrow.

"Okay, I'll have the lox."

That was the last time we had talked. It turned out that I was a witness for both the prosecution and the defense. The prosecution wanted me to tell the story of how Angie shot Sal, and Caroline wanted me to tell the story of how Angie was crazy.

Either way, there would be no benefits until the trial was over.

Maria and I started picking our way down the hill, walking among the snow-covered graves. Most of the stones were still covered by last night's storm, but some had been brushed off. It was Sunday morning and Maria had wanted to come to say hello. Sal and Sophia had been buried in the Rizzo family plot, their names added to a list of deceased Rizzos. My mother's name was on the list.

Maria said, "You brush off your mother's side and I'll brush off my mother's side."

"Deal," I said.

When we were done, Maria looked at the stone. "I miss them," she said.

"I know," I said. "I miss my mother too."

Maria swept her arm across the graveyard. "Do you think all these people are in heaven?"

"Absolutely," I said, hoping I was right.

"My feet are cold," said Maria.

I picked her up. "Can you see your house from up here?" I asked.

"You're silly."

"Yeah, but I'm tall."

"What's that?" asked Maria, pointing.

The base of the black Rizzo headstone had warmed enough to melt the snow around it. A small purple smudge had pushed its way through the snow. A flower.

"That's a crocus," I said. "It means spring is coming."

THE END

© Lynn Wayne

ABOUT THE AUTHOR

Ray Daniel is the award-winning author of Boston-based crime fiction. His short story "Give Me a Dollar" won a 2014 Derringer Award for short fiction, and "Driving Miss Rachel" was chosen as a 2013 distinguished short story by Otto Penzler, editor of *The Best American Mystery Stories 2013.*

Daniel's work has been published in the Level Best Books anthologies *Thin Ice*, *Blood Moon*, and *Stone Cold*. *Child Not Found* is the third Tucker mystery, following *Corrupted Memory* and *Terminated.*

For more information, visit him online at raydanielmystery.com and follow him on Twitter @raydanielmystry.